"You need me just as much as I need you!"

Arcana
Anos's younger sister, who appeared in a dream.
She bears the same name as Arcana the god.

THE MISFIT OF DEMON KING ACADEMY
Keywords

Underground World

An enormous cavern located deep beneath Dilhade and Azesion. It is well governed by the three major nations – Jiordal, Agatha, and Gadeciola – despite their conflicts.

Draconids

Inhabitants of the underground world. They resemble humans and demons though they are not exactly like either. As the name of their race implies, they are believed to be the descendents of dragons.

The first generation of draconids, born directly from dragons, are known as "dragonborn," who possess far more power than other draconids.

Jiordal, Kingdom of the Divine Dragon

One of the three major nations of the underground world. Governed by the pope of the Jiordal Church, the nation worships a god called the Almighty Radiance Equis.

Only draconids live in the nation, but they are warm and welcoming towards humans and demons.

Gaelahesta, the Holy Capital

The holy capital of the underground world, unaffiliated with any of the three major nations. Everastanzetta, the Institute of the Gods, is located at the center of the circular city. A nonaggression pact forbids all conflict within Gaelahesta, excluding inside Everastanzetta.

Pledge Jewel

A divine object used in an ancient ritual called the Summoning Ceremony. Pacts can be made with the dragons and gods summoned through a jewel, allowing the wielder to borrow their power. The pledge jewels used in the Selection Trial are different from those used by others.

Genedonov, Goddess of Absurdity

The blasphemous god that once revolted against the gods. In Jiordal, her name is condemned, and she is thought unworthy of worship.

Draconids who laid eyes on Misha and Sasha's fused form claimed her to be the Goddess of Absurdity, but is that really true?

The Misfit of Demon King Academy

The Misfit of Demon King Academy

story by **SHU**
illustrated by **Shizumayoshinori**

6

jnc
New York

story by † SHU
illustrated by † Shizumayoshinori

Translated by Mana Z.   Edited by Stephanie Buck

This book is a work of fiction. Names, characters, places, and incidents are the product of the author's imagination or are used fictitiously. Any resemblance to actual events, locales, or persons, living or dead, is coincidental.

MAOH GAKUIN NO FUTEKIGOUSHA Vol.6 ~ SHIJOSAIKYO NO MAO NO SHISO, TENSEISHITE SHISONTACHI NO GAKKO HE KAYOU ~
©Shu 2020
Edited by Dengeki Bunko
First Published in Japan in 2020 by KADOKAWA CORPORATION, Tokyo.
English translation rights arranged with KADOKAWA CORPORATION, Tokyo through TUTTLE-MORI AGENCY, INC., Tokyo.

English translation © 2024 by J-Novel Club LLC

Yen Press, LLC supports the right to free expression and the value of copyright. The purpose of copyright is to encourage writers and artists to produce the creative works that enrich our culture.

The scanning, uploading, and distribution of this book without permission is a theft of the author's intellectual property. If you would like permission to use material from the book (other than for review purposes), please contact the publisher. Thank you for your support of the author's rights.

Yen Press
150 West 30th Street, 6th Floor
New York, NY 10001

Visit us at yenpress.com
facebook.com/yenpress ♦ twitter.com/yenpress
yenpress.tumblr.com ♦ instagram.com/yenpress

First JNC Paperback Edition: August 2025

JNC is an imprint of Yen Press, LLC.
The JNC name and logo are trademarks of J-Novel Club LLC.

The publisher is not responsible for websites (or their content) that are not owned by the publisher.

Library of Congress Cataloging-in-Publication Data
Names: Shu (Light novel and manga author) | Shizumayoshinori, illustrator. | Z., Mana, translator.
Title: The Demon King Academy / story by SHU ; illustrated by Shizumayoshinori ; translation by Mana Z.
Other titles: Mao gakuin no futekigosha. English
Description: First JNC paperback edition. | New York : JNC, 2024.
Identifiers: LCCN 2023023705 | ISBN 9781975373054 (v. 1 ; trade paperback) | ISBN 9781975374044 (v. 2 ; trade paperback) | ISBN 9781975374051 (v. 3 ; trade paperback)
Subjects: LCSH: Demonology—Fiction. | Reincarnation—Fiction. | LCGFT: Fantasy fiction. | Paranormal fiction. | Light novels.
Classification: LCC PL875.5.H84 M3613 2023 | DDC 895.63/6—dc23/eng/20230522
LC record available at https://lccn.loc.gov/2023023705

ISBN: 978-1-9753-9106-5 (paperback)

10 9 8 7 6 5 4 3 2 1

TPA

Printed in South Korea

Prologue	✝ The Demon King and His Sister	1
Chapter 1	✝ Mystery of the Magic Eye	7
Chapter 2	✝ Three Memories	15
Chapter 3	✝ Demon King Training	21
Chapter 4	✝ The Demon King's Class Is Pandemonium	29
Chapter 5	✝ The Shape of Love	37
Chapter 6	✝ The Abyss of Love, Crossing the Line	43
Chapter 7	✝ Nation of Dragon Cry	51
Chapter 8	✝ Jiordal, Kingdom of the Divine Dragon	59
Chapter 9	✝ Using the Pledge Jewel	65
Chapter 10	✝ Vessel of God	73
Chapter 11	✝ Ceremonial Hymn	81
Chapter 12	✝ Drifting Memories, Overlapping Dreams, Rising to the Surface	87
Chapter 13	✝ Dora the Liar	93
Chapter 14	✝ Sojourner's Psalm	99
Chapter 15	✝ Demon King Hymn No. Six: "Neighbor"	107
Chapter 16	✝ Prophet	115
Chapter 17	✝ The Pope	121
Chapter 18	✝ Who Will Obtain the Victorious Future?	127
Chapter 19	✝ The Sword Emperor of Agatha	133
Chapter 20	✝ Talks with the Pope	139
Chapter 21	✝ Come, Gospel	147
Chapter 22	✝ The God of Traces' Whereabouts	157

Chapter 23 ✝ The Selfish Nameless God	163
Chapter 24 ✝ An Unfamiliar Visitor	169
Chapter 25 ✝ The Entrance to the Underground Ruins	175
Chapter 26 ✝ The Upstream Corridor	183
Chapter 27 ✝ Where the God of Traces Resides	189
Chapter 28 ✝ Rightful Magic Eyes	195
Chapter 29 ✝ The Fall of a God	203
Chapter 30 ✝ A Promise Made in the Dream	209
Chapter 31 ✝ Contradicting Memories	217
Chapter 32 ✝ The God of Lies and Betrayal	223
Chapter 33 ✝ Flames That Reach the Sky	229
Chapter 34 ✝ The Power of God and Demon	237
Chapter 35 ✝ A Battle of Truth and Lies	243
Chapter 36 ✝ The Divine Dragon's True Identity	249
Chapter 37 ✝ 1,500-Yearlong Prayer	255
Chapter 38 ✝ The Land of Traces	261
Chapter 39 ✝ The Dream a God Had	269
Chapter 40 ✝ The Dragon Lurking Within	277
Epilogue ✝ Sky Barrier	285
Afterword	293

The Misfit of Demon King Academy

§ Prologue: The Demon King and His Sister

Someone was dreaming—of a forest bathed in moonlight. The piercing cries of a dragon filled the air as a small girl ran for her life. She was a demon around six or seven years of age, and while her magic was strong for a child, she was ten years too young to be facing a dragon.

The girl sobbed audibly as she darted between the trees. The dragon pursuing her felled them one after another while baring its fangs.

"N-No!"

The girl's shoes had come off while she'd been running. Her limbs were streaked with blood. She was so absorbed in running away that she failed to notice a large tree root and tripped, slamming heavily against the ground.

"Ugh..."

Enduring the pain, the girl picked herself up. She heard a ferocious growl from behind her and turned to see the dragon's head.

"Eek!"

The girl's knees gave out, and she fell back against the ground. Though she inched slowly away, the dragon's eyes were fixed on her.

"H-Help..."

Its huge jaws opened wide.

"Help me... BIG BROTHER!"

With an earsplitting roar, the dragon lunged towards the girl. Its jaw snapped shut with a sickening crunch, but the girl was not devoured.

"Hmm. Dragons normally avoid this forest," said the demon boy who had appeared. He held one of the dragon's long fangs while stomping down on its lower jaw.

The boy looked to be around ten years old, with black hair and black eyes. If the right person looked at him, they would be able to see he had an abnormal amount of magic hidden within him. His name was Anos Voldigoad—he was yet to be called the Demon King of Tyranny at this stage.

"*Griad.*"

The dragon shrieked as scorching black flames were shot down its throat. Unable to extinguish the flames within its body, the creature was quickly roasted from the inside and crashed to the ground.

"That should do it."

Anos used Gijel to tie up the dead dragon and stored it away in a magic circle. He then turned towards the young girl. Tears were streaming down her face as she sobbed in relief.

"Don't cry," he said. "I've eliminated the dragon that was picking on you." Anos placed his hand on his little sister's head and smiled gently. "There's no need to worry."

The little girl clung to Anos and cried even louder. "Big brotheeer… I was so scared. Big brotheeer!"

Anos rubbed her back reassuringly, but her tears showed no signs of letting up. Unable to stand the sight any longer, Anos drew a magic circle in his palm. "Look," he said, opening his hand to reveal a scarlet gemstone.

"Wow!"

The girl's eyes sparkled as she stared.

"I figured out how to use Iris this morning. You can have this."

"Are you sure?"

"Of course."

The girl beamed from ear to ear. "Thank you, big brother!"

"Well, aren't you materialistic?"

"I'm not a material; I'm a demon! I'm your little sister, after all."

Anos smiled at the childish rebuttal and picked her up in a princess carry. The light of healing magic surrounded her body. Then he rose into the air using Fless and headed deeper into the forest.

"It seems the dragons have sniffed out this place as well. We'll relocate as soon as the sun rises tomorrow."

Prologue — The Demon King and His Sister

"I know of a good place we can go," said the girl in Anos's arms.

"Oh? Where would that be?"

"Do you know what a town is? There are lots of people who live there, and there's a magic wall that protects them, so they're safe from dragons too." She smiled brightly. "If we go to a town, we won't have to run anymore."

"Where did you hear about that?"

"Oh, it was in a book I read. That's why I know there might be a town nearby."

Anos paused to think before answering. "Unfortunately, we can't go to a town."

"Why not? Don't you know where a town is?"

"Do you remember how I told you the dragons will keep chasing us?"

The little girl nodded.

"That was the truth, but dragons normally shouldn't have followed us all the way to this land. This forest, in particular, is full of magic, which they usually avoid. It's because I'm here that they're drawn to us."

"The dragons are after you?"

"Yes. That's why I cannot go to a town—I'll end up endangering the demons that live there. Besides, I won't be very welcome once they realize I'm the one the dragons are chasing."

Although that was how Anos explained it, the truth was that his little sister was the one being targeted. He didn't want to burden the young girl with the blame for their constant running.

"I'm sorry we have to keep moving from place to place because of me. I could have left you somewhere safe, like a town, but I wanted to be together with you despite everything."

The girl's expression brightened. "It's okay! I'd rather be with you than wait alone in a town anyway. I love you, big brother!" She hugged Anos tightly and giggled.

"What's wrong?"

"You know, I thought I wasn't of any help to you. You always have to protect me, but I can't do anything in return." She smiled happily. "But as it turns out, you need me just as much as I need you."

Anos nodded and smiled back warmly. "Yes. You're my only family, after all."

"You know you can rely on me more, right?"

"You spoil me enough."

"Ehee hee!" She grinned shyly. "You know, when I grow up, I'm gonna marry you!"

"Do you know what marriage is?"

"Yup. It's a promise to always be together. I'm gonna marry you because I love you. Will you marry me?"

Anos chuckled. "If you still want to when the time comes."

The little girl giggled. "It's a promise, okay? We'll be together forever and ever!"

"Yeah, that's for sure."

Soon, a wooden house came into view. The two landed, and the girl ran towards it. Just as she was about to open the door, she paused and looked back at Anos.

"Ah, I'm dirty. Is there anywhere to bathe?" She looked down at the dust and dirt on her body.

Anos drew a magic circle and created a bubble of water. A tree grew to surround the bubble, the branches and leaves forming a curtain. It was an impromptu bathtub. "It isn't the most spacious, but it'll have to do."

"Thanks, big brother!" The girl discarded the clothes she was wearing and dived in, but not a moment later, she stuck her head back out. "Do you want to come in too?"

"I've already washed. I'll be preparing for tomorrow."

Anos went into the house and started throwing all their furniture and belongings into a storage circle until only their bedding remained. He then went back outside and drew a magic circle on the ground, retrieving the dragon he had restrained with Gijel. For some reason, the dragons weren't chasing them by scent or sight—they were following his sister's source. With that in mind, he cast Naaz on the dragon, disguising its source to resemble hers. By doing so, he would lure the remaining dragons here after they had relocated. Anos's Naaz still wasn't the most developed, but it could fool a dragon's Magic Eyes to some extent.

He spent his time carefully refining the spell's precision, then returned inside to find his little sister drying her hair with a towel.

"Will this do?" she asked.

"You'll catch a cold like that."

Prologue — The Demon King and His Sister

He drew a magic circle over her head and dried her locks with warm air. She smiled happily at the pleasant sensation.

"We're leaving early tomorrow. Let's sleep now," Anos said, drawing another magic circle to change them into their sleepwear.

"Okay!"

The two siblings proceeded into the bedroom. There were two beds side by side; Anos took the right one, while his little sister took the left. Once the lamplight had been put out, faint moonlight filtered in through the window. Anos closed his eyes and contemplated their next destination.

The dragons chased them ceaselessly. The siblings moved about Dilhade in search of a place the beasts' fangs would not reach, but they had yet to find somewhere safe. The forest they currently occupied hadn't boasted a dragon sighting in several hundred years, but that record had come to an end less than a month after they'd moved there. It felt like the only choice left was to exterminate all dragons, but the young Anos lacked the power to achieve that.

Roughly an hour later, a voice called out from the bed beside his. "Hey, are you still awake?"

Anos's little sister rolled over to face him.

"Yeah. Could you not fall asleep?"

"No," she mumbled feebly. "Can I sleep next to you?"

"Very well."

At Anos's reply, his sister dived into his bed. She happily tangled her feet with his and rubbed her cheek against his. "Where are we going next, big bro? Somewhere hot? Somewhere cold?"

"I'm thinking of heading north. It may get a little cold."

"That means we'll get to wear our winter clothes!" she said happily. She peered closely at Anos's face and grinned. "You know, big brother, I'm not scared of dragons at all. After all, my big brother is the strongest."

Anos smiled. "And my little sister is a liar."

"I'm not lying! I'm not."

"There's no need to put on a brave front after crying so much earlier."

The girl couldn't argue with that. "It was just a little lie. I'm not always a liar."

"You said you'd stay inside, but you sneaked out right away, even after I told you not to walk around at night."

"I'm sorry."

The girl slumped dejectedly. Anos placed his hand on her head.

"There's no need to feel down about it. Your lies are cute."

The girl hugged Anos happily. "Big brother...?"

"What is it?"

"I love you!"

"I see."

"Yup. Dragons aren't scary when you're around, and I can sleep at night. As long as you're here, I don't need anything else." She clung tightly to Anos.

"I couldn't ask for more in a little sister."

"Is that a compliment? Am I a good sister?"

"Yeah. You'd be even better if you went to sleep faster."

"I normally fall asleep fast! I can fall asleep right away if you cast that sleep charm on me."

The young girl grinned at him.

"What a hopeless little sister."

Anos gently held his little sister's head and planted a kiss on her forehead. She happily closed her eyes.

"Hee hee. Good night, big brother."

Anos patted her head and whispered, "Good night, Arcana."

§ 1. Mystery of the Magic Eye

Sunlight streamed through the window, returning me to the waking world. It felt like I'd been dreaming of when I was young. Just then, there was a knock at the door.

"Anos? We're coming in, okay?" Sasha called.

I opened my eyes to a faceful of silver hair. The Selection God Arcana was sound asleep before me, her forehead pressed against mine.

"Arcana," I said. She opened her eyes and stared at me. "When did you sneak into my bed?"

"After you fell asleep."

The door to my room clicked open. Two sets of footsteps approached my bed.

"Are you still asleep?" Misha asked.

"Wake up, Anos," Sasha said, shaking me impatiently. "You said you had something important to talk to us about. I stayed up all night so I didn't oversleep."

Arcana stirred and sat up.

"Huh?"

The sheet covering Arcana slid off her. The god was stark naked, practically glowing with purity.

"Whuh… Whuh…" Sasha's eyes widened in shock. "Why are you sleeping with Anos?!"

Arcana looked somberly back at her. "Is it a sin for god to lie with demon in this nation?"

"Y-You slept together?!" Sasha yelled, upset by the answer to her question.

"Hmm. It must be pretty late if you two are here. My bad. It seems I've slept in later than usual."

"That was my fault. I placed too much of a burden on you." Arcana turned to me. "How was it?"

"How was what?"

"It was my first time, so I don't know if it went well."

Sasha paled and clung to Misha. She seemed to be extremely shaken.

"J-Just because Anos is kind doesn't mean you should take advantage of him! Being a god doesn't give you a free pass to do whatever you want!"

"Take advantage?" Arcana looked at me questioningly, unsure what Sasha meant.

"Wait. Do you mean Anos initiated it?" Sasha asked fearfully.

Arcana shook her head. "I did what I thought best. I believed he desired it too."

At that, Sasha snapped. "Anos wouldn't have wanted *that*!"

"It's what everyone wants. As a god, I wished to grant him salvation."

"H-How dare you lump him in with other men?" Sasha faltered for a moment, then glared sharply at Arcana. "Unfortunately for you, my Demon King has no interest in such things!"

Arcana stared straight back at Sasha with unclouded eyes.

"Hmph! I guess there are immoral gods out there too. You're greatly mistaken if you think such things count as salvation!"

"Why do you think that?" Arcana asked simply.

"B-Because...he's never even asked me..."

Arcana, still confused, looked at Sasha.

"That's why there's no way he'd ask you, whom he just met."

"This isn't something you can do. That's why I did it."

Sasha flushed. "I...I can do it too! If Anos asked me to do it, if Anos wanted me to do it, then I would. There's nothing I wouldn't do!"

"Filling his void isn't easy. Even the body of a god cannot handle it."

"C-Can't handle it?! Is it that much?" Sasha glanced shyly at me, flushed

even redder, and then resumed glaring at Arcana. "What, are you scared? I'm not scared. He can mess me up if he wants. I'd be happy with anything Anos does to me. Besides, I'll get Misha to use her Magic Eyes of Creation to make me stronger!"

Misha tilted her head and muttered quietly, "What do you mean?"

"At any rate, Anos wouldn't want anything like that! Isn't that right, Misha?"

Sasha clung to her sister and looked at her imploringly. Misha blinked several times before looking at me, tilting her head as if to ask if this was yet another chain of misunderstandings. I nodded.

"What did you do to Anos, Arcana?" she asked out loud.

"Exactly what I just said. I was attempting to recover his lost memories," Arcana replied.

Sasha stared at her.

"Anos lost his memories when he reincarnated. My body has consumed Lyeno Ga Roaz, the god that governs memories. I was trying to use that order on Anos's memories, but retrieving those from before his reincarnation isn't easy."

That was what had placed a burden on my body and what Arcana's own body couldn't handle.

"Y-You didn't have to be so misleading about it," Sasha mumbled in embarrassment. "And you didn't have to crawl into bed with him either."

"Memories spill from dreams and drift. Lyeno Ga Roaz is the Keeper of Dreams. The order works the best when inside a dream."

"Then at least put some clothes on..."

"There needs to be no boundary or distinction. The blessing of an order is strongest when god and mortal are in direct contact." Arcana looked at my clothes. "In order to make the most of Lyeno Ga Roaz's order, I should have removed his clothes as well."

"What?! Absolutely not! Why is the magic of gods so immoral?! You said you forgot your name as a god, but are you sure you weren't some immoral god of some immoral order?!"

"Demon girl, I am a god, not a mortal. The undress of a god is sacred and free of immoral concern. Your worries are unfounded."

Sasha looked to Misha for help.

Chapter 1 — Mystery of the Magic Eye

"But you should put on clothes for now," she said plainly.

Arcana seemed to accept that and drew a magic circle over her body. "*Divine garments, materialize.*"

Garments of Jiordal clothed her small body.

"Memories spill from dreams and drift, huh?" I muttered to myself.

Arcana looked at me. "How was it?" she asked.

"I had a dream of when I was young—of back before I was called the Demon King of Tyranny." I thought back to the dream. "I lived with my little sister."

"You had a sister, Anos?" Sasha asked in surprise.

"You said you didn't," Misha said.

"I thought I didn't. I didn't even know my parents two thousand years ago. My mother died when she gave birth to me."

"Are your memories wrong?" she asked.

It would be quite troublesome if they had been altered.

"That, or I've forgotten them. She could have been my half sister from a different mother, or she could have been born from magic. There's no guarantee she was even related to me by blood."

My little sister had been on the run from dragons, but I had never heard of dragons chasing down a single person before—not even two thousand years ago. If those memories were correct, there had to have been something special about my little sister. Why had dragons been chasing her?

"Hmm. It doesn't feel real. Did I really have a sister?"

The fact that her name was Arcana was also quite the coincidence—or was it?

"You merely saw your memories drifting in your dreams," Arcana explained.

That probably meant it wouldn't feel real until I actually remembered.

"I wonder if the god I was before I forgot my name governed an order that conflicted with the Keeper of Dreams'. My compatibility with Lyeno Ga Roaz is bad, so I can't fully control the order. That's why you weren't able to recall everything in one go."

An order that conflicted with dreams, huh? What could that be? It certainly sounded like something to note for later.

"If we continue, you may remember something."

"You want to keep going?!" Sasha yelled.

"My missing memories may be the result of someone's schemes. Like Arcana said, it wouldn't hurt to remember them."

"Th-That's true…"

"There are gods that govern memories more extensively than the Keeper of Dreams," Arcana said. "Using an order like that, you may be able to remember everything."

"If we can meet a god like that so conveniently, sure. Do you have someone in mind?"

Arcana nodded.

"Then please fill me in later. There was a reason I called Misha and Sasha here—I'd first like to confirm something."

"Confirm something?" Sasha asked.

"What do you know about the blasphemous god, Genedonov, Goddess of Absurdity?"

That was what the draconid soldiers had called them upon seeing the Magic Eyes of their fused form. The two girls were demons, but it wasn't impossible for them to have some relation to the gods as well.

"We questioned them like you said, but they wouldn't tell us anything," Sasha said.

"They were angry and scared," Misha added.

"Blasphemous gods are gods that antagonize other gods and seek to destroy order," Arcana explained. "The Goddess of Absurdity was the first god to do so. The Magic Eyes of Absurdity can destroy all magic and reshape all things. The power of the Goddess of Absurdity is said to be able to disrupt logic and recreate the world."

Sasha looked puzzled. "But our eyes aren't the Magic Eyes of Absurdity. They're just the Magic Eyes of Creation and the Magic Eyes of Destruction being used simultaneously. It only looked like one pair of Magic Eyes because we were fused together."

Misha nodded.

"Would you be able to tell if you saw it in person?" I asked Arcana.

"I've never met the Goddess of Absurdity, but I should be able to recognize the divine power of an order."

"Then it's worth a try."

Chapter 1 — Mystery of the Magic Eye

Sasha and Misha nodded. The two linked hands and each drew half of a magic circle, combining them into one. Then they drew another magic circle over it and activated the spell.

"*Dino Jixes.*"

Particles of light rose from the circle and lit up the room. Within that blinding light, their two bodies melted into one. Soon, a single girl with silver hair and silver eyes emerged.

"We just have to show you our eyes, right? *Yeah...*"

Following Sasha's question, Misha created a mock Delsgade in the sky above my house. The silver-haired girl then used the Magic Eyes of Destruction and the Magic Eyes of Creation at the same time. Arcana stared at the magic circle within their combined Magic Eyes, but she didn't say anything.

"Is something the matter?"

"It looks familiar," she mumbled, still staring. She seemed to be surprised at her own recollection. "I think I saw these Eyes somewhere before—before I forgot my name."

§ 2. Three Memories

"Hmm. That's strange."

Sasha wasn't the only one who could use the Magic Eyes of Destruction. The same went for Misha and the Magic Eyes of Creation. Militia, too, had possessed those Eyes—after all, she was the god that governed the order of creation. It only made sense for her to possess every power related to creation magic. At any rate, while the twins' Eyes might not have been unique in and of themselves, Dino Jixes was another matter.

"It would be extremely rare to find two people capable of combining themselves with fusion magic who just so happen to possess the Magic Eyes of both Destruction and Creation. Besides, Dino Jixes is the secret art of the Necron family."

It wasn't common magic.

"When did you lose your memory, Arcana?" I asked.

"One thousand years ago."

"Dino Jixes succeeded for the first time on Misha and Sasha, and that was fifteen years ago. There was no record of the Magic Eyes of Destruction and Creation fusing before then—at least, not in the world aboveground."

If Arcana had seen it somewhere, then it had probably been while underground.

"The Goddess of Absurdity is said to have silver hair and possess the Magic Eyes of Absurdity," Arcana said. "I might have once met the god that destroys order."

"In other words, the fused form of Sasha and Misha. Hmm. Not having a name sure is inconvenient. How about we call you Aisha? Or would you prefer something else?" I asked.

The silver-haired girl nodded. "Aisha's fine. *It's a good name. I like it.*"

"Let's call the fused form of the Magic Eyes of Creation and Destruction the Magic Eyes of Omneity. What you're trying to say is that Aisha could be Genedonov, the Goddess of Absurdity. Is that right, Arcana?"

"Yes. The Goddess of Absurdity continuously defied order. Gods remain gods when they reincarnate, but Genedonov might have resisted that as well. She could have reincarnated after her death, becoming a demon. As a subordinate of the Demon King of Tyranny, she could continue destroying order."

While it was only a conjecture, it was a possibility we couldn't deny.

"The Magic Eyes of Omneity are the Magic Eyes of Absurdity. They merely became the Magic Eyes of Creation and Destruction because they were split with Dino Jixes."

In other words, the Magic Eyes of Omneity hadn't formed through the fusing of Sasha and Misha; it was the Magic Eyes of Destruction and Creation that had been formed through the original Eyes' separation.

"*If Dino Jixes hadn't been used on Sasha, would she have had the Magic Eyes of Omneity?*" Misha's voice asked.

"One source was split into two, but instead of the source's power being split evenly, it was split into the powers of creation and destruction. That's one possible explanation," I said. It certainly wasn't out of the question.

Aisha tilted her head in thought. "We're a god? *That doesn't seem right at all. It's not like we're missing any memories.*"

"There are times when no memories are retained after reincarnation. If Arcana says she's seen those Magic Eyes before, whether you're the Goddess of Absurdity or not, it's possible that you once lived underground."

"As a draconid? *Oh, I get it. We could've been a draconid before we reincarnated into a demon.*"

"I have one question for you, Arcana," I said. "You said you discarded your name as a god, but do you recall how you managed that?"

"I have lost those memories."

So she didn't remember.

"And the Keeper of Dreams was of no use?"

Chapter 2 — Three Memories

"That's right."

This was certainly curious. How did a god go about discarding their name and obtaining a heart?

"Did you reincarnate?"

Arcana mulled over my words for a moment. "Gods remain gods when they reincarnate. Even if they forget their memories, they retain the order they govern. They don't gain hearts. However..."

"The Goddess of Absurdity would have been able to do that. A god capable of reincarnating into a demon would have easily been able to take your name and grant you a heart," I concluded. If Arcana's theory was true, this was another possibility.

"That's correct."

"There's a possibility that you've met the Goddess of Absurdity before and saw the Magic Eyes of Absurdity. Perhaps that was when you were reincarnated into a nameless god." I looked over at Aisha and continued. "Furthermore, the Goddess of Absurdity might have been Aisha. Genedonov reincarnated into the demon named Sasha in order to become a subordinate of the Demon King of Tyranny in this era. Aisha forgot her memories as Genedonov and split into Misha and Sasha through Dino Jixes."

Aisha blinked. It was possible that she had lost her memories because she hadn't expected her source to be split upon her reincarnation.

"In which case, I might have met the Goddess of Absurdity before too," I said.

"You met us...*two thousand years ago?*"

"Misha, do you remember when you first saw the city I'd made beneath Midhaze? You said it looked familiar."

That underground city had been a recreation of Midhaze two thousand years ago.

"That could be proof you still have some vague memories left."

Aisha tried to recall her distant past.

"On top of that, I, too, forgot about the Goddess of Absurdity when I reincarnated. Thus, when I met the two of you in this era, I was unable to realize that we'd met before."

Perhaps I was connected to Arcana somehow too. In the dream I'd had that morning, my little sister's name had been Arcana. That might not have been a coincidence. But even if that were true, I had no idea how a god could end up becoming my little sister.

"The three of us might have met somewhere two thousand years ago. Perhaps we've just forgotten that through our respective reincarnations."

That's why not one of us had recognized each other back when we'd first met.

"Could all this really be a coincidence?"

If Arcana had reincarnated to discard her name, then it made sense for her to have no memories. Genedonov had reincarnated into a demon. Gods normally reincarnated into gods, so the price she had paid might have been her memories. However, my lack of memories was inexplicable. Did that mean Arcana and Aisha's cases could be dismissed as coincidences?

"I don't think so. Someone might have taken our memories," I said.

"Someone… A god?"

"When it comes to enemies of mine, gods would probably be the top contenders, but there isn't enough evidence to say for sure. If someone truly has stolen my memories, they would have taken everything related to themselves as well."

In short, I probably couldn't remember who my enemy was in the first place.

"Someone stole Anos's memories—*and you can't even remember them. Isn't that pretty bad?*" Aisha said worriedly.

"No, it's not a problem. If the culprit erased all my memories of them, I'll eventually find them by following my missing memories."

The blanks in my head were my biggest clues to their identity.

"We'll be underground for the Selection Trial anyway, so we might as well investigate while we're down there."

"Speaking of which, you said you were going to do something about the Selection Trial. What exactly are you gonna do?" Sasha's voice asked.

"The Selection Trial is said to be held by the order of judgment," Arcana answered.

"So we just have to destroy the god of judgment?"

"That's right. But the god that possesses the order of judgment has never appeared before the gods. They are a god no one has seen."

Aisha tilted her head. "How will you find them?"

Chapter 2 — Three Memories

"I don't know. There's no god, but the order of judgment exists. Due to this, the people of the underground—and a number of gods too—deduced the existence of a being called Equis, the Almighty Radiance. That is, they believe that everything is the work of this almighty god and that the Selection Trial is an order personally carried out by Equis, which is why no one has ever seen them."

"So in short, this Almighty Radiance isn't a real god, but a concept the draconids came up with?" Sasha asked.

Arcana nodded. "In a way, that is correct. The Almighty Radiance may or may not exist. It all depends on what you choose to believe."

"Hmm. It would be pretty simple if this Almighty Radiance was the one who stole my memories. I could settle everything in one go."

Aisha shot me a dumbfounded look. "Settle everything? But if this Equis really does exist, they'll be able to use all the powers of the gods at once. What will you do, then? It'd be like going up against the world itself."

"Good point," I said, laughing fearlessly. "I guess I'll just have to destroy the world."

Aisha recoiled in disgust. It seemed my expression was a little more sadistic than I'd thought.

"I'm joking. Even I can't do something like that, but I'll think of something else."

"It didn't sound like a joke. *Fiend...*"

I looked over at Arcana. "You said before that there's a god that governs memories more broadly than the Keeper of Dreams. If we use that god's order, we may be able to recover all our memories."

For now, all this was mere speculation, but if our memories returned, the truth would become clear.

"That god is Revalschned, God of Traces, who governs the order that carves the footsteps of the world. It's believed that Revalschned sleeps in Jiordal, the Kingdom of the Divine Dragon."

Jiordal, huh? That was Ahid's home country.

"Then let's head there."

"Oh. I guess that means this isn't the time to be going to class, right? *Do we call in absent?*" Sasha and Misha asked.

"No, that's not necessarily true. Now that the underground world has been discovered, I need to keep a close eye on the future demon lords of Dilhade."

"I have a bad feeling about this. *Agreed.*"

"You two can head to the academy first. I have something to discuss with Eldmed and Shin before class."

Aisha nodded and drew a magic circle over herself. With a flash of light, Dino Jixes was released, splitting Aisha back into Misha and Sasha.

"See you later," Sasha said.

Misha waved, and the two left the room.

Roughly half an hour later, the bell for the start of class rang. The door to the second lecture hall opened, and the Conflagration King Eldmed skipped up to the podium. Shin, the right-hand man of the Demon King, quietly closed the classroom door behind him and moved to stand beside Eldmed.

"Bwa ha ha! Good news! Good news, everyone!" the Conflagration King cried, raising his arms and clenching his fists. "Today, we'll be holding a special class that has been in the works for a while now!"

He took a running leap, landing before the blackboard and twirling his cane before tapping out a magic circle on its surface. The circle glowed, releasing streamers, confetti, and a dozen doves into the air.

"And that lesson is called"—Eldmed spun rapidly on the spot before dramatically pointing his cane at the students—"Greater Demon King Training!"

A Gatom magic circle appeared on the teacher's podium. I emerged from the circle as Anos Voldigoad, wearing my white uniform. Shin immediately knelt. Eldmed copied him soon after. Chairs scraped noisily across the floor as the students scampered to kneel as fast as they could, nearly smacking their heads against the floor in the process. On the teacher's podium, I opened my mouth coolly.

"I, Anos Voldigoad, the Demon King of Tyranny, will be your provisional instructor for classes starting from today, but there's no need to turn this into a formal occasion." I smiled warmly, like I was greeting old friends. "Long time no see, everyone."

Over half the students pulled faces filled with despair.

§ 3. Demon King Training

The classroom fell silent. Normally, this would be when the class burst into chatter, but everyone remained stiff.

"What's wrong? You're all awfully quiet today. I thought this class would be noisier than this."

The students all opened their mouths at once. The class started stirring like usual.

"W-We've offended him!"

"Quick, everyone, make some noise! Murmur at a volume low enough that Lord Anos can't understand what we're saying!"

"Isn't this bad? We're gonna be in so much trouble," a student in black uniform mumbled at the back of the room.

"I don't know how many times I called the Demon King by his name."

"Dumbass! At least that's all you called him. I called him a misfit the entire time."

"I'm even worse! I kept telling him his blood was worth nothing!"

"Say, do you think he's here to use this class as an excuse to end us?"

"If he wanted us dead, he could just ask Mr. Shin to finish us off. The only reason he'd come here himself would be to watch us suffer in person!"

"But he's the Demon King of Tyranny—*that* Demon King of Tyranny. Surely he doesn't care about demons like us."

"Right! Good point. He's probably forgotten us already. Please, *please* tell me he's forgotten us."

Hmm. They seemed rather nervous.

"Raise your heads. Be at ease."

Shin and Eldmed raised their heads and got to their feet. The students followed their lead, hesitantly returning to their seats.

"There's no need for formalities. Just because you now know I'm the Demon King doesn't mean I've changed. I still clearly remember the time I spent in this classroom with all of you." In order to refresh their memories of me as a fellow classmate, I flashed them a smile. "I remember every single moment—who said what, who did what, everything. They're precious memories of the fun I had with you all. Wouldn't you agree?"

The students in black flinched.

"Oh no. We're doomed! He said he remembers everything!"

"That face... He must be imagining how he's gonna torture us!"

"He's the Demon King of Tyranny, after all—the perfect existence that's both merciful and savage. The legends say he's the most terrifying when he's smiling."

"And what a cheerful smile it is too! Just what kind of horrors is he thinking of?!"

Hmm. It seemed there was a rather severe misunderstanding going on. There was no helping it. I'd have to deny things directly.

"If I could say one thing," I said quietly, looking at each student's face one by one, "in the past, some of you might have spoken to me rudely because of my status as a misfit, but I'm not bothered by that in the least. We were fellow classmates. That means our statuses were equal, and you were free to speak as you wished. I am not so petty as to blame you all for something so trivial."

The Royalist students continued whispering.

"He said he's not bothered by it..."

"That must mean he's holding a grudge against us! We're too late!"

"If he truly wasn't bothered by it, he wouldn't have mentioned it in the first place."

"Being of equal status means he won't have to hold back against us!"

"He's going to do whatever he wants to us. It's over."

"I just hope he'll spare my life!"

Hmm. So that's how it was.

"Sasha, do something."

Chapter 3 — Demon King Training

"Don't just show up and demand things from me! Do it yourself!"

The students in black froze and gulped. "Even Lady Sasha's hesitating."

"What in the world does he want her to do?"

"I don't know, but one thing's for sure: this is the start of our personal hell."

Sasha stared at them with an exasperated look.

I snorted. "Sasha, you're making it worse."

"What are you laughing at?!" she snapped. "You're the one creating this mess! It's all your fault!"

"Well then, Misha, can you do something in the place of your pitiful sister?"

Sasha fumed as Misha got to her feet.

"Please listen," Misha said, capturing the attention of the students. "Anos may not look like it, but he likes mushroom gratin."

Interesting. Emphasizing my love for common food could invoke a sense of familiarity, reducing their fear of the Demon King of Tyranny.

"I often make mushroom gratin for him. I practiced with all my might. I messed up before too, but he always ate it and told me it was delicious. That's the sort of person he is. He's kind."

An anecdote of my daily life was sure to ease the students' fear of the Demon King of Tyranny. They would even see me as a Demon King of the people. With this, they would finally understa—

"M-Mushroom gratin?!"

The Royalist students looked more terrified than ever.

"Wh-What's that? Is it some kind of torture method?!"

"Hey, don't tell me he intends to cook us alive!"

"What?! But we'll melt! Does he mean to disfigure us?!"

"Hold on. If she's made it for him often, has he been making her practice how to torture us?! Oh, the tyranny!"

"And he ate it and said it was delicious! Does he plan on cooking us alive in mushroom gratin and eating us too?!"

"That's not even the biggest problem. Listen…"

The students gulped nervously.

"The biggest problem is that she still considers him kind."

"What'll happen if he truly gets mad?"

"We shouldn't have opposed him. There was no way for us to know his identity, but what have we done?"

The students paled and pressed their foreheads to their desks, trembling in fear. Misha blinked at them, then looked at me. "I made it worse."

"It's fine. It happens."

Looking discouraged, she quietly sat back down.

"It was a good effort, Misha," Eleonore said to reassure her.

Zeshia patted Misha's head from behind. "It's...okay."

Well, it was fine either way. The Demon King of Tyranny name had created needless fear two thousand years ago too. This level of misunderstanding was tame compared to back then. If I remained composed, they would eventually realize the truth.

"Allow me to give you the rundown on Demon King Training," I said.

Eldmed pointed his cane at the blackboard. A cross-sectional map of the world magically appeared there. The map showed the surface and the underground world.

"Just the other day, an underground world was discovered below us. It's roughly the same size as our world and is inhabited by descendants of dragons. The draconid people's culture has been built around worshipping, making pacts with, and summoning gods."

The students listened closely.

"I'm sure you all remember the recent dragon attacks on Azesion and Dilhade. Those attacks were the work of the draconid people. During this class, we will be visiting the draconid nation in the underground world."

The students' eyes widened.

"Um, Lord Anos," Ellen said, hesitantly raising her hand, "does that mean we're going to a country that tried to invade us?"

"That's right. That being said, there's still no telling if every draconid considers Dilhade an enemy. There could be good and bad draconids, just like how there are good and bad humans and demons. Your task will be to head to this unknown nation and judge them for yourselves."

The worried students looked even more uneasy.

"There'll be a risk of death. There's even a chance that you cannot be resurrected, but that's what makes this a worthy learning experience."

"But we'll be fine if you're there, right?"

Chapter 3 — Demon King Training

"I'll have other business to attend to during your training. I may not be able to tend to you the entire time. You must work together with your classmates to survive."

Of course I would make sure they were sufficiently prepared, but they wouldn't make any progress if they assumed I would always save them. A bit of scare would do them no harm. However, the students looked like they didn't want to go at all.

"Well, I won't force anyone to go. It's an unknown nation in an unknown world. There will be many dangers, and it's just as vital to be aware of your own strength. If you think you can't do it, you may ask to be excused."

The fan union girls exchanged looks with each other.

"What should we do?"

"We can't defeat a dragon ourselves yet. Won't it be tough for us?"

"Maybe it'd be better to sit this one out."

"Yeah. I don't wanna cause trouble for anyone."

"Hold it! I just thought of something!"

"Something to do with Lord Anos?"

"Do you think he's testing us?"

"No, that's not it. If it's an unknown nation, Lord Anos hasn't been there either, right?"

"R-Right. Maybe."

"Then if we go together, we'd be sharing an indirect first time with him!"

"Eeeeeek!" they all screamed.

"Besides, if we die while we're there, we'll be dying at Lord Anos's will."

"An indirect first-time trip that ends in destruction?!"

"I want to be destroyed!" they shrieked.

The fan union girls continued squealing, all thoughts of the underground world gone from their heads. As usual, their unwavering resolution was a sight to behold. Those who didn't fear death were the least likely to die. Also, as the girls were among the weakest in the class, the other students found themselves unable to ask to remain absent. In fact, the only person worse at magic than the fan union was Naya. Their pride wouldn't allow them to ask to stay behind.

"Hmm. Well, let me know if you change your minds. We depart tomorrow."

The students seemed relieved to know they still had some time.

"Now, have any of you heard of this story before?" I said, changing the topic. "There was once a Demon Castle in a disastrous situation, surrounded by humans and spirits on the verge of attack. There were two thousand enemies and five hundred allies, but those allies were all newly recruited soldiers with no fighting experience. Even so, it was the demons who emerged victorious. One man led them all to victory. What do you think he did?"

I looked over at Ellen, who scratched her head in thought. "Did he come up with an amazing strategy to defeat them?"

"You could call it a strategy, but that's not quite it."

Ellen pondered further. It seemed she couldn't think of anything.

"What about the rest of you?" I asked.

Misa raised her hand. "I don't know how exactly, but did he use the land to his advantage?"

"No, the geography was irrelevant."

"I know! Pick me next," Eleonore said, raising her hand.

"Let's hear it."

"He tried really hard!"

"I'm sure he did his best, but no."

Zeshia raised her hand in imitation of Eleonore.

"Yes, Zeshia?"

"He tried…even harder!" she answered confidently, clenching her fists.

"In a way, that is correct."

"Zeshia's…correct!"

"Really? You're too soft on Zeshia, Anos!" Eleonore whined, pouting.

No one else raised their hand, so I looked over at the smiling man who was listening to the class like it wasn't his business.

"Let's hear the answer from you, Lay."

His reply was immediate. "He trained the demon soldiers in a single day until they were each capable of taking on four people at once. Then he repelled the human and spirit army."

"Wait, Lay, are you serious?" Sasha asked, frowning.

"He's correct."

"No way. Really?"

Lay smiled wryly. "If I hadn't been on the losing side myself, I wouldn't have believed it either."

Chapter 3 — Demon King Training

"That's kind of unfair," Sasha mumbled, slumping over her desk. "The castle was protected because of that urgently dispatched lone demon—your very own teacher, the Conflagration King."

Eldmed burst out laughing. "What an old story to bring up. And that man over there conquered the castle in the end anyway."

Lay smiled cheekily. He had defeated Eldmed and his impromptu army by repeatedly exceeding his own limits in the midst of battle. His first retreat had been in order to regroup the agitated human army. "The outcome might have been different if you hadn't abandoned the castle and retreated," he said.

The Conflagration King grinned back.

I turned to the students watching in amazement. "A devastatingly powerful enemy could attack us tomorrow. At such a time, it's imperative that we think of this as having a full day to our advantage, not that we have only a day left. A single mindset can be the difference between victory and defeat. If you have no reinforcements, then increase your own strength. That way, you can win even if you're outnumbered. This was what happened during the besieging of two thousand years ago—no, during the besieging of the Conflagration King."

The students stared at me in disbelief.

"Of course, seeing is believing. The class you are about to partake in will be much more dangerous than the Conflagration King's training back then. If all goes well, your abilities will improve dramatically, but if you slip up, you'll perish in an instant. Proceed with caution."

§ 4. The Demon King's Class Is Pandemonium

The enchanted forest behind the Demon King Academy.
Magic circles appeared one after another, followed by the students teleporting in via Gatom.
"Everyone's here. Let's begin."
I drew a magic circle over each student's body. My target was their source.
"Ruminate," I said, sending magic into the sources through a magic link. "Look deep, deep into the abyss of the future you must aim for—the future you will arrive at. I will wake the future sleeping deep within your sources and manifest your ideal selves."
The students peered into their abysses as told, picturing their ideal forms. One after another, their bodies were bathed in light. If the futures they were aiming for were being pictured clearly in their minds, those images would take shape. The outlines of the glowing students blurred and distorted, slowly splitting into two. The more they thought and the deeper they stared into the abyss, the more the separation would progress. Eventually, another body and source before each successful student.
"*Edonica.*"
In an even brighter flash of light, each body turned into an adult version of the student.
"Hey, what's with this guy? He looks exactly like me!" Ramon yelped, leaping back. Before him was another Ramon who'd been created with

Edonica. The Edonica Ramon stood taller than the original and wore armor over a toned body. His face was also far rougher than the real thing.

"Edonica reveals the future self you should strive to become. Using the image you came up with, a part of your source, and a portion of your magic, I manifested your potential."

The Edonicas before them were just one possible destination point for each of them.

"Fight, learn their moves, and steal their strength. Then ruminate again. If your ideal shape changes, Edonica will change accordingly and evolve. However, that shape should never be unachievable. Use your Magic Eyes to look into the depths of your Edonica double and determine your own limits. Experience firsthand what you're suited for and what you don't need."

The students' doppelgängers started running as though to lead the way.

"Hey, where are you going?!" Ramon yelled, giving chase.

"Normally, Edonica can only give shape to your ideal strength and skills. No matter how much magic you use, it won't gain any intelligence or wisdom. The copies are merely masses of fighting instincts. However..."

I held my hand out over the ground. An enormous mass of magic particles rose from Delsgade behind me and gathered at my feet, forming the shadow of a sword. The shadow floated into the air and presented its hilt to me. As my hand grasped the shadow hilt, and the sword transformed into Venuzdonoa. I thrust the Abolisher of Reason into the ground and poured my magic into it.

"I will destroy that reason."

Multiple layers of shadows extended from Venuzdonoa and connected to the doubles. The Edonica copies began to think for themselves.

"Hey, Ramon," Ramon's doppelgänger said.

"Wh-What?"

"You think you're smart, don't you? Just so we're clear, you're an idiot, and you'll always be an idiot."

"What did you say?! You don't know that for sure!"

"I'm teaching you a lesson—that idiots have their own idiotic ways of fighting."

The Edonica Ramon drew a magic circle. A black sun emerged from the center.

Chapter 4 — The Demon King's Class Is Pandemonium

"A-Are you serious?! I can use Jio Graze?!" Ramon retreated, hiding behind a tree.

"That won't defend you from anything; you're not even hidden. You need to do everything you can to block it, since you're too stupid to do anything else!"

Jio Graze incinerated the tree and struck Ramon directly.

"Gyaaaaaaaaaaaah!"

Ramon was burned to ashes and immediately revived through Ingall.

"You can die as many times as you want," I said. "Get used to the sensation of revival. Once you get the hang of it, you can try using Ingall yourself. If you can't, I'll revive you in three seconds."

Ramon looked at the double walking up to him.

"Go on! This is how you cast Jio Graze. If you don't get it, learn it with your body!"

"Damn it! Who the hell are you?! You're definitely not me!"

He charged at his double, ready to die.

Across the enchanted forest, students were fighting their Edonica selves, just like Ramon. Their opponents clearly outclassed them and were thoroughly familiar with their techniques. There was no way for them to win against such enemies, and they all died one after the next.

The source burned stronger and brighter the closer it came to the brink of destruction, but that didn't make it okay to cause suffering for no reason. The experience had to result in worthy development. By experiencing how much of a difference there was between their current and ideal selves, they could train to become closer to their ideals. Their ideals could also be reforged through Edonica. The students would gain strength and skills through the advice and guidance of their ideal selves at the cost of being repeatedly pushed to the brink of destruction. Then, when the part of their source being used in Edonica returned to them, it would become their flesh and blood, leading to an exponential increase in their abilities.

The class quickly became a hellish scene as pandemonium spread across the forest as planned. Among the carnage, I looked over at a certain student—the one Eldmed had nicknamed Bookworm Naya. There was an Edonica double in front of her, but it was completely frozen. It looked exactly the same as her in appearance.

The Conflagration King looked away from the suffering students and cheerfully made his way to Naya. "Bwa ha ha! Why the long face, Bookworm?" he said, leaning on his cane to peer at her.

Her gaze remained fixed on the ground. "I'm no good. Even the Demon King's Edonica of me won't move," she mumbled.

The Conflagration King listened quietly.

"Unlike everyone else's, my Edonica looks just like me and has the same amount of magic. That means I don't have any potential, right?"

Eldmed laughed. "No potential? What makes you say that?"

"If the Demon King's magic and Magic Eyes made me like that, then that has to be it," she said glumly.

"Indeed, you have a point. The Demon King's Magic Eyes are absolute. The Demon King's Edonica is flawless. Anyone who fails his judgment is bound to be lacking in talent. Anyone would think that."

His merciless words discouraged her further. Still leaning on his cane, the Conflagration King stared at her.

"But I, the Conflagration King, am not just anyone."

Naya looked up and met his eyes.

"Have you heard of this story before? There was a demon who took the Demon King Academy's entrance exam and was judged to have no magic at all. He became the first misfit in the history of the academy and was shunned by the entire school," Eldmed said smugly.

"That's…"

"Yes, it's the story of the Demon King of Tyranny, Anos Voldigoad. Someone with as much magic as he has was determined to have no magic at all."

Naya thought for a moment. "But that was because the method of measuring was wrong, wasn't it? Lord Anos had too much magic for it to be measured by modern means," she argued hesitantly.

"Indeed, indeed. That is correct, Bookworm Naya. Isn't that exactly like you right now?"

"Like what?"

Eldmed grinned. "In other words, the Demon King is wrong! Your future holds so much potential, not even the Demon King himself can foresee it!"

Chapter 4 — The Demon King's Class Is Pandemonium

Naya shook her head furiously. "There's no way! Someone like me could never!" She looked over at me worriedly.

The Conflagration King continued. "Someone like you could never? Why not? The Demon King would be delighted to see someone from this academy surpass him. In fact, that man will try to surpass anyone who surpasses him!" Eldmed cackled in delight. "Edonica is merely one means of measurement. It is no more than a single form of training. Perhaps your future is beyond the Demon King's means of measurement. Isn't that marvelous?!"

He looked as if he was enjoying himself from the bottom of his heart. "Do you have no potential, or is it merely unable to be seen by anyone? There's no telling the answer, and an uncertain answer is marvelous! It means there are endless possibilities, no matter how unlikely they may be. Personally, my heart races at the thought of the uncertain!" Eldmed said firmly and cheerfully.

Naya seemed somewhat encouraged, as the life returned to her eyes. Eldmed took off his top hat, reached inside, and took out a long rod. It was a magic tool called the Staff of Knowledge.

"Allow me to teach you how to use this. You are far too young to have reached your limit already. At least reach my age before you say such things."

Naya rubbed at her eyes as though to wipe away tears and then reached for the staff. Her expression was much brighter than before.

"Yes, sir! Please teach me, Mr. Conflagration King!"

As always, Eldmed had a sharp eye for those who could potentially become my enemies. At least Naya should be fine in his hands.

"Say, Anos..." Sasha called. Misha was by her side. "How come we don't have an Edonica?"

Lay, Misa, Eleonore, and Zeshia were in the same situation.

"Why would you? You four have long surpassed the need to train with Edonica."

"So what do we do?"

"I've prepared the perfect practice opponents for you."

I took out my Selection pledge jewel and channeled my magic into it. Magic circles appeared within the jewel, layering on top of each other one after another.

"*Guala Nateh Forteos.*"

With the light of summoning magic, Arcana, the silver-haired Selection God, appeared.

"If we're going underground, you may as well get used to fighting with gods."

Sasha looked at me dejectedly. "I've always wanted to say this, but don't you think your training methods are kind of harsh?"

Misha nodded in silence.

"Use Dino Jixes. Not even you two could face Arcana in your current forms."

Arcana looked around the area, then up at the sky. "We can train up there."

She probably intended to move away from the other students so they wouldn't get caught up in their fight. The three proceeded towards the sky.

"Eleonore, please train alone with Zeshia for a while."

"Got it. Zeshia, we're going over that way. That way, okay?"

"Zeshia will do her best."

The two ran deeper into the forest.

"Now, as for you two…"

Lay and Misa looked at me. Shin immediately appeared behind me.

"The love magic you used against the Royal Dragon was most impressive."

"Ah… Aha ha… I don't really want to be reminded of that. In fact, I'd love to crawl into a hole right at this moment," Misa mumbled, looking down and turning bright red.

The sound of grinding teeth reached my ears.

"What about our love magic?" Lay asked.

"A thought came to me—that perhaps gods are weak to the power of love."

According to Arcana, love and kindness could disrupt order. In fact, it was possible that love magic was the natural enemy of the gods.

"Thus, I've recently spent some time looking into the abyss of love magic. Your love can still reach greater heights, so you'll be training in that today. The fastest way of doing so is to fight against other love magic."

"That sounds great," Lay said, linking hands with Misa and activating their love magic. The light of Teo Aske gathered around them and extended into the sky.

Chapter 4 — The Demon King's Class Is Pandemonium

Misa looked at me curiously. "I know you can use Aske, Lord Anos, but are you able to use love magic? I ask because, you know, it requires two people..."

Shin immediately took a step forward and drew his steel sword from its sheath. He handed it to me quietly and knelt, bowing his head. I solemnly took the sword and pointed it at him then softly tapped the blade on his shoulder. The next moment, light flooded from us, shooting upwards to pierce the heavens.

"Huh? Isn't this... What?!"

"Don't tell me. Anos, you..."

"Did you think you had to be lovers to use Teo Aske?" I asked.

The two immediately recovered from their daze and tensed up. They had realized the point of this training.

"I thought I could take it easy in this class, but it seems we can't afford to lose."

"Right. We have to win no matter what!"

In a battle of love magic, victory depended on the stronger feeling. If their romantic love couldn't amount to the love between Shin and myself, the shame would be immeasurable. That was how their love could grow further.

"My love knows no limits. Come at me with all you've got," I said.

Lay and Misa looked at me with determination. Meanwhile, Shin stood up and moved to my side, calmly prepared to take them on.

"We'll show you two that love can take many shapes."

§ 5. The Shape of Love

Two pillars of light rose from the enchanted forest. One of them was from Lay, who drew a magic circle and summoned the Sword of Three Races. The blade, which had once been transformed into the Sword of the Almighty, had been returned to its original form by Arcana. Lay and Misa's Teo Aske converted their love into magic and wrapped around Evansmana, extending the blade into a longsword. Lay took several steps forward.

"Misa," he said with a gentle smile, looking back at the girl behind him, "wish me luck."

"Um, what to say…" Misa briefly looked down in embarrassment. Then her gaze met his. "I… I want to see you win today, my beloved."

The next moment, in an explosion of light, the Teo Aske around Evansmana shone brighter than ever before. Lay and Misa's love was shining brighter now than it had when they'd faced Avos Dilhevia or fought the Royal Dragon.

Of course, their opponents were none other than Shin and myself. Even though they had lost to us before in demon sword battles, the couple couldn't afford to lose in a battle of Teo Aske. That was why the bond between them—their love—was blazing passionately, but there was one man who was glaring at that glittering fruit with fierce contempt. Shin took a quiet step forward towards Lay.

"I have a humble request of you, my liege," he said to me. "Please allow me to be the first to demonstrate true love to them."

"I'll allow it. Demonstrate to your heart's content." I returned Shin's steel sword to him. Bright light had gathered around the blade—I had activated Teo Aske to convert our love into magic.

"How many times have we faced each other like this, Lay Grandsley?" Shin asked.

"I couldn't say. I lost count some time ago."

The two held their glowing swords at the ready, and their gazes met. The normally smiling Lay was unusually serious even before crossing swords. He had even more drive than he'd had that time he'd said he'd protect me. That was how strongly he felt about this.

"Ever since that demon sword class, I've been thinking. There is one thing I swore to myself—that the next time I faced you, I'd definitely land one hit."

"Save the chatter. I'll land ten hits on you in that time."

Shin's eyes were as cold as a sharpened blade. His bloodlust was as bare as the first time I met him. However, at the same time, there was an emotion contrary to the yearning for death swirling around him. He was about to fight with an emotion he had never fought with, not even two thousand years ago.

Lay was the challenger; Shin was his opponent. Both knew they couldn't lose. Their feelings of love poured into their swords.

"Here I go."

"I'll bring you down."

Lay and Shin raised their swords of love higher. There were no tricks involved—they weren't about to flee using their skills. This was a one-on-one fight between love and love, emotions and emotions. The slightest step back would end in defeat.

With a quick breath, Lay moved first. Lifting his longsword overhead, he charged straight at Shin.

"Haaaaaaaaaaaah!"

His feelings—his love—flowed out of his body, scattering particles of light. Anyone with Magic Eyes would be able to see his determination.

If I win, I'll have you listen to me, father-in-law!

"Howling won't make your love any stronger." Shin kicked off the ground and started running, lifting his blinding sword to repel Lay's emotions.

* * *

Chapter 5 — The Shape of Love

Save your nonsense for after you land a hit, boy!

Two swords of light collided fiercely. Love and love competed for dominance.

You will listen to me!
I shall not.
No! You will listen. I have something important to say regarding your daughter!

Suddenly, there was a deafening explosion of light. Propelled by the force of the explosion, Shin was sent flying back.
"Father!" Misa shouted.
Lay had used a Teo Traloth that had been refined to its limit. It was a pleading blow to the stubborn father who refused to listen to his daughter's lover, which demonstrated the extent of his love.
Believing Shin wouldn't be able to withstand such a blow, Misa stared into the explosion with her Magic Eyes. As the light gradually faded, a figure came into view. Shin was alive. Not only that, but he had blocked their wholehearted Teo Traloth with his sword of love alone.
"Is that the extent of your love?"
"It's not over yet!"
Lifting his sword of emotions and swinging down his love, Lay slammed Teo Traloth into Shin multiple times. However, Shin blocked the blows with ease.

It's something very important. I will make you listen. I swear on this love!
I will not, I will not, I will not! Is that all you've got, boy?!

Shin was affected by neither Lay's words nor his attacks. The next time their swords locked together, Lay was breathing harshly. They crossed blades, sparks flying from the intensity of their gazes.
"Do you get it yet, Lay? The reason Shin's sword can block your Teo Traloth so thoroughly is because this is another shape of love."
Like a boyfriend persistently waiting under the eaves for his girlfriend's

stubborn father to give in, Lay detonated Teo Traloth again and again. With each booming flash, he bowed and pleaded, over and over through rain, shine, and snow.

However, Shin's sword shot those pleads down. Seeing his daughter's lover bowing on his front porch, the father felt unfathomable hatred towards the man attempting to steal his daughter. Despite knowing that his actions would make his daughter hate him, his awkward heart prevented him from allowing the boy inside.

"*Dio Grezeas*," I said.

Lay's sources started exploding one after another. Blown into the air, he died five times, revived five times, died another five times, and then revived the same number of times once again. In the brief moment he staggered as his feet touched the ground, Shin landed ten hits on him.

"Wh-What was that just now?" Lay asked.

"Something new I developed. Dio Grezeas is an explosion of love and hatred. Normally, Teo Aske requires the love of two people, but this version uses both love and hate."

"Hatred... Is that even love magic anymore?" Misa asked.

"Not if it were regular hatred, but sometimes, love that crosses the line turns into hate. That is the love and hatred our Teo Aske thrives upon. Shin's parental love—his feelings towards his daughter's lover, the awkward love that refuses to move out of the way—is the Dio Grezeas capable of shattering Teo Traloth."

Shin's great love for his daughter was what stoked the flames of his hatred for Lay, who was trying to take her from him. However, that hatred wasn't true loathing from the bottom of his heart. If I peered into the abyss of his hatred, I could see love at the very root. His hatred was another form of love. The only flaw to the spell that could easily suppress Lay's Teo Traloth was that to activate it Shin had to face Lay. In other words, it couldn't be used against enemies.

"Now do you understand? The shape of your love is still no match for the love of a parent. There's no need to hold back. Come at us with Ligaro Tir Traloth."

Misa helped Lay up into a sitting position and looked at him for support.

"This may be pathetic of me, but will you lend me your strength?" he asked.

Chapter 5 — The Shape of Love

"Okay," Misa mumbled weakly, averting her gaze. She quietly raised her hand above her head. Blackness spread from her fingertips, enshrouding her entire body with darkness. "But there's no need to ask like we're strangers."

Countless lightning bolts shot through the darkness surrounding her, tearing it apart. Misa emerged in her midnight gown with six spirit wings on her back. When she turned her head, her ocean-blue hair flowed like the deep sea. This was her true form—the great spirit born from the legend of the Demon King of Tyranny.

"You know this body and heart are already yours," she said.

Lay took the hand she gracefully held out and then turned to face forward. The two looked upon the huge obstacle to their love.

"Father."

Shin's gaze wavered from Misa's briefly.

"Please listen, father. Won't you please look me in the eyes?"

"We're in the middle of class. It's not 'father,'" Shin snapped, shutting her down.

"I understand. Then we'll make you listen by force."

Lay stored the Sword of Three Races away in a circle and summoned the Sword of Intent in its place. The pair grasped the sword together.

"With this love, we will defeat you, father. Even if we have to tie you up, today will be the day you listen."

With their breaths in perfect sync, the couple pointed the tip of their sword at Shin. Their hearts and bodies moved as one, making their Teo Aske far more powerful than before. The spell blazed with dazzling light.

"I accept your challenge."

A Teo Aske of love and hatred flowed from Shin's body, swirling upwards in a vortex of light.

"Lay, I'll take the lead today. Will you follow me?"

"I love you."

Misa blushed furiously. She turned her face away and mumbled, "You don't have to say it out loud. I know."

Teo Aske shone brighter and brighter, the light rising like a tornado. Lay was completely in sync with Misa's movements. Acting as one, the couple stood face-to-face with the mighty father.

"*Ligaro Tir Traloth!*"

The sword they thrust forward overflowed with love. Shin planted his feet firmly on the ground, clenched his jaw, and used Dio Grezeas to stop the blow. Light collided with light. Love clashed against love.

"I know you will leave the nest one day, Misa, but for now, you are still a child. I shall teach you that your infatuation is just a game in the face of a parent's love."

Shin forced back their Ligaro Tir Traloth by a fraction. Lay gritted his teeth. Against a spell this powerful, even the slightest advantage would be the key to victory.

Suddenly, Misa murmured, "Ah, mother…"

Shin whipped around rapidly. But of course, there was no one there.

"Now!"

"I'd lose to you too, Misa!"

For just a moment, Shin's guard was down. Looking away in the midst of a battle was unheard of for the Demon King's right-hand man. But the words that had brought about that inconceivable mistake had come from an admirable heart desperate to be acknowledged—no matter the means she had to take.

No man would fail to respond to that. The sword of love rose into the air, burning hot and bright.

"I love you!"

"I love you too!"

With an overwhelming explosion of light, the heat of their love swallowed up Shin, sword and all.

§ 6. The Abyss of Love, Crossing the Line

Enough light to illuminate the entirety of the forest gathered around Shin's body, swelling fiercely with each passing moment. After catching him off guard, the true love of the couple was forcefully prying open the door to his heart. However, just as his sword was about to snap...

"That's quite the love magic, but I cannot give you a passing grade yet."

I created a demon sword with Iris and pointed it alongside Shin's sword of love. The light of Teo Aske emitted by the two swords tripled in size and forced Ligaro Tir Traloth back.

"What?!"

"I can't believe it..."

With looks of shock on their faces, Lay and Misa stood their ground. Putting their backs into defending, they focused their feelings on their sword of love. The clashing swords were equally matched— No, we had the slightest edge.

"What is that? How can Lord Anos and father be capable of casting a Teo Aske more powerful than our own?"

"Do you still not get it, Misa? Love is not exclusive to lovers. There's parental love, fraternal love, the love between master and retainer... This platonic love and respect, the shape of the love between Shin and myself, is another form of Ligaro Tir Traloth."

With our swords outstretched, Shin and I thrust the blades forward. Pushed back by the colossal surge of light, Misa and Lay found their feet sinking into the ground.

"You truly are incredible, Anos," Lay said. "Not only did you cast Teo Aske using platonic love and respect, you refined it to equal the heights of romantic love and unleashed Ligaro Tir Traloth. Such a thing would never have been possible with the logic of hero magic."

The love between a man and woman was superior to any other form of love. That was the unspoken rule written into the spell formula of love magic, but I had discovered a flaw in that structure.

"That is mere prejudice. Love would never be so restrictive. Just look—our platonic love has surpassed your romantic one."

The Ligaro Tir Traloth Shin and I emitted shone even brighter, blowing like a tornado to repel their sword of love.

"There is no love greater than the love I have for my liege," Shin said calmly, pointing his sword together with mine. "Do you understand now, Misa, Lay? Your childish crush will not lead to happiness. Demons live long lives. Your passion will eventually cool off."

Spurred by Shin's words, Lay and Misa's hearts united before the great wall obstructing their love.

"Lord Anos, father, if you say your platonic love surpasses romance…"

"…then we'll surpass romance with our childish crush!"

Unyielding determination flowed from their hearts, blocking the light of our love head-on and pushing it back.

"Look over there, Zeshia! They're up to something incredible. I've never seen love like it before!"

"A platonic Teo Aske…"

"It actually looks a little dangerous. Let's move away, shall we?"

"Understood. Retreating now."

Eleonore and Zeshia, who were well-versed in hero magic, could easily recognize the scale of the magic being used. The collision of Ligaro Tir Traloths had another effect too—on Edonica in the midst of the students' training from hell.

"Hey! Where are you going?!"

"Huh? Mine's running too…"

"Is this because…"

The Edonicas doubles were scrambling away from the center of the explosion and through the enchanted forest as fast as they could.

Chapter 6 — The Abyss of Love, Crossing the Line

"Does this mean we should run?!"

"Uh-oh. If they're running away, it must be serious!"

"Look! They're so far away already, but they're still running for their lives. Are we gonna be destroyed by the shock wave?!"

"I mean… Hey, is this really a class? Lord Anos and Mr. Shin aren't trying to destroy Hero Kanon and Avos Dilhevia, are they?!"

"R-Right? Greater magic like that has no place in class!"

"This is bad! We have to get as far away as possible and put up our wards!"

Trembling in fear, the students started running for their lives. Standing still among their fleeing figures were eight girls staring at the explosion.

"Hey, you guys, did you hear what Lord Anos said just now?" Ellen asked. "You know, that thing about how love sometimes crosses the line into hatred?"

The rest of the fan union gasped.

"He did say that…"

"I heard it too."

"There's no mistaking it!"

"Th-Then does that mean… Does that mean Lord Anos and Mr. Shin's love has crossed that line?!"

"Look! Our Edonicas are—!"

"Eek! They're running towards the light!"

"They must be telling us to follow them!"

Unlike the fleeing doubles of the other students, the fan union Edonicas were charging towards the center of the explosion.

"We have to go!"

The girls made up their minds and started running.

"Hey, you girls, it's dangerous that way! If you get dragged into that, there won't be anything left of your sources!" Eleonore called, but they merely shouted over their shoulders back at her.

"But we have to see it! It is our duty!"

"As the Demon King's Choir—no, as the Anos Fan Union, we are obligated to witness Lord Anos's love from as close as possible and translate that love into song!"

"But you won't be able to do anything if you perish!"

"There's nothing we could wish for more than to perish by Lord Anos's love!"

"Especially if it's love that's crossed the line!"

"This is the best time to perish in this century! If we don't risk our lives here, when will we ever risk them?!"

"This is our fight!"

The fan union girls pressed forward without paying heed to Eleonore's warning.

"I, uh... What should I do? I don't understand them at all."

"Pray...for their safe return."

Eleonore and Zeshia watched as the eight girls disappeared through the trees.

Aisha, who had accompanied Arcana up above, found her gaze fixed on Ligaro Tir Traloth. "Hey, someone's using some ridiculous magic down there. *That's dangerous...*"

"A number of demon students are headed towards the epicenter," Arcana said, pointing at the fan union.

"What are those girls doing?! *Aren't they brave?*"

"Protect those girls. That will be your training, Aisha." Arcana quietly raised her arms and held her palms towards the sky. "*Night falls; day passes; the moon rises; the sun sets.*"

Her order obeyed her divine magic and covered the light with darkness. In no time at all, day had turned to night, and the wondrous Moon of Creation hovered in the sky, radiating a warm light.

"*Snow falls, illuminating the earth.*"

Lunar snowdrops fluttered down from Altiertonoa, covering the enchanted forest. It was almost as if the snow-like flowers were protecting the students.

"Look at the Moon of Creation, Aisha," Arcana said.

The silver-haired girl looked up at the sky.

"The Magic Eyes of Absurdity are said to be able to rewrite a god's order. If your Eyes have that same power, you should be able to change the Moon of Creation from a crescent moon to a half-moon."

Aisha sent magic into her Eyes as she gazed at the crescent moon Altiertonoa. The outline of the moon blurred briefly, but nothing changed.

"Isn't that kind of impossible? *We don't have enough magic.*"

Chapter 6 — The Abyss of Love, Crossing the Line

Aisha focused her magic into her Eyes, but she didn't have enough strength to reshape the Moon of Creation.

"Altiertonoa isn't a crescent moon because of a quantity of magic. It's merely following divine order. However, with the Magic Eyes of Absurdity, you can defy that order," Arcana explained.

"That's easier said than done. We still don't know whether these Eyes really are the Magic Eyes of Absurdity. *It's hard.*"

Arcana held out a hand and sent lunar snowdrops fluttering upwards. "Then I shall give you some magic."

The glittering flowers released silver light.

"Fleeting snow disappears as it melts, leaving its traces in your heart."

Lunar snowdrops landed on Aisha and melted, transforming into magic. The reflection of Altiertonoa in the Magic Eyes of Omneity began to glow slightly.

"I think this'll work. I don't really get it, but all we have to do is make it a half-moon, right? *First, we'll try a quarter moon.*"

Aisha poured all her power into her Magic Eyes of Omneity and glared at the moon. Altiertonoa's outline blurred then slowly began to shift from its crescent moon shape. It transformed into a first-quarter moon, glittering with mystical silver light. The rain of lunar snowdrops intensified, protecting those standing on the ground with greater efficacy.

Inside the enchanted forest, the fan union girls looked up at the half-moon.

"What is that?! It suddenly turned to night!"

"Did Lord Anos and Mr. Shin cross so far over the line, day and night have lost all meaning?!"

"You mean there's no need for day in their world?!"

"Hey, look over there! A silver moon I've never seen before is blessing Lord Anos's platonic love!"

"The battle must be close to the end. Look! Their swords of love are shining so brightly!"

Light collided with light; love collided with love. The explosive sounds of their tremendous struggle for dominance rang out over and over. This was truly the epicenter of love—where love, respect, and affection met in a state of frenzy.

"Misa, I love you."

"I love you too."

Every time those words were repeated, their Ligaro Tir Traloth burned hotter and hotter than before.

"There's no way we can lose. I love Misa more than anything else! No matter how strong you are, Anos, I won't let you win against our love!"

Lay and Misa's sword of love pushed back our own.

"That's how it should be, Lay, Misa. Love burns brighter and more fiercely the greater the hardship before you. There is no limit to that feeling. However..."

In the midst of the fierce struggle, I exchanged glances with Shin. That was all we needed. We understood without words. I slowly moved the sword in my hand. Our two swords touched at the tips, creating a V shape.

"You still haven't crossed the line far enough. Your love still has flaws—the most fatal of which is that your love is so hidden."

We pushed back Lay and Misa's Ligaro Tir Traloth once again.

"Gah... No way..."

"How do they have this kind of love left?"

Lay and Misa gritted their teeth as they desperately tried to hold back the blow.

"I won't say your love is inferior to mine and Shin's. However, you are critically lacking in resolution."

"Resolution?" Lay muttered.

"That's right. The both of you still think love is an embarrassing thing, don't you?"

"Embarrassing? We're long past the stage of embarrassment!"

"I'm not referring to shallow feelings like that. Look deeper into your abyss—deeper, then deeper still. At the bottom of your heart, in the abyss of your love, there's a bashfulness you cannot hide. That is what's creating hesitation and dulling your love. That bashfulness doesn't exist in respectful and platonic relationships and is the flaw of romantic love."

Lay gasped.

"Now do you understand? That is the very depth of love magic. Only when you overcome that shyness will your love reach its full capabilities. And so, there is only one thing to do." I addressed my friend with love. "Bare yourself.

Chapter 6 — The Abyss of Love, Crossing the Line

Expose your true love. Imagine there is no one but the two of you in the world no matter where you go or who you're with."

I took a step forward. Shin mirrored my movement as though he'd known exactly what I was going to do beforehand.

"Let's show them, Shin."

"Understood."

The swords pointed in a V shape were dyed black with the light of love magic and increased in size.

"*Vaviro Varche Triath!*"

Two black swords of love crossed tips. At the end of the blades, a large mass of pure-white light shot forward like a bullet. The bullet of love tore through space, blowing apart Lay and Misa's sword of love and sending it flying.

"Gah!"

"Ah! Eek!"

The explosion of light swallowed Lay and Misa like a flood, flinging them back like bullets. Propelled by the blast, they knocked down tree after tree until they struck a large boulder and came to a stop. Thanks to Arcana and Aisha's lunar snowdrops, their lives would be safe from harm.

"This is the shape of our love laid bare."

§ 7. Nation of Dragon Cry

The next day.
 The first-year students of Demon King Academy class two had gathered at the Ledenor Plain to the east of Midhaze. Thanks to the Edonica combat training that had continued right up until dawn, they had each grown in astounding ways unique to their own individual needs and differences. Being forced to overcome death so many times had completely worn them out both mentally and physically, leaving some looking a little worse for wear, but that was to be expected. If anything, with their training still fresh on their minds, now was the perfect time to set off. After all, there was no telling what would happen in the underground world.
 "All right. It's time to head underground."
 "Um, Lord Anos..." Naya said, raising her hand.
 "What's wrong?"
 "Anosh isn't here today. Is he okay?" she asked curiously.
 "Huh, she's right," someone murmured.
 "Come to think of it, did anyone see him during training?"
 "I sure didn't, but I was kind of occupied with my Edonica."
 The students continued murmuring to each other noisily. I could just say Anosh was absent, but admitting that he was absent only during Demon King training could potentially arouse suspicion. On the other hand, having to control a separate body would be quite the annoyance. I would have to do so in a pretty convincing manner to avoid detection. And so...

"Ha ha, what are you saying? Anosh has been here the whole time," I said, looking into empty space.

"Huh?"

"Is Anosh over there?"

"He is." I walked over to the empty space and spoke to it. "Lynel and Najira, is it? You must think you're quite the prankster to try to hide from me, but you have yet to reach the depths of the abyss. This class will be a good opportunity to change that. Stay hidden this entire trip. I'll give you a passing grade if you can evade my Eyes even once."

The students stared in the direction I was looking.

"Man, I can't see anything at all. There isn't even a hint of magic there."

"Anosh really is a child genius."

"But even Anosh is nothing more than a kid to the Demon King. He's hidden himself so well, yet Lord Anos saw right through him."

That should do it for the Anosh problem.

"Now, let's be off," I said. Arcana, who had been waiting behind me, quietly stepped forward. "I should have introduced her earlier, but this is Arcana. She's from the underground world, but she isn't a draconid. To put it simply, she's a god, and she'll be the one to show us the way to Jiordal."

Arcana vanished, then reappeared several hundred meters away from the students.

"What was that just now? Gatom?"

"It couldn't be. I didn't see a magic circle."

"More importantly, did he say 'god'? As in, she's an actual god?"

"I don't want to believe it, but since it's Lord Anos claiming it, not Mr. Eldmed, it must be true. I mean, she did change day to night earlier just by holding up her hand."

"What was that anyway? That was some crazy magic."

"It was on a completely different level to what we've seen in classes until now. Are we gonna make it home alive?"

While the students chattered, the crescent moon Altiertonoa rose in the sky.

"*Earth freezes; ice melts.*"

The Moon of Creation's silver light poured down on Arcana, its radiance

instantly freezing the ground beneath her. The next moment, that thin sheet of ice shattered to reveal a large hole. It was a tunnel leading underground.

"*Snow falls and becomes wings.*"

Countless lunar snowdrops rained down from Altiertonoa, transforming into dragons made of snow. Scattering glittering silver light, the snow dragons moved towards the students.

"The underground world is quite a distance away. Those who struggle with Fless should get on," I said.

The majority of the students climbed onto the snow dragons.

"Let's go."

Arcana led the way down the hole. I used Fless to fly beside her and was followed by Eldmed and Shin.

"Wow, it's so fun! Look, Zeshia! We're flying!"

"Super…comfy."

Eleonore and Zeshia were riding a snow dragon together. Misha and Sasha flew independently beside them.

"Hey, shouldn't you two be able to keep up using Fless?" Sasha grumbled.

Misha tilted her head. "Is this cheating?"

"Th-That's not it! We just wanted to ride on a snow dragon," Eleonore said. Misha stared at her without saying anything. "Besides, I might be able to use this snow dragon as a reference for a new…" She paused for a moment and gasped. "That's right! I could create a new spell!"

"A great…discovery." Zeshia clapped her hands enthusiastically.

Misha blinked. "So it's not cheating?"

"No, they're obviously cheating. You heard the crappy excuse she gave at first," Sasha said.

Eleonore pointed her index finger upwards, and Zeshia mimicked her. "Sometimes it's *not* about the journey, but about the destination, Sasha."

"The destination!"

Sasha shot them an unimpressed look. "Misha, do you know how to argue with that?"

Misha tilted her head in thought. "Did you really think reaching the destination meant the journey was over?"

"Good one."

Chapter 7 — Nation of Dragon Cry

Everyone chatted among themselves as we made our way down. Before long, land came into view. As we emerged from the tunnel, our field of view widened. Above our heads was the dome of earth, and the underground world spread out down below.

"We've almost reached the airspace above Jiordal," Arcana said. "I'll lead us to Jiorhaze, the capital."

I flew after Arcana. Shin and the students using Fless flew behind us, followed by the students on the snow dragons.

"Say, I was wondering…" Sasha said as she caught up to me. "Jiordal's the place that set those dragons on Azesion and Dilhade, right? Should we really be arriving so openly?"

"According to Arcana, that was all Ahid's work."

"That's right. The Royal Dragon also contradicts the teachings of Jiordal. It actually originated from Agatha, Kingdom of the Royal Dragon," Arcana said.

"Is Jiordal hostile towards Dilhade?" Misha asked.

"That I don't know. Jiordal is ruled by Pope Golroana Delo Jiordal. He's one of the Selected Eight, a draconid bestowed with the title of Savior. Even if he isn't an enemy of Dilhade, he is hostile towards Anos."

"It's also possible that that hostility was Ahid's work," I added.

Misha looked at Arcana blankly then asked, "And what about Revalschned, God of Traces?"

"It is said that certain scriptures are only passed down orally from pope to pope. It's possible that the whereabouts of the God of Traces were also passed down that way."

Sasha brought a hand to her head. "It sounds like we have to meet this pope either way. Ugh, I can feel a headache coming on."

"Don't fret. Since we're already planning on putting an end to the Selection Trial, we would have had to encounter him eventually. A greeting won't hurt."

"It'd better just be a greeting."

"That depends on how the other side responds. The pope could just so happen to be thinking of destroying the Selection Trial himself and offer us his assistance."

Sasha glared at me. "Hey, Arcana, could you give Anos a little bit of your divine advice?" she asked.

"He is correct."

"Aren't gods allowed to lie?!"

Arcana looked back over her shoulder as she flew. "The hearts of mankind drift away from order all the time. Not even the gods can predict their destinations."

"Sure, it might be possible, but there have to be probabilities you can consider. If you had to pick the more likely outcome, what would you say?"

"Considering the hearts of mankind, I would say it's impossible."

"Then say that from the beginning!"

Arcana smiled slightly. "A demon child who doesn't cower before god…"

"She doesn't even cower before me. She's an interesting one," I said.

"It feels like I'm being made fun of," Sasha muttered, frowning. She then pulled herself together and looked back at Arcana. "So will it be okay or not?"

"At this time of year, Jiorhaze becomes a place of pilgrimage for people across Jiordal. We can blend in with them."

"So even if the pope notices us, other people will think we're pilgrims, so he won't be able to lay a hand on us in public. Is that it?"

"That's right. Going in boldly is the safest bet."

Hiding ourselves somewhere secluded would be giving them a chance to dispose of us in secret. However, we still didn't know what the pope was thinking.

"Huh?"

"What's wrong, Ellen?"

"Can you hear something?"

"Well, now that you mention it…"

The fan union girls riding a snow dragon together strained their ears to listen.

"Isn't that music?"

"I don't think so. I've never heard this kind of sound before."

"Is it some kind of instrument?"

"But where could it be being played if we can hear it from this high up?"

"Hey, isn't this a song? I can't say for sure, but it sounds like singing," Ellen said.

Jessica listened to the sound once more. "When you put it like that, it does sound like it."

Chapter 7 — Nation of Dragon Cry

The other girls listened to the tune curiously.

"You are correct, demon of the choir. We have entered Jiordal's airspace. That sound is the song of the Divine Dragon," Arcana said.

The girls raised their voices in surprise.

"So it is a song!"

"Wow, Ellen! How could you tell?"

"Does that mean a dragon's singing, Ms. Arcana?"

Arcana nodded. "The three underground kingdoms—Jiordal, Gadeciola, and Agatha—each have their own dragon that they worship as a messenger of the gods. Jiordal worships the Divine Dragon, the dragon of sound. Its song has resounded throughout the kingdom since its founding."

"There's a dragon singing somewhere?" Misha said, tilting her head.

"So the people believe. The Divine Dragon has been seen only by the popes of each era and the gods they form pacts with. I haven't seen it either." Arcana began to descend. A large city could be seen below us. "This is Jiorhaze, the capital of Jiordal. We will descend on the dragon landing site."

Arcana landed in a vast field in the middle of the city. The field was surrounded by walls, and there were several dragons in the area. They seemed to be accustomed to people, as they showed no sign of attacking. They must have been the dragons pilgrims had ridden to reach Jiorhaze.

The snow dragons landed in the field and let the students down. But at the same moment, the loud rumble of earth cracking rang out from overhead.

"Hey, what's that sound?" Sasha asked.

"Look." Misha pointed at the dome far above. Another tremor rumbled over our heads.

"You know we can't see as well as you, Misha."

"The dome is falling."

"What?!"

One particularly loud rumble later, chunks of earth came crumbling down. It was almost like watching the sky fall with our own eyes.

§ 8. Jiordal, Kingdom of the Divine Dragon

The rumbling from overhead quieted, and the dome stopped falling. Only the sounds of subtle aftershocks remained.

"The sky here can shake and cry. It's called a sky tremor," Arcana explained, looking up at the dome.

"Hmm. I suppose earthquakes occur on the surface as well, but at this rate, the dome will eventually fall."

"The underground world is supported by divine pillars. The fallen pieces of the dome will be raised by those pillars."

So no damage had been done, huh?

"How curious. But the sky doesn't fall aboveground. I'd love to see those pillars if the chance arises."

"The divine pillars are the pillars of order. Ordinary people cannot see them, but you may be able to."

Pillars of order? That meant the cavern the underground world existed in was completely supported by magic.

"Which god created those pillars?"

"The underground was created before the birth of the first dragonborn. The name of the god has since been lost, but that god would have governed the order of creation."

"If it was the Goddess of Creation, then that would have been Militia."

"I've never heard that name."

Since Arcana, too, could call upon the Moon of Creation, it was also possible that she was that god and that she simply didn't know because she'd forgotten her own name. However, in the Selection Trial, gods were able to consume the orders of other gods. It was unclear whether Arcana had participated before she had forgotten her name, but there was a possibility that she had consumed the order of creation from another god. It was also possible that there was another creation god somewhere in the underground world. Well, that would all have to wait until I'd regained my memories.

"Let's get going," I said.

Following Arcana's lead, we made our way towards the bustling city. Other than the odd buildings made of dragon bone and the unfamiliar style of clothing, the landscape wasn't that different from Azesion or Dilhade. There were streets, shops, and stalls. Churches dedicated to the gods they worshipped stood at regular intervals, and figures clad in blue robes could be spotted near them.

"This kingdom is ruled by the pope—that is, by the Church of Jiordal—in the name of the gods," Arcana explained as we walked. "All those wearing robes are clergymen of the church. Those in armor are holy knights."

The students were all looking around curiously. While we walked, the faint hum of the Divine Dragon's song echoed steadily in our ears. It was quiet enough to be unnoticeable unless one focused on it. To the people of Jiordal, the sound was probably akin to the murmur of a creek.

"Hey, do you guys hear a song coming from over there?"

"I can! That's the sound of people singing! What kind of instrument is that? It's got such a pretty tone."

The fan union girls looked into the distance and listened carefully.

"May we go listen to that music, Lord Anos?" Ellen asked.

I looked over at Arcana, who replied, "Jiorhaze is a safe city. Harsh rules are imposed on the people living here, but that's not so much the case for travelers. As long as you don't disrespect their god, breaking those rules will lead only to detainment. There's plenty of leeway before being tried for heresy."

That sounded fine to me.

"Then let's allow for three hours of free time," I said to the students via Leaks. "Go and broaden your horizons. You may do whatever you wish, but I recommend staying away from me—I may be targeted by the pope of this place."

Chapter 8 — Jiordal, Kingdom of the Divine Dragon

"Thank you very much!" Ellen said.

Catha nodded enthusiastically. "I'll go learn a new song!"

"Hmm. I shall look forward to hearing it later."

"Eek! What a reward! Okay, okay, let's do this!" She started running while pumping her fists happily.

"Wait! No fair, Catha! Share the reward!"

"Indirect reward! Indirect reward!"

Catha pulled a serious expression and turned to Nono. "Hmm. I shall look forward to hearing it later," she said.

With the same expression, Nono turned to Maia. "Hmm. I shall look forward to hearing it later."

"Hmm. I shall look forward to hearing it later," Maia said, repeating the same words with a cool expression.

This was repeated by a few more people until every member of the fan union had adopted the expression of a Demon King.

"Hmm. I shall look forward to hearing it later," they said, harmonizing their voices. Then they ran off, squealing happily and singing as though in a musical. The draconids on the street glanced curiously at the singing girls as they passed.

Our song that Lord Anos's ears will receive...
Oh, what kind of emotion will that conceive?
Will it be possible to conceive?
Conceive emotiooon!

The fan union girls left for the source of the song while singing their own impromptu tune with vibrato.

"Why don't they have any sense of danger?" Sasha muttered. "Right, Mish—"

Misha was munching away on a fried dragon skewer that she had just bought from a stall. She had paid with the pocket money that had been handed out to everyone earlier.

"You're right," she said, her voice muffled as she struggled with the piping hot meat. "We need to be careful."

"What are you eating for?!"

"It's a fried dragon skewer."

"I can see that! I'm asking why you're eating!"

"The man at the stall said it was good."

"We're in the middle of enemy territory, you know? Enemy territory! What are you going to do if it's poisoned?!"

Misha swallowed the meat and replied, "I checked."

With her Magic Eyes, Misha was able to detect most poisons with ease.

"I even left some for you." She held out the remaining dragon skewer.

"I wasn't mad because you didn't leave me any…"

"Do you not want it?" Misha tilted her head.

"Fine, I'll take it," Sasha said, accepting the skewer and munching happily on the fried dragon meat.

"Bwa ha ha! What a fascinating city. Surviving on the power of the dragons and gods is an interesting concept. I suspect there will be some exciting encounters to be had here."

Eldmed's cane tapped along the ground as he walked towards a nearby church without hesitation. It was the largest and most extravagant church we had seen so far.

"Um, Mr. Conflagration King, where are you going?" Naya asked, following behind him.

"Bwa ha ha! I'm interested in the church. The draconids living in this world excel at summoning powerful magic beings like dragons and gods. The clergymen in particular possess pledge jewels that anyone can use. Of course, summoning magic also exists aboveground, but the people here are clearly superior at it. It's truly fascinating."

"I see."

The Conflagration King stopped and whirled around to face her. "Do you wish to come along, Bookworm?"

"Won't I get in your way, sir?"

"Bwa ha ha! I would never disregard a student trying to learn! But you must be careful. There's no telling what will happen here."

Eldmed took Naya and stood before the church. He knocked on the door, and it soon opened, revealing a kind-looking draconid. According to what Arcana had told them, the robes he was wearing were those of a bishop.

"You don't look familiar. How can I help you?" he asked.

Chapter 8 — Jiordal, Kingdom of the Divine Dragon

Eldmed leaned on his cane and said boldly, "I've come from the world aboveground to join your religion. So has this girl here."

"Wha— Mrgh?!"

Eldmed's hand covered Naya's mouth, stopping her mid yelp.

"Mmph! Mmph?!"

"Don't be so surprised, Bookworm. I just told you to be careful, didn't I? There's no telling what will happen in this underground world. Isn't that right?"

Naya nodded in her confusion.

"Bwa ha ha! What an obedient student." Eldmed removed his hand and turned back to the bishop. "Sorry for the wait. There's no problem here."

"I'm afraid joining our religion won't be easy. There are many strict rules to follow, and the training will be harsh."

Eldmed maintained a composed smile. He seemed to have expected that.

"I have one question for you," the bishop said. "The road before you branches into a thorny path and a tranquil path. Which path will you choose?"

"Bwa ha ha! The path I choose is the one down which scorpions crawl between the thorns, savage beasts prowl, and the wicked toy with the righteous. It's the path with the possibility of all kinds of danger—the path of carnage."

The bishop stood there gaping for a moment, but he soon pulled himself together and turned to Naya. "And which path would you choose?"

"Um, I'd choose the tran—"

"Bwa ha ha ha ha ha ha ha!"

The sound of Eldmed's laughter drowned out Naya's decision.

"The tranqui—"

"BWA HA HA HA HA HA HA!"

Naya fell silent and looked at Eldmed.

"Will you choose the thorny path *together with the Conflagration King*, or the tranquil path alone? The choice is yours, Bookworm."

Naya looked down and mumbled, "The thorny path?"

The bishop nodded with a solemn expression. "We will extend the hand of salvation to those who knock on our door prepared to offer their lives to our god. Please enter. We will begin with a pledge jewel baptism. If your prayers are answered and you receive a divine call, you will be bestowed with a vocation."

The bishop entered the church.

"Ha ha ha, looks like it went well! The fastest way to obtain a pledge jewel is to join the church and become a clergyman!"

"But what do we do after this, sir? Wouldn't becoming believers of Jiordal cause problems?"

"Hey now, Bookworm, who do you think I am?"

"Um, you're the Conflagration King."

"Precisely! If I had feared the gods, I would never have dared to challenge the Demon King. Although that wasn't enough to avoid being thoroughly defeated by him last time. Bwa ha ha!"

Eldmed marched into the church without hesitation. Naya stared after him in a daze.

"What are you doing, Bookworm? Come along."

She followed the grinning Conflagration King into the church.

Hmm. What was he up to? Although Eldmed hadn't made any odd movements until now, one could never let their guard down when it came to him. He had the potential to be far more annoying than the pope if he tried. Of course, knowing him, he could just be acting on his curiosity, but I decided it best to give him a warning just in case.

"Is something wrong, Anos?" Sasha asked.

"Sasha, Misha, come with me."

Misha nodded.

"I mean, sure," Sasha replied, and we started walking. Eleonore and Zeshia immediately caught up to us.

"Where are you all going? Can we come too?"

"If you want."

I stood before the church Eldmed had entered and knocked on the door. After a brief wait, the bishop from earlier appeared.

"How can I help you, travelers?"

"We'd like to join the church. We'll take the thorny path."

§ 9. Using the Pledge Jewel

We were led to a circular room beneath the church. Beacons were lit at regular intervals, creating a solemn ritual space. The two demons who had entered before us were also there. Naya yelped in surprise when she saw me.

"L-Lord Anos?!"

"Oh? Are you already acquainted?"

Eldmed grinned at the bishop's question. "Bwa ha ha! Acquainted? That man is the Demon King of our homeland!"

"Demon King?" The bishop tilted his head, unfamiliar with the term. "I apologize for my lack of knowledge. What is the name of the nation you hail from?" he asked me.

"It's Dilhade."

"You're not going to hide that?" Sasha mumbled behind me.

"Welcome, and thank you for visiting from afar. The gods must have led you here."

The bishop showed no particular reaction, as though he assumed we were from a small country in the underground world. This meant that the only ones who knew about Dilhade were the cardinal and other church members directly involved in the invasion.

"The Almighty Radiance grants followers who walk the thorny path the right to undergo the pledge jewel baptism. Behold the divine flames before you," the bishop said grandly.

I gazed into the fire to see several floating rings set with clear crystal gemstones.

"Can you see? The rings within the divine flames are pledge jewel rings. As you might already know, pledge jewels have been used since ancient times to form pacts with dragons and gods. According to the teachings of Jiordal, they are ritualistic instruments that deliver prayers to the gods."

The bishop covered the ring on his right hand in prayer.

"Reach into the divine flames and take a pledge jewel ring in your hand. That is the baptism a follower must undergo. Those chosen by the heavens will obtain the ring without being burned. They can then proceed to the Summoning Ceremony."

Hmm. Magically created fire, was it? The slightest anti-magic would be enough to prevent any burns. The baptism seemed to be separating those who had magic from those who hadn't to allow only the magically gifted to proceed to the Summoning Ceremony.

"It is said that only one in ten people will proceed to the Summoning Ceremony. One of you may be chosen by the heavens today. Please attempt a prayer now."

So only one in ten draconids had enough power to use summoning magic, huh? It was a higher proportion than humans, but lower than demons.

"Would it be better for one of us to fail?" Sasha asked.

"No need. It isn't impossible." I plunged my hand into the fire and grasped a pledge jewel ring.

"Oh! How wonderful! And without a single burn. You have most certainly been chosen by the heavens toda— Huh?!"

Eleonore grabbed a pledge jewel ring and claimed it unscathed. "Easy peasy."

"Zeshia's chosen...by the heavens too."

The bishop's jaw dropped. "Three people in a single day?! What is—"

Misha and Sasha also obtained rings without any burns.

"F-Five..."

"Bwa ha ha! What a simple task."

Eldmed picked up a ring. Naya gathered her courage and boldly reached into the flames too. While she was considered an inferior student compared to her classmates, she was still a student of the Demon King Academy. There was

Chapter 9 — Using the Pledge Jewel

no way she would be burned by fire like this; she easily grabbed the pledge jewel ring, which proved it.

"I did it!" she said, sounding relieved. The wide-eyed bishop looked flabbergasted.

"A-All of you were chosen by the heavens. What a day it is! O Almighty Radiance, thank you for allowing me to witness such a miracle through this wonderful encounter."

Unable to hide his excitement, the bishop prayed as though he had witnessed a once-in-several-centuries miracle.

"Now, let us proceed to the Divine Calling Ceremony. Please look over here." The bishop reached into the fire with his right hand and drew a circle. Flames poured out of the pledge jewel ring and formed the shape of a magic circle. "This is the magic circle for Liteld, the foundation for using the pledge jewel. With this spell, faithful followers can summon dragons or gods and have them do their bidding. However, gods are the hands of the Almighty Radiance, so they do not form pacts so easily."

While the spell was similar to a summoning spell of the world above, there were fundamental differences in how it worked. Liteld's spell formula alone wasn't able to summon anything—the spell relied on the existence of the pledge jewel.

"Now, come this way. First, I will tell you all about dragons, the messengers of the gods."

The bishop stood on a magic circle on the floor. We stood inside the circle with him, and he used his magic to teleport us to a room farther beneath the ground. This room was immense in size, the ceiling reaching high above.

"This is the Ceremonial Hall used for conducting the Divine Calling Ceremony. If you can successfully use your pledge jewels to cast Liteld, you will be able to receive a summons. In other words, you will obtain a duty to fulfill for the gods."

It seemed this vast space was used for summoning magic. After all, there was no fitting a dragon in a tiny room. The bishop continued his explanation courteously.

"The pledge jewel, which was brought to this underground world in ancient times, has the power to summon six dragons by the order of the gods. These dragons are Deiro, superior in fire and strength; Sita of flight and teleportation; Garon of strength and durability; Fron of healing and grace; Vista of stealth and concealment; and Dogu of binding and restraints. When summoning a dragon through Liteld, it isn't a dragon from the underground world that gets called. The pledge jewel is actually opening a gate to the Divine Realm and calling a dragon from there. As a servant of gods, that dragon then descends into this land in an appropriate form."

The bishop showed us his pledge jewel ring as he spoke. "Through Liteld, the messengers of the gods appear underground, blessing the lives of the people here. Dragons are the messengers that sustain our lives. They are the house that shelters us, the flesh that feeds us, the feet that carry us. The followers who have received a divine calling are the keys to the gate that brings them to this land."

It seemed that, rather than the dragon itself, it was the source of the dragon being summoned. That explained why Azept allowed the direct use of the dragon's power, while using Liteld made the pledge ring create a physical body for the source. Pledge rings were apparently assigned by the first proxy of the gods—in other words, someone who could use the orders of the gods—so it wasn't impossible. This was probably the reason dragons, who had been on the verge of extinction, had increased in number again. The pledge jewels and summoning magic of the underground had been created in order to prevent them—and perhaps draconids too—from going completely extinct.

"Summoning magic doesn't rely on how much magic one has, but the size of one's vessel. The greater the vessel, the more powerful a dragon that can be summoned. Allow me to show you an example."

The bishop poured magic into his pledge jewel ring. Several magic circles appeared within the crystal, overlapping each other. A large fire rose before the bishop's eyes, within which the faint shadow of a dragon was visible.

"*Liteld Deiro.*"

Suddenly, the flames dispersed to reveal an enormous dragon. It appeared to be under the bishop's control, as it remained still and silent.

"Now, let's see you all have a go. The task may seem daunting at first, but rest assured, you may attempt the Divine Calling Ceremony as many times as you wish. It is a difficult ceremony in which only one in a hundred people succeed on their first try. Your goal for today is to merely touch upon the hand of our god as the first step of your divine calli—"

The bishop's jaw dropped. Misha and Sasha had drawn magic circles

Chapter 9 — Using the Pledge Jewel

within their pledge jewels. The shadows of two dragons were visible in the flames before them.

"I've never used magic like this before. Does this mean it went well?" Sasha asked.

"I think so," Misha replied.

The flames dispersed to reveal two dragons, both larger than the one the bishop had summoned.

"I…I cannot believe it! A dragon superior to mine was summoned on the first try, and there's two of them?!"

The next moment, the bishop's eyes grew even wider. Two more fires had risen, and two more dragons had been summoned. Eleonore and Zeshia had both cast Liteld, and their dragons, too, were larger than the bishop's.

"Heh heh, looks like it worked!"

"Big…dragon…"

They looked up at their dragons excitedly.

"F-Four of you… O Equis, what an incredible day this is! But where are you leading me—?!"

The sight before him silenced him. Eldmed's summoned dragon was large enough to reach the ceiling.

"The sheer size… It's as large as the dragons that have lived for a millennium."

"Now it's your turn, Bookworm."

"Okay!"

Naya drew a magic circle within her pledge jewel and activated Liteld. A small fire appeared before her, the shadow of a dragon visible within. However, the dragon was oddly small, even for a young dragon. When the summoning flames dispersed, a dragon the size of a cat emerged.

"I-It's small, but I made it," Naya said, seeming somewhat ashamed. However, Eldmed approached the dragon with fascination. He stopped right before the dragon and observed its body closely.

"I've never seen such a dragon before," he muttered to himself. The small dragon squawked and opened its mouth.

"Huh?"

The next moment, the six dragons in the room were surrounded by transparent magic bubbles. The inside of the bubbles distorted and collapsed, shrinking the dragons within them before our eyes. Before long, the magic bubbles were each the size of a fist. They flew over to the small dragon's mouth and were sucked inside. The dragon chirped and munched on the small balls. Its green scales gained a slight red hue.

"It ate the dragons?" the bishop murmured, unable to keep up with the situation. "No. I've never heard of a dragon eating other dragons before."

"Hmm. What an odd dragon."

I stared at the small dragon Naya had summoned. It was indeed different from all the others. Even two thousand years ago, there had been no dragons like this. On top of that, it had changed color when it had consumed the other dragons.

"Let's see it consume my dragon as well."

I drew the magic circle for Liteld and looked over at the frozen bishop. "Bishop of Jiordal, you may be in danger over there. I haven't attempted this spell before, so I may not be able to control myself."

"O-Oh..." The bishop finally returned to his senses. "N-No, it's fine. The summoning flames that grant the dragons their bodies would never burn us clergymen."

"Never?"

"Yes, never. We are protected by divine order."

I doubted that was true, but it was possible I was the ignorant one here.

"But it's better to be careful. You may die."

"Rest assured, the protection of the gods will prevent that. Please understand that doubting this is an unforgivable sin for a follower of Jiordal."

"I see. I shouldn't have said that, then."

It was better to follow the customs here. If their faith was strong, nothing I said would make a difference anyway.

I sent my magic into the magic circle and watched as flames appeared before me. They burned fiercely, rising and swelling in the blink of an eye.

"Th-This... I've never even heard of such intense summoning flames! A-Aaaaaaaaaaaaaaah!"

The bishop screamed at the sight of the flames filling the entire room. I placed wards around him for protection.

"Quiet down. You're burning after all."

Despite my warning, the bishop nervously stepped out of the wards.

Chapter 9 — Using the Pledge Jewel

"Rest assured, there is no way I would burn. No matter how fierce the flames look, they are for creating a dragon's body, not harming clergymen—"

"H-Hey, Anos! The entire room is dangerous!"

"The spells of the underground world are a little different from what I'm used to. I adjusted my magic, but it didn't have much effect. Defend yourselves so that you don't die."

"Bwa ha ha! As expected of Anos Voldigoad. This is why you're the Demon King of Tyranny!"

"The bishop burned up," Misha mumbled.

That was why I'd told him to stay still.

"I used Ingall on him," Eleonore informed me.

The next moment, the flames, which had swelled to their limit, suddenly vanished. What appeared before me was a crimson dragon—or rather, the foot of a crimson dragon. Its body was so big, it had broken through the ceiling of the basement, destroying the church as its head broke through the ground above us. Rubble fell from the destroyed bedrock and building, raining down on our heads.

"Now, Naya, make your dragon eat this one."

"What? A dragon that big?!" Naya looked up at the enormous dragon, which was so big, she couldn't grasp its full size.

"If it can shrink other dragons, it can eat this one."

"Ah, right. But... Sorry, I don't know how."

Naya didn't know how to control her summoned dragon. As she looked at it in confusion, the small dragon chirped. A clear bubble began to wrap around the crimson dragon, but it popped before it could completely cover it. The small dragon let out a sad whine.

"Hmm. No chance of that, huh?"

The crimson dragon shifted slightly, further devastating the church. Rubble rained loudly down around us.

"Hey, Anos, do something! We'll be buried alive at this rate."

"There's no need to worry." I fixed my gaze on the crimson dragon. "Fly somewhere out of the way."

"GROOOOOOOOOOAAAR!"

The dragon's mighty roar shook the basement ceiling and church above, sending more debris crashing down around us. Then the huge dragon spread its crimson wings, destroying the foundations of the entire building, and took off into the subterranean sky.

"Hmm."

The church had been destroyed beyond recognition, leaving an open hole all the way to the basement.

"Behold. There's no more rubble to fall upon us."

"Are you stupid?!"

§ 10. Vessel of God

The small dragon squawked happily and started flying in laps around Naya.

"Huh? Eek! Stop... Stop that!"

Naya was running away in fear, but the small dragon playfully stuck by her side.

"Don't be so frightened, Bookworm," Eldmed said. "That's the dragon you summoned, is it not?"

"B-But, sir, this dragon doesn't listen at all!"

"Bwa ha ha! Stop running from it first."

"Um, but, sir..."

"It'll be fine. Just stop. From what I can tell, it has no hostile intentions. Or are you planning on running for the rest of your life?"

Naya made up her mind and came to a stop. She clenched her eyes shut as the small dragon flew straight towards her, chirped, and then landed on her shoulder. She immediately exhaled in relief.

"You've summoned quite the interesting dragon, Bookworm. A dragon that eats dragons—not even the Demon King has seen such a thing before." Eldmed approached the dragon and stared at it with his Magic Eyes. He then shoved his finger into its mouth. "Is it magic that you're consuming? Try and make a bubble like you did earlier."

"What?! That's dangerous, sir!"

"Bwa ha ha! I'm just letting it have a taste of my finger."

The Conflagration King tapped the dragon's snout. A tongue shot out and licked him.

"I see, I see. So a demon's magic isn't to your liking, Cannibal."

"Cannibal? What do you mean?"

"It's this dragon's name. Or did you want to do the honors?"

Naya shook her head rapidly.

Eldmed tapped his cane on the floor and peered into her face. "Well, well, this has become interesting indeed. How about trying to summon a god next, Bookworm?"

"Um, okay... Huh? A god? As in, a *god* god?!" Naya stared at him in confusion.

"P-Please wait a moment," the bishop said, interrupting Eldmed in a hurry. He was still dazed from dying earlier, but he began to explain in order to fulfill his duty. "Your divine callings have all been granted. You have indeed gained the right to obtain a vocation in Jiordal, but that doesn't mean that summoning a god will be easy. After joining the church, you must learn our various doctrines and overcome many trials before you may learn the Liteld spell formula to summon gods. Even if you make it to the pact ceremony, only a handful of followers will ever be able to summon a god. It is far too early for you to obtain that knowledge." The bishop held his hands in a praying gesture. "I can see that you are all blessed by the gods. If you continue to develop your faith, you will eventually be allowed to attempt the pact ceremony. Let us learn and walk the path of faith together."

The bishop looked at us with a pious expression. The Conflagration King burst into laughter.

"No matter, no matter. Now that we've received our pledge jewels, we'll be able to figure out the rest ourselves. If you refuse to teach us the spell formula to summon gods, we'll just have to create one ourselves."

"That's impossible!" the bishop exclaimed.

"Of course, I agree! Not even I, the Conflagration King, could do such a thing."

The bishop exhaled in relief.

Eldmed smirked. "But it's a different matter for the Demon King," he said, turning to me. "Well? Aren't you curious?" He shot a sidelong glance at Naya.

Chapter 10 — Vessel of God

Indeed, the Conflagration King was right—I was curious. That cannibalistic dragon was clearly different from regular dragons, which meant it was highly likely Naya had some kind of gift that allowed her to excel at summoning magic.

"Very well. Let's give it a go." I drew a magic circle in the air. "This is the variant of Liteld used for summoning gods."

The bishop's jaw dropped, and his eyes widened. "It... It couldn't be," he squeaked. "Where did you learn that spell formula? No, you couldn't have learned it from anywhere else. Does that mean... Did you truly write it just now? Is such a thing possible?"

"It was no big deal. I simply took the Liteld for summoning dragons and the pledge jewel and adjusted the formula for use with a pact instead. That naturally led me to the optimal spell formula for summoning gods."

Besides, the base structure of the spell formula wasn't that different from the Guala Nateh Forteos used to summon Arcana.

"While I'm at it, this is Azept." I drew a different magic circle.

"A-Azept as well?!" The bishop gasped. "Such a thing shouldn't be possible, yet... Ah, but knowing the spell formula alone isn't enough to summon a god. You must form a pact with one before you can do so. Unlike dragons, they won't appear if all you do is use the spell."

I marched over to Eldmed, lifted my right hand, and drove it into his chest.

"Gah!"

"L-Lord Anos?! What did he do?" Naya looked at me in confusion.

"Bwa ha ha. No need to panic, Bookworm. The divine body of the Conflagration King cannot manifest order unless on the brink of death." Eldmed coughed up blood and smiled. "Fool who spits on the heavens. Thou wilt face thy punishment for defying order. *Behold the true form of a god.*"

Those were the same divine words Nosgalia had once uttered when creating miracles. Blinding light enveloped the Conflagration King as his magic swelled to an extraordinary level.

"BWA HA HA HA HA!"

Eldmed's body transformed. His hair turned blond, and his Magic Eyes took on a fiery red glow. Particles of magic gathered at his back, forming wings of light. With a low rumble, the earth began to quake. His mere presence was causing the air to burst and the world to shake. Like a mass of tremendous power, the true form of a god had appeared.

"What is this? Azept? No, it couldn't be. He didn't use any magic." The bishop turned his Magic Eyes to the god and cried out in fear. "Don't tell me! It couldn't be, it couldn't be, it couldn't be!" Tremendous shock shot through his heart. "Are you telling me this is a god?! A god sent from the heavens has descended to this land. Oh, what a miracle to behold! O Equis, the Almighty Radiance, please enlighten me on what kind of god he is!"

Clutching his hands in prayer, the bishop fell to his knees before the greatest miracle he had seen today.

"S-Sir, you've grown wings!" Naya murmured. Her focus on his appearance probably meant she was unable to see his current power with her own Eyes.

"Bwa ha ha. You see, Bookworm, I've usurped the power of a certain god. In other words, I, the Conflagration King, am basically a god myself."

"Huh? You're a god?" Naya appeared unable to keep up with the conversation.

"Precisely. Shall I show you some proof?" Eldmed took off his top hat and juggled it a few times. Then the top hat split into four. "Bwa ha ha! Go!" He threw the four pieces forward. After flying a short distance, they suddenly froze in midair. "In compliance with the Heavenly Father, I, the Conflagration King, command four orders to be born. Arise, new Keepers of Reason."

The four silk hat pieces burst into confetti, ribbon, and sparkling light, like a cheap magic trick, that formed the shape of divine bodies. Four new Keepers were born before us.

A girl with unnaturally long hair and a staff in each hand, Nutra Do Hiana, Keeper of Restoration.

A winged lady with the body of a centaur, Reize Na Ile, Keeper of the Sky.

A mountain of a man with an enormous shield on his back, Zeo La Opt, Keeper of Protection.

A black shadow holding a dozen weapons including a spear, axe, sword, and bow, Atro Ze Sistava, Keeper of Death.

The bishop was struck with so much awe and reverence, he couldn't even speak properly anymore. "Go... God... Hah... The order that creates order... The god that emits light closest in resemblance to the Almighty Radiance... The Heavenly Father, Nosgalia!"

Chapter 10 — Vessel of God

Hmm. That insect seemed awfully well regarded in this world.

"Ooh... Ooooooh! What a day it has been! To think I would live to witness a day like this. Oooooooh!" Overcome with emotion, the bishop fell to his knees, tears streaming down his face.

"Bwa ha ha! It seems all went well. Now, Bookworm, exchange a pact with them."

"A-A pact? With these gods?" Naya glanced at the Keepers fearfully. Red eyes appeared on the Keeper of Death, making her flinch. Naya hid behind Eldmed's back to escape the gaze. "I don't think I can."

"No, you can do it. I know you can do it, for you are one of my students. These Keepers are basically my children, and they will obey me. There's no way they wouldn't respond to a pact with you. Just take my word for it and give it a go."

Naya nodded hesitantly and held her pledge jewel ring before the Keepers. "Wh-What do I do?"

"These gods do not understand words. Use your mind. Tell them you want to make a pact for them to become your summonable gods. They may present some kind of condition, but it should be fine to agree to whatever they want."

"I'll try." Naya took a few steps forward and said her words both out loud and in her head. "I...I'll do whatever you say, so will you become my summonable gods?"

Several seconds of silence passed. Then crackling particles of magic began to rise from the Keepers. Their outlines blurred with light before vanishing like they had been called to the heavens.

"Uh..."

Unsure of what had happened, Naya stood there and stared. Meanwhile, the Conflagration King smirked with satisfaction.

"You succeeded! Now try to summon them."

Naya nodded and poured magic into her pledge jewel ring. "*L-Liteld!*"

Fire rose within her pledge jewel. The three-dimensional magic circle within was calling the Keepers. The air crackled as four orbs of light gathered before her.

"Th-This is...!" The bishop reeled with shock, as though trying to use up a lifetime of surprise in a single day. "How... Not only did you exchange a pact with four gods, but you summoned them all at once! Such a thing shouldn't be possible for anyone other than one of the Selected Eight. In the first place, a pledge jewel can handle one god at once. The jewel will shatter if you exceed that limit!"

Contrary to the bishop's expectations, the four lights materialized into bodies—the bodies of the four Keepers with whom Naya had exchanged a pact.

"It's a miracle... O Equis, how many miracles are you going to show me in a single day? Ooh... Ooooooh!"

The bishop resumed bawling as if he had received a divine revelation.

"D-Did it work?"

"I see. I see, I see, I see! I've got it, Bookworm!" Eldmed pointed his cane at Naya in a more lively manner than ever before.

"What have you got?"

"Your potential! You indeed lack magic. If your source was a container and your magic was water, then your container would be practically empty! The water that should be flowing out of your source is nowhere to be seen!"

"Right." Naya looked down dejectedly, but the Conflagration King placed his hand under her chin and forced her to look up.

"Bwa ha ha, what are you feeling down for? You don't get it, do you? I'm praising you! Your source may be devoid of magic, but that's what makes your vessel so vast and fine—enough for you to still have space left after summoning four Keepers!"

"Um..."

"I'm saying you're suited to summoning magic. You lack your own power, but that just makes your vessel perfect for exterior powers to fill."

As the Conflagration King described, it seemed that performing the summoning magic of the underground world required space in the source. That was why adjusting my magic hadn't had much effect when I'd summoned my dragon—because the capacity of my vessel hadn't changed.

Using Liteld and Azept filled the empty space of a source—the unfilled void—not with magic, but with the pact made with a deity and the spell formula used to summon them. Most people didn't have such space in their source, so they used the pledge jewel ring as a vessel instead. The more pacts formed and the more summonings made, the less space there was in the vessel.

Chapter 10 — Vessel of God

When the limit of the vessel was reached, a gemstone would shatter, but Naya was capable of summoning by using the space in her source instead.

"Make a pact with me, Naya. If you become my subordinate, I will become your god and grant you your wish."

"Hmm. That's an interesting idea, Conflagration King," I said, stepping in front of him. "You would indeed be able to evade my Zecht that way."

If his power became Naya's through Liteld or Azept, the order of the Heavenly Father would be free for her to control. Our Zecht didn't apply to Naya, so he would be free to defy me through her.

"Bwa ha ha! Is there a problem, Demon King of Tyranny? Even if my power were to become Naya's, she'd still remain a student of the Demon King Academy, no?"

As long as Naya didn't betray me or Dilhade, I had no problem with allowing her to summon the Heavenly Father's order.

"Hmm."

The Conflagration King was constantly insisting that the Demon King needed an enemy. He was probably planning on raising Naya into my enemy so that he could avoid infringing our Zecht. However…

"Naya," I said.

She straightened up nervously. "Yes?"

"What do you think of the Conflagration King?"

She thought for a moment before replying. "Um, I think he's a very good teacher, and I feel like if I keep up with his lessons, I'll become useful to Dilhade one day."

I nodded. "That's right. There is no better teacher in Dilhade than the Conflagration King. Follow in his footsteps with all your might. I have no doubt he will lead you to where you need to go."

She beamed happily.

"Believe in him, and work your hardest as his student. If you ever feel indebted to him for it, you can repay him with your own growth."

"I will!" Naya replied brightly.

The Conflagration King burst into laughter. "Ha ha… Ha ha ha… BWA HA HA HA HA HA HA!"

That laughter echoed far into the subterranean sky.

"As expected of the Demon King of Tyranny! Not only do you overlook me, you support me in my endeavors! Yes! This is why your words easily surpass the power of the gods! This is what makes you the king of this world!" He clenched his fists and yelled triumphantly. "Never ceding, never faltering, crushing everything from head-on, and always emerging victorious! That is what true tyranny should be—what the Demon King of Tyranny, Anos Voldigoad, should be! Yes! This is what makes you the best!" The wings of light on Eldmed's back glittered as he sang his praises of me. "And so I, the Conflagration King, will meet those expectations with all my strength!" He leaned on his cane and looked at Naya. "Now, Naya, put those Keepers away. Come on! Not even you will be able to keep them summoned while making a pact with me!"

"Um, go back?" Naya said, but the Keepers didn't budge. "Huh? Please go back!"

Although she had the vessel to summon the gods, it seemed she was lacking the magic to control them.

"Allow me to grant you the words of a god, Bookworm. *You can do it. There is no way you won't be able to do it!*"

The Conflagration King's words were laced with magic that transformed them into a blessing for Naya. The next moment, the pledge jewel began to glow. The Keepers were swallowed by the light, fulfilling the earlier command.

"Very good. That will do. Now, state your wish. Let us make our pact."

"Um, what kind of wish?" Naya asked, looking down awkwardly.

"Bwa ha ha! There's no need to hold back. I will grant your every wish."

"Uh, then…" Naya looked up and addressed the Conflagration King. "Will you be my teacher forever, sir?"

Eldmed grinned. "I accept, Naya," he said with an exaggerated gesture as light enveloped his body. "I, the Conflagration King, will drum everything—from the truths of the world to utterly useless trivia—into that brain, body, and tender heart of yours!"

When the light surrounding him eventually faded, Eldmed had returned to his regular form. The pact between Naya and the Conflagration King was complete.

§ 11. Ceremonial Hymn

"Incidentally, I'd like to ask you something," I said to the bishop gazing at Eldmed and Naya with his mouth open. "What do I need to do to meet the pope of Jiordal?"

However, the bishop passed in front of me as if he hadn't heard. He knelt before Naya and Eldmed and started praying. "O great Heavenly Father and the holy saint chosen to form a pact with him, I offer my deepest gratitude to the heavens for this encounter. Will you have the mercy to lend an ear to the woes of this pitiful but devout follower?"

Naya looked over at Eldmed worriedly. He replied in his usual tone. "Hey now, don't get the wrong idea. We're not the ones to be lowering your head to."

The bishop stared at the Conflagration King in shock.

"Our ruler is the Demon King over there. I am just one demon who serves him. Is it the etiquette of this place to ignore one's master and bow to their subordinate? Hm?"

"But gods are superior existences that stand above kings," the bishop argued, clearly confused. "If he is the king as you claim, then his royal authority must have been granted by you. As a follower, I believed it was my duty to first express my respect to the god and the young lady who has exchanged a pact with them."

"Bwa ha ha! Then you'd better remember this: the Demon King stands above all gods. In the first place, the Heavenly Father's order was stolen from

Nosgalia by the Demon King Anos Voldigoad over there. He was the one who granted the order to *me*."

"Oh!" The bishop turned to me with a look of reverence. "He who stands above the gods, granting them and depriving them of power... Is that not the very power of the Almighty Radiance?" He walked in front of me and fell to his knees, clutching his hands in prayer. "In my ignorance, I failed to see the truth. Thus, I will believe the words of a god. He who stands above the gods, Demon King Anos Voldigoad, please forgive me for my belated introduction. I am Mirano Em Sisarad, bishop of Jiordal. Please forgive me for my earlier impoliteness."

"You are forgiven. You may also stand at ease, for I am not Equis. I am merely a demon from the world aboveground, unworthy of your worship."

Mirano nodded quietly. "I understand. However, even if you are not the Almighty Radiance, you still stand above the gods. I cannot doubt the words of a god."

"Then do as you wish."

"Demon King Anos, for you, I will arrange an audience with the pope of Jiordal. I am sure His Holiness will readily accept when he hears that you can control the gods without a pledge jewel. However, before I do so, I ask that you lend your ears to the words of this pitiful follower."

"Speak freely."

The bishop started praying while speaking. "In this pious nation of Jiordal, we worship the gods, revere them, and offer our songs to them, yet there is a fool among us who has fallen to heresy. He utters obscenities about the pope, mocks the faithful, and denies the existence of the Almighty Radiance Equis, all to desecrate the name of our god. There is no one in this city impious enough to believe his words, but he has become such a nuisance to our festivals that we can no longer ignore him."

"Hmm. What is the name of this fallen one?"

"Ahid Alovo Agartze, the former cardinal of Jiordal. After his falling to heresy, the pope stripped him of his baptismal name, so he is currently known only as Ahid."

It was as I'd thought. If he had been stripped of his baptismal name, then he must have been exiled from the church.

"He appears during every festival to desecrate the name of our god. He

Chapter 11 — Ceremonial Hymn

was caught once and sent to jail. Merely recalling his state at that time brings me fear." Mirano shuddered.

"What happened?"

"It was like he was possessed. He deliriously repeated something about being unable to wake from a dream, and his face was like that of a crazed devil. His behavior was so eerie and abhorrent, the congregation hesitated to even look at him. He took that opening to his advantage and escaped."

"Even with less supervision, he shouldn't have been able to escape by himself."

The bishop nodded. "You assume correctly. It seems the foolish Ahid has joined the church of Gadeciola—the church of heretics that worship a blasphemous god. There is no telling what they are up to."

How interesting. So he had joined hands with a heretic church in order to spread the word that the Almighty Radiance didn't exist. That shouldn't have been possible in the short time since I had collared him, so he must have been colluding with them for a while now.

"The Church of Jiordal is currently pursuing Ahid. It will be difficult for him to appear in public, much less leave the city. Starving on the streets will be his punishment. That being said, the city will be hosting a particularly large festival tomorrow."

So they were capable of hunting down Ahid and arresting him, but they didn't want to disturb the festivities, huh?

"And you're asking for my help."

"I wouldn't dare to do such a thing. This is merely a prayer—a wish for our god to turn this way. Whether this prayer is fulfilled depends on the Almighty Radiance."

That aside, they were struggling more over a single man than I'd thought. If the pope was one of the Selected Eight, he should have been able to deal with the now godless Ahid in no time at all.

Were the Gadeciolan draconids that troublesome? Or was there a reason the pope couldn't move?

"What's the festival for?"

"Every one hundred days, Jiordal holds a festival called the Rite of Sacred Song. It is one of the most sacred rituals in Jiordal, during which a holy hymn is offered to the gods in prayer for prosperity in the underground world.

Holding this ritual is extremely important to us, but that fool obsessed with desecrating our god is heedless of danger and he should show up again."

"Where will the festival be?"

"The festival is held across Jiorhaze, but the hymn is sung on the sacred grounds of the Divine Dragon. It's a very short distance from here. Would you like me to show you?"

Arcana probably knew where it was.

"That won't be necessary. I trust you'll arrange an audience with the pope for us."

After saying that, I drew a magic circle that covered the entirety of the destroyed church, aboveground and below. I recreated the building using Iris, completely restoring it to its former glory.

"Oooh! What a miracle. This must be the work of the gods." The bishop started praying again. "As the Almighty Radiance wishes."

His manner of speech was hard to get used to, but it seemed he was willing to arrange our meeting.

"See you tomorrow. I'll bring Ahid as a souvenir for the pope." I turned to leave the church and then stopped. "Come to think of it, are there any good inns nearby?"

The bishop answered nervously. "The Rite of Sacred Song is tomorrow, so there are many pilgrims here in Jiorhaze. Most churches and inns are at full capacity, but I can arrange some rooms to be cleared for you and your party. How many beds are you in need of?"

Hmm. It seemed he was suggesting driving other clergymen and pilgrims out of their rooms.

"There'll be no need for that. Is there any open space we can frequent? It can be underground."

"The nearby dragon landing site is under my management. Feel free to use the space there as you wish."

"That would be great. We'll do just that."

"As the Almighty Radiance wishes." The bishop lowered his head and offered a prayer.

After that, we left the church to find a girl waiting for us outside.

"Arcana," I called. She turned to me. "Where are the sacred grounds of the Divine Dragon?"

Chapter 11 — Ceremonial Hymn

"Follow me."

As we walked behind her, the faint sound of draconids singing grew louder. We eventually arrived at a raised square. At the center was a large but shallow hole where a bonfire was burning. The flames, which reached dozens of meters high, were burning around a tall pillar reaching into the sky. It must have been made of dragon bone. People were gathered around the bonfire, singing an unfamiliar hymn.

"Huh? It's Ellen and the others," Eleonore said, pointing to them.

Sasha looked confused. "You're right. What are they doing?"

The fan union girls were among the Jiordal Choir before the altar, singing their hymn. They couldn't have known the song before today, yet they were singing along perfectly. The song eventually ended, and the girls shook hands with the members of the other choir.

"Your voice is wonderful, Ellen. You mentioned that you girls are a choir as well. Where are you from?"

"We're from Dilhade. It's a nation beyond the dome," Ellen said, pointing upwards.

The woman from the choir looked at her curiously. "Beyond the dome?"

"Stupid Ellen! Are you allowed to say that?"

"O-Oh, right. Um... Aha ha..." Ellen laughed.

The woman from the Jiordal Choir smiled at her. "What an interesting person. I am Irina Als Amina, leader of the Jiordal Choir."

"I'm Ellen Mihace of the Demon King's Choir."

The other girls introduced themselves and shook hands.

"If you'd arrived in Jiorhaze a little earlier, we would have asked you for a Sojourner's Psalm."

"A Sojourner's Psalm?"

"Are you unfamiliar with the term? At the Rite of Sacred Song held in the holy land of Jiorhaze, there is a ceremony in which pilgrims from afar are invited to dedicate a new song to this land. That song is a Sojourner's Psalm."

Ellen and the girls nodded, prompting Irina to continue explaining.

"Once upon a time, the song of a saint who visited this land became a god, who cleared the land of calamity. The event became the beginning of the most important ceremony of the Rite of Sacred Song. The unceasing flow of new songs from outside the city is the god that continues to protect all of us. This is the will of the Almighty Radiance, Equis."

"I don't really get it, but I think it's lovely that a song can be a god."

Irina smiled, pleased with Ellen's response. "I know the song will reach the city, but please stop by tomorrow and watch our hymn from here. May the Almighty Radiance always protect you," she said, holding her hands together in a prayer.

The fan union girls accepted the gesture by bowing, then descended from the stage.

"You look like you're up to something fun," I called.

They shrank back nervously. "P-Please forgive us, Lord Anos. We went off on our own."

"I have nothing to say about how you choose to spend your free time, but I'm impressed. That was your first time hearing that song, wasn't it?"

"Yes! But it was an easy song to sing. Irina and the others are part of the choir of this city—we were watching them because they sang so beautifully, then they invited us to sing along."

So that's how they had ended up singing together.

"Singing is popular in Jiorhaze," Arcana explained. "Draconids connect to each other through their songs."

"Um, will there be free time tomorrow?"

"Do you want to watch the Rite of Sacred Song?"

The girls of the fan union nodded. "Oh, but it's okay if there are other things we need to do! It's totally fine!"

"There's no better chance to experience Jiordal's culture firsthand. We can all come back together tomorrow."

Ellen beamed from ear to ear. "Yay! Thank you so much!"

The girls exchanged high fives with each other in excitement.

"However, there is one thing to keep in mind."

Ellen looked back at me worriedly.

"There's an evil villain scheduled to disturb the festival."

§ 12. Drifting Memories, Overlapping Dreams, Rising to the Surface

After their free time was over, the students of the Demon King Academy toured the city of Jiorhaze together. Aside from the sacred grounds, there were several locations that had bonfires going and where hymns were being offered to the gods. There were so many pilgrims visiting from outside the city, no one treated us with any suspicion—if anything, we were warmly welcomed.

We found a restaurant to have lunch at, then returned to the dragon landing site. There, I drew a magic circle and used Iris to build a Demon King Castle. Although the bishop had given us permission to frequent the area, I made sure to construct most of the floors underground to avoid attracting too much attention during the festival. Only the entrance and first floor were visible from the surface.

"The lowest floor is for teachers. Allocate the rest among yourselves." I opened the front door to let the students inside. "Jiorhaze seems like a safe place, but there'll be fewer people around at night. Stay inside. I won't be coming to anyone's rescue. If you still wish to go out despite that, I won't stop you."

With that warning, I proceeded inside to the magic circle set up on the first floor. Shin, Eldmed, and Arcana stepped into the circle with me. When I sent my magic into it, it teleported us to the bottom floor.

"I'll take the room at the back. Use the rest however you please."

"Understood."

Shin immediately walked forward and opened the door right next to my own. In the unlikely event that an enemy attacked, he would be able to obstruct access to my room from there.

"Then I shall take the room over there," Eldmed said, entering the room farthest from mine.

"What about you?" I asked, turning to Arcana.

She quietly pointed at my room. Unlike other parts of the castle, the door was made of wood. "Does that mean something?" she asked.

"I made it for fun, just in case it brought back any memories. Let me show you."

I walked up to the far room and opened the door. The inside was made entirely of wood and wasn't particularly spacious. The furnishings weren't of the highest quality either, and were in fact rather mundane. It was a recreation of the house in the woods I'd seen in my dream in which I'd lived with my sister. If those were my real memories, I would have made that house using Iris. But though I'd recreated the room, there was nothing particularly familiar about it.

"Is this what you saw in your dream?"

"It was the house I lived in with my little sister."

Arcana's gaze wandered around the interior of the house. "I don't know why, but it feels like I've seen this place before." She took a step forward and touched the door leading to the other room inside. "Is this the bedroom?"

"That's right."

"There'll be two beds." Arcana opened the door. She stared curiously at the two beds placed side by side.

"Come to think of it, I haven't told you my little sister's name yet." I came up behind Arcana, who tilted her head back and looked up at me. Her silver hair swayed with the movement. "It was Arcana."

She paused before responding. "Why is it the same as mine?"

"I don't know. Perhaps we were siblings two thousand years ago."

For a brief moment, Arcana gazed at me curiously, but she quickly turned away and entered the bedroom. After looking at the bed, she turned back to me. "You mean before I became a nameless god?"

"That's the only possibility I can think of, but I understand your doubts. I can't imagine what sequence of events would have led to such a situation

Chapter 12 — Drifting Memories, Overlapping Dreams, Rising to the Surface

either." I walked over to one of the beds and sat down. "That being said, it wouldn't be impossible for you to be different people. The sister in my dream had a significantly different personality to yours." I looked back at Arcana, who seemed lost in thought. "Just to confirm, you do wish to regain your memories, don't you?"

"If it will bring you salvation."

Hmm. So that was the condition.

"You truly are a god through and through." I lay back on the bed and looked up at the ceiling. "You discarded your name of your own will. You might have discarded your memories along with it. If you recall them, you may not be able to return to being a nameless god."

"Discarding my name was my sin. I was the cause of that man's despair."

She was referring to the man she had failed to save after becoming a nameless god.

"No matter what happened in my past, I shouldn't have forgotten it."

"If you hadn't discarded your name, you wouldn't have obtained a heart."

"That is correct, but now that I have emotions, I wish to regain my name and memories. They weren't things I should have forgotten."

Because Arcana had lacked emotions, she'd been able to discard her name and memories. The emotions she'd gained in exchange had then made her desire the name and memories she lacked. It was a hopeless loop.

"You're the one who said it—that there has to be a way to regain my name and memories without losing my emotions. I could atone by continuing to save people," she said.

"If you've made up your mind, then it's fine."

Arcana approached me and climbed onto my bed. "Drifting memories, overlapping dreams, rising to the surface."

"What does that mean?"

"If I was your little sister, we might be able to recall more if we dream together."

That made sense.

"The burden on you will be greater," she said.

"That's fine. If it could help to retrieve our memories, then it's worth trying."

"Thank you."

Arcana straddled my body and placed her hands on my chest. Leaning down, she pressed her forehead against mine, and a magic circle appeared around her body. Her clothes started glowing and fading away.

Just then, the door slammed open.

"H-Hold it right there!"

Arcana turned around. Sasha and Misha were standing in the doorway.

"I knew I had a bad feeling for a reason. This lewd god! I won't allow your inexcusable behavior anymore!"

"Demon child, this is a necessary process to regain our memories. It is not lewd, but holy. It is not inexcusable, but pure."

"I know that, but Anos would have said, *'Do you really think we have to sleep together to regain our memories?'*! He definitely would have said that!" Sasha yelled, her face bright red.

"Well, it wouldn't be impossible," I said, "but using magic in the improper way results in a substantial reduction of both accuracy and efficiency. There's no reason to avoid sleeping together." I looked at Sasha, who remained silent. "Don't look at me like that. I won't ignore the well-intentioned advice of a subordinate. If there's a problem, just say it."

"Problem?" Sasha looked down. "It's just..." She was blushing fiercely, her voice barely audible. "I don't like it."

"Why?"

She closed her mouth, unsure of how to answer, so Misha helpfully chimed in instead.

"Sasha's worried about you."

"Does she think Arcana will do something to me?"

Misha shook her head. "Arcana is a good girl, but Sasha can't help but worry."

Well, I could see her point. It was only natural for a subordinate to worry about their master.

"In that case, you may as well join in. The order of dreams can show you your pasts as well," I said.

"What?" Sasha stared at me blankly.

"If you're worried, stand guard beside me. Watch the dream while you're at it. If you're in direct contact with the order of dreams, you'll be able to detect any suspicious activity."

Chapter 12 — Drifting Memories, Overlapping Dreams, Rising to the Surface

"But doesn't that mean…" Sasha fidgeted restlessly and looked up at me in question.

"…we'll be sleeping together?" Misha asked for her.

"I don't see a problem with that."

"N-No problem?" Sasha mumbled.

"Are you unhappy with something?"

"Oh, no. It's nothing." Sasha looked away again, her cheeks glowing fiercely.

"Then come here. I'd also feel reassured with you by my side."

"R-Really?"

"Really."

"I see… I see. Okay." Sasha nodded to herself slowly, gathering her thoughts. "If you insist, then it can't be helped." Walking awkwardly, she made her way towards the bed. Misha followed behind her. "Um, what am I meant to do?"

"Lie on either side of Anos," Arcana answered.

Misha obediently sat to my left and flopped backwards. Sasha took a seat to my right and lay down stiffly. Misha turned to me and smiled softly.

"What is it?" I asked.

"We're like a family."

"Is that so?"

"Yeah."

Arcana returned her forehead to mine. "No distinction, no borders." She drew a magic circle around us. Our clothes shone bright.

"Wait, isn't this undressing us?!"

"Cancel your anti-magic. I'm merely storing them in your storage circle."

"Th-That's not what I meant. What about a blanket? Would it be okay to put on a blanket?!" Sasha asked.

Arcana nodded. *"Warm snow becomes a bed."*

Lunar snowdrops appeared, transforming the blanket we were lying on into a thin sheet. The sheet was draped over us, and then, in a flash of light, Arcana activated her magic to remove all our clothes. Misha blinked a few times, and the light of the room disappeared. She used her magic to light a small lamp hanging on the wall. I turned to look at her.

"Don't look," she whispered. It was rare to see her normally unshaken self so shy.

"All right."

I looked back at Arcana, who was sitting on top of me, but Misha continued to stare at me while lying on her side. Sasha, meanwhile, was stubbornly turned away, her body stiff.

"Demon child," Arcana called to Sasha.

"What?"

"Relax. You won't be able to enter the dream like that."

"E-Even if you say that, what am I meant to do?" Sasha tried to assume a natural position, but the more she shifted, the more her body tensed up.

"Calm down. It'll be fine," I said, reaching over to turn her head towards me.

"Eek! U-Um... Um... Um...?!"

"Look into my eyes."

She stared at me. "Okay..."

"You came here for my sake, right?"

Sasha nodded.

"I'm glad to hear that, but there's no need to get so worked up—just be your usual self. Nothing will happen. We're just watching a dream."

"Right."

Sasha rested her forehead against my body as if to protect me. She was still a little stiff, but it was much better than before.

"Will this do?" I asked Arcana.

She nodded and leaned forward again. "*Night falls, inviting sleep. Drifting memories, overlapping dreams, rising to the surface.*"

All our bodies were enveloped in a faint light. I surrendered myself to the sleepiness that beckoned me, and my consciousness faded away.

§ 13. Dora the Liar

The dream continued. Arcana staggered towards the fireplace with heavy firewood in her arms. What would have been an easy task for an adult was a huge challenge for the body of a six- or seven-year-old.

"Heave-ho," she said, tossing the wood into the burning fire.

The cold of the billowing snow outside was seeping into the house. Arcana wrapped herself in a blanket and held her hands out over the fire. Just then, two knocks rang from the front door.

Arcana's eyes lit up. "Big brother!" she called happily, hurrying to unlock the door. But when she opened it and saw the man on the other side, she took a step back. "Huh? Who are you?"

The middle-aged man was dressed in blue robes. His expression was haggard, and there was a look of madness in his eyes as he stared at Arcana.

"I've found you. The sacrifice..." he murmured. Two more men in the same blue robes appeared behind him. They looked like evil apparitions.

"She must be offered..."

"The sacrifice to the gods..."

"Now give yourself up as an offering!"

Arcana backed away. The men followed her into the house.

"N-No! Go away!" she shrieked.

But the men reached for her without a care until—

"Gah!"

Firewood went flying through the house, slicing the air and striking the men on the back of their heads. They crumpled over and fell to their knees.

"Hmm. What do you want with my sister?"

A black-haired, black-eyed boy of around ten years of age appeared in the doorway. It was Arcana's older brother, Anos.

"Brother!" Arcana dived into Anos's arms and clung to him tightly.

"Stand back, Arcana. I struck them with enough force to render the average demon unconscious, but it seems these aren't average demons."

The men struggled to their feet, clutching their heads.

"Why do you defy the teachings, boy?"

"That child is the sacrifice. The dragons will not be appeased until she is offered to the gods."

"Ignorant outsiders should stay out of this! The dragons are running rampant because you took the girl!"

Arcana trembled at the men's wrath.

"What are you talking about? If the dragons are out of control, suppress them by force. Full-grown adults like you shouldn't be foisting the blame onto my sister and me."

"Shut up, you dumb brat! An idiot that doesn't understand logic that's already been explained to them has no right to open their mouth!"

The men drew their swords and swung at Anos. He held up a hand and created a barrier, making the swords snap on impact. Then, as a counterattack, Anos used Griad to burn the men, but scales appeared on their skin to block the obsidian flames.

"Hmm. You're unusual demons. I've never heard of anyone who could grow scales. The wavelength of your magic is slightly different too." Anos glared at the men with his Magic Eyes. "Are you really demons?"

"We're not obligated to answer a fool! Die, brat!"

The men opened their jaws, revealing their sharp fangs. Scorching fire shot from the back of their throats, consuming Anos.

"Brother!"

"I'm fine. Today was a little chilly anyway. This is the perfect temperature."

After erasing the fire breath with his anti-magic, Anos drew three magic circles. A small black sun peeked out of each.

Chapter 13 — Dora the Liar

"I just learned this spell. Let's see how you take it."

Jio Graze shot forth from point-blank range. The men tried to deflect the small suns with the backs of their scaly hands, but their bodies were ignited by the black flames.

"Gaaah! This can't be!"

"I'm... I'm burning?!"

"Why does a brat like him have so much power?!"

The scales that had blocked the earlier Griad were completely useless in the face of Jio Graze. The black suns swallowed them, turning them to ash.

Anos gently hugged Arcana's trembling shoulders. "I'm sorry for scaring you. It's okay now."

With her face buried in Anos's chest, Arcana shook her head. "You know, I wasn't scared at all."

"Oh?"

"Because... Because I knew you'd come to save me," she said bravely despite her trembling.

"You're always so quick to lie."

"It's not a lie! I really believed it!"

Anos patted her head softly. "Really?"

"Yes. Really."

"You're strong." Anos drew a magic circle to clean up the piles of ash and repair the damaged house. He then drew another magic circle, reached inside, and pulled out a load of bread. "Let's eat," he said.

After that, he heated some soup in the kitchen, poured it into two mugs, then brought it out to the table in front of the fireplace.

"This cold spell has destroyed a lot of crops. I went to the nearby village, but this was all the food I could get."

"It's okay. I can't eat a lot anyway," Arcana said, holding the mug in both hands to sip the soup.

"I'll try somewhere farther away later."

"You're leaving again?" Arcana looked at him sadly. She didn't want to be separated from her brother.

"I'll be back soon."

"Okay."

She sighed in relief, then picked up her bread and soup and brought them closer to the fireplace. She then patted the floor beside her.

"What a spoiled little sister."

"I can't help how cold it is!"

Anos took his food and sat down beside Arcana. She leaned towards him so that they were touching.

"If it's okay with you, big brother, could you read to me again?"

"I thought you said you could read by yourself now."

"No! I want you to read to me!" She peered up at her brother's face. "Please?"

"The usual book?"

"Yup, the usual one!"

Anos made a beckoning gesture with his finger, and a book flew off the bookshelf and into his hand. The title of the book was *Dora the Liar*. The cover and binding were worn out and peeling from how many times it had been read. Anos began reading the book aloud to his sister. The story was set in a fictional kingdom unrelated to Dilhade.

There was once a girl called Dora.

Although Dora lived in a village, she was actually the daughter of a noble family. Her astounding talent for magic had driven her to a secluded location to avoid being targeted by bad guys. However, every once in a while, famous sorcerers would visit and ask to be her disciple. She cured incurable illnesses when no one was watching. Her noble parents often came to visit her in secret, as they both loved their daughter dearly and dreamed of the day they could live together again.

Of course, this was all a lie made up by Dora.

Dora's constant string of lies had the villagers running about doing her bidding, until one day, a boy the same age as Dora exposed her lies. No longer trusted, Dora lived out the rest of her lonely life all by herself. She was unable to accept her own lies and believed that her nonexistent parents would come for her someday. After lying for so long, she had convinced herself that her lies were the truth. In the end, no one believed her ever again, and she died alone.

"Hmm. As usual, I don't get what's so interesting about this story. What do you like so much about it?"

Chapter 13 — Dora the Liar

"Um, I think Dora's lies were lots of fun! I also like how a small lie could lead to so much trouble and make everyone panic!"

So that's why she likes to lie so much, Anos thought. He couldn't understand young kids at all.

"If you say things like that, you'll end up like Dora one day."

"No, I don't want that! I like Dora, but I don't want to end up like her!"

How honest of her, Anos thought.

"Then you'd better not lie so much."

Arcana puffed up her cheeks. "I have you with me, so I'll be fine!"

"That's a good point."

Arcana giggled happily. "Read more, read more!"

Anos continued reading the book.

"Ah!" Arcana cried, accidentally dropping her bread. The loaf rolled across the floor and into the fire. She watched the flames sadly.

"What's wrong?" Anos turned to her, but she waved her hands.

"Oh, um, it hurt when I took a bite."

"You must have swallowed too much at once."

"Ehee hee. Read more, read more!"

Anos continued reading. When Arcana exhaled in relief, her stomach rumbled. She pitifully stared at the bread in the fireplace, but it was no longer in an edible state. With no other choice, she slowly sipped her soup, unaware of Anos glancing at her as he read.

"Arcana," he said, offering her his bread.

"Huh?"

"Don't drop it this time."

She hesitantly took it. "What about you?"

"Well, actually, I ate something unique in town. I'm not that hungry."

"What? That's so unfair!" she exclaimed, pummeling him with her fists.

"Forgive me. I'll buy you something next time."

"It's a promise! You have to, okay? You can't just eat it by yourself!"

Anos nodded, and Arcana happily chowed down on the bread.

"Your lies aren't like Dora's," Anos said.

Arcana looked at him while munching away.

"You were concerned I'd have trouble finding food again, weren't you?"

"It's so cold outside. You shouldn't have to go."

Anos petted Arcana's head. "Your lies are kind lies that don't hurt anyone. You'll never be like Dora."

Arcana beamed and rested her head on Anos's shoulder. They continued to read the book, pausing every now and then to merrily discuss the mayhem Dora had created.

§ 14. Sojourner's Psalm

A small hand reached through my dozing consciousness and shook me awake.

"Wake up," a soft voice said in my ear.

I opened my eyes to see soft platinum blonde locks. Misha smiled faintly.

"Is it morning?" I asked.

"Yeah."

I sat up, and Misha quietly distanced herself. Sasha seemed to have been woken first, as she was sitting in a chair with a faraway gaze. Both girls were in their Demon King Academy uniforms.

"We watched your dream with you," Arcana said. She was seated on the edge of the bed.

"The dream about draconids coming after my sister?"

"That one."

That had been quite strange. The underground world hadn't existed two thousand years ago. Draconids shouldn't have existed yet either—or had their ancestors lived aboveground?

"Did you recall anything?" I asked.

"I don't know, but it felt like I'd seen that dream before. I wonder why," she mumbled, frowning slightly. "Is it because I really was your little sister?"

If that dream had been the combination of our memories, it would be reasonable to believe so.

"I'd like to see what happened next."

"Tonight," she said.

I nodded. I had plans to attend to. We couldn't be dreaming midday.

"How was it for you two?" Arcana asked the twins.

"We saw the same dream as Anos," Misha answered.

Arcana contemplated for a moment. "What about afterwards?"

Misha shook her head.

"Does the same go for you, demon child?" Arcana asked Sasha, who was still staring into space. Misha walked up to her sister.

"Sasha, did you dream anything?" she asked softly.

"Yeah. I had a dream about a tiny Anos and his little sister," Sasha replied vaguely.

"Anything else?"

"Anything else? Um… Nothing," she said sleepily.

"After they finished watching our dream, I showed them a dream of their past life."

"So why don't they see anything?" I asked.

"Because they have no memory of it. Either they didn't have a past life, or they've forgotten it more strongly than we have."

Either was possible, but at the very least, this meant that Misha and Sasha's memories couldn't be retrieved using the order of dreams.

"It can't be helped. We'll just have to recover their memories by other means, such as finding the God of Traces or something." I got out of bed and headed for the door. Out of the corner of my eye, I saw Sasha's vacant gaze abruptly snap into an alert one.

"H-Hold it, Anos! Clothes! Put on some clothes! I can see everything!" she cried, pointing at me in a panic. I was still wrapped in the sheet, so she shouldn't have been able to see *everything*. That being said, it wouldn't be dignified of me to appear before the students while half naked.

"Don't worry yourself. I had no intention of going upstairs like this." I drew a magic circle and changed into my white uniform. "That aside, you're rather energetic this morning."

Sasha blushed and turned away. "It's not like that. It's just… C-Come to think of it, why are you still wearing your school uniform?" she asked, abruptly changing the topic.

"To remind everyone of how they treated the Demon King as a misfit."

"I see. That is a pretty big warning."

Chapter 14 — Sojourner's Psalm

"It's just an excuse, though."

"Excuse me?" Sasha looked at me blankly.

"I got sick of tailors incessantly offering to make me new clothes. Sending a message like this saves me the trouble of rejecting them all the time."

"But if you do that, won't you have to wear your uniform all the time?"

"I don't mind. You two do the same, don't you?"

"That's true, but…" Sasha curled up on her chair and mumbled something to herself.

"It'll be breakfast soon. Get yourselves ready," I said before leaving the room.

We soon met up with the students of the academy and headed into town for breakfast. After a short break, it was time for the Rite of Sacred Song to begin. We made our way to the sacred grounds. The area was packed with pilgrims offering their prayers to the large bonfire at the center. Following what Arcana had taught me about praying, I covered my right hand with my left while facing the bonfire. Beside me, Sasha looked surprised.

"What's that look for?"

"What happened to you not having faith in the gods? Don't you hate them?"

"I won't deny that. However, people are free to put their faith in what they want as long as they're not harming others. This is a festival for those who have faith. If we're attending, it's only polite to offer a prayer."

"So the Demon King has common sense after all," Sasha muttered, praying beside me.

"Anos is concerned," Misha said.

"About what?" Sasha asked.

"About Ahid trying to disturb the festival."

"Hmm. But it isn't Anos's fault, is it? I mean, if it hadn't been for Nedneliaz, Ahid might not have gone around saying their god didn't exist, but what he was doing before that was way worse. He lied about the gods saying things and tried to control the faithful."

He had also tricked many draconids into sacrificing themselves in order to strengthen the Moon of Creation.

"If he hadn't met Anos, he could have been doing even more terrible things right now."

I burst out laughing.

"What's so funny?"

"I'm just touched to have such a kindhearted subordinate. Indeed, I'm not at fault. I'm under no obligation to deal with Ahid for the sake of this nation. If anything, they should be grateful to me for exposing his connection to Gadeciola."

"As long as you know that." Sasha looked down in embarrassment.

"The responsibility for creating a fool lies with the nation that raised him. There was no guarantee that they wouldn't resent me for defeating a devout follower, even if it was for the Selection Trial."

Stealing Arcana from Ahid had been enough of a blow to his power. The only thing I hadn't expected was for him to be able to escape after being arrested.

"I suppose I could have shackled him to make him a little easier to catch."

Misha looked at me with her unreadable gaze. "Do you feel guilty?"

"Who, me?"

"Just a little, I mean."

"As I just said, if they choose to carry a spark, I'm under no obligation to put out their fires for them. Render unto the gods the things that are the gods' and unto Jiordal the fools that are Jiordal's."

Misha giggled. "Sasha was right," she said, seeing right through me. "It's not your fault."

"You always think too much of me. I'm not as kind as you say."

Misha shook her head. "You're kind."

"Hey, what are you two whispering about? Is it something you can't tell me?"

"It's just idle talk," I responded, accompanied by Misha, who answered at the same time.

"Idle talk."

Sasha narrowed her eyes in suspicion.

"Oh, look! Something's starting!"

Eleonore, who was in front of us, turned around and pointed at the stage. Followers clad in blue robes were appearing from behind the altar. They were the members of the Jiordal Choir. As soon as they stepped out onto the stage,

Chapter 14 — Sojourner's Psalm

they faced the large bonfire and began praying. The melody of a dragon bone harp accompanied their prayer.

"O Equis, the Almighty Radiance, we thank you for another hundred days of safety," Irina said grandly. As the leader of the choir, she was highly ranked and respected among the clergy. Her robes were of a higher quality than those of the other members of the choir. She began to address the congregation. "Since ancient times, the winds of new songs have blown through Jiorhaze thanks to the will of Equis. Those winds have eliminated all kinds of disasters, blessing the citizens of Jiordal. This is proof that our god is always watching over us." Irina raised her hands high into the air. "This is the Sojourner's Psalm. The Almighty Radiance will dwell in our song today and become one with the sacred tune. Close your eyes and pray. Listen closely to the word of Equis."

The choir turned around and exited the stage the way they'd come. The Rite of Sacred Song was performed by pilgrims visiting from outside of Jiorhaze. The choir was probably leaving to allow them onstage.

The followers around us closed their eyes obediently. Then a voice rang out.

"Listen closely, people of Jiordal."

It was a familiar voice.

"The god we all desire does not exist in this world. Gods are merely order; they are not existences that bring salvation. The Almighty Radiance is a fabrication devised by the first pope. The present pope, Golroana Delo Jiordal, knows this and has been covering up the fact this entire time."

The congregation stirred noisily.

"I am Cardinal Ahid Alovo Agartz of Jiordal. As the Oracle, I know this truth, and I have come to you today to share this knowledge. There is no Equis. The Almighty Radiance is a complete deception. As proof, I shall end the Sojourner's Psalm that has continued for two thousand years. If the Almighty Radiance truly exists, the song will not end here. With this, I shall prove that there is no god in this underground world."

He wasn't nearby. His voice was coming through Leaks. The song of the Divine Dragon had an effect similar to a dragon's cry. Because it covered the entirety of Jiorhaze, it was difficult to determine where the magic was being transmitted from.

"The Sojourner's Psalm will come to an end?" one follower murmured.
"Nonsense! The words of a fool fallen to heresy are worth nothing."
"How dare he shamelessly call himself a cardinal!"
"But no one's coming onstage."
"The Psalm Choristers would normally be ready by now!"
"O Equis, please grant us your guidance…"
"Show us the way!"
"Bring your divine retribution down upon the heretic Ahid."

The congregation prayed in unison, but the pilgrims meant to sing the Sojourner's Psalm—the Psalm Choristers—didn't appear onstage.

"I wonder what's wrong," Ellen murmured worriedly behind me.

This was probably Ahid's doing.

"Hmm. Ellen, come with me. We're going to ask the choir leader about the situation."

"Huh? Oh, uh, okay."

I took Ellen's hand and cast my Magic Eyes towards the altar. Behind it, hidden from the audience, was a staircase leading underground. I used Gatom to teleport Ellen and myself there. After starting down the stairs and continuing for some distance, Irina's voice reached our ears.

"What have you done to the Psalm Choristers and Priest Elnora, heretic?! The gods will never forgive acts of violence!"

"Ha ha ha ha! Who needs a god's forgiveness? The gods are only order, nothing more than symbols! When will you understand that?"

The one arguing back was Ahid. His rather dramatic change in personality was probably due to the never-ending nightmare he felt he was trapped in. That, or this was his true self.

"Quit this nonsense! We will never be fooled by such words!"

"In that case, you're free to look all you want, but you'll never be able to find them," Ahid said smugly. "Couldn't you tell? Priest Elnora was me all along. I used magic to change my appearance. You people were completely fooled!"

"You were disguised as a sojourner? How sinful!"

"Sin? Ha ha ha! So what if it's a sin? With this, the Sojourner's Psalm will come to an end. The people of Jiordal will finally realize that the Almighty Radiance doesn't exist. Now, it's about time. With this, I should be able to

Chapter 14 — Sojourner's Psalm

finally awaken from this dream." Suddenly, he began yelling like a madman. "Now wake up! Wake up, wake up, wake up from this dream! There is no Equis! The Almighty Radiance doesn't exist! Wake up already!"

"This lunatic... Feel the wrath of god!"

There was a dull thud as someone was punched.

"Gah!"

We finally reached the bottom of the staircase to find Ahid apprehended by Irina's choir.

"Why...? Why am I still not waking up?! This is meant to be a dream. Why can't I wake up? Why won't it end?! I've done so much already! Why won't I wake?!"

The choir members thrust their swords through the crawling Ahid, pinning him to the floor.

"Gugh..."

Blood seeped from the many wounds that ran along his body, but Ahid merely glared up at them, his vacant gaze distorted by insanity.

"WHY?! WHY WON'T I WAKE?!"

Ahid's body burst into flames, which swiftly spread to the members of the choir.

"Aaaaaah!"

His limbs still skewered by swords, he forced himself to his feet, spewing fire from his mouth.

"Why?! What is the reason?!"

However, the flames rapidly closing in on the choir were tragically erased by my Magic Eyes of Destruction.

"What?!"

"Surely you've started to realize it by now, Ahid. This is reality. You have exposed all the lies you've accumulated until now and lost everything as a result. It's time to accept the truth."

"Misfit..." Ahid clenched his teeth. "No, you're wrong! This is a dream! Reality would never be like this. It could never be this ridiculous!" Ahid opened his mouth to breathe fire again, but I drew close to him long before he could succeed. "Agh... Hah..."

My right arm dug into his abdomen, but something didn't feel right.

"This is a dream, isn't it? It has to be! Otherwise, all my efforts have been for nothing. My position as cardinal, the power of a submissive god, followers who moved exactly as I wished... Do you know how much effort I put into obtaining those things?!"

"Anything we obtain by lying is nothing more than an illusion, which is why you were consumed by your nightmare. From the very beginning, you had nothing." I clenched my fist, crushing his organs. His body turned to dust.

Hmm. As I'd expected, I couldn't grab his source with Vebzud like this.

"A fake created by magic, huh? Then his true body's elsewhere."

"Are you okay, Irina?" Ellena asked, offering the choir leader her hand. Irina accepted the help and sat up. Her body had been burned by the fire.

"This is nothing. What's important now is the Sojourner's Psalm."

"But, ma'am, it's too late to search for pilgrims now."

"No. There's still one option. This must be the will of Equis." Irina gaze fell on Ellen.

"Huh?"

"I have a request for you, Ellen. I believe you will be able to fulfill the duty of the holy Psalm Chorister. Would you please lend us your assistance?"

"What? But there's no time to practice."

Irina shook her head. "Dilhade, was it? Please sing a song from your nation. The singing of the Sojourner's Psalm is a ceremony that ushers new winds to Jiorhaze. If you bring your song, the song of the Demon King's Choir, into this land, the result will be the same. So please, Ellen, consider my request."

Irina bowed her head deeply. Ellen looked over at me.

"I would also like to see how your song resonates with the god-worshipping people of the underground world," I said.

With that single sentence, the hesitation vanished from Ellen's eyes. "I understand, Irina. I don't know how well we'll be able to do it, but…"

"You'll give it a go?"

Ellen nodded. "It'll be a thank you for letting us listen to your sacred song yesterday. This time, you can listen to a song of our nation—the song of a Demon King wishing for peace."

§ 15. Demon King Hymn No. Six: "Neighbor"

The sacred grounds stirred noisily. There was no sign that the Sojourner's Psalm was about to begin. Ahid's earlier words must have flashed through the minds of the congregation.

The two-thousand-year tradition was about to end. Such an event would indeed be proof that there was no almighty god of the underground world. While the people of Jiordal weren't about to believe him blindly, they couldn't hide their agitation and anxiety. Restlessness was spreading through the grounds by the moment.

Just as that restlessness reached its peak, a single girl appeared onstage. It was Ellen. She raised her hand, and the fan union girls before the stage responded in kind. I had informed them of the situation via Leaks.

"Let's go!"

"Okay!"

The fan union girls climbed onto the stage and lined up in their usual formation. I drew a magic circle over their bodies, and ceremonial robes appeared.

"Sorry for the wait, everyone! My name is Ellen, and I'm a member of the Demon King's Choir of Dilhade. We will be your Psalm Choristers for the Rite of Sacred Song."

The congregation looked relieved and began praying anew.

"Our country is located far, far away from here, farther than you could ever imagine. We're ruled by a man called the Demon King, and the people live in peace. We came to Jiordal to learn more about this place. The Demon King told us to look closely at the people who live in this land. He wanted us to see what you all believe in and what kind of future you all dream of." She smiled brightly. "We only just arrived here, so there's still lots we don't know, but there is one thing I'm sure of: the people of this nation love music! Our country is the same. The Demon King of our country loves music as well."

The fan union girls smiled cheerfully in agreement with Ellen's speech. Each of them drew a magic circle that began playing an orchestral tune. The spell was called Synial.

"This is a song for you to learn more about our country and our Demon King. He is a great ruler who loves every aspect of all people. We are the bridge that helps convey that great love of his. That is the purpose of the Demon King's Choir. Please lend us your ear."

"Demon King Hymn No. Six: 'Neighbor,'" the girls said in unison. The elegant sound of stringed instruments began to flow throughout the city. The melody reminiscent of the sky had a different ring to it in this land beneath the earth. It enveloped the city of Jiorhaze like a refreshing breeze.

The draconids prayed as they enjoyed the unfamiliar music. Their magic trembled as though they were captivated by the refined notes. What kind of austere hymn was about to begin? The congregation eagerly leaned forward to listen...

"Oh my!" the girls sang. "I didn't know such a world existed!"

...until the sudden chorus at a completely different key was thrown in as if to ruin the mood.

"In-cum, in-cum, incoming, woo-ooh!"

However, the stark contrast seemed to grab the hearts of the congregation. The Demon King's Choir sang with an upbeat rhythm and melody to keep those hearts enthralled.

"Don't open the door!"

"Woo-ooh!"

"Don't open the forbidden door!"

"Woo-ooh!"

"No, don't open it!"

The Demon King's Choir sang brightly to the rhythmical tune. The

people of the underground world had probably never experienced such a lively hymn before. They all seemed flabbergasted.

"Tell me, gods! What is this? What is this? The ding-dong!"
"Go on. Start with a knock!"
"No, gentle taps are no good!"
"In-cum, in-cum, incoming, woo-ooh!"
"I am a neighbor, just a mere neighbor!"
"It should have been peaceful all by myself."
"But it was extending before I knew it!"
"Like a ruinous hand."
"Your ding-dong!"
"It's the Demon King!"
"Oh, it was the gods who said it."
"'Love thy neighbor.'"
"Go on. Open your heart. Open the forbidden door!"
"Oh, but it's dirty there!"
"The place no one knows…"
"It's dirty there!"
"So please don't come through the door!"
"Saying he won't fit is no good."
"He'll teach you everything the scriptures missed!"
"In-cum, in-cum, incoming, woo-ooh!"
"Oh my! I didn't know such a world existed!"
"In-cum, incoming, woo-ooh!"

The springy rhythm and lively tune had the solemnly praying congregation shifting restlessly. Perhaps they had been yearning for a song like this—a song unlike the strict hymns they were used to.

Ellen made her way to the front of the stage, walking to the beat of the music. "In our country, both the choir and the audience have fun singing the song together," she said, her voice carrying far and wide. "Please sing along with this song from Dilhade. In-cum is a phrase that means 'fun without reason' in the ancient magic tongue. We believe this means that no matter what's going on, why not have some fun?"

The devout congregation listened attentively to her words.

"I don't understand the complex relationship between nations, but I do

Chapter 15 — Demon King Hymn No. Six: "Neighbor"

know that we can all have fun together. You don't have to understand the song to have fun singing, so let's sing together! We believe that relationships between all people can start from there. Let's not sweat over the details until we've had fun!"

"What a wonderful song...I think."

"Yes, but it sounds somewhat irreverent too."

"But if this is a Sojourner's Psalm, then that must be the will of the gods of song."

"Besides, it's rare to hear a song that's so deeply moving."

"How are these lyrics meant to be interpreted? What do they mean?"

"I can listen to it as a Sojourner's Psalm, but singing along is a bit..."

The differences in values among the congregation seemed to be causing them confusion.

"Let's remain calm. The Eight Song Sages, Jiorhaze's experts on Sojourner's Psalms, are here for this purpose."

"Oh yes, that's right. What's their reaction?"

The congregation turned to the special seats reserved in the front row. The sages, dressed in navy robes, all had mysterious expressions.

"It doesn't look good."

"No, look at their fingers!"

"They're bouncing slightly to the rhythm."

"I've never heard of the Eight Song Sages moving to the rhythm before."

Eventually, one of the eight sages broke the silence. "The ancient magic tongue is said to be a language created by the gods."

Another sage spoke up. "In-cum. What a wonderful and profound word we have learned from these foreign visitors today."

"Our people cannot help but think with reason. However, reason means nothing before the gods. Reason is merely decided by people."

"This song reminds us of our starting point."

"And there were other profound words used in the lyrics. Neighbor: this is a word that denotes not only the connection between people, but the connection between nations."

"I agree. We have always hesitated to open the forbidden door between ourselves and nations we know nothing about—nations we have never interacted with before."

"The ruinous hand was merely the hand of a demon. Our misguided judgment and the fear in our hearts made that hand appear ruinous to us."

"But they opened the forbidden door and entered without fear of impurity to reach the other side, passing through the door they shouldn't have fit through. That is when the exchange between nations began. In other words, love thy neighbor."

"It's the dawn of a new world. That courage—the courage to open the forbidden door—is not taught in scriptures, and the Demon King is the one who wanted to convey that."

"Through this song alone, I can see what kind of nation he seeks to lead and what a wonderful person he must be."

"Yes, how blessed we are to hear this song. Listening to it makes joyous emotions overflow from the bottom of my heart. The gods reside in this song. They're telling my heart to dance."

It was a rave review.

"As expected of the Eight Song Sages. What profound observations."

"I knew this song was wonderful! It received such high praise from them!"

With the Eight Song Sages' seal of approval, the congregation began to move their bodies to the music.

"Here we go!"

"In-cum, in-cum, incoming, woo-ooh!"

"In-cum, in-cum, incoming, woo-ooh!"

When the Demon King's Choir sang their line, the Eight Song Sages immediately echoed them. They repeated the words with the exact same melody, albeit deeper and with much more power.

"Again!"

This time, the congregation sang along to the Eight Song Sages.

"In-cum, in-cum, incoming, woo-ooh!"

In no time at all, the girls of the Demon King's Choir had the congregation in a frenzy. Their limited magic meant they couldn't use any impressive spells, but their singing voices touched the hearts of everyone.

As the sacred grounds reached the peak of its excitement, the second half began. The Eight Song Sages turned to face the congregation.

"So please don't come through the door!" the girls called.

Chapter 15 — Demon King Hymn No. Six: "Neighbor"

"Hah!" The sages thrust out their right fists.

"So please don't enter!"

"Hah!" They changed hands, thrusting their left fists out in perfect unison.

"Don't enter with that forbidden key!"

"Hah, hah, hah!"

As one would expect from the highest musical authority of the nation of music, the Eight Song Sages had grasped the essence of the Demon King Hymn in no time at all and created the perfect choreography to go with it. Their adaptability was on another level. The congregation rose to their feet to mimic them.

"Tell me, Demon King!"

"Hah!" Twenty thousand followers faced the altar and thrust their fists out in unison.

"What is this? The ding-dong!"

"Hah! Hah!"

Burning fists of passion flew out, interchanging between right and left. The people raised their voices and shouted along to the lively tune as if training in martial arts.

Music, lyrics, martial arts, and fervor. The miraculous harmony between them enlivened the atmosphere to no end.

"The place no one knows!"

"Hah!" The fists of twenty thousand devout followers were thrust forward with all their might.

"It's dirty there!"

"Hah!"

They thrust and thrust and thrust as though they were trying to break through the forbidden door itself. This was a foreign land that had been isolated until now, but music easily transcended borders. It was the power of in-cum— to have fun no matter what. As though to embody those words, the Demon King's Choir and the followers of Jiordal discarded their reason and yielded themselves to the fun of the hymn.

§ 16. Prophet

The Demon King Hymn playing in the distance behind me was approaching its end. I stared down an alley in Jiorhaze while listening to the merry tune.

"Anos."

A single lunar snowdrop fell before me and transformed into Arcana.

"Did Ahid appear?" she asked.

"Yes. He was disguised as the Psalm Choristers, but that was a fake body as well. I've tracked his magic here." I drew a magic circle on the ground of the alley and blew the dirt away using Deyas. When I beckoned with my index finger, the pledge jewel buried there flew towards us. "It seems he used this as a decoy and fled."

Ahid's magic was contained in the pledge jewel—he had probably used it to activate the spell that shared his magic with the fake body.

"He cast Duggan alongside Azept and Vista to craft a body from earth," Arcana explained. "A Duggan body can be supplied with magic through the pledge jewel, but it cannot think for itself. The caster has to control it."

"In other words, he was connected to his clone via a magic link."

"Yes. He discarded this to run away." Arcana took the pledge jewel into her hands. Her body started glowing brightly. "Forming a pact creates a deep bond that cannot be severed so easily. *Links connect, leading to the origin.*"

I focused my Eyes on the pledge jewel to see a single magic link extend from it. The power of the Keeper of Restoration, Nutra Do Hiana, had restored the magic link. "Hmm. It seems he was prepared for this."

As I'd watched, four more threads had extended from the pledge jewel. More and more threads followed until there were thirty-three threads in total. Ahid's magic could be felt at the end of each one.

"Of those thirty-three threads, at least thirty-two of them should link to a pledge jewel. He must have filled them with his magic to shake off anyone on his tail."

"Does the last one lead to Ahid?" Arcana asked, staring at the magic links.

"That, or they could all be diversions and the real Ahid has fled on foot without using any magic. The song of the Divine Dragon that can be heard across Jiorhaze has a similar effect to a dragon cry. Even my Eyes struggle to see across the entire city."

Following each of the thirty-three threads would be easy enough. Based on that, it would make more sense for the magic links to be further decoys.

Now, how should I go about catching him?

The singing coming from the sacred grounds was growing louder. The Demon King Hymn was reaching its climax. Soon, the group chorus of "in-cum, in-cum" was echoing through the skies of Jiorhaze. The intense passion behind the voices was proof that the girls' song had been accepted by the people of the underground. What a joyful occasion.

Just then, a deep singing voice rang out from the road beside the alley.

"In-cum, in-cum, incoming! In-cum, in-cum, incoming, woo-ooh…"

I turned to see a large man in the crimson armor of a knight, humming along to the Demon King Hymn. Although his hair was on the longer side, his beard was neatly trimmed. On the outside, the man looked to be around forty years of age; however, the air around him was as heavy as that of someone who had lived for an eternity.

"Man, I can't get enough of that." The man chuckled heartily, then met my gaze. "The songs from aboveground sure are something else. Say, could you get them to come sing at my place next?"

Hmm. What a peculiar individual.

"Be careful," Arcana said, glaring at the middle-aged man. "This dragon child is Prophet Diedrich Kreizen Agatha, the Sword Emperor who rules over Agatha. He's one of the Selected Eight."

"Indeed I am. If you know that much, this should be quick." Diedrich

Chapter 16 — Prophet

marched up to me and held out his hand. "As fellow candidates in the Selection Trial, we may end up facing off in a holy battle against each other, but let's hold no grudges, Demon King from above."

He had a rather dauntless personality.

"It's Anos Voldigoad," I said, accepting Diedrich's handshake. He flashed a toothy grin. "If you're here for the Selection Trial, then this is an unfortunate moment. I'm currently pursuing someone. You're free to challenge me, but I won't have the time to play with you."

"Nah, I'm not here to face you today. My business is with the pope of Jiordal and Ahid, the man you're chasing."

"Oh? Come to think of it, Ahid brought something called the Royal Dragon with him when he attacked Azesion. I heard that it belonged to the Kingdom of Agatha."

"Indeed. The Royal Dragon is the guardian dragon of Agatha. I'm here to settle things with the man who stole it and the Jiordal pope."

"I suppose I owe you an apology too," I said. "My subordinate was the one who destroyed it."

Diedrich burst into laughter. "How considerate of you, Demon King, but you're not to blame. The fault lies with the Jiordal cardinal and the pope who overlooked his scheme."

There was no doubt about that.

"So the king himself came all this way to hold the pope accountable for Ahid's misconduct."

"Any messenger I sent would have been ignored, but if I let the matter go unaddressed, my citizens could rebel. At worst, they could start a war with Jiordal, and that's one thing I'd rather avoid."

In stealing Agatha's guardian dragon, Jiordal had spat on their teachings. It made sense that the king would wish to avoid confrontation.

"In that case, this is not the time to introduce yourself to me. You should be visiting the pope."

"While I'd like to do just that, the pope of Jiordal is immersed in his prayers right now. He's got no intention of seeing me anytime soon, so I figured it was best to greet you first."

"Hmm. I'm not seeing your point."

At that moment, a clear voice cut in from behind Diedrich. "The Prophet

Diedrich can see a countless number of futures. His sight extends into the distant future, to factors no ordinary man can see. This allows him to walk the correct path."

The space behind Diedrich warped, and a woman in aqua robes appeared. Her shoulder-length hair was indigo blue, and both her eyes were closed. In her hands was a clear crystal ball. The magic around her wasn't that of a draconid. She was a god like Arcana.

"This is Naphta, Goddess of the Future and my Selection God. You could also say that she's the reason they call me the Prophet."

Goddess of the Future, huh? If Naphta truly possessed the order of the future, the Prophet title was far more credible than Ahid's garbage title had been.

"In other words, greeting me here would lead you to the pope. Is that the future you saw?" I asked.

"Right you are. If I were to make one more prophecy, I would say that Ahid Alovo Agartz will show up at the sacred grounds."

Did Ahid think I wouldn't revisit the areas he had already shown up in? I supposed fleeing among a crowd of draconids made sense.

"When will he show?"

"Around now, actually."

"Then let's confirm that."

I turned my Magic Eyes towards a gap in the dragon domain. This should work.

When I cast Gatom, the scene before me turned white, then a large bonfire came into view. I had arrived at the sacred grounds of the Divine Dragon. The Jiordal Choir was singing before the altar. I shot a glance across the crowd of praying followers and spotted a suspicious figure.

It was Ahid.

He was pushing his way through the crowd, intending to flee as quickly as possible. He marched briskly away from the sacred grounds, doing his best to leave Jiorhaze. As soon as the crowds thinned, someone grabbed his shoulder. It was Diedrich—he must have teleported just like I had.

"Hey there, former cardinal of Jiordal. I hear you had some fun while I wasn't around."

Ahid's face paled. "Diedrich?"

Chapter 16 — Prophet

"You'll be paying for what you did to the Royal Dragon."

"You…!"

Magic circles accumulated inside the pledge jewel in Ahid's hand. Azept Deiro activated. Ahid, endowed with the powers of a dragon, grabbed Diedrich's arm and tried to pull him off, but the man didn't budge.

Ahid opened his mouth to spit fire, but Diedrich grabbed Ahid's jaw as though he knew it was coming and held it shut. Then he cast anti-magic. The flames surged backwards, burning the fool's insides.

"Grrrgh!"

Diedrich hummed calmly as Ahid faltered. He used that brief opening to pin him to the ground.

"In-cum, in-cum, incoming, woo-ooh! That should do it. Now quiet down."

Despite the humiliated look on his face, Ahid started yelling. "Th-There is no almighty one! Wake up, all of you! The Almighty Radiance is a lie devised by the pope! Just think about it! The Divine Dragon's voice can be heard, but no one has ever seen it! That's because it never existed in the first place. Equis does not exi— Bwuh!"

I had teleported over to Ahid and stepped on his head to seal his mouth. "Stop making a ruckus. You're disturbing everyone's prayers."

With his mouth pressed against the ground, he groaned. "Wh-Why? I've done so much already… Why?!"

"Go and ask the pope for that answer."

I kicked Ahid's face up and grabbed the back of his head. The draconids around us were starting to stare and murmur among themselves.

"Sorry for bothering you. Go back to your festival," I said. I then set off towards the church, dragging Ahid along behind me. Diedrich matched my pace as we walked. "I'll be handing this man over to the church. They've agreed to arrange a meeting with the pope for me already, but would you like to come along? As thanks for the assistance."

"That would be excellent. I will gratefully accept the Demon King's generosity," Diedrich said, laughing heartily.

"The ability to see the future sure is an odd one. If I wanted to cause mischief and deviate from the future you saw, couldn't I just say I wouldn't bring you along?"

"Oh, the Goddess of the Future made her prophecy while accounting for your knowledge of her. That means you're a man that prioritizes honor over mischief."

He had known not only Ahid's location but also what it would take for me to feel like bringing him to the pope and that I wouldn't cause any mischief. It seemed his ability was the real deal.

"Why did you let him steal the Royal Dragon if you could foresee it?"

"Seeing the future can be a rather fickle thing. Protecting the Royal Dragon could mean failing to protect something else. It's normally the dangers you can't see that must be removed."

So the best option had been to abandon the guardian dragon of his own kingdom.

"Hmm. How far into the future do those prophecies go?"

"Who knows?" Diedrich said, staring into the distance. "As far as the day the underground world comes to an end, probably."

§ 17. The Pope

By the time we reached our destination, the underground world was growing dark. Before us stood Jiordal Cathedral, the residence of Pope Golroana and a prominent place of prayer. Arcana and I stood at the entrance with Diedrich, the Sword Emperor of Agatha; Naphta, the Goddess of the Future; and Mirano, the bishop who had shown us the way here.

"This way please."

With Mirano taking the lead, we entered the cathedral. The interior was lined with torches, and great pillars supported the high ceiling. We continued towards the back, where we came upon a large door. Beside it, a row of people in blue robes and armor were praying. Mirano stopped before the door and slowly turned to us.

"Behind this sacred door is the Shrine of Sacred Song—a space where the pope prays for the sake of our kingdom." He turned back to the sacred door and touched it. "Your Holiness, I have brought Demon King Anos of Dilhade and Sword Emperor Diedrich of Agatha. The fool who violated our teachings is also here."

Mirano had been astonished to see Diedrich, Arcana, and Naphta together at the same time, but after the prior day's events, he seemed to have become more accustomed to miracles and had promptly sent out a message to the pope. As promised, he had then shown us here after the Rite of Sacred Song.

"Good work, Bishop Mirano," a voice called from the other side of the door. It was an androgynous voice, neither masculine nor feminine.

"As the Almighty Radiance wishes," Mirano said, moving away from the door and joining the line of holy knights. He folded his hands in a quiet prayer. Golroana spoke without opening the door.

"Anos, Demon King of Dilhade, and Diedrich, Sword Emperor of Agatha, I am Pope Golroana Delo Jiordal, the Savior of the Selected Eight. I was told you requested an audience with me. May I ask your purpose here?"

Diedrich turned to me.

"You can go first," I said.

He took a step forward and raised his voice. "This is the Sword Emperor of Agatha, Diedrich Kreizen Agatha. Pope Golroana, are you aware that Agatha's Royal Dragon was stolen by the former cardinal of Jiordal?"

"I am aware."

"I'm here to settle that matter. Prove that Jiordal was not involved with the incident—that Ahid stole the Royal Dragon of his own volition—and accept how Agatha handles his punishment." Diedrich smiled lightheartedly. "If not, we'll have a war on our hands."

"This man, Ahid, has been stripped of his baptismal name. He is not a clergyman to be protected by the church. You may judge him in accordance with your kingdom's precepts. I pledge by our god that it will not violate Jiordal's doctrines."

"Excellent."

Diedrich could see the future. He must have foreseen that Ahid had been stripped of his baptismal name, yet he had come all the way here to hear Golroana's vow anyway. He must have seen a future in which punishing Ahid would have been used against him in some way. That meant the pope must be more than just a blind follower of the gods.

"Hee…" Ahid's head began shaking in my hand. The laughter of a madman bubbled up from within him. "Hee hee ha ha ha ha! I've finally made it to you, Pope Golroana! The time has come for my speech! Listen! Listen closely! Equis does not exist! The Almighty Radiance is just a fantasy made up by our draconid ancestors!"

The area was silent, allowing Ahid's voice to echo even more fruitlessly. The holy knights lined before the sacred door all shot him looks of contempt.

Chapter 17 — The Pope

But Ahid wasn't concerned by that at the moment. A look of utter despair had crossed his face.

"Why... Why won't the dream end?"

He had traveled around Jiordal to spread the word to the people that their god didn't exist, and now he had directly conveyed that to the pope, the head of the church. There was nothing more he could do.

"I don't know what spell it is you're under, but you must have realized it already, Ahid. This is no dream. It is reality."

"Reality..." he muttered slowly, as though he had lost all hope. He must have realized something was off, yet he had desperately averted his gaze. But there was nowhere he could run from here. "Are you saying this is my reality? My efforts... My faith... My position...!"

"The Almighty Radiance sees all. If you wish to know why this happened, ask yourself. You could call this karma for your actions."

"That can't be..." Ahid began struggling fiercely in my grip. I threw him forward, and he clung to the door pleadingly, tears streaming down his face. "Please have mercy, Pope Golroana! You might have heard of what I said in jail about not needing my baptismal name, but that was all a lie! A lie! I only did all that because I thought this was a dream! The truth is that I believe in our god! I am but a pitiful lamb, fooled by this Demon King of Tyranny! Please, please grant me salvation. I am penitent!"

"It is not for you to decide whether or not you are penitent, Ahid," Golroana said coldly.

"But I've repented."

"Even in their dreams, a follower should always remain faithful to the gods. You should have continued to pray. Am I wrong?"

"It was the Demon King of Tyranny here who enticed me! This devil...!"

"Your heart has always been free to do as it wills, no? Believing in Equis isn't something you do with your mouth. If even we can see your true character, there is no way the almighty one wouldn't be able to see through your lies."

Ahid looked horrified at the pope's curt remark. "Please, wait..."

"You are now excommunicated. Never step foot into Jiordal again."

While Ahid remained stunned, Diedrich grabbed him by the head. "All right, then. As punishment for stealing the Royal Dragon, you're going to be a sacrifice for Agatha."

"What?! Equis would never forgive you for such inhuman it— Ack!"

Diedrich's fist had sunk into Ahid's abdomen. The powerful magic packed behind the punch jolted his source and knocked him unconscious.

"Someone who doesn't believe in their own god shouldn't be saying that," Diedrich muttered, tossing Ahid aside before turning back to the door. "There's one more thing I want with you, Golroana. Since I've come all the way here already, let me say it." Diedrich's voice was firm and confident. "There are scriptures that have been passed down from pope to pope of Jiordal. Would you tell me what they're about?"

An unsettled air hung over the cathedral. The holy knights of Jiordal all wore severe expressions.

"Do you know what it is you're asking, Sword Emperor of Agatha?"

"Of course. I'm not asking you to tell me for free. I'm similarly prepared to share the scriptures that were passed down through generations of sword emperors. It'll be a trade. What do you say?"

If I recalled correctly, the three major kingdoms of Jiordal, Agatha, and Gadeciola all had certain scriptures that were only passed down orally, but what was there to gain by sharing those scriptures with each other?

"That is out of the question. The scriptures passed down from pope to pope are for the salvation of Jiordal's followers. Leaking them outside would forsake them."

"Is that what you really think?" Diedrich asked with a heavy tone. "Will Jiordal's followers truly be saved if you follow those scriptures?"

"That is the teaching of the Almighty Radiance, Equis."

Diedrich held his hand to his chin and grunted in thought. "Are you sure about that? Well, I know Jiordal has its own teachings. I'm not asking to see the scriptures directly. Instead, why don't you open this door so we can talk properly? Have a heart-to-heart about the future of the underground world? Well, what do you say?"

After a brief pause, Golroana answered. "I understand your request, Sword Emperor of Agatha, but before I give my answer, I would like to hear from Demon King Anos. Or would you prefer to be called Misfit?"

"Either works for me."

"Then I shall use the title bestowed upon you by the gods. Misfit Anos Voldigoad, what business do you have here in Jiordal?"

Chapter 17 — The Pope

"To speak plainly, I'm here to broaden my horizons. I came to learn how the people of the underground live and think."

"Then what business do you have with me?" the pope asked.

"I have a few questions—about the Selection Trial and Revalschned, the God of Traces."

"I understand." Golroana started addressing us both solemnly, as though imparting a message to his followers. "The Almighty Radiance once said this: He who grants salvation will be sought by many. But there will be no salvation if he accepts every hand and neglects his prayer. By your own means, you must choose which of you will be heard."

"Hmm. You'll only listen to one of us, but it's up to us to decide who that'll be. Is that what you're saying?"

"That is correct."

How annoying. That being said, he wasn't showing any hostility towards me. I could break down the door and force him to talk to me, but the fastest option wasn't always the best. Well, at least he was willing to listen to one of us.

"How unfortunate, Diedrich," I said, turning to Agatha's Sword Emperor. "You came all the way to Jiordal to be turned away. Well, at least the matter with Ahid has been resolved. You still got something to go home with."

Diedrich grinned broadly. "You sure are confident, Anos. We still don't know which of us is going home yet."

"You're the Prophet, aren't you?" I said to the calm man. "If you can't tell that I'll win no matter the match you pick, then that's not much of a prophecy."

Diedrich laughed heartily. "Oh, I don't know about that."

Oh? So he wasn't going to back down despite knowing the future.

"Then you decide how we'll choose," I said.

"We can't hold a proper holy battle in a place like this. How about we each face the other's Selection God, and whoever holds out the longest wins?"

In other words, I would face Naphta, and Diedrich would face Arcana. The Eight were meant to be inherently weaker than the gods. Him suggesting such a match probably meant that he was confident he could last against Arcana for a long time. But how much of my power was he seeing?

"Very well," I replied, turning to find Naphta already waiting. She must have seen this coming too. "Arcana."

Arcana disappeared with a flash of light, teleporting before Diedrich.

"The man will be strong. Fight with all your strength," I told her.

"As you wish."

She raised her hands and slowly turned her palms to the ceiling. The Moon of Creation appeared in the dome above the underground world, though we couldn't see it from inside.

"King of the demons, I grant you this prophecy," the Goddess of the Future said as she turned the crystal in her hands towards me. "When these eyes open, I, Naphta, will be able to see every future. Every possible future, every miracle yet to pass, exists in the hands of the Goddess of the Future. The victorious future you seek will spill from your hands, and you will be deprived of any possibility to resist it." She spoke in a matter-of-fact tone. "People can die of aggravated colds. They can trip over their own feet and lose their lives. Everyone in this world lives by the rolls of the gods' dice. Facing me means facing the worst possible day for you."

"Oh? In that case, I have a prophecy for you too, god who governs the future. The moment you open your eyes, your defeat will be decided."

§ 18. Who Will Obtain the Victorious Future?

With both eyes closed, Naphta filled her crystal ball with magic. "Sinner who stands before the Goddess of the Future, you will now be judged by Kandaquizorte, the Future World Crystal."

The ball floated out of Naphta's hands and distorted in shape, transforming into a spear.

"Your future has been decided. You have been sentenced to impalement," she pronounced like a judge.

"Interesting. Just try it."

The Goddess of the Future held her hands out before her. Divine magic flowed into the surrounding area, shaking the cathedral. The crystal spear turned towards me and shot forward faster than the eye could see. I turned my head to avoid it, but the spear turned at the same time, following my face.

"Hmm. So read the future?"

The spear came to a stop right before my nose. I had grabbed the shaft.

"I can restrict the future. You will be unable to grasp the spear."

The moment the Goddess of the Future said that, the crystal spear slipped from my hand. I immediately dived aside, but the Future World Crystal surpassed my speed by a fraction and bore into my stomach.

"Restrict, huh? I see. I suppose there could be a one-in-a-billion chance of me failing to grasp the spear. You used the Future World Crystal's power to restrict the future and make that happen."

"Kandaquizorte is the future itself. There is no way for you to touch the future."

"Oh?"

I drew a layered magic circle and passed my right hand through it. With my fingertips stained bluish-white with Ygg Neas, I gave it another try, but they still failed to grasp the crystal shaft.

"It seems it won't be so easy to grasp."

The order of Kandaquizorte meant there was no way to touch it, and its power to restrict futures allowed it to slip past my hand.

"The spear can no longer be withdrawn," Naphta said, facing me with her eyes still closed. "You have two options: surrender or let your source be pierced by the spear. The choice is yours."

"Look further ahead, Goddess of the Future, or your crystal will be wasted."

Without any change in expression, Naphta sent more magic into the spear. "Your source shall be executed by impalement."

With a nasty squelch, Kandaquizorte pierced deep into my abdomen. I stared calmly at the god before me. "I did warn you," I said.

The spear that had pierced my body began to blacken with rust at the tip.

"What... What is that?"

The holy knights in front of the door looked baffled by the sight.

"How is that man still alive after being pierced by a god's spear?"

"Kandaquizorte... Rumor has it that anyone pierced by the Goddess of the Future's spear will have all possibilities of their future stolen and destroyed."

"And a mortal was able to resist that miracle?!"

In contrast to the holy knights, there was one person nodding along in understanding. It was the bishop Mirano, of all people.

"Another day of miracles, I see," he said.

I took several steps forward. "Even if I can't touch the future, if you wish to attack me, it must touch me."

As long as it was piercing my abdomen, I was in contact with the spear.

"You'd better take it out quickly—before Kandaquizorte is corroded by the blood of the Demon King," I said.

"The Future World Crystal is the countless futures of this world; it is the shape of the world itself. What you are doing is competing to see who gets destroyed first between the world and yourself. The result should be clear as day."

Chapter 18 — Who Will Obtain the Victorious Future?

"Indeed."

The tip of the crystal spear clattered to the floor.

"My blood can corrupt the world."

Kandaquizorte had completely rusted. Pitch-black pieces crumbled away and dispersed into nothingness. The blood of the Demon King couldn't be used against most attacks. The substance was so destructive that the world itself could be irreparably damaged if the subject couldn't withstand the force of the destruction.

"As one would expect of the Goddess of the Future, you are quite strong. But it's time to get serious and prophesize properly, or you'll be destroyed here."

I walked towards Naphta without stopping. Just then, the crystal spear that had rusted away reappeared in the air as countless glittering fragments.

"I, Naphta, swear to you that as long as we remain in the present, the future will resurrect no matter how many times you destroy it. In order to destroy the Future World Crystal, you must destroy all possible futures."

The crystal fragments rapidly increased in number and wrapped around us like a glittering sandstorm.

"This is one more possible shape of the world. Sinner, you will now be condemned to exile in a restricted world."

The crystal sandstorm dispersed, revealing a whole new landscape. We were standing in an unfamiliar city. Every building, every plant, and every person was made of crystal. The mountains in the distance, the dome far overhead, and the flowing rivers were all crystal too. Each object contained an unfathomable amount of magic.

"A world created by Kandaquizorte, huh? So this is a god's domain."

"I, Naphta, swear to you that this world has been restricted to produce the worst possible result for you in every way. Your victory is not possible in this world."

"Interesting," I said, staring at her calmly. "Come at me then, future. Let's see what you can do."

No sooner had I said that than the ground below fractured with a loud crack. As I floated into the air with Fless, countless crystal spears began flying up from the newly formed rift. I cast Beno Ievun in an attempt to seal the rift, but the spears passed through it easily, striking my body.

The next moment, crystal spears began appearing from the buildings around me. More crystal spears appeared from the dome above until they were being fired from every possible direction. While the spears carved away at my body, the clock tower up ahead separated from the ground and floated into the air. Its pointed spire rotated and shot forward, crashing into me while I was pinned in place. Blood poured from every part of my body.

"It's been a while since I've bled this much."

The black blood of the Demon King rusted the clock tower, the crystal spears, and all the crystal surroundings until everything crumbled away. All that remained was black rust.

"You said that this world would be the worst result for me—that I would succumb to the worst possible day." I held out my hand and drew a layered magic circle, pointing it towards Naphta like a cannon. "That's some terrific authority you have over your order, but if you're that strong, I have some magic up my sleeve too." Black particles overflowed from the magic cannon. "Every possible miracle will befall you. I sentence you to despair."

Countless crystal spears flew at me once again, but the moment they touched the black particles hanging in the air, they crumbled into pieces. Fire, water, lightning, earth, trees, the dome—every conceivable element attacked me. It was like witnessing a miracle. But I wasn't deterred by the world that bared its fangs.

"Using origin magic, I borrowed the power of Militia, Goddess of Creation, Abernyu, Goddess of Destruction, and the Demon King of Tyranny of two thousand years ago." I also added the magic of my current self. "This is a forbidden spell that can't be used in any old place. Even I've only used it twice."

Jet-black particles swirled around like they were alive, enveloping the magic cannon. The reverberations shattered all the crystals in the area, reducing them to dust. Naphta's divine domain had cracked and was beginning to break down.

"So when you open those Divine Eyes of yours, make sure you restrict things properly. Once I release this spell, Kandaquizorte's world will be annihilated at best."

The Goddess of the Future faced me in stunned silence.

"If you don't restrict things, the real world will perish alongside this one."

Black particles formed a seven-layered spiral at the center of the cannon. A bottomless rift opened in the crystal ground. There was nothing to be seen past the rift—it had split the restricted world completely in two.

Chapter 18 — Who Will Obtain the Victorious Future?

"*Egil Grone Angdroa.*"

Flames of doom were unleashed from the magic cannon. The seven layers of spiraling roared as they advanced. Thanks to Kandaquizorte's divine protection, the flames passed through Naphta's body and traveled all the way to the horizon far behind her—where they lit the entire world on fire. The dome burned. The horizon burned. The ground, the mountains, and everything else in the world burned and turned to ash.

There was a reason this spell surpassed Jio Graze yet wasn't considered the highest grade of fire magic: though it took the form of flames, it wasn't truly fire. It could burn the unburnable, destroy the indestructible, and reduce the whole world to ash. It was, undeniably, the magic of destruction—the type of magic I specialized in above anything else.

Before the flames of doom, the restricted world was reduced to jet-black ash. The ash was whisked away by a wind to reveal reality. Naphta and I were standing before the sacred door.

"Hmm. It seems you've finally gotten serious."

Naphta, who was holding the Future World Crystal in her hands, had both eyes open. As the god that governed the order of the future, she couldn't allow the world's possibilities to be closed off. In order to restrict Egil Grone Angdroa, she had gazed at all the futures she could.

"In other words, this match is over."

Naphta nodded quietly. Cracks ran across her body. "I, Naphta, declare defeat. No matter how much the future is restricted, zero cannot become one. There is no world in which you can be defeated."

Cracks ran along the Goddess of the Future's body as she began to break down. No matter how much she restricted the world, the only future in store for one facing me was destruction. That future was fast approaching Naphta.

Gods couldn't defy order. Naphta had kept her eyes closed to avoid seeing this result.

"That's why you should have listened to my prophecy from the beginning."

With my mauve-stained Eyes fixed on Naphta, I slowly walked towards her. I covered her eyes with one hand, shutting out the future. The destruction of her body came to an abrupt halt.

"It would take more than a billion miracles to reach my worst."

§ 19. The Sword Emperor of Agatha

"What the..."

An astonished sound spilled from the lips of one of the holy knights. They had all watched the decisive moment with open mouths and astonished expressions.

"A mortal surpassed the Goddess of the Future. I can't believe my eyes!"

"Are all of the Selected Eight this strong?"

"No, they shouldn't be. Ahid and Gazel were both chosen, but they could never pull off such a feat. The pope has immeasurable power when he summons his god, but even he doesn't have this much power in his normal form."

"Just who is that man?"

Mirano spoke calmly to the holy knights. "There's no reason to be so shaken, gentlemen. Even without a pledge jewel, that man is capable of subduing even the Heavenly Father."

"What?! The Heavenly Father, the order that creates orders, the god closest to the Almighty Radiance, Equis?!"

"Yes, didn't you know?"

"Is that true, Bishop Mirano?!"

"I pledge to the Almighty Radiance that I saw it with my own eyes. Ah, but if I was the first to learn of him in this underground world, then it would make sense that none of you know of him yet."

"Just what kind of miracle did you witness?"

"E-Even so, this is extraordinary! He transcended the norm in every way! Is he truly mortal?! Are you sure he isn't a god in a mortal body?! Or perhaps he's…"

"Don't tell me. Could he be…?"

"Who knows? As the Misfit, he possesses quite the ironic title. Maybe he chose it himself. He could simply be a noble existence beyond our understanding."

Sighs of awe could be heard from the knights.

Anyway, since the winner of the match was determined by which of us could last longer against the other's Selection God, defeating my opponent's Selection God meant there was no way for me to lose.

"Ha! That was something else. The guy you chose is nothing short of outstanding if he could defeat Naphta," Diedrich said to Arcana, who was standing before him.

"I wasn't the first to choose him, but be that as it may, he is more worthy than any other candidate. That is why he strays from the path of the proxy." Arcana fell to one knee as she spoke, her gaze never leaving the Sword Emperor.

"Oh?"

It seemed she was being pushed back. Even as a draconid that relied on the summoning of gods and dragons, Diedrich possessed extraordinary natural strength. Despite being known as a Sword Emperor, he had yet to even draw his sword. As I'd suspected, there was something abnormal about his power.

"*Sleep in the cold embrace of ice.*"

Lunar snowdrops blew violently around Diedrich, releasing a sparkling blast of cold air. That air condensed into sharp ice pillars and shot straight towards him.

"Hmph!"

Diedrich clenched both fists, making every muscle in his body swell. Tremendous magic began to flow from him, wrapping him in a dull phosphorescent glow. Every pillow of ice was deflected by that phosphorescence before it could even touch his body.

"Fascinating. What is that?"

"Nojiaz. Simply put, it's magic phosphorescence that's emitted when the

Chapter 19 — The Sword Emperor of Agatha

wrath of a variant dragon is incurred." Diedrich clenched his right fist, which began to glow slightly. "If I throw a punch like this…"

Diedrich kicked off the ground and sprinted straight for Arcana. Lunar snowdrops gathered in her right hand, forming Locoronotto, the Sword of Divine Snow. The next moment, Arcana disappeared from before Diedrich at the speed of light, and his armor was slashed apart and frozen. Not even Nojiaz could stop Locoronotto, it seemed. No—

"Whoa there. I've caught you now, little miss Selection God."

Arcana gritted her teeth. As soon as she had slashed Diedrich's armor, he had grabbed her blade with his left hand. There was a slight phosphorescent glow. Ignoring his frozen palm and the blood dripping to the floor, Diedrich swung his fist.

"Raaagh!"

Condensing Nojiaz around his fist, he brought it down on the Sword of Divine Snow with all his might. The blade shattered in a single blow.

"No one faces the dragon's wrath and gets away unharmed," he said, charging straight at Arcana, who was creating a new Sword of Divine Snow.

"*Disturbed snow becomes a sword…*"

Locoronotto shone the color of snow.

"*…boring into you and freezing you in place.*"

Diedrich was slower than Arcana. Before his fist could reach her, Locoronotto's blade pierced through the phosphorescence surrounding him and dug into his abdomen. Cold air swiftly spread from the wound, transforming Diedrich into an ice statue. However, if this was all it took, Arcana wouldn't have been pushed back in the first place. As though to prove me right, a faint voice echoed from the other side of the ice.

"I'll take that too!"

A dull glow filtered through the ice statue, then Diedrich moved. Nojiaz took the shape of a dragon's jaw, snapping closed around the sword of snow. When I focused my Eyes, I could see that Nojiaz's fangs had broken down the magic of the ice that had frozen Diedrich and the snow that formed the Sword of Divine Snow to devour it for itself.

"It's consuming the magic," Arcana murmured, attempting to retreat.

"That's right!"

The consumed magic was channeled right back into the spell, allowing Diedrich's Nojiaz-covered fist to move even more rapidly as he struck Arcana's small body. The impact made a thunderous noise and sent her flying into the sacred door.

"The light of restoration heals wounds."

Arcana tried to use the Keeper of Restoration's power, but the wounds she had received were slow to heal.

"To be more precise, Nojiaz consumes the source. Even a god will struggle to recover when their source has been torn into."

Consuming the source, huh? It almost sounded like a dragon's womb. But he hadn't shown any sign of using Azept.

"The Sword Emperor of Agatha is said to be a dragonborn."

"That's right. By some turn of fate, I was born from a dragon. Thanks to that, I ended up with more power than I know what to do with." Diedrich casually approached Arcana, who had fallen to her knees before the door. He stopped before her, canceled his Nojiaz, and grinned. "Well, it's my defeat," he said, offering her a hand up.

She accepted his hand and got to her feet. "There's no need to declare defeat. The moment you inflicted a wound I couldn't easily recover from, it was my loss."

"Unfortunately, this is a match between me and him. If I had killed you with that last hit, I might have been able to claim a draw, but that wasn't the case." Diedrich looked over at me.

"The agreement was based on who lasted the longest. You made Arcana surrender, so there's no way to decide. It's a draw," I said.

He laughed heartily. "Everyone saw how you defeated Naphta first. As the king of Agatha, I'd be setting a bad example if I insisted we drew on a technicality. Besides"—he pointed to the sacred door—"he has no intention of speaking to both of us."

I chuckled in spite of myself. "What an honorable thing to say. Diedrich, you've piqued my interest in your kingdom."

He grinned. "If you drop by Agatha, I'll prepare you a warm welcome. In return, could I request you bring along that choir of yours?"

He had mentioned that earlier too.

Chapter 19 — The Sword Emperor of Agatha

"Have you taken a liking to them?"

"Gah ha ha! I can't get enough."

What a refreshing man.

"I can get behind that," I said.

Diedrich grabbed Ahid from where he'd been discarded and tossed him over his shoulder. Naphta made her way back to his side.

"I have one question for you, Diedrich."

He looked back at me.

"If you can see the future, you must have already been aware of this result. There's the Selection Trial to consider too. Why would you purposely reveal your own hand?"

By facing Arcana directly, everyone present had witnessed Nojiaz and Naphta's order. However, even without facing us, he should have been able to see my cards using the power of the Goddess of the Future.

"If you don't wish to answer, you don't have to."

"Well, there's this thing called the trial of the Goddess of the Future, you see," Diedrich said, holding his chin in his hand. "Suppose there's a fight you have to win no matter what, but when you look into the future, you find there's no possible way to win it. What do you do?" He answered his own question calmly. "It isn't the job of the Prophet to turn tail and run. There's no meaning to a prophecy if it cannot be overturned."

So that was it. To him, I was the symbol of a prophecy that could never be defied. That was why he had challenged me. He was determined to overthrow the future even if doing so would be unfavorable for him.

"Your resolve is admirable, king of Agatha."

Diedrich laughed loudly. "I have a prophecy that may be of interest to you."

"Oh?" I straightened up and stared straight at him. "Let's hear it, Sword Emperor."

The smile vanished from Diedrich's face. In a serious tone, he said, "Demon King from above, the one who chose you, the Misfit, as their candidate for the Selection Trial was the Goddess of Creation, Militia."

A whirlwind of conflicting emotions swirled through my chest. He didn't seem like the kind of man who would lie about this.

"I'll throw in one more thing as a bonus. This one involves my circumstances as well. If you face Golroana, it'll be better to destroy him completely—if you don't want to expose Dilhade to danger, that is."

"Hmm. I appreciate the warning, but you know my answer already."

Diedrich grinned and turned around.

"See you in Agatha, Demon King," he said over his shoulder, waving as he left with his god. As he strolled away, he continued humming "in-cum, in-cum" happily to himself.

§ 20. Talks with the Pope

A heavy clang rang out from behind me. I turned to see the sacred door slowly swing open. The dazed holy knights closed their eyes and clasped their hands together in prayer.

"Enter, Misfit Anos Voldigoad. May you find salvation," Pope Golroana's unfiltered voice called from past the doorway. It echoed oddly in my ears.

Arcana and I walked through the door and into the Shrine of Sacred. The interior was lined with pillars shaped like tuning forks. Each one was a magic object that contained as much power as an artifact from the Mythical Age.

The sacred door slammed shut behind us. Each step forward I took echoed loudly through the room. At the very back was a lone draconid clad in blue robes—the pope. His hair was neither long nor short, and his androgynous face made it difficult to tell his gender at a glance. His well-refined features made him both handsome and beautiful at the same time. He was kneeling at the center of the pillars, his left hand covering the pledge ring on his right as he prayed.

"It's a pleasure to meet you, Misfit and the Selection God Arcana. I am Golroana, the pope of Jiordal," the pope said, his quiet voice echoing loudly through the shrine. He retained his posture the entire time he greeted us. I walked right up to him.

"It's Anos Voldigoad," I said, holding out my hand for a handshake, but the pope's hands remained folded before him.

"Please forgive me. As the pope of Jiordal, I must never cease praying for the sake of the kingdom," he said.

"Excuse my ignorant greeting, then." I knelt down to lower myself to Golroana's eye level and assumed the same praying pose. Arcana stood behind me.

"You said you wished to know about the Selection Trial and the location of Revalschned, the God of Traces."

"Yes. More so the latter."

The pope fell silent for a moment before responding. "The god that governs memories and records lies dormant here in Jiordal. As the order that brings salvation to this underground world, he will not wake until the right moment."

"Hmm. He should try waking up and stretching his legs from time to time. He'll get better sleep that way, which will make for much smoother salvation."

Golroana's expression remained unchanged. "There is no telling what calamities will befall us for waking a sleeping god."

"There's nothing to fear from a god whose order is just to look back on the past, and you can always pacify him if he wakes up grumpy."

"Revalschned is capable of reproducing the marks of the entire world. In that regard, he is most certainly capable of recreating the worst calamities ever to befall this world."

"You can just use a bigger calamity to defeat him."

The pope fell silent again. "I know about you. I was in the Holy Seat Hall the first time you visited Everastanzetta," he said.

That was the place where I'd met Jiordal's holy knight, Gazel. It wasn't that surprising to hear that candidates close to Ahid had been in attendance.

"I also know that you overcame the trial of Leviangilma, Sword of the Almighty, and that you possess more power than the gods." Golroana's tone harshened. "However, that does not mean you have a just reason to awaken the God of Traces. If Revalschned is as weak as you say, then there would be no need for you to rely on him in the first place. If you wish to rely on the power of a god, you must treat them with due respect."

"You make a valid point. In short, you're telling me that if I awaken Revalschned in an agreeable way, you won't have any complaints."

Chapter 20 — Talks with the Pope

Golroana's expression remained unchanged, but there was a clear air of astonishment about him. "How do you intend on getting a sleeping god to agree with you?" he asked.

"I'll think of that later. At the very least, I can promise you that I won't beat it awake. You shouldn't have a problem with that, right?" I grinned, staring straight into the pope's elegant face. "So where is the God of Traces?"

The pope shifted slightly, turning to look in my direction.

"Surely you know the location, considering everything you just said," I added.

"I do. However, the location of the God of Traces is part of the scriptures passed down from pope to pope. It cannot be revealed to someone who doesn't believe in the teachings of Jiordal." After stating that, Golroana continued. "However, I would make an exception for you, Misfit Anos Voldigoad. I will tell you the location in exchange for your god."

Behind me, Arcana's magic trembled.

"You'd exchange the content of the popes' exclusive scriptures for a nameless god?"

"The God of Traces is the god that will bring salvation to the underground world, but Arcana is the god necessary for its rebirth. She is the reincarnation of the god who created this land—the Goddess of Creation, Militia."

I narrowed my eyes reflexively. Was he saying that after I had created the wall, Militia had abandoned her name, turning into Arcana? If so, who did that make the little sister I'd seen in my dreams? The answer was unclear, but Golroana had to have a reason he would claim Arcana was Militia.

"Where did you learn that?" I asked.

"From the Almighty Radiance, Equis."

He probably meant he had heard from a god, but it seemed he wasn't going to discuss the details.

"So what will you do?" he asked.

"Unfortunately, I've made a promise with Arcana. I cannot break that agreement."

"I expected as much," Golroana said in a melodic voice. "However, Arcana was originally a god of Jiordal. The Almighty Radiance will not bring us any salvation if she remains exploited by you."

"You have things wrong, dragon child," Arcana said. "I am not being exploited, for I chose to go with him of my own will. I believe he is worthy of fighting alongside me in the Selection Trial."

"Are you saying it is the will of the gods to make him the proxy?"

"That is also wrong. I am fighting with him to bring an end to the Selection Trial. This divine ritual that only seeks to maintain order was a mistake. We have been repeating that mistake ever since. It is time for that to come to a stop."

Golroana's expression turned grim. He quietly shook his head. "Selection God Arcana, I say this with all due respect, but by abandoning your name, you must have forgotten your duty as a god. Please reconsider your decision and refrain from taking such action until you regain your name and memories."

"Why is it a sin to defy order? What good is a god that lets evil orders run free?"

Golroana's answer was immediate. "To defy order is to become a blasphemous god. Any god who does so will fall into the hands of Genedonov, the Goddess of Absurdity."

"Will anyone be hurt by that?" Arcana asked quietly.

"I will. Every follower in Jiordal will be overcome with sorrow."

Arcana seemed saddened to hear that, but she didn't argue.

"Pope Golroana, you are not a child. This matter poses no real harm to you. Keep your nose out of a god's affairs," I said.

The pope just barely turned in my direction.

"You believe in the Almighty Radiance, do you not?" I added.

"Yes, I do, which is why I pray like this. There is no follower who wouldn't grieve a god's fall from grace."

"That's ridiculous. What good is a follower who does nothing but cry and cling to the gods? Perhaps you should be the one being prayed for for once," I said, dismissing his words.

"I understand your perspective as one who does not believe in god," the pope said firmly. "However, please remember that we have dedicated our hearts and our lives to these matters you call ridiculous."

"You mentioned Arcana regaining her name and memories—that just so happens to coincide with our goal. Will that not serve as a reason to wake the God of Traces?"

Chapter 20 — Talks with the Pope

Golroana thought for a moment. "Very well. If you return Arcana to Jiordal, we will restore her name and memories using the God of Traces' order."

"Fool. I already refused that."

"I am discussing a compromise with you, Misfit," Golroana said gently.

"By taking Arcana from me?"

"By awakening the God of Traces for your benefit, we will be violating our precepts and scriptures. Such an action would normally be out of the question, but in this case, Arcana would be returned to her rightful place, and you would have your wish granted while being pardoned of any sins. If you don't call this a compromise, what would it be?"

"If you're being serious, then I question your sanity. There are better ways of handling a negotiation. If Arcana wanted to return to Jiordal, she would do so. Does Jiordal's teachings involve controlling gods to do one's bidding?"

"I said this was a compromise. When it comes to other matters, we obey the will of the gods without interference. However, you and Arcana declared your intention of ending the Selection Trial."

"I see. So you're discontent with that."

With his hands still clasped in prayer, Golroana opened his eyes and glared at me. "The Selection Trial is Jiordal's most sacred ritual. It allows draconids to become gods and protect the faithful. This salvation, which has been passed down for generations, is vital to the underground world."

"You make it sound good by calling it salvation, but people suffer for it. What's the harm in ending that suffering?"

"Every living being in this world suffers to an extent. Without the Selection Trial, even more will suffer."

"And why would you think that? Even without the Selection Trial, gods exist in this world. The lives of you draconids shouldn't be affected."

Golroana exhaled quietly before speaking in a tranquil voice. "That is explained in the scriptures."

"What exactly?"

"The will of the Almighty Radiance, Equis."

So he wouldn't reveal the contents of the scriptures. Perhaps there was no foundation for them in the first place.

"If you want to convince me, you'll have to find better excuses than that."

The pope glared at me. There was anger in his gaze. "For the Misfit who cannot understand the word of Equis, I shall explain things your way," Golroana said firmly. "Please keep what I am about to say in mind. You demons who lived peacefully on the surface have no right coming to the underground world and acting like you own the place. We follow our own teachings here."

"People go mad when they obtain power beyond their means. Both Ahid and Gazel from your nation gleefully tried to kill me. They attacked Azesion and Dilhade because of it. You allowed your men to run free while you were too busy praying—how will you take responsibility for invading my land? Surely you won't say you were unaware."

The pope, seemingly lost for a response, didn't respond right away.

"You're free to do whatever you wish within the underground world, but I will not overlook your attempts to harm Dilhade," I said.

"Ahid's invasion of the surface was most regrettable for both of us. That was unrelated to our teachings. As the pope of Jiordal, I apologize sincerely for his actions." Golroana bowed his head.

"Pledge to your god that it won't happen again. You may feel spiteful about it, but the same applies to me. If you're willing to compromise with me on this, I won't rush my decision about the Selection Trial."

Golroana sighed and looked at me. "Misfit, an apology is the greatest compromise I can offer. Of course, I have no intention of aggravating things either. I will vow to make every effort to obey your laws. However, please understand that I must prioritize the teachings of my god."

I burst into laughter. "In other words, you'll show us a little consideration, but at the end of the day, Dilhade's laws mean nothing compared to Jiordal's teachings."

"That is not what I said."

"Can you pledge not to harm Dilhade as part of the Selection Trial?"

"I cannot foresee the intentions of the Almighty Radiance."

"So when the time comes, you'll set Dilhade ablaze without hesitation. I wouldn't call that a compromise."

"Then allow me to suggest a solution that will benefit us both." Golroana looked at me sincerely.

"Oh? I'll hear you out, but I won't expect much."

"How about Dilhade joins the religion of Jiordal?"

Chapter 20 — Talks with the Pope

It sounded like a joke, but both the pope's tone and expression were utterly serious.

"As long as you have faith, the Almighty Radiance will solve all your problems."

"I've thought of an even better solution. How does this sound?"

Golroana listened with a skeptical look.

"Unite Jiordal with Dilhade. Come under my rule and swear fealty to the Demon King, and I will resolve all the problems of the underground world."

"That is a foolish suggestion," Golroana replied with a solemn look. "We are followers of Equis. It would be impossible for us to obey anyone else."

"Now do you get it? The same applies to us."

Golroana closed his eyes and prayed. "It is inevitable that there will be times when nations and their people fail to understand others. We will merely continue down our path, trusting in the gods."

It was a roundabout way of saying so, but that basically meant he would invade Dilhade as soon as doing so aligned with his god's teachings.

"That's why I'm going to destroy it. Without that absurd trial, the world aboveground won't be in any such danger."

Of course, that danger wouldn't be completely gone, but the draconids wouldn't be as much of a threat without the borrowed power of the Selection Gods.

"With all due respect, this is as much of a compromise as we're willing to offer a foreign nation," the pope said angrily. "If you demand any more than this, you will be punished accordingly."

It seemed I had my answer. I stood up and looked down on Golroana. "Get up. I will destroy your god. If the Selection Trial is as holy as you say, you shouldn't have any objections once you lose here."

§ 21. Come, Gospel

Pope Golroana remained on his knees as he spoke. "You and I both are candidates in the Selection Trial. If it is a holy battle you wish for, then I am ready to face you. However, I will not be cajoled. No matter how much you beat this body, the faith in this heart will not waver." His unwavering will could be felt from his honest expression. "You will never recover the scriptures and find your way to Revalschned."

"Sorry, but you saying that only makes me want to disprove you even more," I replied, looking down at him from above. "How long are you going to pray? You can't fight me while sitting."

Without breaking his pose, Golroana spoke in a songlike voice. "Would that be a problem for you?"

"Oh?"

"I am Golroana Delo Jiordal, pope of Jiordal and the one bestowed with the title of Savior. I must continue praying until the day of salvation arrives in the underground world." He glared up at me. "Please, come at me without reservation. My body is protected by the miracle of Equis, which eliminates all that might cause me distress."

"Interesting. Then I shall do just that. *Zola e Dypt.*"

A huge magic circle appeared on the floor as he spoke. Jet-black flames emerged from within, forming chains that wrapped around Golroana's kneeling body. The hellfire chains burned intensely, morphing into a magic circle used for greater magic.

"Thou shalt learn fear. No one may restrict our god."

Divine light gathered around Golroana's pledge ring. A flame lit up inside the jewel, and a three-dimensional magic circle appeared. The layers piled on top of each other, and his magic reached a godly level in no time at all.

A strange sound echoed through the air as the tuning fork pillars reverberated. The sound grew louder and louder, ringing out at irregular intervals like an unfamiliar melody. A god began to manifest behind the pope.

"Come, Gospel. *Guala Nateh Forteos.*"

With another series of loud tones, a long-haired god in blue robes appeared.

"*Azept Doldread.*"

The god that had descended was absorbed into Golroana's body. The pope's magic swelled, and Zola e Dypt's chains swayed like a mirage and then vanished. Another tone later, Golroana's body teleported ten meters behind me.

"Doldread, the God of Gospel, is Pope Golroana's Selection God," Arcana said, standing beside me. "As the god that governs sound, Doldread can take the form of sound itself."

"Hmm. So they can't be restrained by fire or chains. That aside"—I looked over at Arcana—"how's the wound you received from Diedrich?"

"Healed."

"Then let's deal with this swiftly."

I drew a magic circle and cast Badorom. The room turned into a vacuum, and silence enveloped the area. However, the gospel broke that silence, resounding despite the vacuum. Its melody bounced between the tuning fork pillars, filling the room with magic. Doldread, the God of Gospel, was the god of sound—which was why their magic grew each time the melody hummed from the pillars.

"On the day of resurrection, the gospel will bring temporary life to fallen followers," Golroana said in a songlike prayer. "O mighty god, thank you for your miracles. *Book of Gospel*, First Movement: *'Egred.*'"

With each booming note, a new blue-robed figure like Golroana appeared. There were thirty-three of them in total, each wielding their own sword shaped like a tuning fork.

Chapter 21 — Come, Gospel

"The gospel resonates even in a vacuum," Arcana explained. "As long as the song can be heard, Doldread is immortal."

"A phonetic magic circle, huh? How unusual."

Changes in the gospel's tune had drawn the magic circle of sound and activated the spell. Magic circles triggered based on pitch, volume, and rhythm were far more troublesome than regular magic circles, as the spells wouldn't activate unless the full melodies were played. However, it seemed the order of gospel allowed those melodies to be played in an instant.

"See for yourself, Misfit. These are the former popes of Jiordal, devout followers who spent their lives praying. You shall now fall before the miracle of a god."

The dead followers that had been resurrected through Egred charged towards me, swinging their tuning fork swords.

"*On the night of a blizzard, everything freezes,*" Arcana said. Lunar snowdrops whirled around her, the cold air freezing the legs of the undead assailants.

"If the former popes have returned from the dead, I'd like to respectfully take this opportunity to ask them a question," I said once their movements were sealed. "Is this kingdom striving for war or peace with Dilhade? State your opinions one by one."

In response, the Egred visitors made their tuning fork swords resound with a hymn. The phonetic magic circle hummed with powerful anti-magic that shattered the ice around them. They then raised their swords and continued charging through the blizzard.

"There should be no need to ask the obvious," Golroana replied. "All that binds the dead are their dying wishes. Never before has there been a pope who has wished for anything beyond offering our songs and prayers to the gods."

"Departed souls who return to fulfill their dying wishes, huh?"

Black lightning enveloped my right hand, swiftly expanding until it was crackling throughout the room. Struck by Jirasd, the thirty-three undead bodies were annihilated. Not a scrap remained.

"The dead cannot be killed twice. In other words, they are immortal."

The gospel rang out, and the undead were resurrected through Egred once more.

"On the second rebirth, gods descend into the bodies of the dead. Countless gods will manifest here, driving away the darkness and bringing light to the world."

The former popes of Jiordal drew magic circles and cast Azept. Their magic was elevated by a divine order of magnitude.

"Mirahi Ide Jizm, Keeper of Sound," Arcana said.

The thirty-three popes pointed their tuning fork swords towards me. Masses of magic-filled waves of sound were launched in unison.

"*Snow falls, illuminating the earth.*" Arcana's falling lunar snowdrops formed a barrier, blocking the sound to protect us.

"Before thirty-three popes and thirty-three gods, all living beings will fall to their knees and hang their heads. Find faith, heretical ones," Golroana sang. "Believe in the work of the gods. Merely praying will bring one salvation."

The thirty-three tuning fork swords sounded even louder, resonating with the order of gospel to strengthen the phonetic magic circle.

"*Book of Gospel*, Second Movement: '*Zabioz.*'"

Sound waves tore through the vacuum like a dragon's roar, making the lunar snowdrop barrier creak like it was about to break.

"It seems they're quite the devout popes, but did they truly sacrifice everything to the gods?"

"There is no need to ask the obvious," Pope Golroana replied. "The popes of this nation would never act on their own self-interest."

"Shall we make a bet, then? I will expose the self-interest of the pope. If I win, you'll tell me the location of the God of Traces. If I lose, you can have Arcana."

"I already said I won't be cajoled by you."

"If you can land a single scratch on me, it'll be your win. I'll even give you Dilhade while I'm at it." I drew a magic circle for Zecht. The pope let out a quiet sigh and looked at me. All he needed was one more push.

"You seem pretty confident in your singing. What if our battle was through hymns alone? I'll immediately remove this barrier too."

At that, the pope replied, "I pledge in the name of the Almighty Radiance."

With those words, the Zecht was signed. Arcana's lunar snowdrop

Chapter 21 — Come, Gospel

barrier vanished. Zabioz raged towards me, but I now held a magic flute I'd made with Iris.

"*Goldros.*"

I sent my magic through the flute and began to play a hymn. The sound waves collided with Zabioz, canceling out both melodies.

"Hmm. It's pretty effective for an impromptu creation. It seems the best way to fight sound is with sound." I handed the flute to Arcana. "Use it."

Arcana accepted the flute and brought it to her lips to play the hymn. A barrier, much stronger than the one before, rose to block Zabioz. Altiertonoa shone down on her, illuminating her with sparkling light. The silver glow passed through the ceiling, creating a bridge connecting the dome to the ground.

Slowly but surely, the Moon of Creation descended. The half-moon's light drew closer and closer until it completely enveloped the flute.

"*Swallowed by the moon, awaiting the snow's thaw, a new form is revealed.*"

Altiertonoa and the flute blended together, creating a divine flute with the power of the Moon of Creation. Arcana blew into the flute and crafted a melody that immediately erased the Zabioz released by the tuning fork swords. The tune didn't stop there either—the sound waves released by the divine flute swallowed the popes, eliminating them completely.

"Next is Doldread. Are you ready?"

Arcana blew into the flute. A solemn but frightening tune filled the air, assaulting the gospel. The tune interfered with the gospel's booming melody, making it drop in volume.

Possessed by the God of Gospel, Golroana grimaced. "Tsk..."

"Hmm. It seems it's working. Don't tell me you've stopped praying out of the self-interest of keeping yourself alive."

Pope Golroana gritted his teeth and continued praying. "As I told you already, the dead are immortal."

The gospel rang out, and the undead resurrected possessed by the Keepers of Music once again.

"On the third rebirth, the fallen followers dedicate a sacred song to the gods. The holy tune passed down through the generations will become a divine fire that burns all calamities."

The thirty-three popes with gods in their bodies sang their hymn loud and clear. Their voices resonated together, forming a multilayered phonetic magic circle. Pillars of divine fire rose around us. They slowly pushed against the Arcana's musical barrier, closing in little by little.

"Earlier, you asked why we prayed this much. The Savior answered, 'I am not praying alone. The prayers of those who have departed for the gods already—followers up until now—have left their prayers here.' The Savior sings together with the dead of the past and that divine song itself is salvation. Everything that defies the gods will burn in sacred songfire."

Golroana sang loudly and clearly. As he did, the songfire intensified, smothering the flute's tune in an attempt to burn us.

"Hmm. Music is indeed better when sung and performed together. You were right there, Golroana," I said. I traced a magic link to send a Leaks. "Can you hear me, girls? I've come upon a great opportunity for you. It's time to test just how effective love is against gods."

"*Yes, Lord Anos!*" eight voices immediately responded. They were the voices of the girls of my personal choir, who were waiting back at the Demon King Castle.

"Sing for me. Send me all your love."

"*As you wish!*"

"*Gard Aske.*"

The spell dived into the abyss of their love, converting even their deepest emotions into magic. Black light overflowed as that love that bordered on madness transformed, becoming a thick, viscous liquid that swirled and coiled around me.

"*Book of Gospel*, Third Movement: '*Lanrez.*'"

"We shall use this," I said to the praying pope. "Demon King Hymn No. Six: 'Neighbor.'"

Arcana began playing the accompaniment to Neighbor. The magic flute, powered by the Moon of Creation, produced the tune perfectly.

"Everything is fleeting before prayer. Everything falls before the gods. You shall burn in this songfire and be purged of sin."

Blazing songfire swallowed both me and Arcana. The flames roared towards the ceiling and broke through the roof, reaching the top of the dome. They truly were the flames of a god, purifying fire that burned everything in the world until not even ashes remained.

Chapter 21 — Come, Gospel

"O transgressor, may your sins be burned away with this sacred song— What?!" Golroana's eyes widened. He must have heard the singing traveling via Leaks. The next moment, Gard Aske's sludge-like light expanded, corrupting the flames. There wasn't a single burn on me.

"*Oh my! I didn't know such a world existed!*"

The undead popes—who had been focused on singing their hymn until now, focused on fulfilling their dying wishes—screamed in anguish as they were blown away. Bathed in thick black light, their bodies shriveled up and decayed.

Golroana could only look on with wide eyes, doubting his ears. Gard Aske could corrupt both the flames and the dead. It was a fearsome spell that rotted the target with love. In terms of pure corrosive power, it was almost as potent as the blood of the Demon King.

"A song powerful enough to make my predecessors forget their prayers and hymns..."

"Do you get it now?"

"It's not over yet. They might have screamed reflexively, but there's no evidence of self-interest!"

"Then I'll make it clear."

"*In-cum, in-cum, incoming, woo-ooh!*"

"Gaaaaaaaagh! O gods!"

But the current pope was a formidable opponent. Golroana remained in his praying pose as he endured the Gard Aske that ruthlessly attacked him. Then he began singing a hymn, calling more songfire to counter the light. The past popes also began to pray and sing, making their song resonate to use Lanrez against us.

"Your hymn isn't bad, but praying alone isn't enough. After all"—the Demon King Hymn synchronized with the tune of Arcana's flute—"ours has choreography!"

I started running to the rhythm of the music.

"*Don't open the door!*"

"Hah!" I thrust my Gard Aske-clad hand forward, punching away the divine songfire.

"*Don't open the door!*"

"Hah!" I changed hands, pulling my right fist back while thrusting my left fist forward. The black Gard Aske shot forward, sending the undead popes flying.

"Gaaaaaaaaaaaaaaah!"

"Aaaaaaaaaaaaaaah!"

"Don't open the forbidden door!"

"Hah, hah, hah!" Three more thrusts, and the sacred song burst apart before the Demon King Hymn.

"It can't be! The sacred song is...!"

"What is this forbidden tune?!"

Completely shocked, Golroana stared at the screaming undead. "Do not fear, my predecessors," he said. "What is there to be afraid of? The dead cannot be killed. As those invited to join the gods, you are already immort—" He fell speechless as one of the popes completely rotted away and vanished. "Why...? Why isn't he resurrecting? What's happening?"

"Can't you tell?"

Arcana and I stood before the praying Golroana. The Demon King Hymn echoed around us.

"It's because in-cum, incoming, woo-ooh."

"I don't get it at all!"

"It means I have no idea what's going on, but it's fun, so it doesn't matter. This song awakened their true desires and allowed them to rest in peace."

"Rest in peace...?" Golroana looked at me in disbelief.

"People cannot live for the sake of their nation alone. Everyone has their own heart. What kind of life would it be to only pray without any fun?"

"No, that couldn't be!"

"Still can't believe it? The girls opened the forbidden doors of your predecessors." I raised my right fist into the air. "Get ready. The forbidden key will open your heart next."

"So please don't enter!"

"Hah!"

The magic flute sounded, and Gard Aske wrapped around my fist. I thrust that fist forward, blowing away the God of Gospel.

"Gaaah!"

My right fist sunk into Golroana's solar plexus, which should have been made of sound, and lifted his body into the air. It was sound against sound,

Chapter 21 — Come, Gospel

love against gods. Gard Aske, the magic flute, and the choreography to Neighbor ate away at the God of Gospel immune to attacks.

"Stop! Don't corrupt the hymn with that racket. The God of Gospel is…!"

"*So please don't enter!*"

"Hah!" My left fist sunk into the pope's abdomen, folding his body in half.

"Gah! The gospel… The gospel is disappearing!"

"*Don't enter with that forbidden key!*"

"Hah! Hah! Haaaaaah!"

I continued beating Gard Aske into him—into his abdomen, into his throat, into his face. The pope flew backwards, smashing through several pillars before hitting the wall and coming to a stop. Doldread, the God of Gospel, rotted away and perished.

I spoke to the pope, who had lost his divine power. "I don't know what's so good about your gospel. Did you really think a song with no choreography would have an impact on me?"

§ 22. The God of Traces' Whereabouts

I walked leisurely over to the pope, who was lying on the floor. Despite being unconscious and beaten ragged, Golroana still held his hands folded in prayer. The other popes throughout Jiordal's history had forgotten their prayers before the Demon King Hymn.

"Hmm." I cast Ei Chael to heal Golroana. His wounds receded immediately, and his eyes snapped open. "You told me you never stop praying for the sake of the kingdom. It seems those weren't just empty words."

After taking on Gard Aske and the magic flute rendition of Neighbor, complete with choreography, Golroana had remained praying. If he hadn't used both hands to protect himself, he might have perished alongside his god, yet he had thrown aside his self-interest at the last moment.

"Out of respect for your faith, I won't force the God of Traces to do anything against his will."

Golroana sat up and resumed his praying pose.

"Tell me the location."

The signed Zecht magic circle glowed.

"I cannot go against my vow to the gods. You were right when you said the past popes didn't pray wholeheartedly."

Perhaps Golroana had failed to notice that because he had been capable of doing so.

"Two hundred kilometers west of Jiorhaze lies the ruins of Ligalondrol. The God of Traces is said to sleep deep below the ground there. At white night, the place where the Divine Dragon sings will become the entrance to Ligalondrol."

"Is white night rare here?" I asked Arcana.

"There's no sun in the underground world, so our day isn't the same as the world above. Morning is called dawn; day is called white night; and night is called polar night."

So what he meant was day. That should be enough to find the God of Traces. I looked at the pope before me.

"Now, Golroana, you know why I'm here, right?"

"The Selection pledge jewel is a gift from the gods. If you wish to take it, you must first take my life."

"I don't need it."

The pope looked perplexed.

"What are you so shocked about?"

"You won the holy battle. Surely you don't intend to leave after destroying my Selection God."

"Hmm. I don't see your point."

"Why aren't you presenting the God of Gospel as an offering?"

In the Selection Trial, Selection Gods were able to consume other gods, like how Arcana had once consumed Gazel's god and gained the god's order for herself. Golroana probably couldn't understand why the same wasn't happening to the God of Gospel.

"Like I said, my goal is to destroy the Selection Trial."

"Isn't that all the more reason to need a god's miracles?"

"In the Selection Trial, gods can consume other gods. It almost feels like it was designed to pit the Eight against each other even though there should be ways of settling things without holy battles."

Golroana looked bewildered by my words. "What are you implying?"

"The standard way of winning the Selection Trial is to defeat the enemy gods and have them consumed. In other words, the being that created this trial, this Almighty Radiance of yours, wants gods to eat each other."

Was such a system really necessary to maintain order?

"There must be a reason for creating a god that possesses multiple orders. Maybe it makes the orders sturdier, or maybe there's another reason. Either

Chapter 22 — The God of Traces' Whereabouts

way, there's some intention behind all of this, and if someone wanted this to happen, it's in my nature to defy them."

Besides, there was no need to make my god consume others. I could handle everything myself.

"Then are you here to kill me?"

"I'm not interested in your life."

"Then what could you possibly want?"

"Of course, it's to continue from where we left off."

The pope's elegant features twisted into a frown. "I don't understand. You've already won, so you can kill me and do what you wish. No one in Jiordal will criticize the results of the Selection Trial."

"I'm addressing this matter as the Demon King of Dilhade. It might have been a different story if you were an oppressive tyrant or incompetent leader, but at the very least, you care for this nation and rule it peacefully. Your death would unsettle the kingdom and tempt Agatha and Gadeciola to invade."

"Even if they did, that wouldn't be your problem."

"I wouldn't dismiss the happiness of this nation's people. The sight of so many smiles being steeped with sadness would be too much to bear."

I had explored Jiorhaze with the students of the academy, and while there were many things we still didn't know, it was clear that the people living here were in good spirits and great health. They had happily sung along with the Sojourner's Psalm and earnestly prayed for the Rite of Sacred Song to succeed. Although we had our cultural differences, Jiorhaze wasn't that different from Dilhade.

"I won't forgive any hostility, but as long as you're cooperative, I am willing to join hands," I said.

Golroana stared at me as though to search for the truth in my face. "Are you really saying that after destroying my Selection God?" he asked bluntly.

"Bwa ha ha! There's no point in speaking of ideals. Only once you knew there was nothing you could do to me would my words reach you. Our conversation began the moment you realized words were more effective than power against me."

"What an arrogant thing to say."

I grinned. "You finally understand one thing about me. That's right: I'm arrogant. I'm sick and tired of enemy nations. I want peace—true peace."

Golroana closed his mouth. He didn't have anything to say in return.

"Ask your heart. My words should be reaching you better than before."

The pope sighed. It almost sounded like affirmation.

"Two thousand years ago, there was a great war aboveground," I said. "Just like how the three underground kingdoms faced conflict, the three races aboveground were constantly killing each other. Many soldiers died—many civilians as well. With power and conversation as my last hope, I marched into the enemy nation."

The pope listened silently as I continued.

"The world is now at peace—far more so than it was two thousand years ago, at least, but I still think about that to this day. If I had communicated with them earlier, would there have been fewer sacrifices?" I spoke with genuine emotion. "I cannot repeat that mistake. That's why I will continue to make conversation while fighting. I'll keep talking with my fists and punching with my words until you give in."

"What do you want me to do?"

"Compromise. I will respect your beliefs, but you mustn't let your beliefs cause harm to Dilhade. Let's make a pact between nations."

Golroana shook his head. "I can't compromise any more than I previously stated. Jiordal is a nation of the gods. We cannot defy our teachings."

"Then think of a way to avoid harming Dilhade without defying your teachings."

Confusion filled Golroana's delicate face. "That doesn't sound like a very wise solution. It's essentially no different from before. It is only because of our teachings that we would ever think of harming Dilhade in the first place."

"I'm not asking for everything all at once. Every time you mess up, I'll teach you a lesson and have another conversation with you."

Golroana closed his eyes and prayed for a few seconds before opening them again. "In order to survive in the harsh underground, we have had to rely on the power of the gods and their messengers, the dragons. We are unable to live without faith. People from the surface who can live on their own power could never understand that."

"That lack of understanding is why we fear each other. We feel no

Chapter 22 — The God of Traces' Whereabouts

hesitation in destroying the unknown, which is why we each see the other as fiends."

Eventually, a long chain of hatred would build up, dragging everyone into the bottomless bog of war.

"Don't you think we should start with getting to know each other? Even if we truly can't understand one another, we can at least say we tried."

"I cannot stand by and watch as you destroy the sacred Selection Trial. The people of Jiordal will not allow it either."

"If you still don't comprehend my strength, then you may do as you wish," I said, not backing down. "I'll teach you as many times as it takes. You'll learn that in this world there are worse things to offend than gods. Your scriptures will change whether you like it or not."

"You may never be able to understand this," Golroana replied, looking more sorrowful than he had until now, "but our hands are for praying to the gods. We will never join them with the people from aboveground." The pope continued with emphasis. "I did not accept the hand you offered me when you came here. That is all. There will never be a day when we shall join hands."

"The hungry only pray to the gods when there's no food to eat. If the fruit tree grew right beside them, they wouldn't continue praying."

Golroana listened without any change in expression.

"Some things cannot be saved by praying alone. The time will come when you must reach out and grasp something yourself. The popes of the past were the same. That's why they reacted to that hymn." I turned on my heel. "There's no rush for an answer. I'll humor you until you run out of ideas."

With that, Arcana and I left the Shrine of Sacred Song.

§ 23. The Selfish Nameless God

Jiorhaze, the dragon landing site.
We were currently in the wooden bedroom on the bottom floor of the Demon King Castle. It was dark outside, as it was currently polar night. It had to be white night to access the ruins of Ligalondrol, so we had to wait until the next day.

"Well, we've almost reached the God of Traces, but there's no harm in watching the rest of the dream. Even if the pope wasn't lying, there's always a chance the God of Traces has long vanished from Ligalondrol."

"That is correct."

I lay back on the bed, and Arcana climbed on top of me. She moved to press my forehead to mine but paused partway and stared at my face.

"May I ask a question?"

"Go ahead."

"You spared Savior Golroana. According to Diedrich's prophecy, he will expose Dilhade to danger. Why didn't you eliminate him?"

I answered without hesitation. "No matter how accurate the prophecy may be, the future is yet to take place. You can't judge someone for a crime they have yet to commit."

Arcana nodded quietly. "That is correct."

"As I said to the pope, if he dies, Jiordal will become unsettled. The smiles of the people living here will be lost. It would have been one thing if he were a foolish king that only caused the people pain, but that isn't the case." I recalled the smiles and sound of the people singing the Sojourner's Psalm. "It's also not that simple. He may be an enemy of Dilhade, but to the people of this country, he is their king."

"You said you wanted true peace."

"Achieving peace in Dilhade alone would be simple. If I wanted that, all I'd have to do is destroy the rest of the world."

Arcana listened closely.

"But a world like that would not be kind," I added.

"Is it a kind world that you desire?"

"I made a promise a long time ago. I have to prove it to them."

Arcana gazed into my eyes. "Prove what?"

"That this world is warm and full of love and hope."

Arcana's expression brightened. "You gave me a chance at redemption. Then, after you granted a god forgiveness, you spared your enemy."

"It's not that big of a deal. I only had one thing in mind."

"Should I know what that was?" Arcana asked hesitantly, searching her godly emotions.

"That I have no use for a world that isn't the way I want it."

Arcana's eyes widened.

"I said I was arrogant."

"I've been thinking," she said slowly. "Ever since becoming a nameless god, I've been alone. Gods don't often join hands with other gods. People cling to the gods with hands that beg for salvation, but they never offer their own in return. That is because they are mortals, and I am a god."

With the exception of a select few, gods were supernatural beings. They were no more than objects of worship and faith.

"That also applied to Ahid, another member of the Eight."

If anything, he was probably worse than the others.

"For the first time, I am trying to achieve something together with someone, standing shoulder to shoulder, working towards the same goal." Arcana's warm emotions lingered in her pure voice. She spoke as though she was fumbling to grasp them. "What would you call this emotion?"

"What do you think?" I asked.

"I…" Arcana trailed off in thought before replying. "I think it's called happiness. I think I'm happy right now. Meeting you has saved me."

Chapter 23 — The Selfish Nameless God

"Don't rush to conclusions."

"Am I wrong?" Arcana looked at me questioningly.

"Something as trivial as that shouldn't be called salvation."

"Trivial," she mumbled thoughtfully.

"Yes, it couldn't be more insignificant. You should seek keenly, desire more, ask for help if you need it."

"Because I am a god, I feel no greed. The selfishness of a god is a sin. Salvation alone is enough fulfillment for me."

I smiled at her earnestness. "Where there's a heart, there's greed. You can direct your selfishness towards me. No one will be harmed that way."

"Do you need my selfishness?"

"That's right. You can't save someone without knowing what's in their heart. Many gods lack that understanding, which has often led to the desecration of humans and demons in the world aboveground. I can't imagine the underground world being much different with all that power borrowed through pacts."

Grief filled Arcana's face as she recalled her past sins. She closed her mouth and thought for a long moment, her gaze cast downwards. After a while, she looked up at me. "I think I wish to see more of that dream."

"The dream of our memories?"

"Yes. That dream felt very comforting. The Arcana in there wasn't alone. Her brother was always there to protect her." Arcana smiled softly as she thought about the dream. "You always protected me," she said slowly, reflecting on her memories with each word she spoke. "If the dream was real, if that Arcana was me and her brother was you, then that makes you the ultimate form of salvation." She touched her pale fingers to my chest. "That is what I desire."

"You want a brother?"

Arcana nodded. "I want to know I'm not alone. I want to believe someone cares for me. Knowing that there's a single person who worries for me is enough for me to walk this path of salvation with my head held high."

"I see."

"Is that too greedy of me?" Arcana asked worriedly.

"What are you saying? It's still so trivial, I could cry."

Arcana fell silent for a moment. "If I am the Arcana from the dream, why did we end up parting ways?" she then asked.

"Who knows? Unwanted farewells were common two thousand years ago."

Perhaps that also had something to do with why she was currently a nameless god.

"I want to know more about myself," Arcana said plainly, "and about you."

So that was the desire she'd suppressed.

"If I truly am your little sister, there's something I'd like to say."

"What's it?"

"I'm glad… I'm glad we met again, brother," the god in the form of a little girl whispered shyly.

"Then come. Let's continue this dream."

Arcana pressed her forehead to mine, and a magic circle surrounded us. But just then—

"Hey! Hey, I said!" a voice cried from the chair.

"Have you forgotten we're here?!" Sasha snapped. Misha nodded furiously beside her.

"What are you saying? Hurry up and get over here. You'll accompany us in our dream again today, won't you?"

"Of course, but that's not what I meant." Sasha climbed into the bed beside me, still grumbling. "She's a little sister… Just a sister…" she mumbled over and over to herself.

"Do you accept me as his little sister, Sasha?"

"What?! Oh, um, yes, I do. I mean, you were his sister in the dream, right? And I think it'd be nice if you really were his sister," Sasha answered in confusion.

"I thought you were wary of me."

"In a way, yes."

"Thank you."

Sasha averted her gaze. "Y-You're welcome," she said, clinging to me. Misha took her spot on the opposite side.

Arcana activated the magic circle, removing our clothes in a burst of light and storing them in storage circles.

"Hey, at least replace them with a blanket!"

Chapter 23 — The Selfish Nameless God

At the same moment Sasha yelped, the door to the bedroom swung open. Two figures came charging in.

"Anos, Sasha, we're here to help!"

"Zeshia will fight in the dream too!"

Eleonore and Zeshia had appeared, beaming from ear to ear. They were immediately greeted by the sight of us stark naked.

"Wow!"

"Butt naked."

Several beats later, lunar snowdrops formed a thin blanket that covered us. For once, even Eleonore was frozen in surprise.

"Hmm. What did you mean by 'help,' Eleonore?"

"Oh, well, you know how Sasha and Misha hung out in your room yesterday? I asked them what they'd been doing in there, and they said something about fighting in a dream."

"Zeshia wanted to fight too."

So that's what this was about.

"We're borrowing the power of the Keeper of Dreams to recall my memories," I explained.

"Aaah, I get it. Being naked helps the magic act more effectively, just like when casting Eleonore!"

As the result of a spell of similar requirements, Eleonore had come to understand pretty quickly.

"The dream isn't particularly dangerous, but you can watch too if you're worried."

"Totally! I don't like being left out!"

Eleonore drew magic circles over her and Zeshia. Misha quickly turned off the light before anything could be seen, leaving only the dim glow of the lamp. Once the two girls were in their optimal forms for the spell, they dived under the blanket.

"Hmm, it's kind of cramped."

"This bed was never that big to begin with. There's no way I can fall asleep with everyone in it," Sasha grumbled.

"Heh heh. I've got just the spell for that!"

Eleonore drew a magic circle, and an orb of water surrounded us. I floated in the center with Sasha to my left, Misha to my right, Arcana before me, and Eleonore and Zeshia behind my back.

"What's this spell?" Sasha asked curiously.

"It's called Relyme. The buoyancy of floating the water reduces the strain on your body, allowing for a peaceful night's sleep!"

Sasha looked around at the magic bubble. "Human magic sure is weird."

"But doesn't it feel good?"

"Um, well, now that you mention it, my body feels pretty relaxed."

"Right?" Eleonore put her arms around my neck and hugged me from behind. Two firm symbols of peace pressed up against my back. "What do you think, Anos? Feels good, right?"

"Hey, what are you doing, Eleonore?" Sasha said in a fluster.

"What? What do you mean?"

"Th-That... That! I mean that!"

Eleonore giggled. "There's nothing wrong here. If you want to cling to him too, go right ahead. Isn't that right, Anos?" She leaned her face close to mine.

"You won't be able to enter the same dream without physical contact. Don't hold back."

"R-Right." Sasha blushed in embarrassment and brought her body a little closer than before.

"Sorry for the wait. Looks like we're ready."

"I want to try gathering the magic of everyone here," Arcana said.

"In order to make it easier to continue the dream."

"That's right. It's to enhance the Keeper of Dreams' power. The deeper the sleep, the further we can dive into the dream and into the abyss of your memories."

It was worth a try.

"What do we have to do?" I asked.

"Link your magic and join sources." Arcana's magic circle covered the Relyme orb. Our magic connected with each other's, bonding our sources together. After signaling with a look, Arcana continued. "*Night falls, beckoning sleep. Drifting memories, accumulating in dreams, floating to the surface.*"

Just like before, a faint light enveloped our bodies. Overcome with sleepiness, our minds drifted somewhere far away.

§ 24. An Unfamiliar Visitor

The dream continued.
It was a clear afternoon after the snow had melted. Arcana was seated in a chair, reading a book. An owl flew over, hooted once, and then dropped a letter on the window ledge. Arcana looked up curiously and opened the window. While the weather was a lot warmer than before, the air outside was still chilly. She quickly retrieved the letter and closed the window.
Looking down at the letter, Arcana saw the words "Invitation from Midhaze Castle" printed on the envelope. Even a girl as shut off from the world as she was knew that Midhaze was the largest city in Dilhade. The letter was addressed to Anos.
"Brother!" Arcana called to her older brother, who was sleeping by the fireplace. Anos slowly sat up and looked at her.
"Is something wrong?"
"It's an invitation from the castle! An owl brought it here."
"Hmm. Another one, huh?"
Arcana placed the envelope in Anos's outstretched hand. He immediately threw it into the fire. Arcana's eyes widened in surprise. "Y-You're burning it?"
"They always say the same thing."
Arcana stared into her brother's face curiously. "What do they say?"
"In short: come to the castle. I made a bit of a fuss in Midhaze not too long ago. They must still be offended by it."

"Is everything okay?"

"Don't worry. I won't be caught by castle grunts. Besides, if I did go, the dragons would follow me. They wouldn't want that kind of trouble either."

"Oh, I see." Arcana sighed in relief.

"I'm going back to sleep. Wake me if you need anything."

"Okay. I'm sorry."

"Make sure you don't wander off where I can't see you," Anos warned.

Arcana shook her head furiously. "I wouldn't do such a thing!"

"As long as you know."

With that, Anos closed his eyes. It wasn't long before he drifted off again. Arcana nervously poked his sleeping face, but he showed no signs of waking.

"He's already asleep."

Arcana returned to her chair and put the book she'd been reading back on the shelf. She then made her way over to the front door and opened it quietly. After a big stretch and taking a deep breath of the outside air, she set off walking through the forest. Of course, she stayed within range of Anos's Magic Eyes, just like he'd instructed.

She was strolling along, observing the new plants beginning to sprout, when an owl descended from overhead. It was the same owl that had delivered the invitation earlier. The owl swooped low enough to brush against the ground and was enveloped in light as it transformed into a black cat.

"Whoa!" Arcana cried, staring at the cat.

The cat looked back at her, then started walking slowly through the forest as though to tell her to follow.

"Hey, wait!"

Arcana shot a glance back at the cabin, but figuring she'd be fine as long as she stayed within sight, she promptly went after the cat. After walking for some time, she was met by an unfamiliar sight. A man was seated below a tree, leaning against the trunk. He had purple hair and blue eyes, and wore a cloak draped over his shoulders. The black cat ran up to him and hopped onto his lap. Petting the cat, the man turned to Arcana.

"Hello, Arcana."

Arcana flinched.

"There's no need to be afraid. I'm not here to harm you," he said in a

Chapter 24 — An Unfamiliar Visitor

gentle tone, smiling earnestly. "Besides, although your brother may be asleep, he'd notice me if I took another step forward."

The space between Arcana and the man was precisely as far as Anos's Magic Eyes could reach. He had identified that limit with ease.

"How do you know my name? Who are you?"

"We've met before, back when you were younger. You probably don't remember, but I'm Ceris. I have a favor to ask of you, Arcana."

"What is it?" Arcana asked warily.

"I want you to give this to Anos."

Ceris took out a letter and flicked it with his finger. The letter fluttered through the air and landed in Arcana's hand. It was the same invitation Anos had disposed of earlier.

"Are you here to catch him?"

"Catch him? Why would I want to do that?"

Arcana struggled to find the right words to reply. "Because, uh... Because he made a fuss in Midhaze."

"Oh, that. He did indeed make quite the fuss. His magic is abnormal for someone so young. The extraordinary amount of power he bears is still too much for him to handle. The slightest loss of control could incinerate the entire nation. His power is so great, in fact, it's holding him back from using magic freely." Ceris smiled without a hint of ill will. "I've come to collect him. He has what it takes to become the king of Dilhade and needs to learn how to wield that power of his in an appropriate setting."

Arcana stared at Ceris curiously. It didn't look like the man was lying, but at the same time, she couldn't imagine her brother lying to her either.

"I believe that's what Anos would want too. Do you know what he gets up to so late at night?" Ceris asked.

"He's been studying magic."

"That's right. The progress he's made in this remote location is quite remarkable, but it seems he's come to a bit of a standstill." Ceris watched Arcana carefully, but it felt like his blue eyes weren't seeing anything. "That's only natural though. Any child, especially one with such unprecedented power, would struggle to learn from the wisdom of his predecessors all by himself. Reaching the abyss of magic through self-study alone is an exceedingly difficult task, but if he were offered the right opportunity, I'm sure he'd be diving deeper than ever in no time at all." Ceris was merely listing the facts without expressing any awe or fear. "And I am able to give him that opportunity."

"My brother can't go to the castle. He's being targeted by dragons, so he'll cause trouble for everyone there," Arcana said nervously.

Ceris nodded in understanding. "Oh, I see. So that's why."

Arcana looked at him in confusion. "Why what?"

"Have you heard of *Dora the Liar*?"

Arcana nodded.

"Why do you think Dora kept lying so much? There was nothing for her to gain from telling those lies."

"Because it was fun?"

"Perhaps that was one reason. But I think she wanted to give the villagers in the boring countryside a little amusement in their lives."

"Was Dora telling gentle lies?" Arcana asked, recalling her brother's words.

"I believe so. What about you?"

"But if she was telling gentle lies, she should have done it to achieve happiness. Instead, Dora died alone without anyone believing her."

Ceris nodded in agreement. "In other words, telling gentle lies doesn't always lead to salvation. I can only pray he doesn't end up like that." Ceri turned his gaze towards the house. "So how about it, Arcana? If you help me persuade him, I'll grant you one wish. What do you say?"

"Whatever I wish for?"

"That's right. You can ask for anything you like. You've lived here in the middle of nowhere for a long time now. Don't you want to go into town?"

Arcana thought for a moment, then shook her head. "My brother would feel lonely if I did. Besides, I promised him."

"Then is there anything else you wish to do?"

"Wish to do…" Arcana looked down and thought for a while. Eventually, she raised her head. "Could I learn to do magic as well?" she asked nervously. "You see, I always feel bad watching my brother fight the dragons all by himself. If I could use magic too, I'd be able to defeat the dragons instead of him! I could build our cabin and start the fire too."

Chapter 24 — An Unfamiliar Visitor

"That's so considerate of you, Arcana," Ceris said, still smiling.

Arcana grinned happily in return.

"You can't use magic because of the seal preventing your power from leaking out."

"Seal?"

"If you come over here, I'll break the seal for you."

Arcana thought carefully.

"It'll only take three seconds. He won't notice anything."

"Hmm. Okay."

Having come to a decision, Arcana slowly walked up to Ceris. He immediately drew a magic circle on her body. The spell formula was designed to disrupt the magic seal that had been placed on her. Light entered her body, and the next moment, particles of magic started flowing from her source.

"What...?"

"Have you ever learned a spell formula before?"

Arcana nodded. "But I couldn't use it."

"You'll be able to now. Give it a go."

Arcana the magic pouring from her to draw a circle. The spell formed exactly how she'd imagined it, and fire burst from the center. It was Grega, but the power was immense. Ceris used his anti-magic to erase the flames, which were large enough to burn a large tree down.

"See? You did it."

Arcana nodded happily.

"If you want, I can also teach you spells to escape the dragons."

"There's spells like that?"

"Of course. In exchange, will you help me persuade Anos?"

"Yup! I'm sure he'd agree to go to the castle if the dragons stopped attacking! He loves magic after all!"

"That's good to hear. You're a big help." Ceris smiled in relief. His expression exuded kindness. "I need to make some preparations, but I'll be back here tomorrow at the same time. I'll return your seal until then."

Ceris removed the magic circle he had drawn on Arcana. Her seal immediately reactivated, suppressing her magic once again.

"Oh, that's right. The invitation I gave you has something extremely important to Anos written on it. You must not read it."

"Oh?"
"Can you promise me that?"
"Okay."
"All right. I'll see you tomorrow, then."
Ceris used Fless and rose into the air before flying away.

§ 25. The Entrance to the Underground Ruins

The next day.

It was white night in the underground world, and we had made our way to a wasteland west of Jiorhaze. There wasn't a single blade of grass or tree in sight. The only thing that existed in this area devoid of all life was the singing of the Divine Dragon.

Arcana, Lay, Misa, Misha, Sasha, Eleonore, and Zeshia were accompanying me today. I had ordered Shin and Eldmed to watch over the remaining students.

"I heard things got out of hand again while I wasn't around," Lay said as he listened to the Divine Dragon's singing.

"Oh, it was just a brief match against Agatha's Sword Emperor and a squabble with Jiordal's pope. No one died."

"Aha ha… So why were Ellen and the others singing 'Neighbor' like crazy in their room?" Misa asked. She seemed to have guessed the answer already.

"I developed a spell called Gard Aske, which converts their bottomless love into magic, and used it to destroy the pope's Selection God. As I'd suspected, love is pretty effective against the gods."

"So you went on a complete rampage," Sasha muttered under her breath.

Misha nodded repeatedly beside her in understanding.

"Come to think of it, I didn't see either of you earlier," Eleonore said, smiling suggestively as she peered into Misa's face. "What were the two of you up to?"

Misa's cheeks flushed. "I'll leave it to your imagination."

"Oh? If you say that, I'll imagine something amazing!"

"Zeshia will imagine too." Zeshia clenched her fists enthusiastically. "They went to eat really yummy food. Zeshia is jealous."

It seemed that was the limit of her imagination.

"We were practicing our love magic, since we'll probably face more gods in the future," Lay said cheerfully.

Sasha shot him an unimpressed look. "You say that with a straight face, but you were probably just flirting with each other."

"Speaking of which, I heard you guys have been visiting Anos's room these last two days. What were you doing there?"

The unexpected comeback had Sasha boiling red in an instant. "What do you mean?! We weren't doing anything. Right, Misha?"

Misha tilted her head in thought. "We'll leave it to your imagination?"

"Are you stupid?!"

Misha laughed. "I wanted to try saying it."

"Jeez…"

Arcana, who had been walking in front of us, came to a sudden stop and turned around. "This is where the dragon sings," she said.

Sasha paused. "Huh. It's echoing weirdly here. How does it work?"

"Maybe there are two Divine Dragons," Misha suggested.

"But it sounds like there might be three of them. Try over here, maybe."

Misa walked forward while listening closely. Indeed, there were three voices singing.

"It seems the voice of the Divine Dragon echoes into multiple voices from where the God of Traces sleeps. My guess is that it's doing more than just pointing out the location of Ligalondrol." I looked over at Arcana, who nodded.

"I believe that is correct. That may be the reason Revalschned remains in this land rather than returning to the Divine Realm."

"Oh? What do you mean by that?" Eleonore asked.

"The Divine Dragon has already passed, but the God of Traces governs the order of records and memories. Revalschned continues to leave traces of the Divine Dragon's song after the dragon's death."

Chapter 25 — The Entrance to the Underground Ruins

"Oh, I see!" Eleonore replied. "It has to recreate the singing, so it constantly remains in Jiordal."

"The song of the Divine Dragon is like a dragon's domain. It serves as armor protecting the kingdom from outside enemies."

As long as the Divine Dragon's song could be heard, it was difficult to see across the kingdom with Magic Eyes and use spells like Gatom and Leaks. Any attempts at invasion would be stunted when the enemy tried to gather information.

"The God of Traces is also known as the guardian god of the underground world," Arcana explained.

"You say that, but it seems the only place it's guarding right now is Jiordal." I cast my Eyes around the area and found the point with the most overlapping voices. "Hmm. The Divine Dragon's song resonates the most below here."

Arcana disappeared in a flurry of lunar snowdrops and reappeared before me.

"But I don't see anything that resembles underground ruins," I said. "Even with the Divine Dragon's song in the way, shouldn't I be able to detect that much?"

"That's probably because the ruins don't exist anymore," Arcana said. "The order of traces connects the ruins of the past to the present."

"Are you saying Ligalondrol only exists in the past?"

"That is correct." Arcana held out her hand, and the Moon of Creation appeared overhead. "*Land freezes; ice melts.*"

Silver light shone down on her. The glittering rays froze the ground around her to form a circle. There was a cracking sound, then the ice shattered, and a large hole opened in the ground. From what I tell with my Magic Eyes, it was completely hollow all the way down.

"If we can construct a bridge to the past, we'll be able to cross into the underground ruins," Arcana said.

"Hmm. In other words, something like this?"

I drew a magic circle in the hole—it was for Rivide. As I rewound the time of the space, dirt shifted and returned to stone. A large building formed below us. Eleonore and Zeshia stared in awe.

"Wow! It's a huge ruin!"

"It looks...like a temple."

"This is the farthest back I can go," I said. The stone building was so big, only a portion of it could be seen through the hole. "That seems to be the entrance."

We flew over to a ruined structure that looked like a tower. Upon closer inspection, the circular floor of the tower appeared to be a large gate.

"How do we open it?" Sasha asked, staring down at it.

"Things like this are generally designed to open with brute force. Just give it a good kick."

"Of course the Demon King would say that."

"Float over the floor or you'll fall in when it opens." I lifted my foot to stomp down on the gate, when I spotted something from the corner of my eye.

"What's wrong?" Sasha asked.

"Look."

There was a footprint embedded in the gate close to where I was about to stomp down.

"These ruins are a thing of the past, so it's a little difficult to say for sure. However..."

Misha came up from behind me and peered at the footprint. "It's still fresh."

"So it seems."

"Hold on. What does that mean?" Sasha asked.

"Someone entered already, or at least they attempted to do so. Either way, someone else arrived here before us."

The moment I said that, the magic of multiple entities could be detected overhead. I looked up to see a row of figures lining the edge of the hole. They were soldiers—around a dozen of them. They were clad in deep-green armor that gave a dragon-like appearance and appeared to be using some kind of cloaking device that concealed their magic. They glared down at us with open hostility.

"Identify yourselves. What's your purpose here?" I asked, but there was no reply. They summoned bows and aimed their arrows.

"I've seen them before," Arcana said. "They were once the nameless knights of Gadeciola. At some point, they came to be known as the Phantom

Chapter 25 — The Entrance to the Underground Ruins

Knights. Their existence has never been publicly acknowledged, but they're rumored to be the direct subordinates of Gadeciola's overlord. They move in the shadows, eliminating Gadeciola's enemies."

Gadeciola, huh? If they'd had Ahid's help, it wouldn't be strange for them to be in Jiordal.

"Are you after the God of Traces too?" I asked. At the same time, the soldiers loosed their arrows. They rained down upon us, laden with a vast amount of magic particles. "That confirms it."

I drew as many magic circles as there were soldiers and fired a black sun from each one. The dozen or so Jio Graze swallowed the incoming magic and set the soldiers ablaze, armor and all. However...

"Oh?"

The soldiers shook off the black flames. Not a single one of the Phantom Knights was wounded.

"Ahid's forces were nothing compared to these soldiers. With this much power, they should have had no trouble getting in."

There was probably another force already inside, meaning these guys were just the lookouts.

"Anos," Lay called, "we'll take care of this lot. If they destroy the God of Traces first, we'll have come here for nothing."

Misa stood beside him and raised a hand. Darkness surged forth from nowhere, enveloping her and revealing her true form.

"Get going," the great spirit said.

"I'll leave them to you."

I raised my foot and brought it down on the floor. The circular gate was forced open with a resounding *thunk*. Lay and Misa remained at the entrance while we proceeded down through the gate.

"Wow, this goes down deep," Eleonore said, staring ahead.

Roughly ten seconds into our fall, the floor finally came into view. As soon as we landed, Sasha cried out.

"Anos, behind you!"

A soldier in deep-green armor appeared from the darkness and stood behind me. A white blade flashed—but I moved faster. My Vebzud-covered hand pierced through the armor and grabbed the soldier's source.

"Did you think you had caught me off guard?"

Chapter 25 — The Entrance to the Underground Ruins

"Just die..."

Magic surged from the soldier's source like it was about to self-destruct. The magic took the form of a jet-black sun that swelled and swelled in an attempt to swallow me. With a mighty boom, the soldier's source was enveloped in black flames and burned to ashes, but the black sun he'd released at the cost of his life was still raging fiercely around me.

"No you don't!" Sasha cried, glaring at the flames with her Magic Eyes of Destruction and erasing the magic around me. My index finger was left with a mild burn.

"I'll commend them for landing a scratch, but with Jio Graze, huh?"

The soldier's body had already disintegrated. I stared at the remaining source that was about to burn away. After one look into the abyss, his identity became clear.

"It seems these guys aren't draconids, but demons."

§ 26. The Upstream Corridor

We proceeded down a corridor of the ruins. By observing the stone flooring with my Magic Eyes, I could see many minute marks that were undetectable to the naked eye. They were marks made by walking, and they were relatively fresh.

"Hmm. Someone's already passed through here. Be on your guard; they may be waiting to ambush us."

We continued as fast as we could while remaining aware of our surroundings. Ligalondrol was vast, and even a single corridor took a long time to traverse.

"Did those Phantom Knights get here before us after all?" Sasha asked.

"That's certainly possible."

"But why would there be demons in the underground world?" Eleonore asked, raising her index finger. "Do you know, Arcana?"

"I don't. At the very least, I know that the rumors of the Phantom Knights have existed since shortly after Gadeciola's founding. They didn't have a name back then, but there has always been a group of mysterious knights on Gadeciola's side."

"They weren't fazed by my Jio Graze either," I said. "That armor of theirs probably has some kind of dragon power to it, but even without that, they weren't weak by any means. They were most likely demons from the Mythical Age."

"Did they come here two thousand years ago?" Misha asked.

"Most likely."

Perhaps shortly after the underground world had been created, they had noticed its existence and descended.

"But what did they come here for?" Sasha asked.

"I have no clue. If I recall correctly, Gadeciola worships a blasphemous god."

Arcana nodded. "That's right. The citizens of Gadeciola are people who oppose the gods and their orders. Despite the kingdom being smaller than Jiordal or Agatha, powerful draconids have gathered there. Those draconids claim there is danger in relying on the power of the gods."

"Shouldn't that make them our allies? They're demons, and they oppose the gods," Sasha remarked.

"But they attacked us out of the blue," Eleonore pointed out.

Sasha hummed in thought.

"If they're demons from two thousand years ago, they should know Anos," Misha said.

"Oh, good point!" Eleonore exclaimed. "They should recognize Anos's face and magic. It's not like he's hiding it or anything."

"They attacked...knowing it was Anos?" Zeshia asked, looking a little angered.

"So it seems. I should have been able to recognize anyone strong enough not to fear me, but it's possible there were powerful demons hiding away during the war."

After I'd created the wall and sacrificed my life, a number of demons had traveled underground. If they had neither resurfaced nor alerted anyone to the underground world's existence, then everything made sense. It wouldn't have been peculiar for one or two people to leave the group over the years, so the fact that no one had broken away hinted at quite the impressive feat of leadership.

"Gadeciola is a mysterious kingdom. Unlike Jiordal and Agatha, it isn't easy to enter. It's said that once you enter, only a special few may leave."

"What? That doesn't sound like a good nation at all!" Sasha cried.

Arcana nodded. "Indeed. Gadeciola makes no contact with other kingdoms. It is the final destination for those who have lost their faith—the only

Chapter 26 — The Upstream Corridor

place of salvation for those who don't believe in the gods. Thus, not even I know the details."

Gadeciola was a kingdom that didn't believe in gods. It made sense that only a blasphemous god would be welcomed.

"I have no idea what the Phantom Knights' objective was in coming here, and the same goes for why they've remained here to this day. However, the fact they're here at the ruins means they're currently after the God of Traces. If they are a group that means to defy order, then they most likely want him destroyed."

"That sounds correct," Arcana said.

If they didn't want him destroyed, their presence here could be related to my lost memories. Perhaps my finding a way to regain those memories would prove inconvenient for someone.

Suddenly, Eleonore froze. "Hm?"

The rest of us came to a stop.

"The water's flowing weirdly!" she exclaimed.

In front of us was a T-intersection. The corridor connected to ours was inclined, but for some strange reason, the water was traveling up the slope. It was flowing in reverse. There seemed to be some spell at work, as the water never flowed into our corridor.

"Look." Misha pointed to a stone slab up ahead.

"What does it say?" Sasha asked. It was written in prayer runes, so she couldn't read it. I read it aloud.

"'The upstream corridor is the only path to the past. However, the corridor will only accept the past from thirty-three days prior; it will reject everything else. Time within the ruins of Ligalondrol remains stagnant while always facing upstream. Take the key, open the door, and use the boat inside to travel upstream against the flow of time. In thirty-three days, all the traces of the world shall await you in the depths of Ligalondrol.'"

Sasha tilted her head. "The door's right here, isn't it?"

Beside the stone slate was a door, a magic circle, and a keyhole.

"Do we use this magic circle?" she asked.

"Let's give it a go." I touched the circle and sent my magic into it. A key was created before us. I inserted it into the keyhole and turned it, but nothing happened. "Hmm. It won't open."

"Just break it," Eleonore said, holding up her index finger. "Use that strength of yours to take it down with a bang!"

"If only it were so simple." I clenched my fist and slammed it against the door, but the door didn't even make a sound, much less break apart.

"Time flows differently here," Arcana said. "This door is a trace of the past. The upstream corridor only accepts the past from thirty-three days prior. In other words, you have to bring the key from thirty-three days ago to open the door."

Eleonore frowned in thought. "Huh. How do we fetch it from thirty-three days ago? If we traveled back in time, the key would disappear."

Sasha was the one to answer her. "Time's stagnant in Ligalondrol though, right? If we leave the ruins, our time will continue flowing again. The slate said that time in the ruins always faces upstream, so the past becomes the future and the future becomes the past. In other words, if we leave the ruins and wait a day, we would be one day in the past when we return."

"Aaah, my head hurts!"

"At any rate, if we take this key outside and wait thirty-three days before returning, this key will become a key from thirty-three days ago. That should open the door, right?" Sasha asked.

"That sounds correct," Arcana said.

"Huh. The boat's on the other side of this door, so we'll have to take that out too," Eleonore remarked. "Then we'll have to wait another thirty-three days and then spend an additional thirty-three days traveling to the depths of the ruins."

"A total…of ninety-nine days…" Zeshia said.

Sasha held her head in her hands. "If all the traces of the world are waiting in the depths, that should mean the God of Traces is there too, right?"

Misha nodded. "But we won't be able to catch up to the Phantom Knights."

"Of course, so there has to be some other way to—"

With a click, I opened the door. There was a magic circle drawn on the floor of the room inside.

"Wait, what did you just do?!"

"Did you think I couldn't wait thirty-three days in an instant?"

Sasha gasped in realization. "Right! Of course. If you use Rivide to speed up the key's time, you can make a key from thirty-three days in the past."

Chapter 26 — The Upstream Corridor

I stepped inside the magic circle on the floor, and a boat appeared. It was a two-person canoe. Since there were six of us, I summoned two more and cast Rivide on all three of them, speeding up time by thirty-three days. In other words, to Ligalondrol, they became boats of thirty-three days prior. I picked up the canoes and carried them out of the room.

"Now let's get going."

I set the boats down on the upstream corridor for us to board. Arcana and I sat in one, Sasha and Misha sat in another, and Eleonore and Zeshia sat in the last. The canoes immediately began descending the upstream corridor, traveling against the flow of water.

"I know you've sped things up a lot, but it'll still take thirty-three days to get there, right?"

Sasha was right; logically speaking, whoever set sail first would be the first to reach Ligalondrol's depths.

"Can we make the boat go faster?" Misha asked.

"There's no oars to paddle with. From what I can see, these boats can't do anything but follow the flow of time."

"Can't you speed up the flow of time with Rivide?" Arcana asked.

"To an extent, but unlike with the key and boats, the flow of this water is the work of the God of Traces itself. We'd be at a disadvantage competing with a god in their own field of expertise."

Sasha frowned. "Will we make it at this rate though?"

"Don't worry. I made another key earlier. This one will open the door to the depths." I showed her the key. Arcana looked confused.

"What do you mean?" she asked.

"Where's the door to the depths?" Sasha asked, looking over at Misha, who shook her head.

"The upstream corridor only accepts the past from thirty-three days prior."

I raised the key above my head and then slammed it into the floor of the corridor. At the same time, I used Rivide to make the motion of the key faster by thirty-three days. Accelerating the time of only the key meant its speed would surpass the speed of light. The next thing we knew, a thundering tremor could be heard, and the boats accelerated. The thrown key opened a large hole in the floor of the corridor, and water came gushing out.

"See? The door opened."

"Door? This is a hole!" Sasha screamed as the boats approached the void.

"Bwa ha ha! Don't sweat the details. Whether it's a door or a hole, we can still pass through it, no?"

Traveling in reverse to the water spewing furiously out of the hole, the canoes were rapidly sucked in.

"Heeeeeeeeeeeeeelp!"

Accompanied by Sasha's scream, our canoes tipped and fell, plunging into the depths of Ligalondrol.

§ 27. Where the God of Traces Resides

Water surged upwards from the gaping hole. The three canoes traveling upstream plummeted faster and faster downward.
"Wow, I think I'm seeing stars!"
"So many...boats."
Traveling with the flow of the water, in the opposite direction to us, were rising stars. By peering into their abyss, I could see the twinkling stars were actually canoes. All kinds of draconids—young and old, male and female, some wearing armor, and some wearing robes—were riding the boats that rushed past us.
"This must be a record of those who have visited here," Arcana said.
Apparently, this water bore traces of those who had once visited the depths of Ligalondrol.
"Look," Misha said. Her gaze was directed towards an androgynous figure in blue robes. It was the beautiful clergyman, Pope Golroana. He must have followed the scriptures and visited Ligalondrol too.
"The farther we go, the further back in time we get, right?" Sasha asked, looking at Arcana in confusion. "How far does this go exactly?"
"All traces return as far as the beginning of time. That is where the God of Traces resides."
"You mean we're traveling to the beginning of the world?"
Arcana nodded. "That is correct."

"My head hurts."

"Don't worry. Everything only applies within Ligalondrol. The order of time is maintained here, so time will not be distorted. The order of traces overflows here alone, in the heart of Revalschned."

Sasha put her head in her hands in apprehension. "If the pope was right, won't we be in trouble if we make the God of Traces angry?"

"Bwa ha ha! The order we're up against is capable of turning back time this far in their sleep. It isn't merely a god that changes things into traces."

She tightened her grip in concern. "How can you laugh in this situation? There's still the Phantom Knights ahead of us to worry about."

"It's okay," Misha said. "Anos is here."

"I know that, but if our opponents are strong enough, Anos's attacks might go flying off course. I'm more worried about that."

I chuckled. "Don't worry. My followers aren't that fragile."

Sensing the implied order to evade it herself, Sasha looked at me, unimpressed. "Yeah, yeah, if you say so."

"Brace yourselves for impact. We'll be landing soon."

The end of the current was reflected in my Eyes. The next moment, the canoes shot forward and passed through a large hole. The flow of water suddenly ceased, and the canoes were thrown into the air.

We had arrived in a vast space where the floor was covered by a shallow pool of blue water. The edge of the room was lined with waterfalls flowing in reverse, but despite the current, the swaying water surface was not disturbed.

Before long, the canoes came to land on top of the pool. Thanks to the water absorbing the momentum, the impact wasn't as great as expected, and the canoes came to a stop.

"So this is the depths of the ruins."

We disembarked from the canoes to find the water was shallow enough to stand in. The room was overflowing with a tremendous amount of magic, and it didn't take long to find where it was coming from. Its source was a large ripple on the water's surface. I set off straight towards it, but then…

"As usual, you make the most unexpected appearances," a familiar voice said.

A faint black mist began to drift before me, and two demons appeared from the haze. One held a crimson demon spear in his hand and wore an eye

Chapter 27 — Where the God of Traces Resides

patch that concealed half his face—it was Aeges Code of the Four Evil Kings. The other was a man with six horns protruding from his head—it was Aegis's fellow Evil King, Kaihilam Jiste.

"Oh? If it isn't the Netherworld King and the Cursed King. What an odd place to be meeting the two of you. Since when were you part of the Phantom Knights?"

Netherworld King Aeges held his spear at the ready in response. "Leave, Demon King. Arguing with you would be a waste of time."

"Are you in agreement with him, Kaihilam? Or are you Jiste right now?"

The Cursed King answered me quietly. "I'm sorry, Anos. This is Kaihilam's request. I know you helped me out just recently, however..."

The Cursed King had two personalities: Cursed King Kaihilam, and his lover Jiste. It seemed that Jiste was currently in control, but by the sound of it, it was only a matter of time before Kaihilam made an appearance.

"Anos," Misha said, her gaze focused on the large ripples spreading across the water's surface. I could force my way past the two Evil Kings, but if I caused too much of a commotion, the God of Traces could wake up.

"I know." I stepped forward, heading straight for the heart of the ripples. Aeges and Jiste blocked the way. "What's your objective?" I asked.

"You already know. We will destroy the God of Traces here before he awakens."

"Unfortunately, I have business with him. Wait your turn."

Aeges lowered his center of gravity, glaring at me from his single visible eye. He pointed Dehiddatem, the Crimson Blood Spear, at the left side of my chest. "Have you forgotten my warning? If you underestimate the gods, what happened to Avos Dilhevia will happen again."

"Hmm. Avos is outside playing with your friends right now. Is there a problem?" I asked.

"Even if there were, it would be too late. We're here to nip the bud before it opens."

"What a wasteful thing to do. A lovely flower could bloom, you know?"

Aegis's eye narrowed. "Like I said, arguing with you is a waste of time."

Dehiddatem glinted as it shot forward. Space distorted, and the front half of the spear vanished. It had transcended dimensions to appear before me. I grabbed the shaft with Ygg Neas.

With a grunt, Aeges swung the spear upwards. My body rose into the air with the shaft.

"Oh? You've grown stronger since last we met."

"I told you I wasn't playing around!"

Dehiddatem crossed dimensions once again, carrying me high into the air. I quickly released my grip on the demon spear, but the blood flowing from it encased my body in a sphere.

"Fly to the ends of this dimension."

A copious amount of blood began to flow from Crimson Blood Spear. The blood emitted an ominous power as it interacted with my body—it was attempting to do just as Aeges had said. The next moment, Aeges withdrew his spear and leaped to the side. The Teo Triath Eleonore had fired struck where he'd been standing, sending up a spray of water.

"What an annoyance."

"If you move, you'll die," Sasha said from behind Aeges, pressing her Vebzud-covered fingertips against his back.

"*Ice prison.*"

Misha enclosed Jiste in a cage of ice. Jiste released a black mist that attempted to swallow the ice, but Misha repaired the ice faster than Jiste could destroy it. More and more ice formed around the prison until it was many layers thick.

"Anos," Misha said.

"Right. Come, Arcana. We will subdue the God of Traces first."

The sphere of blood around me had burst when Aeges had withdrawn his spear. I controlled my fall with Fless and immediately headed for the heart of the ripples. Arcana appeared beside me in a flurry of lunar snowdrops, and the two of us jumped into the water together. As we swam forward, we heard a voice.

"I'm impressed. You would sacrifice your lives just to buy time against two of the Four Evil Kings."

The Netherworld King appeared unaffected by the Vebzud pressed against his back. His gaze followed Arcana and me as we moved. Apparently, he thought Sasha was no match for him.

"You got that last part right, but the rest is wrong," Sasha declared loudly,

Chapter 27 — Where the God of Traces Resides

her Magic Eyes of Destruction at the ready. "I don't know how strong the Four Evil Kings are, but I am a subordinate of the Demon King."

Aeges shot me a look of anger, twisted his entire body around, and hurled his demon spear like a bolt of lightning. At the same time, Sasha read his breathing and sank her fingertips into his spear-wielding arm. Their movements overlapped. Dehiddatem flew through the air and missed its target, grazing my cheek.

"Good job."

We reached the center of the ripples and made a splash as we sank below. What should have been a shallow pool of water suddenly stretched out deep below. I gazed into the water with my Magic Eyes, but I couldn't see the depths.

"Arcana."

"I can detect a god's magic—most likely that of the God of Traces. Because he's asleep, he doesn't have a form."

So all this water *was* the God of Traces.

"You said you would make Revalschned acknowledge you and convince him to wake up," Arcana said.

"If he's dreaming, it should be possible to speak to him without waking him up. If he's a reasonable god, he should be able to evoke my memories on the spot, no?"

"That is correct. However, the God of Traces governs a wider order of memories. In order to make the god dream, a large amount of magic will be needed. Even if we succeed, we may only join him for a short time."

"It's worth a try. Use my magic."

Arcana nodded and touched my body, drawing a magic circle. Our clothes disappeared in a flash of light. Then she pressed her forehead against mine. "*Night falls, inviting sleep. Drifting memories, overlapping dreams, rise to the surface.*"

Sinking into the traces of the past, we quietly fell into the dream.

§ 28. Rightful Magic Eyes

We were in an unfamiliar place—a never-ending wasteland with no sign of life. A dome covered the sky above, and polar night cloaked the land in darkness.

Arcana was beside me. Both she and I were clothed. Was this the God of Traces' dream?

"This is both my dream and hers. I am Revalschned, God of Traces. I govern the order of this world's records and memories, and inscribe their traces into my body."

As the voice resounded, the ground of the wasteland rose, revealing huge bookshelves that reached all the way up to the dome. Before I knew it, a man was standing before us. He had a white book in his hand and wore formal robes befitting a god.

"Here in the depths of Ligalondrol, I sleep at the end of time, waiting for a certain day to come. What business do you have here, Misfit and Arcana, the nameless god?"

Arcana took a step forward. "We wish to retrieve our lost memories. They should be inscribed into your order," she said.

"Memories are pain; to forget is to receive salvation. I am the god that bears the burden of this world's pain. The memories you retrieve will torment you."

"The sins I committed belong to me. If they caused me agony, then I should not have healed that pain. I wish to carve those scars back into my own body."

"This is where all the records and memories of this world end up. Look into the abyss of your memories, Arcana. If you truly seek the truth and do not avert your Eyes, you shall regain those memories."

Numerous books fell silently from the vast bookshelves that stretched endlessly into the wasteland. They hovered around us and opened midair, pages tearing themselves out one after another and fluttering around like confetti. Those millions and millions of pages were the traces of records and memories of the world.

Just then, there was a deafening roar of thunder. Countless bolts of purple lightning flashed, striking the books hovering in the air. Paper caught alight and began burning fiercely. The fire jumped from the books to the shelves, turning the entire dreamworld around us into a sea of flames.

Revalschned's brow furrowed. Purple lightning coiled around his body. "Uninvited guests—fools that worship blasphemous gods—have released lightning upon my sleeping body."

"Hmm. They were waiting for the God of Traces to be distracted."

This purple lightning's magic belonged to neither Aeges nor Kaihilam. I'd figured they weren't the only Phantom Knights here, and it seemed I was right.

"Should I wake up?" Arcana asked.

"No; I'll stop this fire. You keep searching for your memories for as long as you can."

"I shall do as you say." Arcana drew a magic circle over me. *"From a droplet of snow, he wakes from his dream and returns to the present."*

A single lunar snowdrop fell on my cheek. The next moment, the wasteland before me disappeared. Arcana was in my arms, stark naked. Purple lightning crackled through the water, eating away at the God of Traces. I drew a magic circle to change into my white clothes and then wrapped a blanket around Arcana.

With that, I glared at the lightning with my Magic Eyes of Destruction. A single glance was only enough to erase one third of it. The spell was pretty powerful. I continued glaring until the lightning completely vanished.

After cleaning up the place, I searched my surroundings. My Eyes fixed on a figure lurking in the darkness.

"I found you. Who are you?"

Chapter 28 — Rightful Magic Eyes

I drew a layered magic circle and reached inside. Once the pale blue of Ygg Neas had covered my hand, I used it to grab the lurking figure. Suddenly, I felt resistance on my left shoulder. An invisible hand had grabbed me—the figure was using Ygg Neas on me in return. Ygg Neas was a spell from the world aboveground, so the culprit was most likely a demon.

"Sorry, but I won't let you do as you please here," I said.

With the figure still in my grasp, I jumped into the water. One loud splash later, I had returned to the room with the waterfall.

For a brief moment, the people in the room glanced over at me. My followers were still locked in combat with two of the Four Evil Kings.

"Who was it, Jiste? Who locked you in here?" an angry voice muttered. It came from the body of Jiste, who was trapped in an ice prison. The magic flowing from her source was on a completely different level than before.

The Cursed King had an abnormal physical constitution that caused his source to change along with his personality. Now, it was no longer Jiste who stood before us—it was Kaihilam, the Cursed King.

"I see." Black mist gathered before him, forming a magic circle. "This is unforgivable!" Hatred flowed from him as particles of magic, which rose into the air, shattering the ice. "I'll never forgive you!" He reached into the magic circle and drew out an ominous-looking bow.

"Hmm. Be careful, Misha. That's Netrauvus, the Demon Bow. Its arrows will never miss the cursed—and from the moment you laid a hand on Jiste, you were cursed."

At that moment, Aeges, who had been facing Sasha, made a move. Dehiddatem flashed, piercing Sasha's abdomen. As the Phoenix Mantle's flames wrapped around her, healing her wound, she jumped aside and reached for her sister. "Misha!"

"Got it."

The two halves of the magic circle they drew connected.

"*Dino Jixes!*"

Their bodies melted together, becoming one. The silver-haired girl, Aisha, turned her Magic Eyes towards the Cursed King.

"Now perish!" he roared angrily, shooting the Demon Bow. Its arrow immediately vanished from sight only to reappear embedded in the left side of Aisha's chest.

"This is your punishment for laying a hand on my Jiste. Be cursed to death."

However, no sooner had the Cursed King said that, than the arrow turned to ice and shattered.

"Unfortunately for you, Mr. Split Personality—*ice arrows can't hurt us!*"

The Magic Eyes of Omneity had turned the arrow into thin ice the moment before it pierced Aisha's skin. Kaihilam's hatred grew, and he glared murderously at the silver-haired girl. He had a short temper when it came to Jiste—there was no talking sense into him.

"We'll finish you in one go—*Magic Eyes of Omneity!*"

Aisha glared at Aeges and Kaihilam. The Magic Eyes of Omneity broke through their defenses and interfered with the demon bow and spear.

"You dare…!"

"Those Eyes are as tremendous as the tales say!"

Dehiddatem and Netrauvus were promptly transformed into ice crystals. The Netherworld King and the Cursed King leaped aside to avoid the effects of Aisha's Magic Eyes.

"You can't escape. *No matter how far you run, you're still within our sight.*"

Aisha sent more magic into her Eyes as she glared at them again, but at that moment, the sensation on my shoulder disappeared. A giant bolt of purple lightning came crashing down, blocking Aisha's view.

"It's just as I thought," a lighthearted voice said. It didn't belong to either Aeges or Kaihilam. "Those are the Magic Eyes of Absurdity."

A shadow appeared amid the purple lightning. The bolts scattered and dispersed to reveal a purple-haired, blue-eyed man dressed in a coat. It was the man we'd seen in our dream—the demon who'd been speaking to Arcana. If I recalled correctly, his name was Ceris.

"Long time no see, Genedonov. You seem to have been reborn, but do you still remember me?"

Aisha glared at him sharply. "As if!"

But the man glared back at the Magic Eyes of Absurdity. His pale-blue eyes changed into mauve-colored Magic Eyes.

"Why didn't it work? *Those Eyes are similar to Anos's Eyes,*" Sasha and Misha murmured in surprise.

"That would be a misleading statement, Goddess of Absurdity," he said

Chapter 28 — Rightful Magic Eyes

with a friendly smile. "His Eyes are similar to mine. I'm Ceris Voldigoad, Anos's father."

"Oh?" I stepped before Aisha and stared into his familiar mauve Eyes. "That's news to me."

Ceris chuckled softly. "You've simply forgotten, Anos. This was the work of Militia, the Goddess of Creation. She stole your memories of me and created false memories in their place."

He made it sound like Militia was the enemy.

"I won't dismiss the possibility, but why would she do that?"

"You wouldn't believe me even if I told you. Otherwise, I would have shown myself long before now and told you everything."

That all sounded plausible enough, but there was no guarantee it was the truth.

"Something doesn't add up. If you wanted me to regain my memories, why would you destroy the God of Traces?" I asked.

"Because the God of Traces would get away if we waited for your memories to return."

Ceris raised a hand and drew a layered magic circle. The air immediately changed. The formerly calm water's surface surged wildly. Here, at the beginning of time, every drop of water was a mark that had been left on this world. That order was reacting violently to a spell Ceris hadn't even activated yet.

"That's some mighty impressive greater magic."

"You should step aside," Ceris said in a kindly manner, his Magic Eyes on me. "You may not die, but you could end up injured."

"Make me."

"Oh? So you wish to rebel."

"If you truly are my father, this much should be easy."

"Goodness, what a disobedient child."

The layered magic circle in front of Ceris morphed into a sphere, but just as he held his hand over it, the crashing waves before him fell silent, leaving not a single ripple behind. The water became transparent and vanished, taking the tremendous amount of magic in the room with it.

"It looks like your god has interfered. She's awakened the God of Traces."

Ceris exhaled and erased his magic circle. The tremors in the underground ruins came to a sudden stop. I turned to see Arcana standing there with a blanket wrapped around her. With the water gone, she must have flown here.

"I let Revalschned flee," she said. "That demon isn't someone you can fight while protecting others."

She had a point. At the rate things were going, I would have had to protect both Revalschned and the sleeping Arcana.

"I wouldn't have minded. It was the perfect handicap."

"As a god, I can't be a burden to you."

I'd figured she'd say something like that.

"Did you remember anything?" I asked, looking at Arcana while remaining wary of Ceris. A dark look crossed her face.

"I..." She bit her lip. "I couldn't remember."

"There's nothing to feel down about. You prioritized helping another over fulfilling your own wish. That's why you're the god I chose."

Arcana dropped the blanket by her feet and drew a magic circle to don her usual clothes. She then looked at Ceris. The man was smiling innocently.

"Why don't we have a chat?"

"Oh?"

"I am the commander of the Phantom Knights. Gadeciola is at war with the gods. You don't think too highly of the gods either, isn't that right? On top of that, you are my son. Our interests might not have aligned this time, but there's no reason for us to fight." He retained his cheerful look. "We should be able to cooperate with each other."

If things could be resolved without fighting, that would be for the best, but for some reason, when I looked at him, I had a feeling it would be better for the sake of the world if I destroyed him right then and there.

I looked over at Aisha, who gave me a small shake of her head.

"*I can't see it*," Misha's voice murmured.

She meant that she couldn't see into Ceris's heart.

"When it comes to dealing with me, seeking conversation over battle isn't a bad choice," I said. "There are too many fools who resort to violence without talking things through."

He smiled good-naturedly. "Indeed, there are many bad people in this world. I get that. Differences are best resolved through discussion. Peace is the best option."

Chapter 28 — Rightful Magic Eyes

"Exactly. However, there are also people who can make regular scoundrels look cute."

"Oh really?"

"The lowest scum are those who approach you while pretending to be good people."

"That's a scary thought," he said, seemingly unaffected. "I'd better be careful myself. Well, there's no need to rush your answer. When you feel like talking, come to Gaelahesta. I'll await your presence there, in the Holy Seat Hall of Everastanzetta." He drew a new magic circle. The Netherworld King and the Cursed King stood beside him.

"Ceris," I said just before he used Gatom, "keep this in mind. Whether or not you are my father, if you're planning on causing trouble, I won't let you get away with it."

He smiled at my warning and teleported away.

§ 29. The Fall of a God

The dragon landing site, Jiorhaze.
We had returned to the furthest room on the bottom floor of the castle.
"So the knights you faced were demons too," I said, having just heard Lay's report.
"They were abnormally wary of the Sword of Three Races, so I broke their armor and confirmed it. Their magic was definitely that of demons—though I didn't check every single person," he answered with a cool smile.
Beside him, Misa added, "They were really strong too. We fought pretty seriously, but they escaped before we could finish them off."
Even though the goal hadn't been to kill them, no ordinary demons could have gotten away from Lay and Misa so easily.
"Were they subordinates of the Four Evil Kings?" Sasha asked, tilting her head. "Or maybe they worked for that Ceris guy."
"Either is possible."
"That demon said he was Anos's father. Do you think that's true?" Lay asked. "I've never heard of the Demon King having a father. Even if Anos's memories are incomplete, my memories shouldn't be affected. If so, then the situation is much worse than we thought."
"Well, I couldn't have been born from nothing. I must have had a father at some point. If he never revealed himself to anyone, then it wouldn't be that odd for humans to be unaware of him. As for the Magic Eyes, they're easily inherited by children."

That being said, they weren't always hereditary. To inherit powerful Magic Eyes one must bear a suitable source. That was why out of my many descendants in this era, only Sasha had inherited my Magic Eyes of Destruction—although in Sasha's case, her Eyes could have come from elsewhere.

"He called our fused form the Goddess of Absurdity," Sasha mumbled.

Misha nodded. "He said the Magic Eyes of Omneity were the Magic Eyes of Absurdity."

Back when we'd spoken with Arcana, we had discussed that possibility, but it was unclear just how much we could trust what that man said.

"You took a look at his heart, right?"

Misha nodded. "But I couldn't see anything. His heart was a void, like he was completely empty," she said, recalling when she had tried to stare into the abyss of his heart. But she soon shook her head. "Maybe I just couldn't see it."

"Well, I didn't like him either," Eleonore said.

"This isn't a matter of liking him or not," Sasha muttered.

"How do I put it? He said we should cooperate, but his words felt so untrustworthy, it was kind of scary."

"I agree that he's untrustworthy," I replied. "If he's part of Gadeciola, he must have been facing the gods until now, but that isn't necessarily his true objective."

Lay grinned. "At the very least, the Netherworld King has always hated the gods."

"The fact that he was trying to destroy the sleeping God of Traces suggests that Ceris has no intention of showing any mercy. He and the Netherworld King have that in common."

But at the same time, this new demon didn't seem like the type the Netherworld King would willingly obey. Perhaps he was only a subordinate as a formality and they were more like cooperative allies.

"He also appeared in your dream, right?" Sasha asked.

I nodded. In the dream, Arcana had been targeted by dragons. I had been hiding the truth, but that man had been trying to reveal it to her. Still, without seeing the continuation of the dream, there was no proof.

"He didn't seem like Anos and Arcana's father at all," Sasha said.

Chapter 29 — The Fall of a God

"He probably wasn't a good one. Not all children in this world are born out of love. That was especially the case two thousand years ago."

"That's a fair point." Sasha thought to herself. Her disgust for Ceris was written all over her face.

"Let's get back to the dream. Anything we can remember about Ceris could become the key to our discussions with him—especially since he believes I've forgotten everything."

If he told any lies about things I remembered, we would end up one step closer to identifying his objective. It was even possible that he was the one who had stolen my memories.

"Everyone...gets to sleep together again!" Zeshia said happily, looking at Arcana, but Arcana was vacantly gazing into space. Her normally clear expression was dark with worry. Her heart didn't seem with us.

Misha came closer and whispered in my ear. "Let her rest."

That certainly would be for the best. There weren't any urgent matters to attend to.

"I'll go talk to Ceris, but I want to organize my thoughts first," I said. "You should all get some sleep."

"Okay," Misha said, leaving the room with Sasha. Lay and the others also stood up and headed for their own rooms, leaving only Arcana and me behind. Arcana was completely silent.

"Are you tired from using too much magic?" I asked, walking up to her.

"I used too much, but that isn't the problem."

She was a god, after all. Only in extreme circumstances would she run out of magic.

"So what are you so depressed about?"

Arcana finally looked at me. "Am I depressed?"

"It looks that way to me."

"I see." Arcana hung her head in thought.

I waited until she felt like speaking.

"I had time," she finally said. She began recalling events angrily. "I was in the God of Traces' dream. In order for me to regain my memories, you woke up and bought time for me. There was time between when Ceris targeted the God of Traces and when I allowed the god to escape. The traces of records were dancing in the dream, but out of all the records of the world, I was unable to find my page. I must have averted my eyes." She continued in a matter-of-fact tone. "Remembering would have been my atonement, yet I felt fear. I got cold feet at the last moment because I didn't want to lose myself. I have committed yet another sin."

"You didn't avert your eyes on purpose."

She stared at me without confirming or denying my words. "Was I right to let the God of Traces go? You would never lose to anyone. Should I have believed in you and watched the rest of the dream? Perhaps by letting the God of Traces escape, I was the one running away." Arcana fell silent for a moment before speaking again. "Maybe I was using salvation as an excuse."

"I don't know about that. My magic is ill-suited to protecting others. We didn't see the full extent of Ceris's powers, so we can't say for sure that you did wrong."

Arcana opened her mouth but couldn't find the words to speak.

"I won't tell you not to fear. It's only natural to feel that way after choosing to abandon your name."

"If a god feels fear, people will feel uneasy."

"What good is a god that can't understand fear? If you can't comprehend their hearts, you can't bring them salvation."

Light returned to Arcana's eyes. "You said the same thing yesterday."

I nodded. "You wanted kindness, right?"

"Yes. That much is for certain."

"That's what you desired. You've made no mistakes."

Arcana's gaze met mine. "Is fear a form of kindness?"

"People are weak. Extending your hand towards that weakness is kindness. Thus, you must know weakness yourself." I smiled at her clear, untainted expression. "I find it comforting to hear you speak of the weakness of people."

"What do you mean?" she asked.

"It's a form of salvation to me."

Arcana looked back at me in surprise. "But what should I do?"

"If you're scared, just say it. Take my hand without reservation."

Still thinking, she stared at my face. Then after some time, she spoke. "I can't sleep like this," she said, "but if you put me to sleep like my brother did back then, I may be able to get some rest."

Chapter 29 — The Fall of a God

I recalled the very first dream I'd had of my little sister.

"That is my weakness."

"I guess it can't be helped," I said, replying like I had in the dream and offering her my hand. She took it, and we climbed into bed. Arcana snuggled under my blanket just like she had back then.

"I've learned selfishness," she said, clinging to me tightly. She buried her face in my chest while mumbling to herself. "I've learned weakness. I am a god, yet I have fallen."

At that, I laughed. "Did you think gods were incorruptible?"

"I think I now know why you're called the Demon King. You erase fear like a tyrant." Still hugging me tightly, Arcana drew a magic circle over the two of us. "If you were my older brother, I would have nothing to fear."

With a flash of light, our clothes vanished. Arcana brought her face close to mine.

"Can I call you the same as I did in the dream?" she asked.

"Do as you wish."

Arcana grinned bashfully. "Big brother..." she said in her crystal clear voice.

"What's up?"

"May I fall a little more today?"

"I'll allow it."

She gazed into my eyes. "Can you cast that spell to put me to sleep?"

I cupped the back of her head and planted a gentle kiss to her forehead, just like in the dream. A faint glow surrounded us and lulled us to sleep.

"Good night, Arcana."

"Good night, big brother."

§ 30. A Promise Made in the Dream

In the dream...
Arcana was walking through the forest. Her usually bright expression was somewhat glum. Pushing her way through the foliage, she moved steadily forward until she left the range of her brother's Magic Eyes. There, a man appeared before her. It was Ceris, the purple-haired demon wearing a coat.
"Hey, you're here," he said, greeting her with a friendly smile.
"Um..." Arcana quickly got to the point. "Teach me magic! You said there's a spell to run away from dragons, right?"
For some reason, she was much more desperate to learn magic than she had been the day before.
"Of course that's what I intend, but that's rather hard to do here." Ceris offered his hand to her. "You'll have to leave Anos for a while. Would you be okay with that?"
Arcana hesitated, but the next moment, she made up her mind and took his hand.
Ceris smiled with satisfaction. "Let's go."
He drew a magic circle, and the two rose into the air before setting off faster than the eye could see. After a while, a great mountain came into view. Ceris held his hand out towards the middle of the mountain, and a magic circle appeared. He flew them towards the magic circle and directed them through it.
Having entered the mountain, they arrived in a large room made of stone. The structure was so large, in fact, that the walls couldn't be seen.

Countless pillars and torches stood in neat rows, and at the center of it all were silver flames.

Arcana trembled in fear at the sight of the fire. The room was blazing hot, and the heat only increased the closer they got.

"This is the Bonfire of Judgment," Ceris said. "It's said that by throwing yourself into its silver flames and withstanding one thousand pains, you can gain tremendous power. With that power, you'll not only be able to run away from dragons but annihilate them yourself."

"But I'll die in the fire."

"Don't worry. First, I'll teach you the spell to flee from dragons." Ceris draped a necklace around Arcana's neck. There was a clear stone attached to it.

"What's this?" she asked.

"A charm to help the spell succeed." Ceris drew a magic circle in front of himself. "Now you try."

Arcana tried to copy the circle as told, but she found herself struggling.

"Let me help."

Ceris held his hand over Arcana's magic circle. Using her magic and the magic in the crystal, he drew the rest of the circle. It was the formula for Liteld. Layer upon layer formed within the interior of the crystal—the pledge jewel—attached to her necklace. A huge pillar of flame rose up behind her. The shadow of a dragon swayed within.

"GROOOAAAAAAAAAH!"

The summoning flames dispersed to reveal a golden variant dragon.

"Ah… No!" Arcana backed away in fear and fell to the floor.

"There's nothing to be afraid of, Arcana. You are a dragon core that can be reborn in a dragon's womb once eaten. Dragons seek the sources of those that can become the cores of their children. That is why you have been targeted by dragons until now."

Arcana looked at Ceris in surprise.

"You looked at the invitation, didn't you? It's about time you remember the memories Anos stole from you—and the lie he told you."

"I…" Arcana shook her head in confusion.

"Once you become dragonborn, the memory-loss spell will be broken. You'll recall everything in an instant. Anos took pity on you because you

Chapter 30 — A Promise Made in the Dream

constantly had to flee, but there was no point in his actions. Even if you're consumed, you will just be reborn."

"Stop," Arcana whispered, barely able to find her voice, but Ceris tilted his head with the same friendly look on his face.

"Stop? But why? I'm not telling you any lies—I swear on my life! Once you're reborn, you will no longer be hunted by dragons. You won't have to flee anymore. Isn't that what you wanted?" Ceris asked, confident in his own goodwill.

"But it'll hurt if I'm eaten."

"Ah. Indeed, having your source merged with others in the womb of a dragon will be agonizing beyond belief. This dragon is freshly summoned and has yet to consume a single source. It'll probably need to eat one thousand people before you can be reborn, but the pain will only last until then."

In the face of Ceris's obstinance, Arcana was filled with despair. "Save me…"

He smiled cheerfully. "I get it. It's okay; you'll be saved soon. Your days of living in fear are almost over."

"Save me, brothe—!"

"GROOOOOOOOOAAAAAAAAAAAAAAH!"

Arcana's scream was drowned out by the dragon's roar as the golden beast swallowed her tiny body whole. Ceris looked on in satisfaction. "Anos has no idea where we are right now. Besides, the pain of being eaten by a dragon is nothing compared to the pain of the Bonfire of Judgment. The flames are connected to the land where the gods pass their judgment, so the agony it inflicts is out of this world. Consider this a rehearsal." He grinned again. "You were born for this."

"Hmm. What lies are you feeding my sister?"

Ceris turned, his gaze harshening. The space creaked and then black flames filled his view. The black sun that had smashed through the magic door struck Ceris directly.

"Oh?" Ceris deployed his magic wards and glared straight ahead. Anos appeared from within the black flames. "That's quite the powerful spell you've learned, but your Eyes are still lacking when it comes to judging the skills of others."

Ceris's anti-magic had easily defended him against Anos's point-blank Jio Graze.

"You cannot save her. That is why I'll save her for you." He pointed his left hand at Anos and fired Vera. Purple lightning broke through Anos's anti-magic and tore up his body. Anos's expression twisted fiercely.

"Listen closely, Anos. There's nothing to be worried about. She will be reborn. Struggling like this is futile."

Anos glared at Ceris with his Magic Eyes. His expression was full of hatred. "Move..."

"What was that?"

"I said move!"

Magic gathered in Anos's Eyes, which turned mauve as a dormant part of his source awakened. His magic immediately intensified, and a vast magic circle appeared. Jio Graze blasted from the circle and pushed Ceris back. The man's eyes widened.

"Huh, so you can actually push me by force. Bravo. But don't you get it? Your Jio Graze is no match for my—"

"Have you finally noticed? Moron."

The Bonfire of Judgment burned behind Ceris.

"Good grief. Such petty tricks won't work on me." He evaded the black sun by twisting his body into the air. The next moment...

"GROOOOOOOOOAAAR!"

Right on cue, the golden variant dragon charged and knocked Ceris flying.

"What?!"

"I've been playing tag with dragons a lot recently, you see. Along the way, I couldn't help picking up a few tricks to attract their attention."

Ceris attempted to maintain his balance using Fless, but Anos fired another Jio Graze for good measure.

"I don't know who you are, but if you love the land of judgment so much, you can go there alone."

Flames engulfed Ceris's body as he was swallowed by the Bonfire of Judgment. Sensing he couldn't escape the silver flames once he was caught in them, he stood still and lowered his arms. "Dear me. Well, whatever. This isn't a bad outcome either."

Chapter 30 — A Promise Made in the Dream

With that, he was completely engulfed in flames and vanished. A low growl echoed as the golden variant glared at Anos.

"Stop growling. I'll put you to rest soon." He drew a magic circle and stained his right hand black. "*Vebzud.*"

"ROOOOOOOAAAAAAAAR!"

Golden dragon breath beat down Anos as he leaped towards the dragon, thrusting his Vebzud-stained hand through its chest. "Give her back." He cut through tough scales and sturdy skin to reach into the dragon's womb and grasp Arcana firmly. "Did you think I'd let a mere lizard eat my sister?"

He yanked his hand back. As a dying wail left the dragon's maw, a torrent of blood poured from its body. Its huge frame tilted slowly and then fell to the floor with a mighty crash.

A battered Arcana lay in Anos's arms. He cast Enchel, and light surrounded her body, but Anos's gaze remained grim. Her wounds showed no sign of healing. Perhaps because he had forcefully removed her from the womb in the middle of the rebirth process, her source was still deteriorating by the moment. Anos gazed down at her body with his Magic Eyes.

"How did you know?" Arcana asked, opening her eyes weakly.

"You left this behind when you went out, didn't you?" He reached into a magic circle and took out the note Arcana had written. The words "For your birthday tomorrow, I'll give you the thing you want most. Look forward to it!" were written on it. He continued casting healing magic as he searched for a way to cure her. "That's why I figured you were up to something reckless. I placed a magic mark on you to track you wherever you went."

As soon as she'd vanished from his field of view, he'd immediately set off after her.

"I'm sorry, big brother."

Anos patted her head. "It's okay, Arcana. I'll definitely save you."

He poured all his magic into his little sister and cast Enchel, but no matter how much he exhausted himself, Arcana's wounds didn't heal at all. Her source was still deteriorating. Anos clenched his teeth and poured more magic into his spell. Panic spread across his young face.

"It's okay, big brother. I'm all better now," Arcana said with all the courage she could muster. She could tell Anos was pushing himself.

"Your lies are as poor as ever."

Anos was using enough magic to whittle away his own source, yet he didn't relent even for a moment.

"I never noticed…"

"Don't talk. You'll worsen your wounds."

Arcana smiled sadly. "It wasn't you the dragons were chasing. It was me. You were protecting me this whole time." She desperately fought to form the right words as the strength drained from her body. She could sense the end was near. "I wanted to become stronger. I thought that if I were able to run from the dragons alone, you wouldn't have to worry about me anymore."

She gazed at her brother with sorrowful eyes. "I know what you truly want to do is study magic, but because of me, you couldn't go to the castle and had to study alone. That's why it's okay now. I'll be okay alone, so go and study. That was my gift to you." Tears spilled from her eyes. "But I was a liar."

"I don't need that. All I need is my adorable little sister with me."

"But…" One after another, tears streamed from Arcana's eyes. "But I'm not really your little sister!" That was what had also been written on the invitation she'd stolen a glance at. The despair must have spurred her into action. "And you're not really my brother."

"Arcana," Anos said quietly, "forgive me. I'm not strong enough to save you."

"It's okay."

"I'm going to use Syrica, but I'm still inept at source magic. Your source was altered within the dragon's womb. I won't be able to control when or where you're reincarnated, or whether you'll have any memories. I don't even know if I'll succeed."

Arcana nodded firmly. She held back her tears and smiled with all her might. "That's okay. If that happens, you'll finally be free. I'll be fine—I'm not afraid of being alone."

"I'd like one last gift from you."

"What might that be?"

"Become my little sister."

The tears she'd been holding back started streaming again.

"I won't tell you to forget. Please, remember. Remember no matter what. You are my sister. We may not be related by blood, but the days we spent

Chapter 30 — A Promise Made in the Dream

together weren't lies." Anos hugged his tearful sister and drew the magic circle for Syrica.

"Big brother..." Arcana said desperately, "next time...next time I'm born, I'll definitely, definitely be strong. I'll be strong enough to be helpful to you... because any little sister of yours has to be strong too, right? I'll come find you again! This time, it won't be a lie! Okay?" She looked up at her brother worriedly. "You do believe me, don't you?"

"Of course I believe you." Syrica activated, and Arcana began to fade into light. "Come find me no matter what. No matter who you become, you'll always be my one and only little sister."

Anos gripped the hand Arcana reached out at him. His fingers slipped through hers as she vanished into particles of light. His sad eyes remained fixed on the empty space. Overcome with a mix of frustration and determination, Anos made a vow to his little sister.

"Next time, I won't allow anyone to make you cry. I'll do everything I can to become strong enough to protect you, and until then, I'll wait for you, Arcana."

§ 31. Contradicting Memories

The next morning.
　I woke up to the sight of neat silver hair and an innocent sleeping face. While she was different in appearance, there was something about her that resembled my little sister in the dream.
　"It doesn't feel quite real yet, but I suppose I owe you an apology for forgetting I told you to come find me," I mumbled, softly patting Arcana's head.
　Even without her memories, she had managed to find me. I wondered if somehow, in the reaches of her source, she remembered that promise.
　Arcana groaned softly and opened her eyes. Her golden eyes looked at me sleepily. "Thank you," she said to me.
　"What for?"
　"I was able to sleep last night thanks to you."
　She stood up and drew a magic circle over herself. Light enveloped her body, and her clothes appeared. I got out of bed and put on my white uniform.
　"You saw the dream, right?" I asked.
　"I did."
　"Do you think you reincarnated as a god after that?"
　Arcana thought quietly. Her expression seemed almost somber. "Syrica can't turn a demon into a god."
　"That's true. I wouldn't be able to reincarnate into a god myself. However, the dreamworld Arcana had her source altered in a dragon's womb. She was

targeted by them for her source—the dragon core—so she wasn't a normal existence to begin with. It's not entirely out of the question."

But if it was true, her reincarnation had probably been the result of many miraculous coincidences coinciding. There wasn't enough information to know for sure yet.

"Pope Golroana called me Militia."

"If that's the case, then you already found me two thousand years ago."

"We still don't know the truth," Arcana mumbled uneasily.

"Do you want to check?"

"How?"

"There's a way to confirm whether you're Militia, but it won't return your memories. If you're fine with learning the truth, then it may be worth trying."

"I think I'd like to know," Arcana mumbled, but then she shook her head. "No. I want to know," she said firmly.

"Then come."

I left the room with Arcana following beside me. As I climbed the stairs, I contacted the others via Leaks. *"Today's Demon King Training is suspended. We'll be going to Gaelahesta. Come to the castle's training arena once you're ready."*

We walked until a double door came into view. I opened it to reveal a large room. This was the training arena. It had been constructed to allow for a decent level of magic and sword training. I walked to the center and turned to Arcana.

"Origin magic cannot affect that which it borrows from. If I use Militia as an origin to cast it, we can find out for sure if you are Militia or not."

"Will that apply to a god who abandoned their name?"

"That's what I'm unsure of. Without your true name, you may not be classed as the exact same being as before, and the spell could have an effect on you anyway. But the fact you can use the Moon of Creation means there is some connection between you."

"Will you decide based on how much I'm affected?"

I nodded. "The magic I can wield depends on the origin. In the case of using the Goddess of Creation as an origin, it becomes very difficult to control my magic. I'll unfortunately be limited to attack spells."

Chapter 31 — Contradicting Memories

Simply put, the borrowed magic spiraled out of control. I would have to subdue it by force and unleash it.

"It's okay. Do what you believe is best." Arcana moved a short distance away from me and lowered her anti-magic.

"Here goes."

I drew a magic circle and named the Goddess of Creation Militia as the origin. Black lightning crackled and wrapped around my right arm. It was Jirasd. The lightning swelled to the extreme, exceeding my expectations as it rumbled and cracked over the entire arena. The next moment, it struck with enough force to destroy the room.

The air crackled as the mountain of rubble scattered around us settled. I had managed to suppress the spell at the last moment, so Arcana was unharmed.

"What's wrong?" she asked, staring at me curiously.

"Hmm. It failed."

Origin magic was difficult to control without a proper understanding of the chosen origin. It was even harder when that origin was a god—even channeling a keeper was enough to make the magic unstable. Successfully casting the spell was a demanding feat. Calling upon the Goddess of Creation made it all the more challenging to succeed, but I was normally able to control the rampaging magic by letting it run wild. A good example was Egil Grone Angdroa—the spell combined the Goddess of Creation and Goddess of Destruction's magic at maximum output to create a stable equilibrium. However, dropping that output to Jirasd's level required delicate control that made stability near impossible. Still, if I knew Militia's source well enough, I shouldn't have had a problem. After all, I'd been able to use it two thousand years ago. That could only mean one thing.

"I've forgotten something, or perhaps I've remembered something wrong."

"About the Goddess of Creation?"

"Yes. Under these conditions, we won't be able to determine whether you're Militia."

Arcana kept her mouth for a moment, then opened it again. "There's no helping it."

"At least we know there's a discrepancy in the Militia I remember and the real Militia."

But what had I forgotten?

"You'll remember once we find the God of Traces."

"Do you know where he is?"

"I do not."

The god had dwelled in the underground world all this time. He wouldn't return to the Divine Realm so easily.

"Whoa, what happened here? It's a wreck," Sasha said as she entered the arena.

"Was it Jirasd?" Misha asked curiously beside her.

"Sorry for the wait! We're ready to leave whenever!"

"Preparations...complete."

Eleonore and Zeshia had arrived too. Lay and Misa were right behind them.

"It'd be nice if things could be resolved peacefully."

"Aha ha, if only."

Just then, the tap of a cane could be heard. "Bwa ha ha! Things have taken another interesting turn, I see. The Netherworld King and the Cursed King, here in the underground world? I was wondering where they'd run off to, but who would have expected them to be preparing to defy the Demon King?!" Eldmed laughed heartily. "That sure was a risky choice. Wouldn't you agree, Mr. Shin?"

"I only have one opinion: it was foolish," Shin replied beside him.

"Indeed, indeed, they are fools, but that's why this is so interesting! After all, the wise would never defy the Demon King!"

Eldmed's vaguely treacherous words constricted his throat and had him excitedly struggling for breath.

"Say, Anos Voldigoad," he wheezed, "this new opponent is formidable enough to gather your subordinates beneath him, no?"

"The demon named Ceris is apparently my father. Don't let your guard down."

Eldmed's mouth twisted with delight. "I see. I see..."

"Well, the blood relation doesn't matter. The problem is what that man is plotting. Last night, Arcana and I had a dream in which he had a rather twisted view of good and evil."

Chapter 31 — Contradicting Memories

On top of that, he had joined forces with two of the Four Evil Kings, and he possessed powerful enough magic to destroy the God of Traces.

"Also, he's from Gadeciola, so he probably knows something about the Goddess of Absurdity."

Sasha's gaze harshened, and Misha squeezed her hand. Pointing at them, Ceris had addressed them as the Goddess of Absurdity.

"I'll go hear him out. If he's a fool, I'll destroy him then and there."

I doubted he would give me a proper answer, but there were still things we couldn't explain. At the very least, it was worth checking out.

"Let's go."

I drew a magic circle for Gatom. Everyone glanced at it and drew their own. We activated the circles and teleported, and the next moment, we were standing before Everastanzetta.

Arcana held out her hand, and the front gate opened. We proceeded through it, heading straight for the heart of the Institute of the Gods. At the end of a corridor, I opened a door to a circular room—it was the Holy Seat Hall with its eight seats positioned at regular intervals.

"Hey, you're here."

Ceris was waiting there. The Netherworld King and the Cursed King stood beside him.

"I have a question for you," I immediately said to Ceris. "What is your goal?"

"It's hard to put it in a single phrase, but let's see." He smiled good-naturedly. "First off, I'm thinking of overthrowing Jiordal."

§ 32. The God of Lies and Betrayal

Ceris spoke with the lighthearted tone of someone announcing they were disposing of a broken chair. That being said, it didn't appear to be a threat or a bluff. He was serious about overthrowing Jiordal.

"That's rather hasty of you. Or have you been preparing up till now?"

"Your unexpected arrival was rather troubling, Anos," he said, not seeming troubled at all. "What we prepared for was to destroy the God of Traces. The plan was to have that accomplished yesterday."

"I understand harboring animosity towards the gods. However, there are many gods out there. Revalschned was sleeping. What reason did you have to destroy him?"

"A god is a god," he replied simply. "Don't you think that's enough reason?"

"I do not. A sleeping god poses no danger. Just let him sleep."

"Then let me put it this way," he said swiftly. "The God of Traces is the guardian god of the underground world. The underground world will never coexist peacefully with the world aboveground. They will eventually invade beyond their dome, so I'm preparing for that moment by dealing with them now. I'm just a demon that wants to protect my homeland."

Despite the patriotic statement, his words sounded light and detached. It was almost like he didn't care if either world were destroyed.

"If I try to overthrow Jiordal, Revalschned will show up to protect it. If I can destroy either one, two threats to the surface will be erased." Ceris held up two fingers.

"You sure enjoy conflict."

"Oh, I'd never. There's no better outcome than resolving things peacefully, but the other side doesn't seem to think the same. Peace sure is difficult to achieve, huh?" He smiled again. "You're the king of Dilhade right now, Anos. Won't you join hands with me to protect your homeland?"

"If that's what you want, then obey me. I'll protect Dilhade without destroying Jiordal or Revalschned."

Ceris sighed in disappointment. "Dear me. What a rebellious child. It's hard to believe we're related."

"I concur. I never imagined such a weak man could be my father."

His eyes widened curiously for a moment. "Oh?"

"If you want to call yourself my father, prove it with your strength. A coward that has to kill innocent civilians to protect his homeland has no business calling himself the father of the Demon King."

"You're too naive, Anos, but you are still a child. In a way, this was inevitable."

"Naive? You merely lack capacity. We may be connected by blood, but my real father in this life is far more broad-minded than you."

Ceris narrowed his eyes. "You hopeless child. I didn't want to stoop to your level during our long-awaited reunion, but it seems we need to deepen our parent-child relationship."

"Oh?"

"How about a bet? If the desire to overthrow Jiordal rises within you before the end of today, it's my win. If that happens, you'll turn a blind eye to my destroying Jiordal and Revalschned."

"Interesting. Then if I don't feel the urge to overthrow Jiordal, you'll keep your hands off Jiordal and Revalschned."

I drew a magic circle for Zecht, and Ceris signed it without hesitation. Did he know some kind of truth that would make me change my mind? Then again, perhaps this was nothing more than a game to the deranged man.

"Incidentally, Anos, I see you've brought a blasphemous god," Ceris said suddenly. "I really do think you'd agree with Gadeciola's teachings." He looked over at Sasha and Misha. "I never expected the Goddess of Absurdity to split

Chapter 32 — The God of Lies and Betrayal

into two and reincarnate on the surface. It's no wonder I couldn't find you down here."

"Unfortunately for you, those two are my subordinates. I didn't bring them because of their past, and I have my doubts about whether that's the truth." I glared at Ceris, searching for his true intentions. "After all, that information came from you."

"How much do you know about the Goddess of Absurdity?" he asked calmly.

"A blasphemous god is a god that opposes other gods, no? I've heard that she isn't very highly regarded in the underground world, but if this is about Gadeciola, Arcana didn't know much about that."

At that, Ceris smiled kindly. "Genedonov, Goddess of Absurdity, bears an order that opposes order. She defies her own order, deceives gods and mortals alike, and turns against them. She is the god of lies and betrayal."

Sasha's gaze turned grim. Misha gently took her hand and squeezed it.

"Genedonov was a god of Jiordal. Legends say that she, alongside her devout followers, fought in the very first Selection Trial in order to bless the underground world. As a result of her victory, pledge jewels were introduced to this desolate land. Jiordal became a powerful nation with vassal states and flourished for a long time."

So Genedonov had been the first Selection God. The fact that she adhered to the order of the Selection Trial meant that she hadn't been the Goddess of Absurdity at the time.

"But Genedonov betrayed Jiordal and took half the pledge jewels with her to Agatha. She was originally a god of Agatha, you see—she had been deceiving the pope of Jiordal the entire time. Thanks to that, Jiordal went to war with the newly empowered Agatha in order to retrieve the jewels. Many lives were lost, and despite their religious differences, the two exhausted nations agreed to avoid further conflict with a ceasefire."

He continued in a matter-of-fact tone. "Peace prevailed for some time. Draconids survived in the harsh underground world through the power of summoned dragons and gods. But this time, Genedonov betrayed Agatha. No, it wasn't just Agatha. The god decided that order was wrong and turned her sword on order itself. She rebelled against both draconids and the gods and eventually became known as the blasphemous god, the Goddess of Absurdity."

I could understand her view that order was wrong, I supposed.

"Soon after, draconids from Jiordal, Agatha, and other small nations began to gather, having lost their belief in the gods. As the god that opposed all gods, Genedonov led them to war against Jiordal and Agatha. Eventually, she gained a large enough following, and Gadeciola, Kingdom of the Supreme Dragon, was born."

So the nonbelievers had gathered around the god that opposed gods. The Phantom Knights were probably like them—on the outside, at least.

"However, the Goddess of Absurdity betrayed even her own people. In the war against the gods, she would shoot her own allies in the back. In the end, Genedonov was slain by the people of Gadeciola. The one who delivered the finishing blow was declared the overlord. But in the Goddess of Absurdity's absence, Gadeciola suffered an enormous blow…"

"I don't get it. Gadeciola still worships the god that betrayed them, no? I was told they believe in the blasphemous god."

"That's right. Genedonov was a god of lies and betrayal. Gadeciola worships her as the god that cannot be believed in. That's because they don't believe in the gods, you see, but as long as they live underground, they have to rely on the power of the gods to survive. Thus, the people of Gadeciola live by the teaching of not believing in the Goddess of Absurdity—in other words, believing that Genedonov will always betray them."

It was confusing to say the least, but borrowing the power of the gods they didn't believe in was the only way they could survive in the underground world.

"In short, a god that always lies is the same as a god that always tells the truth."

"That's right. So you should be careful trusting those little followers of yours. The Goddess of Absurdity will always betray you."

Sasha glared sharply at him. "Unfortunately, even if I was the Goddess of Absurdity, that would never happen."

"We are Anos's allies," Misha said plainly but firmly. "We always wish for his victory."

Ceris smiled brightly. "I believe he said just yesterday that the lowest scum are those who pretend to be good people. Am I wrong?"

Sasha bared her teeth and snarled. I held out a hand to stop her from leaping at Ceris.

Chapter 32 — The God of Lies and Betrayal

"That wouldn't happen," I said.

"I don't blame you for believing that. People see what they want to see, even if it means turning a blind eye to reality. I suppose that applies even to the Demon King."

"Those who turn away do so because they're powerless. Inconvenient realities can be destroyed with a glare and changed into ideals."

Ceris shrugged. "The Goddess of Absurdity will always betray you. She will even betray your ideals. Genedonov is the god of lies and betrayal. Everyone who once believed was deceived and betrayed without fail. You will realize the meaning of that one day, and it won't be too long now." He smiled again. It was a smile that seemed far from genuine. "I'm worried for you, Anos. You believe that power allows you to make all your ideals come true. This may sound harsh, but it's my duty as a parent to teach my grown child reality."

"And?"

Ceris narrowed his eyes and spread his arms as though to welcome me. "I know it may be hard to accept me right now. Though it was short, we once spent some time together as parent and child. I'm sure my words will be able to reach you when you remember that."

"Don't get too delusional."

I took a few steps towards him. Arcana matched my pace. The Netherworld King and the Cursed King braced themselves for combat, but Ceris stopped them with a wave.

"Do you know her?" I said, signaling Arcana with a glance.

"She's the Selection God you made a pact with, I assume. The pope of Jiordal claims this nameless god to be Militia, Goddess of Creation, but I don't know the truth of that claim."

"If you wish to act like my father, you should at least remember my little sister."

He was convinced I had no memories, so I made my declaration boldly to unsettle him.

"There's one thing I do remember: that time we had fun playing with fire." I laughed at the blue eyes watching me. Then I stared into his abyss to catch every shift in his heart and said, "Did you enjoy the Bonfire of Judgment, Ceris?"

§ 33. Flames That Reach the Sky

"You remembered," Ceris mumbled. "Or did you really?" He stared straight at me, his expression unchanged. He showed no sign of discomposure, and his tone was as calm as always.

"I've never met your little sister before. In fact, this is my first time hearing of such a thing. Do you know what that means?"

"It means you're lying."

Ceris's eyes narrowed. "Perhaps. But it could also mean your memories are wrong." He pointed at me. "The Goddess of Creation meddled with multiple layers of your memory. It's only natural for one to believe the first memories they manage to recall, so she must have prepared fake memories for when that happened."

I couldn't imagine that this shady man was telling the truth, but it was possible he was actually telling the truth to trick me into turning away from it. At the very least, I couldn't dismiss the possibility that my memories were incorrect.

"In that light, the nameless god you exchanged a pact with could potentially be the Goddess of Creation. What could she be up to?" He looked at Arcana.

"I seek salvation. That is all I require as a god," Arcana replied.

"Really now?" Ceris continued before she could answer. "Just now, you mentioned the Bonfire of Judgment. If that is one of your memories, you must have seen it aboveground."

"Yes."

"In that case, I have something interesting to show you. Follow me."

Ceris used Gatom. I saw through the formula with my Eyes and conveyed it to Sasha and the others using Leaks. The Netherworld King and the Cursed King teleported soon after Ceris, and we followed behind them.

One white flash later, we arrived on one of the middle floors of Everastanzetta. The room was so vast, the walls were out of sight. Endless rows of pillars and torches lined the room, and an eye-catching silver fire stood at its center. Ceris stood before the flames.

"This is the Bonfire of Judgment," he said, raising one hand. "This bonfire, placed here by the gods themselves, only exists here in Everastanzetta. Now think carefully—why would it have been aboveground?"

Both the room and Bonfire of Judgment were exactly as they had appeared in the dream.

"Perhaps Everastanzetta once stood aboveground," he said, immediately offering an answer to his own question. "But would a castle with a three-dimensional magic circle as big as Delsgade really be able to remain hidden from the Eyes of you and the other demons of that era?"

Indeed, it was hard to imagine myself overlooking it. Perhaps I might have as a child but certainly not as an adult. Many others of that era would have noticed too, so it didn't make sense if my memories were merely sealed.

"Let's assume Arcana truly is your sister. That would mean that after the two of you were separated, she became a god of the underground world, where you miraculously reunited two thousand years later. What a moving story! It's enough to bring me to tears." Of course, Ceris remained emotionless. "Could such a convenient thing really happen by chance? Gods govern order. Order means everything is inevitable to some degree. Are the memories you recall truly consistent with reality?"

Indeed, there were some inconsistencies. In the first Selection Trial, which had been held underground, the first proxy had been selected and pledge jewels had been brought to the underground world. That was the history recorded on the stone tablets in Everastanzetta, and Ceris had said the same earlier. The underground world had come to be two thousand years ago, after my reincarnation. If it had been around before that, I definitely would have

Chapter 33 — Flames That Reach the Sky

noticed it when I'd been wiping out the dragons. So why had pledge jewels existed during my childhood? The three draconids that had invaded our cabin had clearly used Azept to summon dragons into their bodies.

"Perhaps it's possible to explain the inconsistencies, but how many miracles would it take for that to happen?"

If pledge jewels had existed aboveground over two thousand years ago, their existence would have had to be hidden this entire time, and the summoning magic that depended on the jewels had to have been kept a secret. It would have been a coincidence that Arcana had been reborn as a god and a coincidence that she had discarded her name. She had coincidentally reunited with me and coincidentally agreed to our pact. The chance of all of that happening indeed sounded like a miracle.

"Of course, there's nothing wrong with miracles, but if a miracle did happen, then the gods might have been involved."

"So what if they were?"

"I know the past that you've forgotten. I could fill the blanks of your memory, and I could do it in a way that would make you sure of the truth." Ceris drew the magic circle for Zecht. "Do you wish to know?"

"State your price."

He raised a hand. Another magic circle appeared over the Bonfire of Judgment. It was for Limnet. Reflected in the flames was a distant view of Jiordal. Jiorhaze Cathedral was the size of a mere speck.

"I received a report from one of my undercover knights. The song of the Divine Dragon has grown louder."

He snapped his fingers, and sound started playing through Limnet. The song of the Divine Dragon, which constantly echoed through Jiordal like the murmur of a stream, was currently echoing loudly throughout the nation.

The next moment, the cathedral went up in flames. It was songfire. The flames were far larger and were flaring up with far greater intensity than when I'd fought Golroana. The purifying fire reached into the air, melting holes into the dome above. But it didn't slow there. The songfire continued burning past the dome, rising higher and higher.

Sasha looked shocked. "Wait, isn't that...?"

"The direction of Midhaze," Misha murmured.

The songfire suddenly subsided. Pieces of the broken dome came crumbling down in a rain of stone and dirt.

"It seems the first shot has been blocked by the barrier shielding Midhaze's underground. I can't see it clearly because of the Divine Dragon's song, but a barrier created by you would only be half worn down by that, right?"

The magic barrier surrounding the underground of Midhaze was by no means weak, but the songfire had carried tremendous power behind it. In my absence, the city wouldn't be able to withstand multiple blasts.

"At most, it'll hold for one more shot. The third will cause the barrier to break."

"The increased volume of the Divine Dragon's song is probably to prevent anyone from using Gatom to approach whoever's casting the songfire."

With the song this loud, we wouldn't be able to see the situation with our Magic Eyes, much less teleport towards it.

"Now that you know what's happening, I have a proposal for you, Anos. I am going to cast a spell to destroy Jiorhaze. The pope is the culprit behind the songfire."

"Even if the songfire originated from Jiorhaze, there's no guarantee he's still there."

"Indeed. That's why I'm going to destroy not just the cathedral, but the entirety of Jiorhaze. Do you understand? Without a kingdom to protect and followers to save, the pope will have no reason to fight. If destroying Jiorhaze doesn't work, then Jiordal is next."

Ceris looked completely unaffected as he spoke. "You can easily protect Dilhade without dirtying your own hands—you just have to allow me to destroy the threat. Of course, I'll wait until all your followers in the city have fled. Then, once it's all over, I will tell you the truth of your past." He added conditions to the Zecht. "If you sign this, Dilhade's enemies will perish, your nation will be protected, and you will learn of your lost past. There'll no longer be any reason to go after the God of Traces. That sounds good, doesn't it?"

"It does sound like the smart choice to make," I said.

Ceris smiled.

"But it's far from ideal." I glared outside with my Magic Eyes, searching for the closest point that Gatom could reach. "It's as the Zecht says, Ceris.

Chapter 33 — Flames That Reach the Sky

I have no intention of destroying Jiordal. Back off from Jiordal and Revalschned."

"You have until the end of today to sign. You may still change your mind."

"That's not happening," I stated firmly, drawing a magic circle for Gatom. It would be a rather difficult journey to make, so I extended my hand for Misha and the others to grab on.

"Shin, Eldmed, stand watch over those two. Ceris was the only one who signed the Zecht, so they could still attack Jiorhaze at any moment."

"Understood."

Shin took a few steps forward and drew the Pillage Blade and the Sword of Severance from a magic circle.

Ceris looked on calmly. "Just the two of them? I can't attack Jiordal because of our Zecht right now, but that doesn't apply to my men. Wouldn't it be better for you to stay here and send your followers to put out the songfire?" He smiled as if he were doing me a favor. "Otherwise, you may regret your decision."

"Don't underestimate them. Even if you do have the power to destroy a nation, my right-hand man wouldn't fall to the likes of you." I glanced at the Conflagration King, who was grinning behind me. "And this one here's a pain to silence."

Eldmed waved a hand in denial.

"When I faced him, I had every chance to destroy him, yet here he stands here with that arrogant look on his face. Hopefully you can avoid falling for his tricks."

Eldmed tapped his cane against the floor. Shin took that as the cue to send his magic into his demon swords, drawing the attention of Ceris and the other Evil Kings.

"I suggest you remain still unless you want your head to be separated from your neck," Shin said as we vanished. We had teleported close to Jiordal.

The Netherworld King pointed his crimson demon spear at Shin. "If you think the two of you can take on the three of us, you would be quite arrogant."

The Cursed King pulled Netrauvus from a magic circle and nocked three arrows at once. "Watch me, Jiste. I'll punish the people who hurt you!"

"Good grief."

Sighing, Ceris raised a hand and drew a layered magic circle. He was merely drawing a spell formula, yet the air around him crackled and trembled, shaking the whole of Everastanzetta. Purple lightning escaped the magic sphere and spread through their surroundings.

On the verge of confrontation, Ceris and his subordinates glared at Shin and Eldmed.

"Bwa ha ha! Who would have foreseen a class reunion like this in the underground world!" Eldmed started walking forward leisurely, exposing himself to their weapons and magic without a care. "This sure brings back memories. You're as stubborn as ever, Netherworld King. Cursed King, you're even more off your rocker. Now if only the Scarlet Stele King were here, we could have had a fun little chat. Well, at least we have a substitute."

Eldmed leaned on the cane in his hands. "I, the Conflagration King, have been searching high and low for an enemy to the Demon King when you were here all along, Ceris Voldigoad. I see, I see." He smirked suggestively, as though he knew all about Ceris.

"What are you trying to say?"

"Oh, no. I'm actually trying to say *nothing*, but at this rate, I could slip up. That aside, being outnumbered against an opponent that can destroy an entire nation sounds rather unfavorable for us. How about we make a Zecht where I buy you time in exchange for my silence regarding your secrets?" Eldmed smiled gleefully. "What do you say? You wouldn't want your plan to be spoiled here either, right? I've finally found a worthy enemy for him, and it won't be any fun if you don't act the part."

"You're an interesting one," Ceris replied with a smile. "Of course, I have my secrets—things a child need not know—but I'm pretty sure you're not privy to them."

"That's exactly right! But on the slightest chance that I *do* know, you wouldn't want me to say anything, right? I'm quite the chatterbox, so you'd be better off silencing me sooner than later. Otherwise, an unexpected situation might ruin your plan." Eldmed returned Ceris's thin smile with a smug grin. "It'll just be ten minutes. If you and your men can wait ten minutes, I will sign a Zecht to protect that information with my life."

It was unclear if the Conflagration King truly knew anything or was

Chapter 33 — Flames That Reach the Sky

merely bluffing—but if he did know something, he would certainly use it for his own advantage as soon as he had the chance. Buying time for a powerful opponent didn't count as defying me, and he could foster new danger towards me at the same time.

"In fact, I would beg to sign that Zecht," Eldmed added cheerfully.

§ 34. The Power of God and Demon

The Bonfire of Judgment burned fiercely. Ceris and his two subordinates were still glaring at Shin and Eldmed. The Conflagration King opened his mouth to break the tension.

"Bwa ha ha! What's wrong, Ceris Voldigoad? If you won't sign the Zecht, you'd better silence me quickly—unless you want to make this another boring battle during which the Demon King tramples over everyone, that is."

Ceris watched Eldmed calmly as he continued chattering.

"Or is it part of your plan for me to reveal *that* to everyone here?"

"Say it, and we can find out," Ceris replied, unperturbed.

Eldmed cackled. "Precisely. That is the correct answer. Signing the Zecht in a fluster would only imply you have a secret. I expected no less from the man who will become the enemy of the Demon King! Then I shall speak without holding back. You are— Gwahah!"

A crimson demon spear pierced Eldmed's throat.

"You're careless as always. You make less sense than the Demon King."

The Netherworld King pushed Dehiddatem forward, the Crimson Blood Spear traversing through dimensions to reach Eldmed in an instant. The head of the spear pierced the Conflagration King's throat.

But despite being covered in blood, Eldmed remained smiling. "Did you stab me because I was careless, or did you stab me because you didn't want me to finish what I was about to say?"

"What nonsense."

Aeges tried to withdraw his spear and lower it, but the Conflagration King grabbed the end before he could do so.

"Face the wrath of my arrows and perish."

Kaihilam released three arrows from the Demon Bow. Pinned in place by Dehiddatem, the Conflagration King had no means of evading. He was struck in the head, heart, and abdomen.

"Curse him, Netrauvus."

At Kaihilam's words, black mist rose from Eldmed's wounds. The demon bow's curse ate away at his body, weighing down his magical and physical strength.

With a grunt, Aeges thrust his spear forward again, making fresh blood spurt from the Conflagration King's body. "Are you sure about this, Thousand Swords?" he asked. "If you keep your eyes on our commander, your comrade will end up dead."

But Shin held his stance against Ceris. "Feel free to finish him off," he said coldly. "We may fight on the same side now, but the Conflagration King will turn against my liege. Having him eliminated here would be a blessing."

Ceris made not one careless move before the sharp bloodlust before him. It would be three against one once the Conflagration King was out of the picture, so he must have thought waiting out the battle would be advantageous.

"You should keep your guard up yourself, Netherworld King," Shin said. "If the man were a fool who exposed himself easily, he would have died by my blade long ago."

The Conflagration King smirked. The divine words to create a miracle fell from Eldmed's lips. "Fools who spit on the heavens, face your punishment for defying order. Behold the image of god." Eldmed was enveloped in light as his magic swelled to a phenomenal level. "Bwa ha ha ha ha!"

His whole body transformed. His hair turned gold, his Magic Eyes became a glowing red, and particles of magic gathered at his back to form wings of light.

Everastanzetta shook with a deafening rumble. The true form of a god and his tremendous magic burst into the atmosphere, shaking the world. Dehiddatem snapped and Netrauvus's arrows crumbled away in the face of his overwhelming magic wards.

The Netherworld King immediately thrust his hand through the left side

Chapter 34 — The Power of God and Demon

of his chest and created a new demon spear with his blood. His single Magic Eye stared into the Conflagration King's abyss. "Hmph. You..."

"Bwa ha ha! Do you get it now, Netherworld King? I have finally obtained what I have sought for the past two thousand years!" The Conflagration King took off his top hat and juggled it in his hands. Each time it changed hands, it increased in number. "But to be honest, I'm not quite used to this divine body yet. Which gods come out is still a roll of the dice. Do we have any bets?" Eldmed threw ten top hats into the air. "I, Eldmed, the Conflagration King, order you in the name of the Heavenly Father: be born, ten keepers of reason."

Glittering light burst from the top hats like confetti and streamers. Keepers began to form like a party trick. The keepers that appeared wore pure-white robes with hoods that covered their faces. They wore white gloves on their hands and each held a Scythe of the Timekeeper—because every one of them was Eugo La Raviaz.

"Oh my, who would have guessed it?! Just when I wanted to buy time, I summoned ten Keepers of Time! It's almost like a cheat!"

By making a pledge with Naya for her to do the summoning, Eldmed had become capable of creating divine bodies at any time. He must have been testing his order out behind my back.

"Now, why don't we relocate to the Garden of Time?"

The world turned white. The floor, ceiling, and walls—even the Bonfire of Judgment—turned white. Created by Eugo La Raviaz to regulate the order of time, the Garden of Time was a divine domain rid of any outside elements.

"You should be familiar with this. If you defeat Eugo La Raviaz in this garden separated from the rest of the world, you will arrive several hours in the future. There is no way of returning to your original time, and everything will be over by then." Eldmed turned to Ceris. "Well? Do you feel like signing the Zecht yet? If you wait just ten minutes, you'll not only have my silence, but freedom from this place too! Offer available for a limited time only!"

"Dear me. Did you think Gadeciola would yield to mere keepers?" Ceris held one hand out over his spherical magic circle. Purple lightning flooded the area, striking all around them. "*Gavest.*"

Countless bolts struck across the white world and began to swell in size. With an ominous rumble, they dyed the white world dark purple, as though to force the frozen Garden of Time back into motion. The floor, ceiling, and walls were torn apart by the lightning as the Garden of Time blew apart. The world regained color, and they returned to their original world without a single Eugo La Raviaz being defeated.

"It's as you can see."

"How wonderful!"

The Conflagration King beamed and applauded at how easily Ceris had defeated the Keepers of Time. "But you'll eventually have to pay for all the order you defy. You cannot return to the exact time we left. A minute has already passed, you know?"

The Keepers of Time created another white space around them.

"I know that isn't your limit, Ceris Voldigoad. Show me your true power! Otherwise, sign the Zecht!"

Ceris immediately fired Gavest, destroying the Garden of Time.

"Now it's been two minutes. The Zecht only asked for ten minutes. How much time do you think I can buy at this rate?"

"Two minutes is all it'll take," the Netherworld King said. All ten Eugo La Raviaz found their bodies pierced by his crimson spear.

"Crimson Blood Spear, first hidden art," Aeges muttered quietly, "*Dimension Drive.*"

Holes opened in their chests. All ten Eugo La Raviaz were sucked into those holes and vanished. Frozen in time, their bodies couldn't be hurt, so they were instead flung to the end of time.

"You might have obtained the power of a god, but don't get too full of yourself."

"The Divine Sword will bring you judgment, Netherworld King."

Gold flames burst from the Conflagration King's hand. The flames formed the shape of a golden sword, Roduier, which shot in the direction of Aeges.

"Hmph!"

Dehiddatem struck Roduier and knocked it away, but the Divine Sword turned in the air and slashed at the Netherworld King once again. The golden sword that had once cornered Shin attacked the one-eyed demon with a fury.

"Crimson Blood Spear, second hidden art—*Dimension Burst.*"

One brandish of a red spear later, the Divine Sword flew to the end of time too.

Chapter 34 — The Power of God and Demon

"Bwa ha ha! I should have expected as much of the Netherworld King. I shall answer your expectations!"

Pillars of gold flames rose around them, half of which transformed into dozens of Divine Swords that shot towards the Netherworld King. As Aeges braced himself, black mist drifted before him. Roduier pierced through the mist.

"Gah..."

The golden sword had pierced the body of the Cursed King, Kaihilam. Once one sword made contact, the rest of the swords were drawn towards his body and pierced him one after another.

"Ah! Aaagh!"

Black mist flowed from the bloodless wounds and coiled around the Divine Swords like a sinister curse.

"You have wounded me, Conflagration King," Kaihilam said with resentment, "and I won't forgive you for it."

At the same time, the black mist formed a magic circle and activated. It was Degded, a curse that used magic-inflicted wounds as a catalyst to curse the owner of the magic and draw that magic towards the caster.

"Bwa ha ha! I see you're still a masochist, Kaihilam. No worries, no worries. I, the Conflagration King, will play along with your fetish all you want!"

Eldmed drew a magic circle with his cane. The gold fire that emerged transformed into more Divine Swords, which were all drawn towards Kaihilam's body like a magnet. Each one that stabbed him released more black mist from the wound. Most of Kaihilam's body had turned black by this point.

"I know your tricks, Kaihilam. If your entire body turns into mist, Degded will be lifted! The Demon King told me himself!"

"I won't wait that long, Conflagration King."

A profuse amount of fresh blood sprayed the air. Countless crimson spears burst from within Eldmed's body. He had been pierced from the inside.

"Crimson Blood Spear, third hidden art—*Fang from Within*."

Aeges rotated a tipless Dehiddatem. The spears protruding from Eldmed's body started tearing him to shreds. Any attack or healing magic Eldmed cast would be drawn to Kaihilam through the curse. He was unable to heal himself or counterattack—or so the Netherworld King believed.

"With this, it's over—"

Just as Aeges swung the rotating Dehiddatem to make the finishing blow, the spear flew out of his hands. Aeges fell to his knees weakly, as though all his power had suddenly been drained.

"What...What is this?" he mumbled, using the last of his strength to look around. The floor was burning with the golden flames. Hidden within the flames were forty-four Hourglasses of Conflagration. All the sand within them had fallen, activating the curse to steal the Netherworld King's life.

"Bwa ha ha! The order of the Heavenly Father might have been usurped, but Kaihilam failed to curse my own magic."

Eldmed had used his own magic to cast Ei Chael and heal his wounds. To avoid drawing attention until his curse activated, he had continuously allowed the Netherworld King's hidden arts to strike him.

"A fatal blunder..." Aeges collapsed to the floor. He had used Ingall, but as long as the Hourglasses of Conflagration remained active, he would immediately die upon revival.

The Conflagration King tapped his cane on the floor and laughed. "You like to remind people not to take the gods lightly, but you forgot all about me, the Conflagration King!"

§ 35. A Battle of Truth and Lies

Instead of reviving the Netherworld King immediately after he'd been defeated, Ceris held out his hand towards Eldmed.

"*Gavest.*"

Ceris's voice echoed alongside the deafening roar of raging thunder. Purple lightning pierced the Conflagration King's body faster than he could respond, mercilessly eroding his divine form.

"Bwa ha ha! You've finally noticed it. Why don't we play some more, Ceris Voldigoad, father of the Demon King?"

The next moment, Ceris stood before the Conflagration King. His hand reached out and seized Eldmed's face. "Playtime's over," he said in a friendly tone.

"You've finally left an opening," a voice responded.

A bare blade glinted. Having read Ceris's breath to determine the moment he would step forward, Shin slashed at the spherical magic circle with perfect timing.

"Think again," Ceris replied.

Purple lightning flickered. Rumbling thunder accompanied the Gavest that struck Shin's Pillage Blade, snapping it in half. The reason Gilionojes had snapped so easily was because Shin's magic had vanished at the same moment.

Deltoros, the cursed demon sword that absorbed magic, became nothing more than a cold yet beautiful blade. Its hidden art, which could decapitate an enemy in a single swing, was faster than the speed of light.

"Sword of Severance, second hidden art—*Decapitation.*"

"*Galvedul.*"

But Ceris didn't move one step in the face of the fearsome hidden art. He swung his right arm up at it. The purple lightning flowing from the spherical magic circle wrapped around his arm and became a giant battle-axe that could both attack and defend. The axe met the incoming Sword of Severance like a bolt of lightning.

Deltoros's blade collided with the lightning axe with an earsplitting boom. Ceris's Galvedul was split in half, while Shin's Deltoros was charred black.

"Want to try again?" Ceris poured magic into his hand to repair the broken Galvedul.

"Bwa ha ha! Splendid, just splendid! There aren't many people out there who can do that to Shin Reglia's sword!"

From behind Ceris, gold flames rose from Eldmed's hand.

"Now, show me more of your power!"

A Divine Sword shot towards Ceris but veered off course partway.

"Kaihilam's Degded is still in effect," Ceris said.

"Which saves me the effort of handing it over in person. Right, Shin Reglia?"

Shin grabbed Roduier as it was flying towards Kaihilam.

"You should have no trouble using it."

The master of the sword was overwritten in an instant. Shin charged at Ceris and swung down on Galvedul with crushing force. The fast and heavy battle-axe of lightning clashed with Shin's Roduier. They struck each other three times, each strike just as loud as the earlier impact, but this time, both weapons were unharmed.

In one flowing motion, Shin broke out of their deadlock and knocked the battle-axe away. Galvedul was powerful, but when it came to swordsmanship, Shin was far superior. No sooner had he stepped within striking range than Roduier flashed between them. He had aimed at Ceris's right shoulder—and severed his Galvedul arm from his body. Blood sprayed through the air as Ceris's right arm sailed in an arch.

"Oh?"

Ceris backed away, but Shin moved after him in an attempt to sink

Chapter 35 — A Battle of Truth and Lies

Roduier into his heart. However, Galvedul came swinging down with a thunk. Ceris's severed right arm had moved by itself, using the lightning axe to cut off Shin's right arm, which was wielding Roduier. Ceris retrieved his own arm and reattached it to his body.

"Did you think I'd finally left an opening?" he said with a smile, but he quickly realized something and looked at the arm on the ground. The arm turned into mist.

At the same time, Shin's body also turned to mist. Then the mist split and transformed back into two copies of Shin. Ceris looked baffled. There were plenty of spells out there that could fool the Eyes, but he couldn't see any magic circle when he peered into the abyss of Shin's body.

"Tee hee hee!"

The high-pitched laughter of children rang through the air.

"You missed; you missed!"

"We're not Sword Uncle!"

"Common sense! Common sense!"

Tiny winged fairies called titi fluttered around the two copies of Shin. Footsteps sounded, drawing Ceris to look behind himself.

"They're children from my homeland. When I told them I was going to an unknown, underground world, they insisted on coming along."

A third Shin appeared a short distance away. Just before Shin had been cut by Galvedul, Gennul, the Wolf of Hiding, who had also come along, had spirited him away and swapped him out for titi.

"We learned…"

"…a new prank!"

"Which one…"

"…is the real one?"

The titi turned into mist that covered the entire area. The three copies of Shin also melted into the mist, transforming into twenty-two copies of Shin. Even by straining the Eyes, it was impossible to tell who the real one was.

"Spirits of Aharthern…" Ceris said.

"Yes," said both Shin and the fake Shins at the same time. "Although you may not be very familiar with them after all that time you've spent underground."

"What does it matter? If I can't tell the difference, I can just erase all of you." Ceris reached into the spherical magic circle. He poured his magic directly inside it, making it crackle and spark wildly with purple lightning. "Now…"

Clenching his fist, Ceris compressed the magic circle and cloaked his hand in condensed lightning, resulting in the feeling of pure destructive power. This must have been the same power he intended to use to destroy the God of Traces and Jiordal.

"I shall reduce everything to ashes."

The next moment, the world turned black-and-white, but it wasn't from Ceris's magic. He enhanced his Magic Eyes and looked around sharply.

"The Garden of Time…"

Eldmed cackled. "I said ten keepers should be born, but I didn't say there couldn't be eleven."

Ceris carefully cast his Eyes around the area, but he failed to spot the Keeper of Time.

"It's not that complicated. The mischievous titi decided to hide the keeper until they wanted to disguise it as Shin Reglia." Twenty-two copies of Shin carefully surrounded Ceris. Eldmed grinned. "Now there's one jackpot, twenty duds, and one super dud. If you pick the super dud, you'll be sent several hours into the future."

Ceris drew a magic circle with his free left hand. "*Gavest.*"

Purple lightning bolts filled the room, destroying the Garden of Time. At the same time, one Shin ran forward to swing Roduier at Ceris's face. Ceris evaded at the last moment but failed to dodge completely. Blood spurted from his neck.

"There you are."

With the destruction of the Garden of Time, one of the twenty-two Shins showed a faint reaction. Ceris assumed that it was Eugo La Raviaz and fired Gavest at him.

"You can't fool me with this child's play."

Just as he finished his sentence, he looked around with his Magic Eyes. They were still in the black-and-white world of the Garden of Time.

"Bwa ha ha! I said there could be eleven"—Eldmed smirked with delight—"but I didn't say there couldn't be twelve."

There had to be another Eugo La Raviaz disguised as Shin. But how many more were there? Ceris must have found himself thinking hard.

Chapter 35 — A Battle of Truth and Lies

"You really do resemble that Demon King. Is it like father, like son? You both have so much power that you inadvertently end up destroying things you don't mean to. That magic in your right hand can indeed blow away the Garden of Time multiple times over, but if you do that, you'll destroy the Keeper of Time in the process."

Destroying the Keeper of Time would cause several hours to pass. By then, the bet would be over.

"Of course you can destroy each Garden one by one using Gavest, but do you have any idea how many keepers I created in total?"

Eldmed's question purposely avoided the true matter at hand: that if push came to shove, Shin could always kill a Keeper of Time to shoot Ceris forward in time himself. With no idea which Shin was Shin and which was a Keeper, Ceris had no means of defending himself. Even if he did, the Conflagration King most likely had another card up his sleeve. That was what his words were implying, anyway.

"That is where my Zecht comes in. In exchange for ten minutes of obedience, you'll be able to silence me. Oh, but my ability to create Eugo La Raviaz means I can rewind time to easily confirm what happened. I'll even seal that as a condition. That doesn't sound bad, does it?" Eldmed redrew his magic circle for Zecht. "You don't have to force your way out of here; you just need to wait ten minutes, and you'll be free. This way, even if you sign the Zecht, it won't imply that you have anything to hide. You have great justification!"

Glaring at the fake Shins around him, Ceris sighed. "Good grief, I guess it can't be avoided. Anos was right about how troublesome you are."

Ceris erased the magic circle on his right hand and signed the Zecht. Perhaps he thought he'd be able to use Eldmed to his advantage.

"*The contract is signed, Demon King,*" Eldmed gleefully told me through Leaks. "*He was a formidable opponent. It was so close, I had no choice but to exchange my useful information to buy you time. Oh well, at least I'm closer to my ideal! Bwa ha ha!*"

Just what did he know about Ceris?

§ 36. The Divine Dragon's True Identity

While Shin and Eldmed faced Ceris, we had teleported near the dome, just outside of the dragon song's range. Before us was the sight of Jiordal ablaze with songfire. The blazing flames of purgatory shot upwards like a spear, piercing the dome to reach Midhaze. Although there was a barrier under the city, this was the second shot. It wouldn't be able to withstand another.

"Let's get going."

As quick as a flash, I flew through the subterranean sky. Arcana was the only one who could just barely keep up. I turned my Magic Eyes towards the ground below and caught a glimpse of the third flame.

"*Perish.*"

I glared at the raging songfire. The flames approaching me from below weakened and died out.

"The second and third shots were from different locations," Arcana said, having caught up.

"So it seems. The songfire spell targeting Midhaze was similar to Lanrez. It's much stronger than when I last saw it, so the pope must have used Egred to resurrect even more followers this time."

"Gods that perish in the Selection Trial can't be resurrected until the trial ends. Casting Egred should require the God of Gospel's power."

"I destroyed that god already."

I'd seen it with my own Eyes, so there was no mistaking it.

"Lanrez is a phonetic magic circle, right? If enough of Jiordal's followers gather and sing together, would they be able to produce that fire?" Sasha asked. In order to increase her flight speed, she had fused with Misha to become Aisha. Misa, too, had changed forms to keep up, transforming into Avos Dilhevia.

"That's not impossible. If they can't use Egred, that would make the most sense."

Because of the Divine Dragon's song, I couldn't see the draconids within Jiordal from this distance.

"This may also be why they didn't inform the people of Jiordal about the world aboveground."

If they knew that above the dome there were nations that lived just like they did, even the most faithful of followers would hesitate to do such a thing. Was the truth being hidden so the people could fire at the dome without doubting the gods?

"Why would the pope fire at the surface?" Arcana asked.

"Who knows? It's not like I'd give up on ending the Selection Trial even if he did. There should be no reason to needlessly create conflict."

What did he intend on doing once he destroyed Midhaze? He had to know that firing at my nation would only serve to anger me.

"We're going to do what I informed the pope I'd do. Once we've stopped this songfire and sealed his means of resistance, I will interrogate him myself." I stared at the city below.

"Oh? They've stopped firing now," Eleonore said, looking confused.

"Are they...out of ammunition?" Zeshia asked, humming along in thought. But if that was all the magic they had, they wouldn't have fired in the first place.

"Maybe they know it's pointless to fire with us up here," Lay suggested.

"That's one possibility. No matter where they fire from, anything aimed towards Midhaze has to pass through here. Firing will notify us of their location, allowing us to take them out. Considering the interval and origin points of the first three shots, there are at least three squads. We're looking at an army of a thousand or so."

There were most likely other squads as well.

Chapter 36 — The Divine Dragon's True Identity

"They've probably ceased fire to move the squads that have fired already. There'll be no one left at the earlier firing points," I said.

Descending carelessly would only weaken our defense, but we also had to worry about further shots.

"Normally, we'd be fine in a test of endurance, but…" Lay trailed off with a troubled smile.

"It'd be a fine plan for us but maybe not for Shin and Eldmed. There could be more Phantom Knights than just the three we saw. If they intervene, what could have been settled peacefully may not end that way."

Although we still had no clue as to the extent of Ceris's power, the two of them should have been able to buy us time. However, there was no telling who would emerge victorious if the two sides went at each other seriously. Our only choice was to stop this magic bombardment at the source while Ceris's movements were sealed. If we didn't, he would only stir up this situation and force me into destroying Jiordal.

"Arcana will remain here. The rest of us will find the followers creating the songfire and crush them."

"I can block it, but there's a limit," Arcana said calmly.

"That's the point. If there's a benefit to firing, then they will do so. That way, we'll be able to locate the source and defeat them before they move again. We'll neutralize all their squads before they break through Arcana's defense."

Arcana thought for a moment. "Are you sure you should entrust the fate of your country to me?" she asked.

"You're the best suited for it. Also, the followers of Jiordal will hesitate to fire at a god."

"If someone else can do it, they should. The fate of your country is too heavy a weight for me to bear. The role should be given to your most trusted follower."

She had a point, but something felt odd. Ever since we had returned from Ligalondrol, Arcana had begun to show signs of hesitation. She had said she didn't remember anything, but perhaps that wasn't the whole truth.

"What was your wish, Arcana?"

"Salvation," she replied quietly but firmly. "I wished for the people of this world to receive salvation."

"Then there's no one more qualified than you. Stand your ground and protect the wish behind you."

Arcana stared into my eyes and nodded. "If you insist."

"Let's go. Lay will take the east, Misa the west, Aisha the north, and Eleonore and Zeshia the south. I will descend in the center. If a shot goes off, whoever's closest to the firing point will head there."

We exchanged looks and swiftly descended towards Jiordal. They seemed to have some means of observing the dome, so if we moved farther away, they were more likely to fire again.

The ground drew closer and closer. Just as I was about to reach the dragon landing site, the air above the east of Jiordal glowed—and another pillar of songfire shot into the air.

"*Snow falls, illuminating the sky.*"

Altiertonoa, the Moon of Creation, appeared in the sky above. Glittering lunar snowdrops fell from it, creating a silver barrier that covered the dome.

The roaring songfire crashed ruthlessly into the barrier. Sparks and snow rained upon Jiordal like in a scene from a fairy tale.

"I'll head over," Lay said. He departed for the source of the shot. Another blast rose soon after, this time coming from the west.

"I'll clean it up," Misa said.

Two more blasts were fired right after.

"It's Zeshia's turn..."

"We'll kill them till they're dead!"

Zeshia and Eleonore headed south.

"It was the followers after all. *There's 1,012 of them in total*," Sasha and Misha said from the same body as they headed for the north point.

I stepped onto the dragon landing site. The students of the Demon King Academy were gathered around the entrance of the castle, staring in awe at the songfire and the silver moon blocking it.

"Ah! Lord Anos!" Ellen called when she noticed me, and the rest of the fan union girls turned my way. The other academy students followed their gazes.

"Get inside the castle and wait. Midhaze is being attacked, and this place may become a battlefield. Let the others know."

"U-Understood!"

Chapter 36 — The Divine Dragon's True Identity

The girls set off running for the castle. Since there was no songfire near me, it was time for me to find the pope. It would be helpful if he was still in the cathedral.

That aside, this was an odd series of events. They must have known we were luring them to attack, yet they had fired four blasts of songfire at once. Was it because they had more troops in ambush? However, the songfire was powerful greater magic. Considering the power of Jiordal's draconids, they shouldn't have that many forces left. Despite that, they were using those precious fighting forces without any hesitation. It was almost as though they wanted us to find them as quickly as possible.

Indeed, Arcana was protecting Midhaze by herself right now. If they were lucky and with enough songfire, they'd be able to break through her barrier. But it was hard to believe that was the best option available to them. Were they firing so openly as a diversion? In that case, their true target was elsewhere.

"No, Cani! Get back inside!"

There was a cute growl. I looked back to see Naya chasing the tiny Cannibal. Naya somehow managed to grab the dragon and hug it to her chest.

"S-Sorry! He always wants to escape and eat other dragons."

"But there are no other dragons right now."

"Huh?" Naya looked around the dragon landing site. There were normally a few dragons around, but none were here right now.

Cannibal growled, and a large magic sphere appeared in the dragon landing site. The sphere gradually shrank in size until it was no larger than a fist. The magic sphere flew up to Cannibal. The tiny dragon cried once and swallowed it. The next moment, there was silence. The noisy song of the Divine Dragon had vanished.

"C-Cani, what did you just eat?" Naya asked worriedly.

For a brief moment, the tiny dragon disappeared, but its infant growls continued to echo through the area.

"Cani, where did you go?! Come out, let's go back to the castle already!" Naya called nervously. Cannibal immediately replied with a cry. The tiny dragon was still on her shoulder—it hadn't gone anywhere.

"Huh?"

"Hmm. It seems this dragon takes on the traits of those it consumes."

"What?" Naya looked utterly confused. The tiny dragon who only ate other dragons had eaten the singing voice. That could only mean one thing. The singing voice that echoed through Jiordal came from the Divine Dragon. According to Ahid, no one had ever seen the Divine Dragon before. He had been half wrong and half right. The Divine Dragon had always been present in this land. Everyone had been in contact with it, for it was an invisible dragon of sound. In other words, the Divine Dragon was the song itself. Jiordal had been inside a giant dragon's body this entire time.

§ 37. 1,500-Yearlong Prayer

The faint sound of singing filled the air. The sound grew louder and louder, until the song of the Divine Dragon could be heard at the same volume as before. Cannibal had only eaten a portion of the vast Divine Dragon—the equivalent of a scratch on the surface. I turned to Naya, who was standing in confusion.

"It's dangerous here. Go back to the Demon King Castle."

"R-Right! Sorry for the trouble. Let's go, Cani. Behave this time, okay?"

Cannibal chirped in response. Naya clutched the dragon and hurried inside.

I flew up with Fless and observed Jiordal from the air. The four pillars of songfire were already dying down—or so I thought. New pillars of fire were rising from all four locations at once. The songfire struck the Moon of Creation and its barrier of lunar snowdrops, creating a shower of sparks. I followed the magic link of Gyze to look through everyone's Magic Eyes. They were all in combat with the troops from the Jiordal Church. The enemy had large numbers on their side, so we wouldn't be able to stop the holy song right away, but it would only be a matter of time before we did.

The Divine Dragon's song obstructed our Magic Eyes, hiding the army from view. If the songfire was truly being used as a diversion, there should be more squads hidden elsewhere—and Pope Golroana had to be commanding them all somewhere.

He wanted me to think they were vigilantly watching for the right moment to fire, which was why he had aimed at Midhaze, the largest city in Dilhade. But that had all been in order to focus my attention on the songfire.

The pope's true aim had something to do with the song of the Divine Dragon. It was singing so boldly, it gave the impression that its purpose was to conceal their troops, but the song wasn't enough to hide them completely. Whenever the dragon of sound did anything, it made a loud noise that couldn't be hidden by magic. The songfire was to make that sound seem natural.

The song of the Divine Dragon had a similar effect to dragon's domains, but as a dragon of sound, that was more of a side effect of its cries. It should have an ability other than that—and that ability was most likely what the pope was after.

I cast my Magic Eyes over Jiordal. My vision was obscured by the song, but it was enough to find where the voice was echoing the loudest—I just had to look for the areas with less magic.

I cast my eyes across the kingdom to see a point with no magic towards the west. It was two hundred kilometers away from where I was, at the ruins of Ligalondrol. I flew west using Fless at my highest speed and arrived above Ligalondrol in no time at all.

The Divine Dragon's song echoed in multiple voices at a deafening volume. I descended and smashed through the door, charging into the underground ruins. I went down deeper and deeper, but unlike the last time we were here, there was no end in sight.

Eventually, despite being inside the ruins, a sky appeared before me. A dome stretched out overhead. It was the same wasteland I had witnessed in the God of Traces' dream: an endless space with bookshelves extending into the horizon. At the center of the bookshelves was a robed god with a book in his hand—it was Revalschned, the God of Traces.

Knelt in prayer beside the god was Pope Golroana. I landed in the wasteland and looked right at them.

"So the God of Traces has already formed a pact with you," I called.

Golroana quietly opened his mouth. "Yes. The God of Traces is the guardian god of Jiordal, succeeded by generations of popes. I had a pact with Revalschned before I was chosen by the Selection God Doldread."

Chapter 37 — 1,500-Yearlong Prayer

The underground world relied on the support of the gods, so what he said was convincing enough.

"The Divine Dragon's song is a dragon of sound. When I look into its abyss, I can see the phonetic magic circle," I said.

As a dragon of sound, the Divine Dragon was incessantly activating that magic circle.

Without breaking his praying pose, the pope opened his eyes. I faced him and continued. "A phonetic magic circle was once used somewhere in this land. By picking up those traces and piecing them together over and over again, the popes of Jiordal were able to spread the phonetic magic circle throughout the kingdom. They passed down the pact with Revalschned, preparing for the day to come."

And that day was most likely today.

"I don't know when the Divine Dragon's song first started, but that phonetic magic circle has been playing nonstop for at least one thousand years. A greater magic spell of that scale that uses the God of Traces' order would be able to create its own miracle."

"If Ahid hadn't disobeyed our teachings, you wouldn't be standing here right now," Golroana said with a solemn look.

It seemed he no longer had any intention of hiding the truth.

Agatha's Prophet Diedrich had said I would be exposing Dilhade to danger if I didn't eliminate Golroana. That prophecy was probably why the pope had attempted to delay me with songfire rather than feign ignorance.

"Your goal isn't Midhaze; it's Dilhade. Actually, no. Considering the size of this phonetic magic circle, it'd be the entire world aboveground. Is it the teachings of your god to blow away the entire dome, pope of Jiordal?"

"If the teaching of Agatha's Royal Dragon is for people to reincarnate into dragonborn through a dragon's womb, then the teaching of Jiordal's Divine Dragon is for the world to be reborn through a dragon's womb," Golroana said solemnly. "The world will be swallowed and recreated into its rightful form in the womb of a dragon. The border between underground and aboveground—the dome—shall transform to sky. That is the duty of the Divine Dragon, the messenger of the gods. Blessed rain will fall from the newborn sky and turn the underground world into paradise."

"Turning the dome into sky means the complete destruction of everything above the dome, no?"

"Rest assured; the world will be reborn without borders. Those who live aboveground will not die. Although we reside in different nations, they are fellow residents of this world. The gods will show them mercy."

"That's nonsense. You want them to live underground once their world is gone? That would be the same as destroying their lives. Are you so desperate for your paradise that you'd steal the happiness of innocent people, Golroana?"

"I told you we would never be able to join hands. The people of Jiordal haven't even been able to come to an understanding with Agatha or Gadeciola—our fellow nations underground. It would be impossible for that to happen with the people aboveground."

The pope was probably responding to me because the Divine Dragon needed time to activate the phonetic magic circle. The more Galroana spoke, the more time he'd be able to buy.

"What a pathetic excuse."

"The world is divided, king from above. The border between our worlds is a gap that can never be bridged." Golroana glared at me with unshakable resolution. "You saw the vast wasteland on your way here yourself," he said calmly. "The people of the underground world live on the blessings of summoned dragons and gods. In other words, we would be unable to live without them. Compared to the blessings and order of the world above, we receive far too little. Why should the innocent people of the underground be less blessed than the people from above?"

The pope continued without waiting for an answer. "A person's happiness should have no boundaries. In order to achieve equality between all living people, we must lose that boundary. The gods will make that dream a reality."

"Do you truly think the people who have lived aboveground should live underground just because they received blessed rains? In the end, only more inequality will be born. Tell your gods they made their move too late. If they wanted equality, they shouldn't have made the border in the first place." I glared at the pope and spoke firmly. "Why should the people aboveground pay for the mistakes of the gods?"

"The inequality created right now is for the sake of the future. Even if this

Chapter 37 — 1,500-Yearlong Prayer

prayer cannot come true right now, as the pope, I will pray for the sake of this kingdom one hundred years later."

"The only thing that will bring sudden change is war. Even if intrinsic equality were to be introduced to this land, the minds of the people wouldn't change so easily. You can gloss over it all you like, but in the end, there'll be villains and victims. Will you bind your people to a chain of hatred lasting thousands of years?"

Golroana didn't seem like a fool who couldn't understand that. It was almost like he was possessed by something.

"If you wish to change the world, you must change it slowly. Make life tomorrow a little better than today—there's no other shortcut to it."

"Would you be able to say the same thing if you were a king of an underground nation?"

"Then tell the people of the underground the truth."

Silence fell over Ligalondrol for a brief moment.

"Demons, humans, and spirits live above the dome, just like the people underground," I said. "You want to take their blessings for yourselves—tell your people that."

"This is one of the teachings passed down in the scriptures of Jiordal. Only the pope needs to bear the burden of the sin. That makes it my duty as pope to carry the sins of the people and offer my prayers." Golroana closed his eyes in deep prayer.

"Why must you face misfortune for being born in a different place?" I asked. "I get what you're trying to say, but if you feel that strongly about creating an ideal world, stop praying to the gods and take my hand." I walked up to him and held out my hand. "I'm not the only one who'll help you build that future. Join forces with Agatha, Gadeciola, and the other nations as well. I promise you'll reach a better future like that rather than if you continue along this foolish route."

Golroana glanced at my hand and continued praying.

"You can always blast through the dome if I break my promise."

At those words, Golroana remained silent and prayed in thought. He then opened his eyes and stared straight at me. "Unfortunately, it is too late for that. It's too late to even consider that. Today is the only day the Divine Dragon can spread its wings and take to the true sky. There will be no second chance. I believe in Equis. The Almighty Radiance is the only one who can save the underground world."

It seemed that today was the only day the phonetic magic circle of the Divine Dragon's ancient song could be used to its full potential.

"My father, my father's father, and my father's grandfather all perished here while praying for salvation. From the day we received the divine revelation, the teaching has been passed down through generations of popes. Their prayers spanned 1,500 years, and fate has now entrusted the revelation to me. I will not allow their dearest wish to go to waste."

The pope raised his voice, expressing his firm refusal to concede. "I have retired from the Selection Trial, but I will fulfill my last duty as the Savior. Misfit, your intent to destroy the Selection Trial is wrong. I will deny your god, remove you from your seat as one of the Selected Eight, and bring you salvation."

"Oh?"

"Anos Voldigoad, I will prove to you that I am right and teach you what this 1,500-yearlong prayer truly means."

"Just try it." I drew a magic circle and stained my fingertips with Vebzud. "Blinded by the length of your prayer, you all became convinced you were right. It isn't easy to go back on 1,500 years of effort. But even then, all you needed to do was find the courage to accept your mistake." I glared at Golroana and the God of Traces standing beside him. "I will destroy your prayers, your god, your everything—and prove to this kingdom that those 1,500 years were for nothing."

§ 38. The Land of Traces

Particles of magic rose into the air. They flowed out of our bodies and crashed into each other, blending and sparking like fireworks signaling the start of war.

I thrust my Vebzud-clad hand towards Golroana. He remained in the same kneeling position and showed no sign of evading the incoming attack. My black-stained fingertips mercilessly blew apart the pope's face. His source was shredded, and his body was reduced to dust.

"This is the ruins of Ligalondrol. The land here is engraved with the traces of the past," the God of Traces said somberly.

I looked to the side to see Golroana appear in the same praying pose. The source I had shredded was completely unharmed. "You distorted time," I said, looking into the abyss.

"Indeed. In the land of traces, there is no future. My devout follower's life is carved into the past, so he will never die."

"He will if I deal with you first."

"Indeed. But I, too, am undying. As the order of traces, I am the past of everything in existence. You can rewrite time all you wish, but the past that existed won't change."

As the order of the records and memories, the God of Traces was the past itself. Destroying him would require altering the past, but there was little chance of that happening against the god of such an order, even with time magic.

Revalschned existed here. That truth could never be changed. This was what made the God of Traces immortal and was the reason Ceris had wanted to destroy him while he was still asleep.

"I have one question, Revalschned," I said to the god. "Is your goal for the Divine Dragon to consume the dome?"

"I am the order that inscribes records and recollections. For generations of popes, I have carved the prayers and pain. The choice is not up to me but is the will of Pope Golroana, with whom I made the pact. I merely carve the path they have walked—the history of this world—into my body."

What a godlike answer. So the song of the Divine God was entirely the will of the popes.

"Demon King of the world above," Golroana said in a songlike voice, "when judgment visits you, your body will be torn apart by the blade of divine light. *Book of Traces*, Chapter One: '*Azbef*.'"

Revalschned opened the white book in his hand. That was probably the *Book of Traces*. Light surrounded the book as it floated into the air and transformed into a holy sword—Evansmana, the Sword of Three Races. The god took the sword into his hand.

I was already within reach of his sword, but I stepped forward anyway, sinking my Vebzud-stained fingertips into him. His heart was crushed in my palm, and his source was destroyed along with it.

"Even if you destroy me now, the past will live forever," he said. Revalschned's body regenerated in the blink of an eye, allowing him to swing the Sword of Three Races. I cloaked my left hand in Beno Ievun and attempted to catch the blade. "Traces make the blade."

My eyes widened. The God of Traces swung the holy sword just like Lay, reenacting our past battle.

"*Heaven Splitter.*"

White light gathered around Evansmana before bursting out as blinding beams. In the span of a single breath, countless slashes tore apart my body. The first hidden art that could severe fate—Heaven Splitter—drove into me faster than the sword itself. The blade left numerous wounds on my source. The blood of the Demon King could corrupt all attacks, but its one weakness was the holy sword created to destroy the Demon King.

I wrapped my entire body in Beno Ievun and endured the demon sword's attacks. However, just as I was about to hit back, Revalschned used the Sword of Three Races once more.

"Traces make the blade—*Heaven Splitter.*"

The hidden art struck multiple times, tearing my body apart and chipping away at my source. Not even Lay could use Heaven Splitter so many times in succession. The God of Traces' inexhaustible magic and physical strength allowed him to brandish the sword relentlessly over and over again.

"From the traces of this world, I have chosen a blade that can defeat you," Golroana announced. "Hero Kanon, the enemy you acknowledge yourself, will be your never-ending trial, Azbef. This blade will continue until only traces of you remain."

"Hmm. That is indeed Lay's sword."

By layering Ygg Neas and Beno Ievun, I caught all the sword slashes aimed at me.

"But at the same time, this is not Lay's sword."

"Guh..." The God of Traces groaned. I had caught the blade of the Sword of Three Races as it came swinging down. He continued using Heaven Splitter while the blade was locked in my grip, but the brandishes of the sword were sealed by my Ygg Neas and Beno Ievun.

"You are capable of recreating traces of the past. Heaven Splitter was indeed what Lay once used. However, his sword grows with every slash, moving towards the future. Every swing surpasses the one before it, making his moves impossible to predict. But your sword merely traces the past."

Because Revalschned was the God of Traces, he was unable to swing the sword in a new way. This was not Lay's sword.

"Did you think you could reach me with a poor imitation of the Hero?" Using my hand, I chopped off the God of Traces' right arm. Then I sunk my jet-black right arm into his abdomen. "*Degzegd.*"

A black snake mark appeared on Revalschned's body, rampaging fiercely as it tried to consume him. It was a curse that caused one's magic to fly out of control, driving the subject to death. Just as expected, the god's magic ran wild, rapidly decaying his body. I grabbed the magic circle with my right arm and forcefully yanked it out of his body along with his source. Once his source was out of his body, I crushed it in my hand. The God of Traces' body immediately rotted away, turning into air.

Of course, it was only a temporary solution. He wouldn't die just from that.

"I've witnessed the whole scheme now. In order to destroy you, I have to destroy the land of traces first," I said.

The order of time was twisted here, but using a little more of my power shouldn't be a problem for me. I held out my hand and drew a layered magic circle. Individual circles piled on top of each other to form a turret pointing at Revalschned. Black particles gathered at the mouth of the magic circle turret. It was Egil Grone Angdroa, an origin spell borrowing the power of the Demon King of Tyranny, Anos Voldigoad; Militia, Goddess of Creation; and Abernyu, Goddess of Destruction.

"Misfit," Revalschned said, appearing some distance away. The *Book of Traces* was still in his hand. "All traces are on my side. This origin magic you use as your trump card will have no effect against the order of traces."

The black particles flowing from the magic circles suddenly scattered. The magic borrowed from the past vanished before my eyes.

"Know this, Demon King from above. The past will never be on your side. There is no future for you here," Golroana said like he was singing. "The greatest form of destruction in this world will befall you in your greatest trial. *Book of Traces*, Chapter Six: 'Azael.'"

Revalschned's *Book of Traces* opened and transformed into a magic circle. Black particles overflowed from the turret of magic circles that were formed. One particularly violent scrap of magic coiled around the magic turret like a living creature.

The mere aftershock of that movement shook the land of traces, causing books to come tumbling down from the giant bookshelves and through the air.

"Oh? Egil Grone Angdróa, is it?"

"You may think that origin magic won't work on those it borrows magic from, but every past takes the side of the God of Traces."

So it could work on me too. Considering the God of Traces' order, it didn't sound like a mere bluff. The turret of magic circles slowly turned to aim at me.

"I shall allow you an opportunity to repent. Pray to the Almighty Radiance and express your repentance. Only then shall you receive salvation. If not, you will have to bear the destruction of the world with your body."

Chapter 38 — The Land of Traces

"Sure, if you can hit me. If you miss, this entire land may disappear."

"All is as the Almighty Radiance wishes," Golroana replied immediately.

Black particles of magic formed a seven-layered spiral around the turret. A bottomless rift appeared in the land of traces, splitting the world into two.

"Traces of destruction—*Egil Grone Angdroa*," Revalschned said in a deep voice. Flames of doom appeared from the turret of magic circles. The jet-black flames covered the seven-layered spiral and fired with a deafening boom. The next moment, my limbs were weighed down.

"Traces of restriction—*Gicherge*."

Transparent chains appeared out of nowhere and restrained my limbs. No, I was already chained. My body was already restrained by Gicherge as though the past had been altered. Before I could tear the chains apart, the flames of doom closed in on my body and burned me up. Fire that could destroy the world pushed my source closer to its end, but at the same time, my magic grew and grew.

"Revalschned and this land are immortal because they are the past of everything—in other words, they are the traces of everything in this world," Golroana said while watching me burn. Then his eyes widened. "Why?" he murmured in disbelief, unable to understand how I hadn't immediately been destroyed.

"No matter how far back in time one goes, footprints are permanent," I said, looking down at my own footprints on the ground. "Footprints can be carved into this land, but they can never be erased. So how can they be destroyed?"

Revalschned stared at me blankly, expecting me to perish.

"This is the answer."

I casually lifted my foot and brought it down on the ground. The footprints on the ground vanished without a trace. The magic in my step left a giant footprint that covered the land.

"They just need to be covered up by a bigger footstep. The original footprint disappears beneath the new footprint, and the bigger footprint is greater than the world can fit. In other words, when it's too much for the order of traces to handle."

"That's impossible. The entire world can fit into the land of traces. Seven hundred million years have passed from the beginning of time, yet this land can hold a hundred times more with ease. There is no trace that could possibly be larger than that," Revalschned said grimly.

"You mean in the past, right?" I drew a magic circle over my dying source, bringing the flames of doom into my body. "Unfortunately, I'm only interested in moving towards the future."

It was a close call, but I'd made it in time. Egil Grone Angdroa had pushed my source close to destruction. It had been a long time since I'd felt this close to death. The end was near. In other words, it was similar to how a flame burns brightest just before it goes out. This was the rule for every source, but the effects were all the more powerful when it applied to my source of destruction. The closer I got to destruction, the stronger I became, ultimately overcoming my eventual demise.

Under normal circumstances, it would have been impossible for me to ever be on the receiving end of Egil Grone Angdroa. Thus, I had exposed myself on purpose.

"Here's a spell that hasn't been carved into your traces—a spell I created at this very moment."

The power of destruction in my body flowed out. The seven-layered spiral of obsidian flames wrapped around me. I quietly recited the spell.

"*Gilieriam Naviem.*"

It was enhancement magic that momentarily raised my strength and released the destructive magic condensed in my source. I slowly walked towards the God of Traces. All I had to do was walk.

On my first step, all the bookshelves stretched across the land collapsed, sending all the books recording the traces of the world into the air. Each page that opened had a trace of this world written on it. The shadows of countless people appeared in the wasteland and then vanished, destroyed by my footstep.

On my second step, the books in the air tore apart, scattering their pages everywhere. Groups of various animals appeared on the water while birds and dragons filled the skies. Then the traces of all living creatures were crushed under my foot and destroyed.

On my third step, the land shook, and the scattered pages burst. The

Chapter 38 — The Land of Traces

dome vanished, and the sky appeared, followed by the sun, the moon, and the stars. Their shadows all disappeared under my step, banished beyond the skies.

On my fourth step, the torn scraps of paper disintegrated. The land cracked into pieces, lakes dried up, and all plant life withered away.

On my fifth step, countless bookshelves rose once again, recording the traces of destruction until now. The bookshelves shook violently before being crushed into pieces. Broken by my footstep, the shattered sky flickered overhead.

On my sixth step, there was nothing left in the land of traces as it shook. The only light left before me was crushed by my footstep, enclosing the world in darkness.

On my seventh step, I froze before bringing my foot down. The land of traces had vanished, and I was back in the room with the stone floor. If I had finished taking my seventh step, I would have destroyed the world a thousand times over.

"Hmm. I made this spell with the intent of conquering the land of traces in seven steps, but it seems I've failed. If I had taken seven steps, nothing would remain."

The land of traces had reached its limits at the sixth step, unable to record any more traces of destruction. The divine realm had broken down. I canceled Gilieriam Naviem and set my foot on the floor.

"That can't be..." Despite seeing it with his own eyes, Golroana trembled in disbelief. "The land of traces... The infinite world created by the gods..." he mumbled in a daze.

"Not even the land that could record seven hundred million years of traces could withstand seven of my footsteps, it seems?"

§ 39. The Dream a God Had

A song could be heard. The song of the Divine Dragon was echoing through Ligalondrol.

"Are you trying to say that the magic you created on the spot destroyed the world of a god? That the wisdom you came up with yourself was superior to the wisdom of our ancestors?"

I laughed at him. "Did you think that just because I made it on the spot, it was born in an instant?"

Golroana looked confused.

"The past isn't something to be fixed upon, but something to build on. The countless traces accumulated from the past were what allowed me to take a step forward and create Gilieriam Naviem."

Having witnessed me crushing the supposedly indestructible land of traces underfoot, Golroana was no longer able to ignore my words.

"As long as you do nothing but pray, Revalschned's power remains nothing but a trace of the past," I said. "You won't be able to surpass the answers accumulated by your ancestors and arrive at a better solution beyond them."

Golroana remained silent.

"How can you preach about an equal world when you refuse to acknowledge your mistakes and correct them? Can you really say that your thoughts—your ideals—have no borders after 1,500 years of prayer?"

The pope clenched his teeth.

"Before removing the dome over your head, try removing the limits in your mind." I sent my magic into my right hand and clenched it. "If you can't do that, I will destroy that god next."

"I said it was too late." Golroana clenched his Selection pledge jewel and covered it with his right hand in fervent prayer. "While you were stomping the land of traces into pieces, Revalschned's role was already over. Destroying my god will make no difference at this point. The song of the Divine Dragon will continue traveling upwards until it swallows the dome. The world will lose its disparity and be born anew. That is Beherom, the final gospel." He glared at me with unshakable determination. "You possess an enormous destructive power. But that is why you were too slow. No matter what you destroy, you cannot protect that dome."

"Indeed, it is as you say. If I tried to destroy the phonetic magic circle for Beherom, the world aboveground would be affected as well."

At best, the land would change drastically. At worst, it would be destroyed.

"But that's only if I use my power alone." I called out through Leaks. "Were you listening, Arcana? It's too late to stop Beherom, but we can still defend against it."

Her reply was immediate. *"What do I do?"*

"Use Leviangilma, the Sword of the Almighty, to make the dome eternally unchanging. Not even Beherom can have any effect during Leviangilma's trial."

My attacks and Nedneliaz had been ineffective against Ahid when he had been in his eternally unchanging state. All harmful magic would be repelled.

"Leviangilma's eternally unchanging state only affects me and whoever I make a pact with. I can't alter the state of anything other than you."

"Then I shall destroy that reason." I released the magic in my right hand upwards. It arrived at the dome near Arcana and formed a magic circle. "Delsgade."

Black particles rose from the magic circle as the Demon Castle Delsgade appeared. The shining black sword before it was Venuzdonoa, the Abolisher of Reason.

"Fuse that demon sword with the Moon of Creation and turn it into Leviangilma. Even if Venuzdonoa changes shape, it should be able to change what Leviangilma applies the eternally unchanging state to."

Chapter 39 — The Dream a God Had

Arcana flew through the air and approached the Abolisher of Reason. I confirmed that before looking back at Golroana. "If you cooperate with the retrieval of my memories, I'll spare the God of Traces. What do you say?"

"I'd have to ask a question first," Golroana said with a meaningful tone. "Which is that you wish to know?"

"Hmm. What do you mean by 'which'?"

"Do you wish to know the memories that Arcana has already retrieved or the memories that she has yet to retrieve? Which is it?" he asked quietly. "The last time she came to Ligalondrol, she witnessed a portion of her memories in the God of Traces' dream. Why do you think she failed to inform you of that?"

He continued without waiting for my reply. "This is the truth that the God of Traces' order revealed. I vow to return my life back to the gods if I speak any lies," he said, drawing a Zecht magic circle and signing it. "Arcana is the god of lies and betrayal, Genedonov, the Goddess of Absurdity, and as her name suggests, she will one day betray you. That time may be now."

The Zecht was in effect, and Golroana was still alive, which could only mean one thing.

"You thought you were following your memories through the power of the Keeper of Dreams," he said, "but that was all a lie. You do not have an adopted sister named Arcana. The dream was to fool you."

The Zecht remained intact, and Golroana remained alive. The dream I'd had was a lie—he had proved this was the truth.

"It is true that she had lost her memories," he said. "However, after she regained them, she never informed you she was the Goddess of Absurdity. She dragged you back into pointless dreams just so that she could be your little sister, but what reason did she have to lie? What purpose did she have in playing your fake little sister? Everything was for this moment—to betray you."

With a devout expression, the pope spoke in an admonishing tone. "Think about it, Misfit. Should you really be entrusting the fate of the world above to the Goddess of Absurdity? She is the god of betrayal. What proof do you have that she won't eradicate what you wish to protect?"

This was the moment the pope had been waiting for. He had read the past using the order of traces and predicted how I would move until the end. By taking away the time to think things through—and the time for negotiation—he could corner me into making this compromise. He knew from the beginning that he couldn't win. By playing the fool until the end, he had bet everything on this single chance.

"My god already declared that Beherom won't take the lives of those above. Only the border between our worlds will be removed. Considering how much power you possess, the removal of the border shouldn't make much of a difference to you, no?"

There was no denying that fact. As long as people were alive, as long as no one perished, we could rebuild as many times as necessary. The tragedies brought about by the absence of the dome and the relocation of so many homes could be crushed by force.

"But if you leave everything in the hands of the Goddess of Absurdity, the many demons and humans may perish forever. Can you truly believe in your god? Can you, who doesn't believe in the gods in the first place, entrust such a thing to someone who wasn't even your real little sister? Compromise. Make a concession. You told me not to be fixed upon the past, but there isn't even a past between you and your god to be fixed on. There are only fake memories, fake dreams—such a fleeting bond could never compare to our 1,500 years of prayer."

The pope looked up with solemnity. Ligalondrol's door was open, and the dome could be seen far in the distance.

"Please, go and confirm this with your god first. There's still some time until Beherom will be activated."

I focused my Eyes on Arcana, who was floating overhead near the dome. I could clearly see her expression through the magic link between us.

"Anos..."

It was the same as back then. When she had first woken from the God of Traces' dream in Ligalondrol, she had worn the same dark expression.

"*That dragon child speaks the truth. I remembered it. I am Genedonov, the Goddess of Absurdity, the god of lies and betrayal that opposes order. Anos...*" She bit down her lip with a downcast look. "*You must never believe in me.*"

Her voice sounded awfully sad. Tears spilled from her eyes and wordless cries escaped her lips. However, her heart reached me through our link.

Back then, in the God of Traces' dream, I found my memories. I remembered that I was Genedonov, the Goddess of Absurdity. I remembered that there was

Chapter 39 — The Dream a God Had

anger within me, a bottomless anger that scorched my body and burned my source.

In the end, I couldn't become a kind god. The proof lies in how I continued to deceive you. I didn't say a word about the memories I'd regained, just so I could remain your little sister.

I thought I'd be happier that way. But now I know. The dream we watched was indeed a dream. They weren't memories. It was merely all that I had wished for.

I was once chased just like in the dream. Ever since I was little, dragons and draconids have been after me. I was persecuted in this underground land. Everyone was my enemy. Not a single person protected me. That's why I wanted an older brother.

When I was attacked by dragons, when the draconids forced themselves into my house to sacrifice me, when I was swallowed by the dragon, I wished I had an older brother who would rescue me. But I was unable to accept my memories and averted my eyes until the end. I held my silence, unable to tell you the truth.

I wanted to watch this dream for a little longer. At least in my dreams, I wanted to forget that I was a foolish god. Everything was a lie, everything was fake. I am a god made of pomposity and pretense. I will betray you one day. I will hurt you one day. After all, these emotions, this desire to bring people salvation…they're all fake feelings I made with the Moon of Creation. When the time comes and I regain my memories and my heart, I will betray even myself in order to fulfill my goal. That's why I'd like you to destroy me before that happens.

Anos, I was never your little sister. I was a foolish, lonely, blasphemous god. I lied to myself until I believed my own lies. I was Dora the liar.

The pope before me spoke. "With this, I shall grant you salvation. You will no longer be betrayed by the blasphemous god." Golroana closed his eyes in prayer. "All is as the Almighty Radiance wishes."

"Golroana," I called quietly, "is this what you wanted with the God of Traces?"

He opened his eyes and looked at me.

"If so, you've missed the point."

The pope frowned. "What?"

"My little sister would never betray me."

"What are you saying? She's not your little sister. It was all a dream."

"That's right, which is why I'll make it happen. Dreams can come true, you know? Or did you fail to look inside people's hearts when you looked into the past, Great Pope?"

"She is the god of lies and betrayal, not a person! She continued to show you her dream in order to deceive you! Arcana said it all herself!"

"Fool. Can't you tell the difference between lies and wishes? That was her dream. Arcana wished for an older brother. The god no one believed in desperately sought a brother who would believe her no matter what." I confronted the man seized by the Goddess of Absurdity's past. "Did you fail to see the traces of that loneliness and sadness, Golroana?"

"Anos..." Arcana's voice called out. It was a sorrowful voice filled with tears.

"Do you remember our promise, Arcana?" I called as gently as I could. "I told you to remember no matter what. You are my little sister. We may not be related by blood, but you are still my sister."

"*The days we spent together were fake. That promise was fake too.*"

"Even so, there were no lies in the wish we watched together."

Tears fell from Arcana's eyes, just like they had in her dream.

"You said you'd get stronger when you were reborn, right? Strong enough to help me. Now is the moment to overcome that weak heart of yours. Be strong. I don't care if you're the Goddess of Absurdity or the god of lies and betrayal. You told me in your dream that this time, there would be no lies."

If her wish failed to reach anyone, it was up to me to grant it.

"Did you think a dream couldn't become reality?"

"*I lied to you.*"

"It wasn't a betrayal. No matter what happens, I won't let you betray me."

The pope prayed earnestly. The song of the Divine Dragon echoed even louder through the subterranean sky. The dome was about to be reborn.

"*Book of Gospel*, Final Movement: '*Beherom.*'"

The sky flickered violently as a light too bright to look at covered the dome.

"I will believe in the words of my god, in the wish of my little sister, until

Chapter 39 — The Dream a God Had

the end. If that isn't enough, then I will say it one more time." I put all my heart into my plea. "Become my little sister."

One beat later, the air shook with her teardrop.

"*Big brother...*" Arcana reached out and grabbed Venuzdonoa. The Abolisher of Reason fused with the Moon of Creation. Golroana's face fell.

"How foolish can you be, believing in the Goddess of Absurdity?! Destroy that sinner, that walking disaster, Revalschned!"

The God of Traces opened his pure-white book and held his hand over it. A rumbling tremor resounded through the ruins, and a divine sword came falling from above. It was the Sword of the Almighty, Leviangilma. The sword made from the Abolisher of Reason and the Moon of Creation landed in my hands. I held the sword up in its sheath and grasped the hilt. My body and magic shifted to and fro like a wave.

"Traces make the blade—*Heaven Splitter.*"

An infinite number of Revalschned's sword strikes struck my body. I took a large step forward to face them directly.

"*Veneziara.*"

My shifting body crossed positions. There was a brief moment of silence. Then, part of the God of Traces' body started to slide. His divine body had been split into two. Leviangilma was still in its sheath, but its blade of possibilities had slashed apart the Heaven Splitter and enemy before me.

The God of Traces couldn't avoid death against the sword that possessed Genedonov's power, the order that opposed order.

"Pope Golroana, I will leave your prayers here..."

The next moment, the god shattered into pieces. Only the pure-white book in his hand remained, a faint trace of what once was.

I slowly looked up at the dome. Beherom had activated, but the dome was still there, and nothing had changed in the world above. The Sword of the Almighty had made it eternally unchanging, repelling Beherom.

When I listened carefully, the song of the Divine Dragon in the skies had been replaced with Arcana's soft sobs.

§ 40. The Dragon Lurking Within

The dome glittered white. That light fell upon the underground world, illuminating the ruins of Ligalondrol. Knelt in prayer, Golroana lifted his head and looked up.

"The prayers of 1,500 years..." he mumbled in a daze. "They've..."

The song of the Divine Dragon had vanished. The phonetic magic circle broke off, and with the God of Traces destroyed, it was impossible to use Beherom again. I picked up the *Book of Traces* from the ground and walked over to Golroana.

"Is this the answer?" he muttered with a self-deprecating smile. His vacant gaze was still fixed on the dome. "My prayers, my god, and Beherom have all been crushed. The Goddess of Absurdity who should have betrayed you did not, and the dome still stands in our way..." Golroana clenched his jaw. Tears welled in his vacant gaze. "The Almighty Radiance, Equis, will lead us down the proper path. But the path I walk has come to an end. Without our prayers and our god, Jiordal has lost everything." He looked up at me. "Were we really trying to make a meaningful lesson out of meaningless efforts for these past 1,500 years like you said?" the pope asked.

With all his prayers gone down the drain in an instant, he was clinging to a new hope.

"If I had stopped praying at the Shrine of Sacred Song and accepted your hand, would we have attained salvation today?"

"No clue."

Golroana looked surprised at the unexpected answer.

"All I denied was your ridiculous plan to invade and reincarnate the entirety of the world aboveground. That was your only wasted effort—everything else was irrelevant to me. I never denied your hearts that have prayed for the salvation of the underground world this entire time."

Golroana blinked blankly, unable to process his thoughts. If I said the right thing here, he would probably end up worshipping me. With 1,500 years of prayer ending in vain, he was likely to depend on me for having shown him an even greater miracle. An even stronger bond would form between Dilhade and Jiordal.

Not that I would accept that. That would only change the object of worship.

"Jiordal attempted to invade the world aboveground. I, as the king of Dilhade, put a stop to it. There was no meaning to this fight beyond that."

He prayed, but there was no salvation. He had started a fight and lost. Those were the facts I had thrust before him.

"I only have two demands of this nation. Don't invade others. And, to the best of your ability, protect the happiness of your citizens."

He slowly shook his head with a look of resignation. "Unfortunately, I no longer have the right to promise that." Golroana released his hands from prayer. Then he drew a magic circle. "There is only one moment when a pope is allowed to rest from praying." He reached into the magic circle and withdrew a dagger. "Rest assured, this is a sword of repentance. It is used when a pope has strayed from the correct path, so that he can offer his life for his sins and beg forgiveness from the gods. 1,500 years of prayer failed to lead to salvation. My prayer was insufficient, and this is my sin."

Golroana grabbed the dagger and held it up to his throat. He reduced his own magic as much as he could, in preparation to kill himself.

"This sinful soul will depart for god. I pray that my blood will wash my sins away and lead Jiordal towards the correct path."

Fresh blood sprayed the air, more traveling down the dagger and dripping to the floor.

"Gah... Hah..." he gasped.

The agony of death ate at Golroana, whose expression twisted in anguish.

Chapter 40 — The Dragon Lurking Within

Despite that, he linked his hands in one last prayer. Golroana was holding back all forms of resistance towards the sword of repentance. Without using healing magic within the next few seconds, he would be dead. Under normal circumstances, that is.

"Agh... What? Why?" Shock and horror filled the pope's face. "How am I alive?"

"I used Indol on you. No matter what state you're in, you won't die."

"What?"

Deep sadness crossed his face.

"If there's only one moment when a pope can stop praying, with this, you can no longer wash yourself of your sins."

The hands held in prayer trembled uncontrollably.

"Your goal was to remove the border between worlds without taking the lives of the people. You showed mercy to your enemies. Thus, my mercy to you is to only take your means of repentance."

"A-Aaah! What have you done?! Cancel the magic right this moment!"

"No." I reached out and pulled the sword of repentance from his throat.

"Gahah!"

Golroana's body was surrounded by light. I healed his wounds using Ent.

"If you want to die, pick up the sword once again. This time, by defying your teachings."

Golroana clenched his teeth, unable to do such a thing.

"This soul that failed to fulfill a 1,500-yearlong prayer is tainted. If I do not return this life to the gods, Jiordal will be unable to wash these sins away. We will be doomed to destruction!"

"Then as the first sinful, tainted pope that failed to repent, live in disgrace."

Despair filled Golroana's face. The pope had failed to die in accordance with the teachings—who knew how many followers would criticize him behind his back?

"Suffer, struggle, and survive while coming up with a way to atone yourself. Once you do that, you may come to an unexpected realization: that something as trivial as your blood won't wash away any sins."

Golroana trembled at the fate that awaited him.

"Sins aren't so light that they can be redeemed with mere death. Try dealing with the cleanup yourself instead of relying on god for once."

I sent magic into my Eyes and forced Golroana's storage circle open. I then returned the sword of repentance and Revalschned's *Book of Traces* to him. Golroana's face twisted in confusion.

"You and your god were both in search of your memories. With the God of Traces gone, the *Book of Traces* should be able to provide a hint, limited as it may be. Why would you return it to me?"

"Did you forget the God of Traces' last words?"

The god had said he'd leave their prayers here.

"This book is packed with 1,500 years of your nation's wishes. I'd have no right to talk about peace if I tried to lay claim to that over a few forgotten memories."

Items like the Scythe of the Timekeeper broke in my hands when I used them. The same would probably happen to the *Book of Traces*.

"What do you want in return?"

"My two demands are what I stated earlier. As long as you stick to them, then whether you believe in god or not, your path is your own. I will not interfere."

I held up a hand and clenched it lightly.

"But I believe that one day, we will be able to join hands. Not only between Dilhade and Jiordal, but with Agatha, Gadeciola, and Azesion too."

"I don't know how things are aboveground, but the disputes here are deep-rooted. I can't imagine people who follow different teachings ever understanding each other."

"I thought the same during the great war of two thousand years ago. That demons would never join hands with humans," I said. Golroana listened on with a confused look. "Your god and your prayers have only just come to an end. While bearing your sins, you have a mountain of things to consider. I will not offer you my hand right now, but organize your thoughts and prepare yourself for the next time we meet."

I drew the circle for Fless and poured magic into it, preparing to depart. "I have one last question. There's no doubt that Arcana is the Goddess of Absurdity. But you once called her Militia, the Goddess of Creation too."

The pope stared at me.

Chapter 40 — The Dragon Lurking Within

"Was that a lie to fool me? Or was she the Goddess of Creation as well?"

Technically speaking, the Goddess of Absurdity wasn't the name of a god. The people of the underground world had merely dubbed her that for defying order and betraying others over and over again. In that case, Genedonov should have another name as a god. And it wouldn't be too odd for that to be the Goddess of Creation, Militia.

"That's..." Golroana mumbled quietly. But before he gave his answer, I noticed his right arm with the pledge ring was turning black before my eyes.

"What are you doing?"

"What do you mean?"

Golroana looked genuinely confused. When I focused my Eyes on his right arm, I could see the magic had risen to an abnormal level.

"Hmm. There's something lurking inside your body."

No sooner had I said that, I used Leviangilma to slice off his right hand.

"Ugh! Aaaaagh!"

A purple dragon's face appeared from the open wound of his right arm. I braced myself for its approach, but it went for Golroana's severed hand instead.

Two blue flames flickered in my Eyes. The dragon had consumed the God of Traces and Gospel God that resided in the Selection pledge jewel after their defeat.

"Whose god are you? Name yourself."

Leviangilma flashed with Veneziara. The head of the dragon fell to the floor.

"Guh... Gaaaaaaaaaaaah!" Golroana screamed.

It seemed like the dragon had been a parasite living off him. Their pain was shared.

"Th-The Supreme Dragon... It must be Gadeciola's overlord," Golroana said between groans. A pair of dragon wings burst out of his back. "Foolish heretics. This body is dedicated to the gods alone. You will not have free rein over it!"

A giant spear appeared from a magic circle the pope drew. He then used Fless to send it into the air and towards him, piercing himself through the chest and pinning his body to the floor.

"Gah!"

"Well done. Stay just like that."

I sliced off the dragon's wings with Leviangilma.

"G-Gaaaaaaaaah!"

"It'll hurt a bit. Endure it."

My Vebzud-covered fingers sank into the pope's body. I grabbed the Supreme Dragon feeding on his source and pulled it out by force.

"Kreeeeeeeeeeeeee!"

A dragon's screech rattled my ears. As I drew my right arm back, an enormous dragon emerged from the pope's body.

"Hmm. This is one large dragon to be hidden inside a body."

I lifted the giant Supreme Dragon and slammed it into the floor, but it didn't even flinch. The purple dragon opened its jaw and lunged at me. I bisected it using Leviangilma. The source of the dragon split cleanly into two and vanished. But the next moment, the two pieces of the dragon's body distorted, transforming into two dragons. I ran forward and slashed the two dragons lunging at me from the left and right. The two sources disappeared, but their bodies turned into four more dragons.

"Gaaaaaah!"

I glanced over at the screaming Golroana to see half his body had transformed into a dragon. He took off into the air.

The four dragons leaped at me, but I cut them away with Leviangilma. Once again, their bodies transformed into eight more dragons. The moment I cut them down, Golroana opened his mouth and breathed a purple fire at me. Instantly, sixteen more dragons stood before me. By the time I cut them all away, Golroana had disappeared from sight.

"He got away."

I was sure I had torn out the dragon source that was within Golroana and destroyed a total of thirty-one sources. Which meant the Supreme Dragon was either an aggregation of multiple dragons, or had multiple sources like Lay.

It seemed that Gadeciola's aim had been Golroana from the start. They had been waiting for the moment he lost his divine power and was unable to resist.

The God of Traces should have been able to spot anything lurking within his body though. Was it the power of the Supreme Dragon that had stopped him from noticing?

Perhaps it had been hoping to eliminate me in the process, but judging by

Chapter 40 — The Dragon Lurking Within

how it hadn't made any move on me, it was smart enough to recognize the gap in our power.

There was Ceris to consider too. It seemed I'd have to go give Gadeciola's overlord my greetings after all. The fact Golroana hadn't been killed on the spot meant they would keep him alive for a while.

Well, at least I had an excuse to visit now.

§ Epilogue: Sky Barrier

Using Gatom, I returned to the dragon landing site in Jiorhaze. Eleonore, who was waiting before the Demon King Castle, caught sight of me and beamed.

"Oh, Anos is back. Good work!"

Zeshia pointed at herself and mumbled quietly, "Zeshia was first."

She probably meant that she'd been the first one back.

"Well done," I said, and she hurried over to me. She looked up at me and pointed down at the ground a few times. It seemed she wanted me to crouch down.

"What's up?" I asked, crouching down to Zeshia's eye level.

"The reward for first place," she said, looking at me with her round eyes, "is Anosh!"

Hmm. It was only right to reward my hardworking followers.

I drew a magic circle over my body and shrunk to my six-year-old form using Kursla. "Will this do?"

Zeshia smiled with satisfaction. She turned around and stood before me as though to protect me, puffing up her chest proudly. "Zeshia...protected him!"

"Well done, Zeshia. That's how a follower of the Demon King should be!" Eleonore said, patting Zeshia's head. She reached out and patted mine at the same time. "You did well too, Anosh. Both Dilhade and the rest of the surface were protected."

"Of course."

Eleonore giggled and ruffled my hair. "When you say it at that size, you sound even more cheeky than usual."

Just then, two magic circles appeared before us. Lay and Misa emerged from them.

"That aside, I didn't think they'd target not just Midhaze, but the entire surface," Misa said, joining the conversation. Everyone had been looped in on my conversation with the pope through Gyze.

"If we hadn't come to the underground, our world might have been destroyed before we noticed," Lay said with a cheerful smile.

"Don't even joke about it," another voice called out.

It was Sasha. She had teleported over with Misha.

"Anos would protect us," Misha murmured, looking at me.

"I don't know about that. Maybe I was just lucky this time."

Just before Beherom activated, the song of the Divine Dragon had spread far enough to affect magic aboveground as well. As long as I noticed that, I would have been able to do something using Leviangilma.

"But it's a bit of a shame, isn't it?" Sasha muttered. "Just as we win against Jiordal and can begin holding negotiations, the pope gets abducted. It feels like a wasted effort."

"Bwa ha ha! What are you saying, Witch of Destruction?" Eldmed exclaimed. He made his way over with Shin. "You protected the world aboveground against a greater magic 1,500 years in the works. What more of a result could you ask for? We haven't even lost anything on our side. It's a perfect victory!" He spread his arms and clenched his fists. "The Demon King has even obtained a new power! Gilieriam Naviem! Just what was that magic?! A world formed by the past of the entire world, crushed underfoot! *This* is what makes the Demon King of Tyranny who he is! Bwa ha ha! BWA HA HA HA HA HA HA!"

"Incidentally," I said, interrupting the Conflagration King's manic laughter, "did you really know something about Ceris's plan?"

"Of course not. It was all a mere bluff, yes, nothing more than a bluff. How would I know anything about such a strong man? If I did, I would have tried to inform you. Oh, what a shame it is. Bwa ha ha!"

Due to their Zecht, Eldmed was unable to say anything unfavorable for Ceris. He would have to say it was a bluff whether it truly was one or not.

"How clever of you."

"Bwa ha ha. I ensnared him just as the Demon King of Tyranny wanted." At any rate, he had bought us time without any risk. Considering that the extent of Ceris's power was unknown, this had been for the best.

"Oh right, I have a message from Ceris Voldigoad. Although you might have been listening anyway," Eldmed said with a smirk. "'That was beyond my expectations. Since it seems it's my defeat, I'll go home quietly for today.'"

Beyond his expectations, huh?

"Now, how much of that do you think was the truth?"

Sasha looked thoughtful. "He called us the Goddess of Absurdity. Was that a lie he told on purpose?" she asked me.

"Most likely. He's from Gadeciola, the nation that worships Genedonov, the Goddess of Absurdity. He might have known that Arcana was the true Goddess of Absurdity too."

He'd known that, and he'd known the pope's intentions, so he'd called Aisha the Goddess of Absurdity instead. There was no telling what his goal was.

"Or it could have just been a trifling prank to him."

"Your memories may also play a part, my liege," Shin added.

Revalschned had perished, and the *Book of Traces* had been abducted by Gadeciola. It indeed seemed like they were trying to prevent the retrieval of my memories.

"Say, what happened to Arcana?" Eleonore asked. She looked around, but Arcana was nowhere to be seen.

Misha pointed at the dome. "She's over there."

Arcana was still where she was when she prevented the songfire from reaching Midhaze.

Eleonore held a hand over her eyes and squinted at the dome. "Oh, she's so far I can't see her!"

It seemed her Magic Eyes couldn't pick up Arcana's figure.

"Why isn't she coming back?" Zeshia asked curiously.

"That does seem odd," I agreed, then sent Arcana a Leaks. "Did something happen?"

After a moment of silence, she replied. "*It's nothing. I'll be over later.*"

So that's how it was.

"What are you embarrassed for? Get over here."

"Am I being embarrassed?"

"If you aren't, then you can hurry on over."

Arcana paused again. "*You'd probably say it's fine for a god to feel embarrassed.*"

"Naturally."

"*Then...I won't go. This must be what people mean when they say they can't show their face.*"

"Bwa ha ha! It seems you've learned quite a bit about the weakness of mankind. But I won't allow that, Arcana."

I used Kurst to return to my Anos form. The pledge jewel ring I had stored in a circle appeared on my finger.

"Learn this as well: overcoming weaknesses takes courage. *Guala Nateh Forteos.*"

Layers of magic circles formed in the pledge jewel. Light gathered before me in a humanoid shape before fading to reveal Arcana, head cast down in shame.

"I question your judgment in using Guala Nateh Forteos for a matter like this," she muttered unhappily. She avoided looking me in the eye.

"It was the perfect spell to drag out my shy little sister out of hiding."

I stared at her as she remained still.

"You feel sorry towards everyone, right?"

Arcana nodded.

"There's no need to worry about that. So what if you're the god of lies and betrayal? No one in this world is perfect. All of my followers have made some kind of mistake before, yet they still stand here now."

With her head still cast down, Arcana shot a quick glance at me.

"Sasha, who looks like the perfect example of a loyal follower right now, actually picked a fight with me the very first time we met. Even after she became my follower, she betrayed Misha by stabbing her in the chest."

"I-It's all in the past now!" Sasha yelled in a fluster.

"Misha just lay there and accepted her death, so she isn't one to talk either. It also took some time before she believed I was the Demon King of Tyranny."

Misha blinked. "I've reflected."

"Lay is probably the biggest liar you'll ever meet. He tried to take the place of the Demon King of Tyranny and start a war between Dilhade and Azesion."

Lay laughed awkwardly. "Can't deny that."

"As a result of his actions, Misa was born as Avos Dilhevia, the fake Demon King of Tyranny. She was the order that could destroy the Demon King, and she brainwashed all the demons against me."

Misa pouted unhappily. "I can't help what rumor or legend I'm born from. It's all the Heavenly Father's fault!"

"And when it comes to betraying me, even Shin, who's always ready to risk his life for me, has pointed his sword at me before."

Shin turned his face away. "I am most ashamed."

"As for Eldmed, well, he's probably plotting how to betray me right this moment."

The Conflagration King burst into laughter. "Betray the Demon King of Tyranny? I wouldn't dare!"

"Got it?"

Arcana looked embarrassed, but she stared straight into my eyes.

"I don't care if you're Genedonov. What lies you've told and who you've betrayed in your past are trifling matters to me. There's only one thing I care about."

"And that is?"

"That I am your older brother, and you are my little sister."

Tears welled in Arcana's eyes. I gently wrapped my arms around her in a hug.

"There was one time when Misha pointed at you and said you were like someone wandering endlessly through a dry desert."

Tears fell from the small god's eyes.

"Were you lonely?"

"I didn't have any memories," Arcana mumbled, "but for some reason, I could feel loneliness. There was a vacant feeling within me. When I remembered I was the Goddess of Absurdity, I realized that feeling was the scars of sadness."

"There's nothing to worry about anymore. No matter how lonely you feel or what sad memories you remember, you'll always have your big brother by your side." I hugged the frail body in my arms tighter. "Don't forget that. Whatever memories you recall are of little consequence."

"Even if this heart is fake…"

"It's all trivial to me. You're dear to me even when you lie."

Arcana wrapped her arms around me and squeezed. "Big brother…"

She cried into my chest, soft sobs slipping out here and there. Tears fell from her golden eyes like a spring in a parched desert. Everyone looked on with warm smiles as she made no attempt to separate from me.

Several minutes passed like that until eventually, Sasha broke the silence. "Um, it's been a while now," she muttered under her breath.

Behind her, Misha peered over her shoulder. "Are you jealous?"

"Th-That's not it!" Sasha snapped. She clenched her fists and began mumbling to herself while nodding. "They're brother and sister, and Arcana only wants to be his little sister anyway. Yup, I win."

Misha giggled in amusement.

"Arcana," I called.

Arcana quietly stepped back and looked up at me with teary eyes.

"Let's go back to the surface for now."

I drew Leviangilma from my storage circle and handed it to Arcana. Under the blessing of the Sword of the Almighty, nothing would be able to pass the dome. In its current state, it was impossible to make a hole in the dome.

"Okay."

She took the sword into both hands and bent down on one knee. Lunar snowdrops swirled around her, sparkling with light.

"Moon rises, and the sword falls, waiting for the next judgment."

Leviangilma glowed brightly. The light of the Moon of Creation, Altiertonoa, illuminated the surroundings. Then…

"Huh?" Eleonore said, a confused look on her face.

The light had receded, but Leviangilma remained in Arcana's hands.

"Um, is it over?" Sasha asked.

Arcana shook her head. "I can't turn it back."

"Can't turn it back? But why?"

"I don't know. There's some kind of limitation on my body."

I observed Arcana's body with my Magic Eyes. "Is it something placed on you before you lost your memories and became the nameless god?"

"I think so. It might be something I cast upon myself, as the Goddess of Absurdity."

So the Goddess of Absurdity would betray even herself.

Arcana looked up at the dome with a troubled look. "Only the wielder of Leviangilma may pass," she said in a worried tone. "The dome has turned into an eternally unchanging barrier."

The End

Afterword

I've liked games from a young age. I don't have as much time nowadays, but back when I was a child, I would play for around sixteen hours a day. My favorite single-player games were role-playing games, and I can still remember the excitement I felt whenever I arrived at a new town.

Since this volume features a visit to an unfamiliar nation in an unknown underground world, I tried to capture the same feeling of excitement from those childhood games. I hope you all enjoyed it.

In a change of topic, I will be supervising the anime production of this series as the original creator.

There are a lot of tasks to be done as a supervisor, but the storyboard meetings are probably the most tiring of them. After receiving the storyboards, I have to check them before attending a meeting to go over them. This check involves pointing out any specific issues and how to correct them. I'm given plenty of time to make this check, but I tend to add more and more corrections up until the last moment, so I worry I'm actually making more work for everyone involved.

To be honest, I don't know much about anime, but I was told that anime faithful to the original work and anime that deviate from the original work both have their good points. After discussing this with the production team, it was decided that this anime adaptation will faithfully follow the original. That being said, the adaptation will be short and uses a different form of media, so following the exact structure and dialogue line for line would only result in a dull anime.

Thus, the structure and dialogue need to be adjusted to suit the anime. Of course, many problems emerge as a result of this, and it's my job as a supervisor to make corrections to make it more in line with the foreshadowing, background, characters, and theme of the scene in the original work. Most of the corrections are accepted, so as long as I haven't messed up anywhere, it should be pretty faithful to the original. Not all of it is complete yet, but I believe with the way things are going so far, it will be pretty good.

Avid readers may find a few details off here and there, but I will continue making every effort to ensure the work respects the core essence of *The Misfit of Demon King Academy*. Please look forward to it!

I will also continue working on revising the next volume for your enjoyment as well, so I hope to see you again then.

SHU
15 Jan 2020

HEY ///////
▶ **HAVE YOU HEARD OF J-Novel Club?**

It's the digital publishing company that brings you the latest novels and manga from Japan!

Subscribe today at

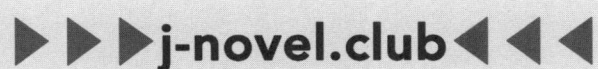

▶▶▶ **j-novel.club** ◀◀◀

and read the latest volumes as they're translated, or become a premium member to get a *FREE* ebook every month!

── Check Out The Latest Volume Of ──
The Misfit of Demon King Academy

Plus Our Other Hit Series Like:

- ▶ Welcome to Japan, Ms. Elf!
- ▶ Mercedes and the Waning Moon: The Dungeoneering Feats of a Discarded Vampire Aristocrat
- ▶ Knock Yourself Out! The Goddess Beat the Final Boss in the Tutorial, So Now I'm Free to Do Whatever
- ▶ The Brilliant Healer's New Life in the Shadows
- ▶ They Don't Know I'm Too Young for the Adventurer's Guild
- ▶ The Apothecary Diaries
- ▶ Isekai Tensei: Recruited to Another World
- ▶ Campfire Cooking in Another World with My Absurd Skill
- ▶ My Quiet Blacksmith Life in Another World

...and many more!

In Another World With My Smartphone, Illustration © Eiji Usatsuka   *Arifureta: From Commonplace to World's Strongest*, Illustration © Takayaki